Praise for The Guest List *and Melissa Hill*

'Brilliantly written and full of twists, rows and tears' *Closer*

'There's plenty of family drama . . . a good gift for the bridezilla in your life.' *Heat*

'If you need to turn off from all the worries and stresses of the week and get away from it all, *The Guest List* is the perfect light read. You'll quickly get sucked into Cara and Shane's soap-opera-style story and author Melissa Hill cleverly keeps throwing another twist in here and a turn in there to keep you hooked. It's so easy to read, even when I was sardined on the tube with a random man's elbow in my back I was still able to lose myself in the world of bridesmaids dresses and bouquets!' *Fabulous*

'Extremely readable . . . I always read Melissa Hill's books very quickly as I always want to know how everything turns out in the end. As with all her books, there is also an unexpected twist but she writes in such a clever way that you don't suspect for one moment what it will be.' *Curious Book Fans*

'Stylish and uplifting . . . Perfect froth for whiling away a few hours' *Irish Independent*

'Blissfully escapist' *Marie Claire*

About the Author

Melissa Hill lives with her husband Kevin, daughter Carrie and dog Homer in Co. Dublin. Previous titles including *The Charm Bracelet*, *Something from Tiffany's*, *The Truth About You* and *Please Forgive Me* have all been bestsellers, and her books have been translated into twenty-three different languages. Melissa is a Number One bestseller in Ireland and Italy.

For more information, you can visit Melissa's website at www.melissahill.info, like her Facebook page www.facebook.com/melissahillbooks or follow her on Twitter twitter.com/melissahillbks.

The Guest List

Melissa Hill

HODDER

First published in Great Britain in 2013 by Hodder & Stoughton
An Hachette UK company

First published in paperback in 2013

1

Copyright © Melissa Hill 2013

A CIP catalogue record for this title is available from the British Library

B-format Paperback ISBN 978 0 340 99345 3
A-format Paperback ISBN 978 0 340 99346 0

Printed and bound by Clays Ltd, St Ives plc

Hodder & Stoughton policy is to use papers that are natural, renewable and
recyclable products and made from wood grown in sustainable forests. The
logging and manufacturing processes are expected to conform to the
environmental regulations of the country of origin.

Hodder & Stoughton Ltd
338 Euston Road
London NW1 3BH

www.hodder.co.uk

Acknowledgements

Massive thanks to Francesca Best and Isobel Akenhead for fantastic editorial input, and to the Hodder team in Ireland and the UK who always work so hard on my behalf – I'm very grateful.

Thank you to Sheila Crowley for being an amazing agent, wonderful friend and true force of nature. Thanks too to Katie McGowan, Rebecca Ritchie, Tally Garner and all the lovely people at Curtis Brown UK, who continually work their magic.

Big thanks to readers, booksellers, reviewers and bloggers everywhere for being so supportive of my books, and to those who've been in touch to say how much they enjoy them. I love hearing from you so please do keep the feedback coming at www.melissahill.info, www.facebook.com/melissahillbooks or Twitter @melissahillbks.

I very much hope you enjoy *The Guest List*.

To Kevin and Carrie, with lots of love

Chapter 1

You are invited to attend the nuptials of
Audrey McCarthy and Joseph Bourke

The bride and groom kindly request the following:

- *No female guests to wear white; this includes clothes,*
  shoes and/or accessories.
- *Guests should refrain from wearing garments from Coast*
  or Karen Millen clothing stores.
- *Guests should please visit laceconfetti.com/mccarthy–bourke*
  to review the colour scheme of the wedding and dress
  accordingly.
- *Single male invitees should not bring as dates female*
  guests who are unknown to the bride and groom.
- *All non-local guests should stay at the hotel in which the*
  wedding reception will be held (prices and information
  available online at www.themanor.com).
- *No gifts on the day unless in the form of cash or cheques.*
  Preferred method of gifting is via the wedding list (see
  attached notification card for details) or through
  deposits to the couple's joint bank account (details below)
  by the date of the wedding.

It was more of an edict than an invite, and Cara Clancy
didn't think she'd ever come across anything more obnoxious.

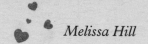

Engraved on expensive wedding stationery below the date, time and place was that long list of what could only be described as *demands*.

She knew that her old college friend Audrey McCarthy was a show-off, but this was taking it to another higher level. Even as a person who wasn't easily offended or slighted, Cara couldn't help but feel her hackles rise at this utter lack of tact and taste, not to mention blatant money-grabbing tendencies.

So much for 'for richer for poorer' . . .

She shook her head as she sought out the wedding list 'notification card' mentioned in the invite, and wasn't in the least bit surprised to see that the list was at one of Ireland's most expensive luxury stores, Brown Thomas. Of course.

No run-of-the-mill chain store would be good enough for these two and she made a mental note to check it out to see what the cheapest item on the list would be. She was sure she wouldn't be the only one doing so.

But just in case guests didn't subscribe to the wedding list, the couple were also kind enough to allow you donate to them personally, should you be so inclined.

Her eyes widened. The cheek of it . . .

The inclusion of the bank account number was a brazen appeal for cash, and Cara wondered when weddings had become less about the commitment two people were making to spend the rest of their lives together and more about money and gifts.

As much as she wanted to throw the invite in the bin and compose a response that regretfully informed the couple of her inability to attend an affair that seemed geared to padding their pockets (and which would undoubtedly help with the financial burden of any future divorce), she found that she didn't have it in herself to do so. Instead she placed it aside, wondering what Shane would think when she showed it to him.

Probably much the same as she did. Despite his moneyed background and privileged upbringing (his father, Gene Richardson, was a hugely successful Dublin property developer), her boyfriend wasn't in the least bit flashy, and wasn't a fan of ostentatious displays of wealth.

Not that Audrey McCarthy was wealthy. From what Cara could remember, she was pretty sure that her old friend had, like herself, come from a normal working-class background. Maybe the hubby-to-be was minted? Although if he was, they'd hardly be sending out glorified begging letters in the guise of wedding invites – would they?

And who was the groom anyway? Cara glanced back through the invite for the mention of him and found the name. Ah, a 'Joseph Bourke.' Maybe Mr Bourke didn't have any demands for the wedding day, or maybe Audrey thought of him as simply another wedding-related accessory.

Her thoughts resting on the idea of weddings, Cara wondered what her and Shane's wedding would be like, if one day he decided to ask her.

She certainly knew what her answer would be if he did, and she also knew for certain that their big day would be an out-and-out celebration of their love for each other, and a million miles from what Audrey McCarthy seemed to be planning.

Cara and Shane had been together for almost three years. They'd first met at a mutual friend's dinner party and had immediately hit it off. He was fun and laid-back and had a wickedly dry sense of humour that really appealed to her. Not to mention that he was very good-looking with fair hair, green eyes and a broad rugby-player physique from his days playing at Blackrock College. By the end of that night the chemistry was almost palpable and she knew that if Shane asked her out she wouldn't hesitate for a second. Turns out he did, and the pair embarked on a budding romance that turned to full bloom within months.

At five foot nothing, Cara always felt tiny in Shane's arms, but more importantly, she felt safe.

She glanced at a photo on a nearby side table, of her and Shane taken the previous winter on a weekend trip to Barcelona. Smiling, she suspected that when the time was right, Shane would ask. Now twenty-nine years old, Cara was certain she had found the man she was supposed to be with. Marriage was just the next natural step, wasn't it?

Turning her attention away from thoughts of marriage, she began the process of organising herself after a day's work. She placed her laptop case on the coffee table, ready and waiting for later when she had some additional work do to.

As someone who was naturally artistic and creative, Cara adored her job as a graphic designer at Octagon Design, a small firm based in Greygates, the small Dublin coastal suburb in which she had grown up. It was also a plus that she had a stellar relationship with her boss, Conor Dempsey, whom she'd always known from the area, and was proud of the fact that she was not one of those people who constantly lamented that their boss was a pain in the ass or out to get them. Cara knew that he respected her and the job that she did for his company and as such, he gave her a relatively free rein.

She glanced at the time and knew that Shane would be home soon. While Cara was a million miles from being a domestic goddess, she was at least confident in her ability to whip up some tomato soup . . . even if it was just from a can.

4

She went into the small galley kitchen of their cosy one-bed apartment and started pottering about, first deciding to open a bottle of red and let it breathe while she waited for Shane. Although the place was by no means palatial, it had modern and stylish features that complemented their lifestyle. Located just on the fringes of Dublin city centre, it was handy for them both for work, while also ideal for bustling city living, which they both enjoyed. Having decided not to follow in his father's footsteps and go into the building industry, Shane had instead trained as an accountant and worked in a city-centre firm, and her own office in Greygates was just a short commuter-train ride away. They were both thrilled with the place when they'd picked it out together the year before, aware that it was a real demonstration of their commitment to one another and the future they were working on creating, one step at a time.

Within minutes, she heard the front door of the apartment open, and listened to the usual rustlings indicating that Shane was getting rid of his work things and making his way to the kitchen.

She had her head down, buttering bread and getting ready to place it in the frying pan, when he came in.

'Ahh . . . what kind of culinary masterpiece do I smell tonight?' he teased. 'Could that really be grilled cheese sandwiches and tomato soup? Ah the memories that are flooding back to me . . . all involving being five years old. You really are a domestic goddess in disguise,' he said, coming up behind Cara and encircling her with his arms.

She let loose a snort of laughter. 'Yep, that's me, cooking for you in such a way that you think of your mum.' She turned in his arms to face him and planted a kiss on his lips. He was six foot two and with those blond good looks

Cara really couldn't get enough of him. Her pulse still quickened when he kissed her.

'Mmm . . .' he sighed into her long hair. 'Actually, my mum never made grilled cheese, but Lillian did.'

Lillian had been his nanny. Shane had grown up in a huge house located on a large country estate outside Kildare. To say that the family was wealthy would be a huge understatement, and his parents, especially his mother Lauren, enjoyed flaunting their money and social status. The fact that Shane didn't was yet another quality of his that Cara admired.

Giving her another brief kiss on the forehead, he stood back and idly checked through the post. 'Crikey, what the hell is this?'

Seeing that Shane was holding Audrey McCarthy's wedding invitation in his hand, she shook her head. 'I know. Tacky isn't it?'

Shane read the invitation, his eyebrows climbing higher with every sentence.

'Christ on a bike,' he guffawed. 'Single male guests should not bring female guests the bride and groom do not know?' Who *are* these people?'

Cara walked to the cabinet and removed two wine glasses. 'Well, I only know the bride.' She poured two glasses of wine and handed one to Shane as she took a sip. 'Look at this. They've even included their bank account number.' She pointed at the series of numbers lining the bottom of the invite.

'This really is tacky. Where did you meet this girl? At a fundraiser or something? She seems to have a good understanding of the concept in any case.'

'Stop it,' Cara smiled as she swatted at him. 'And when did you ever see me at a fundraiser? I think you're mistaking me for your mother again.' She threw the invitation on the countertop. 'We don't have to go to that wedding; I would prefer it if we didn't actually.'

'Ah don't say that, we'll go and have a bit of craic,' Shane said wickedly. 'Surely you don't want to miss the ice sculptures, or the doves, or the fifty-piece orchestra serenading the beautiful bride as she walks down the aisle in a dress that probably cost the same as this place?'

'Sounds like you know plenty about the goings-on on at weddings these days,' Cara joked. 'I'm still not sure about going, though. When I opened up the invitation, and read all those demands . . . honestly I felt like telling Audrey McCarthy where she could stick her wedding list and bank account number. And I wouldn't mind but I have a wardrobe full of Coast and Karen Millen, and she's telling me I can't wear any of it?' And if Audrey expected Cara to go out and spend even more on something new she could go sing. Money was tight for everyone these days, so such a demand truly was a bit rich. 'Seriously, I thought that kind of nonsense was finished with nowadays.'

Elaborate wedding celebrations and one-upmanship had been rife throughout Ireland's Celtic Tiger days, when the banks were happy to lend for such excesses as helicopters for the bride and groom, but the ensuing recession had put a welcome stop to the worst of it.

'Ah, you really shouldn't let people like that bother you.' Shane shook his head and paused briefly. 'I've never understood it myself though, these couples who go into massive debt for just one day – especially now. I understand that a wedding is a big deal, but really, shouldn't it be all about the commitment you're making to the one you're marrying, rather than trying to impress some relatives you don't even know by flying in beluga caviar from Moscow?'

Cara smiled. This was why exactly why she loved him so much; they felt the same way about so many things and were always completely in tune with each other.

'I knew I was with you for a reason. You are so smart.'

'And I know I'm with you for a reason. Sadly one that definitely doesn't involve your cooking.' He sniffed the air, and nudged her arm as she turned to place her wine glass on the counter. 'Sorry to break it to you, but I think your grilled cheese is burning.'

'Oh no!' Cara exclaimed, quickly turning her attention to the stove. Shane laughed as she grabbed the frying pan and removed it from the hob. The cheese was nicely charred and looked deeply unappetising.

Shane raised his eyebrows. 'So what'll it be then – Indian or Thai?'

She blushed guiltily. 'I suppose a takeaway might be a good idea at this point.'

'My thoughts exactly,' he grinned as he pulled her close and kissed her on the forehead. 'Cooking is way overrated anyway. Don't worry; I know you have a great phone voice.'

'Ha! Conor says the same thing,' she laughed, reaching for the phone.

A slight shadow crossed his face at the mention of Conor, and Cara mentally cursed herself for mentioning him. Shane had never quite been able to get his head around her close relationship with her boss. She supposed they had a rather unorthodox employer/employee relationship, but Conor Dempsey had taken her on straight out of college when he was first setting up Octagon, and she'd been working for him for close to a decade. But notwithstanding the fact that Conor must be almost twice her age, Shane never seemed especially comfortable with their easy-going friendship. Possibly because Conor was still unmarried, drop-dead gorgeous and had most of the female half of Dublin chasing after him.

Truthfully though, Cara never thought of her boss as anything other than just that, but it seemed Shane remained unconvinced.

She winked, hoping to deflect his attention away from that last remark. 'Good to know I have *some* redeeming qualities.'

As she dialled the Indian restaurant down the road she noticed Shane once again pick up the wedding invitation from the countertop. '"The bride and groom kindly request . . . "' he read out loud, shaking his head. 'At least that won't be us.'

Cara was on the line waiting for the restaurant to pick up, but Shane's words made her turn suddenly and face him. What on earth did that mean?

'I'm sorry, what?' she asked.

Shane looked steadily back at her. 'I said . . . no way will that be us.'

'Oh.' Cara didn't have much time to think about it just then, as the restaurant answered her call.

But as she placed their order, she couldn't help but wonder what Shane meant. Did he mean that they wouldn't dream of creating as much fuss around their wedding as Audrey McCarthy – or, more worryingly, she thought, gulping, that a wedding wouldn't be them at all?

Chapter 2

Heidi Clancy looked at the pink and white plastic wand in front of her, and waited for the oracle to announce her future.

Or at least for the two pink lines to show.

She *would* be pregnant. After all, she had willed it to be so. It was the way things were supposed to happen. She'd been married almost a year now, this was the next natural step, and heaven forbid someone or something cross her in her quest.

She stared expectantly at the pregnancy test that rested on the marble counter of her master bathroom, and then looked at her watch, tapping her foot impatiently on the porcelain-tiled floor.

'Anything yet?' called out Paul, her husband, and Heidi looked nervously at the door. She knew he was just as excited by the prospect as she was and she didn't want to let him down.

'Still waiting.' She turned to the bathroom mirror and exhaled heavily, just as her yoga instructor had told her to do. It would help her circulation and ultimately promote a healthy pregnancy. She studied her reflection – while her chestnut (albeit artificially enhanced) hair was always glossy, today it had an additional sheen to it, and her skin looked clear and dewy. Heidi nodded satisfactorily.

She had to be pregnant.

She glanced down at the counter again, but there was no change.

Hmm . . .

Heidi reached for her make-up bag and grabbed her MAC lip-plumping gloss. Quickly she swiped her lips and fluffed her bouncy hair and prepared to become a mother. It had to happen this year, and preferably this month. She was tired of waiting around now, and this was the fourth test she'd taken this year.

She had played by all the rules, followed all the tips and invested a small fortune in the techniques and strategies for conceiving or 'getting knocked up' as her sister-in-law Kim would so tackily put it.

What her brother, Ben, saw in the woman she would never understand. She was so crass, so vulgar. She remembered the way Kim had been all throughout her last pregnancy, acting as if it was no big deal, as if it was simply something that was completely run-of-the-mill.

The woman hadn't even held a baby shower, for heaven's sake! Heidi shook her head. She couldn't think of a better reason for getting gifts and being smothered by attention – it was called a *shower* after all.

She knew for sure her baby shower would be a great celebration of life – the fact that she was giving life to another human being. She imagined herself sitting in the midst of friends and family, tummy swollen, face glowing, surrounded by gifts and being waited on. Or no, wait, being massaged would be even better. That's what she'd do, Heidi decided: it could be a baby shower weekend at a spa hotel and there would be massages and lots of relaxation. Perfect.

She smiled with excitement at the thought of it. Yes, she simply *had* to be pregnant.

Heidi took another deep breath and considered the test

in front of her. *Just one more minute and then I'll look,* she decided – really, the suspense was killing her, and she didn't think she could wait much longer.

'Honey?' Paul asked again from the other side of the door. 'Anything?'

'Not *yet*,' Heidi replied somewhat testily. 'When there is of course you'll be the first to know. Now better leave me be, you are disrupting my aura. We need to be surrounded by positive energy when we learn of our impending child,' she continued. 'I don't need any extra tension just now, honey. The baby will immediately sense its mother is anxious and stressed. And what kind of start in life is that?'

'You're right, you're right, I'm sorry, of course we don't want any of that, please relax. Would you like a foot rub while you wait? I could come in,' he offered lamely.

'No Paul, just . . . go and sit in the living room, and watch the rugby on TV or something,' she replied reassuringly. 'I'll be out shortly.'

There was silence from the other side of the door, and Heidi guessed that her husband had taken her suggestion and was – hopefully – somewhere far away from the bathroom. Paul was wonderful, but he did have a tendency to fuss.

She thought of all the things she would have to do once the test came back positive. Or rather, she thought of all the lists that she would have to make during the nesting process. She wondered if she should hire a nanny soon, to assist her with getting the house ready and going about buying all the things that they would need for the baby. And the nursery . . . oh the nursery! Heidi couldn't wait. It would be great to have another room to decorate. Truthfully, she'd been kind of bored, now that she'd finished decorating the house and there were no more interior designers to meet with or builders to keep in check. She could have great fun organising a nursery, going to Mamas and Papas and all the baby stores to pick out the paraphernalia. She'd need help though, especially as Paul was always so busy with his work at the bank. Yes, Heidi would need someone, preferably a professional.

Would coming along to baby stores and organising a nursery be in a nanny's job description though, or would it make more sense for her to go and hire an assistant for the duration of the pregnancy at least? Heidi wondered. Actually, that seemed like a better idea, and would make much more sense, she decided.

A nanny might just get in the way if there wasn't actually a baby to deal with just yet, whereas an assistant would be there to assist in every sense of the word – they'd be someone who would do exactly as Heidi pleased. After all, she would need help; she couldn't be expected to do much of anything once the pregnancy was confirmed, could she?

She wondered how much help her family would give her. She could depend on her mother Betty, of course, but not Cara. Never Cara. Her older sister was so career-focused and selfish, not to mention completely consumed by that boyfriend of hers.

Heidi harrumphed. She had to admit though; her sister had done well in nabbing the likes of Shane Richardson, heir to the Richardson millions. As for what he saw in Cara, she'd never know.

It had also slightly miffed her that Cara hadn't actively entered into the spirit of competition a couple of years back when Heidi was intent on getting engaged to Paul. She didn't seem to care that Heidi would be the first Clancy sister to reach the altar. Their oldest sister Danielle didn't count; she was swanning around in Florida somewhere, and for all they knew she could be married by now – possibly three or four times over for as much as they knew about her life.

But back then, when Heidi was doing her utmost to make sure Paul put a big diamond ring on Heidi's finger, Cara herself acted like she didn't care that her little sister was moving miles ahead of her in the relationship stakes.

Didn't she understand that stuff like that was important? That these things – and not stupid work - was what life was all about? Milestones – diamond rings, wedding showers, big weddings, even bigger houses, then pregnancy, babies and all the rest of it . . .?

Heidi looked again at the pregnancy test. She frowned. Was that a *single* line that was forming? There was only a hint of a shadow on the second line . . .

Shit, she thought, concentrating harder. She knew she had control over this. She grabbed the box with the instructions. She was looking for two lines, wasn't it? Not a single. She read quickly and confirmed that yes, she was indeed looking for two pink lines. She glanced back down at the pregnancy test again.

The second line was indeed developing and becoming more pronounced. Two lines.

Two solid pink lines.

Yes, yes, yes! She smiled, satisfied, impressed by her own intuition.

Two lines. Pregnant.

She was actually pregnant! Heidi cheered to herself and watched, fascinated, as the second line became even clearer. Two parallel twin lines.

Twins . . . Maybe she would have twins! What could be better than one baby but two? Heidi thought about the attention she would get. Everyone adored twins, and if she had them it would be almost as if she had more talent for childbearing than women who only produced one baby at a time.

And of course they would be identical, rather than fraternal twins. Identical girls preferably, as everything in pink was so much lovelier and prettier than boring old blue. Oh, and think about the presents she'd get at her baby shower, she thought gleefully. Double everything!

Heidi picked up the pregnancy test and looked at it again. *She was with child*, she confirmed sagely. She wondered if her own mind power had assisted in the conception; she wouldn't doubt it. She was strong like that, had a great ability to make things happen, merely by concentrating hard on them. Like Paul, for instance. She'd known right away that they were perfect for each other, and had concentrated very hard on making sure he knew it. And look at them now, barely married a year and now pregnant with their first child.

Heidi placed the pregnancy test back on the counter, feeling very impressed with herself. She was so calm about it all, so self-assured and confident. She had known deep down of course, had known for a very long time that she was destined to be a mother. From as long ago as childhood, really, when she used to push her immense doll collection around in her toy pram. She loved dressing them up in all the pretty little clothes, and styling their hair. Oh, she would be the most fantastic mother, Heidi reassured herself, thinking of all the fun that was sure to be had with a real baby. And unlike her own mother, she wouldn't play favourites with her children. It was obvious to anyone with half a brain that goody-two-shoes Cara was the golden child in the Clancy family, despite Heidi being the youngest.

She bit her lip, and tried again not let such negativity creep in, concentrating instead on her happy news.

Heidi knew exactly when the conception had happened

too. Six weeks ago, right in the middle of her cycle, just like the books advised. While it wasn't the most romantic situation (Paul had been tired and rather unenthusiastic), it had got the job done and that was the most important thing, wasn't it?

She couldn't wait to tell everyone. And right away too, none of this waiting for three months or twelve weeks or whatever foolishness some people chose to subscribe to. Heidi wasn't in the least bit superstitious. No, she would announce the big news straight away so she could make the most of every last minute of her pregnancy.

Six weeks pregnant.

She smiled at herself in the mirror as she patted her still flat tummy and remembered that her family was planning on getting together this coming weekend at her parents' house for Sunday dinner. It would be the *perfect* time to share her news, and of course a family dinner ensured that she would have the undivided attention of everyone, all at the same time. She could only imagine the big fuss a new baby in the family would cause. There hadn't been one for ages – not since Ben and Kim's youngest daughter Lindsay was born. There had been some big commotion back then too surrounding the birth, but Heidi couldn't remember much about it, as she didn't trouble herself too much with Kim's dramas. To say that she and her sister-in-law had little in common was putting it mildly. In fact, as she often said to Paul, as far as Heidi was concerned the only good thing to come of that marriage was her adorable nieces.

And thinking of Paul . . . Heidi couldn't wait to see his face. Her beloved husband already treated her like a princess, but now he would treat her like an absolute queen. After all, she was carrying his child; she was the one responsible for giving life to his son or daughter.

Her mind flitted off in another direction at that thought. Which would she prefer? she wondered. A boy or a girl?

Her heart said girl so that she could dress her up in pretty little dresses and show her off, and of course when her little girl grew up they could be best friends.

But she didn't really need to think about that just yet. Plenty of time – well actually seven short months or so – before she would have a tiny baby in her arms.

Once the baby arrived it would get plenty of attention, whereas right now was *her* time. In order to make sure the baby was safe and arrived healthy, it was Heidi's responsibility to make sure she took good care of herself and, more importantly, made sure everyone else understood what was expected of them now that she was in a delicate condition.

Time to start with her husband.

Heidi turned toward the closed door of the bathroom with the pregnancy test in hand. She exited into the dark panelled hallway that led to the master bedroom, crossing it regally, as if she was a queen off to tell the king that she would be producing him an heir.

She turned on her heel at the door of the bedroom and walked down the hallway, head held high, shoulders back, walking slowly. After all, you never could be too sure when carrying such delicate and precious cargo . . .

She covered her tummy protectively with one hand.

Coming into the well-lit, high-ceilinged living room, she found Paul waiting obediently on the chaise longue across from where she stood. He looked at her hopefully and Heidi recognised awe and wonder on his face. Even he could see that she was already glowing.

'Well?' Paul asked, a half-smile on his face, eyebrows raised.

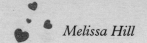

She took a deep breath, savouring the moment. Time to share her news with someone else. Time for her pregnancy to begin. He truly would be over the moon when he heard.

'Yes, darling,' she said dramatically, holding up the pregnancy test and feeling fully aware that this was exactly what was meant for her – this was precisely how her life was supposed to be. 'I am indeed pregnant.' She smiled. 'You are looking at the mother of your unborn child.'

Chapter 3

Cara woke early the next morning. Creeping out of bed while Shane slept, she glanced lovingly at him and blushed as she recalled the night before. The curry they'd ended up ordering from the local takeaway wasn't the only thing that had been hot and spicy.

However, as she tiptoed into the bathroom to get ready for work, she couldn't shake the feeling of confusion that now plagued her. They didn't speak about weddings again last night after Shane had made the comment about how Audrey McCarthy's tacky and overblown wedding 'wouldn't be them', and Cara was still wondering what that meant.

Did it mean that a proposal would soon be forthcoming? Or that it would happen somewhere down the road? Worse yet, and while she couldn't imagine this being the case, what if 'that *won't* be us'— meant them *not* getting married, ever?

She shook her head in an effort to banish her bleariness and try to clarify her thoughts. No, she thought, she wasn't in a big hurry to get married and surely it wasn't a case of 'if' but 'when'? She reaffirmed her thoughts from the day before. When the time was right, Shane would ask and she would say yes.

She took a deep breath and tried to put the thought out of her mind, instead focusing on the day ahead. She had a mountain of work to get through for Octagon and thanks to the night before (and the fact that she was otherwise

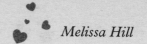

Melissa Hill

distracted), she hadn't gone near any of the files that she had brought home with her.

Just as she was putting the finishing touches to her make-up, swiping her eyelashes with mascara, the bathroom door opened and Shane shuffled in, bleary-eyed, bare-chested and wearing pyjama bottoms covered in characters from *The Simpsons*.

'Looks like someone had a rough night,' she teased.

Shane smiled and leaned in to plant a kiss on her cheek. 'Thanks to you, you little minx.'

She smiled. All too easy when Shane simply looked like *that*.

He pulled aside the shower curtain and started the water, waiting for it to heat up. As he removed his pyjama bottoms and jumped in, Cara was quick to throw an appreciative glance at his rear in the reflection of the mirror.

'So,' Shane said from the confines of the shower. 'Do you have a busy day ahead?'

'Yep' Cara told him. 'Conor handed me a pile of work before I left last night – which of course, simply adds to the pile that was already on my desk. I was hoping to get started on it last night but . . .'

'Hmm, sounds like he's working you a bit hard.'

'Ah, you know Conor isn't like that,' she said quickly, anxious not to get into a conversation with him about her boss. 'Still, I was hoping to have lunch with Kim later, but I'm not sure if I will have time for that now.'

Kim was Cara's sister-in-law, married to her older brother Ben. While she had sisters of her own – the older Danielle and younger Heidi – Cara had felt closer to Kim since well before she married into the family, and by all accounts had more in common with her than she had with her own flesh and blood.

Of course, much of this had to do with the fact that Danielle had been living in Florida for as long as she could remember, and rarely returned for visits. Truth be told, Cara didn't have too many memories of her older sister, as she'd moved out of the family home when Cara was still very young, first getting her own place in the city centre, and eventually moving onwards to the US.

The last time she saw Danielle, on her most recent visit home to Dublin a few years ago, it had looked as though her sister was doing her best to single-handedly support the American plastic surgery industry. By all accounts she enjoyed a fabulous life in south Florida, promoted by her wealthy boyfriend Zack and her own apparently successful career as a real estate agent.

Cara (or indeed any of the Clancy family) had never met Zack, but from what little they knew about him through Danielle, it seemed he was some kind of globetrotting aficionado with business interests in pretty much every sector in the US.

She knew her sister worshipped wealth, youth and material possessions and clearly she loved life in America too, as every time Cara spoke to her she thought she sounded like a character in some soap opera. She had developed a pronounced American accent over the years, now considered herself a 'Floridian' and sadly seemed all too happy to have left her Irish roots behind.

Cara never quite understood that part. Her parents Betty and Mick were great people, hard workers who had formed a quality life and built a family together. Cara felt that was something to be proud of in parents, not something to shun and hide the way Danielle did. Her parents weren't flighty or superficial, and they certainly didn't put on false airs and graces like Danielle did. Sometimes Cara couldn't believe

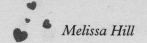

that she was actually related to her older sister, they were just so dissimilar.

And as for her younger sister Heidi . . . well, Heidi was almost a different species altogether. At twenty-seven, two years younger than Cara, she was the baby of the family and as such had always been spoilt rotten. Heidi was practised in getting her own way and, if ever she didn't, there was hell to pay.

They all knew that Heidi, married now for just over a year, and evidently already bored with playing newlyweds, was currently dead set on becoming pregnant ASAP. When she was planning her wedding just over a year before, she'd been the ultimate bridezilla, and now the world revolved around her becoming a mother.

She probably wouldn't be so spoilt if her husband would put his foot down with her occasionally, but he indulged and treated her like the princess she believed herself to be. Paul held a senior management position at one of the country's biggest banks – one of the reasons (if not the only one, Cara sometimes thought) Heidi had pursued him so relentlessly when they first met.

Still, thanks to Paul's income, Cara's baby sister now lived in a fabulous home in one of Dublin's most upmarket coastal suburbs, and didn't have to worry her pretty little head about work. What Heidi did all day (other than obsess about getting married – and now getting pregnant) was a mystery.

Shane spoke again, bringing her thoughts back to the present. 'Too much work to do to grab a bite with Kim?' he asked. 'Surely Conor doesn't expect you to work through lunch too?'

'He doesn't expect anything of me other than to get through the work, which I plan to do,' she said with an easy-going smile. 'You keep forgetting, what I do isn't the same as working with numbers –' she teased, referring to his profession '– there are few absolutes.'

'Ah yes, I sometimes forget that you creative types are a different breed altogether,' he said, winking. 'Honestly, though, don't work too hard.'

'I know; I'd prefer not to have to cancel –I was really looking forward to seeing Kim – but I honestly don't think I can spare the time now. You know, we should really organise a night out with her and Ben, or at least arrange to get together for lunch or dinner some weekend. It's been ages since I saw the girls.'

Kim and Ben were parents to Cara's nieces, the lively and precocious Olivia and the inquisitive and curious Lindsay.

'Good idea, why don't you set up something soon? I'd like to see them all, too.'

Cara smiled. She was delighted that Shane got along so well with her family. While he wasn't keen on Heidi and all her posturing, he was never anything but polite and respectful to her, something Cara herself had problems with when it came to her baby sister.

He also carried on a lively relationship with Ben and Kim, another reason Cara enjoyed spending time with her older brother and his wife.

And most importantly, her parents Betty and Mick adored the ground he walked on and vice versa. While Cara in turn had a good relationship with the Richardsons, she was always slightly intimidated by them, compared to the relaxed and easy-going rapport Shane enjoyed with her family. Cara anticipated that if they did get married themselves, those family ties would be the ones that would matter the most, especially when they had their own children. The thought brought her straight back to her confusion over the night before. Surely Shane wouldn't set so much store by spending time with her family if he didn't plan to be around for the long haul?

'Shane?' she said nervously to the shower curtain. She was reluctant to ask because she didn't want to be viewed as some kind of marriage-obsessed psycho, but she knew that this would probably just eat at her for the rest of the day if she didn't say something now. And she and Shane were usually straight with one another about anything that was on their minds.

'Yes?' He peeked his head out from one side of the curtain. He had suds in his hair that were streaming towards his eyes, and he brought a hand up to brush them away quickly.

'Well, I was just wondering . . . look, it's silly really, I know it is, but I just have to ask.'

'Ask what, hon?' he asked, squinting at her. Apparently some soap had made it into his eyes after all.

'It's stupid, but well . . .'

'Cara, what is it?' Shane reached a hand out of the shower and grabbed a towel, bringing it to his face and wiping it. He looked concerned.

'Well, remember when you said last night that "it won't be us" with regard to that stupid wedding invitation? Did you mean that it's not going to be us because we aren't materialistic and crazy like Audrey and her fiancé? Or that it's not going to be us because you're not just interested in getting married? To me, I mean.'

There, she'd said it. She had diverted her eyes as she asked the question and now she raised them hesitantly to meet Shane's. He was looking at her with a smile.

'What?' he replied, his tone full of humour. 'You think I am not interested in making an honest woman out of you?'

Cara exhaled the breath she suddenly realised she'd been holding.

'No, it's not that, it's just . . . oh, just forget about it.' She felt a blush creeping up her neck and immediately regretted bringing the subject up. Feeling stupid, she dropped her gaze and focused on studying the pattern on the porcelain-tiled floor.

'Cara, look at me,' Shane urged, and she slowly brought her eyes up to meet his. 'I can't believe that you even had to ask me that question. You should know that I love you and of course I'm in this for the long term. It's you and me; you're mine, I'm yours and as far as I'm concerned that's the way it will always be. And, when the time is right, we'll move forward. You know that, don't you?'

Her heart soared and she nodded somewhat dumbly, willing herself not to blubber. Sometimes, Shane truly had a way with words.

'It's you and me, and what I meant last night when I said that, is that when we do it, when we get *married* – assuming you agree to be my wife,' he continued, emphasising the word, and Cara felt her heart skip. Partly because of his tone; it was so self-assured and sexy, 'we will do it our way. I thought you got that.'

She took a couple of steps towards him till she held his wet face in her hands. 'I'm sorry, I do know that, and I shouldn't need reassurance. I love you.'

'And I love you. Now go,' he added with a grin, 'unless you're willing to get very wet and join me in here.'

She giggled, all worry set aside. She knew she was being silly, but then again, she was also glad she'd asked – at least now she could put the stupid thought out of her head and get on with her day. It was wonderful to be in a relationship where you didn't have to play games or hide your true feelings. Everything was out in the open, which Cara supposed was how a mature relationship should be.

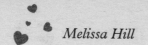

'All right, have a good one.' She leaned in towards Shane again for a kiss, unconcerned that the humidity of the shower was probably wreaking havoc on her hair.

'You too.' He returned her kiss, then smiled and pulled his head back under the spray of the water.

Feeling giddy, Cara turned on her heel and reached for the bathroom door. Oh well, she would just have to worry about her hair on the way in to work.

'Oh Cara?' Shane suddenly called out as she was about to leave the room. He poked his head back out of the shower curtain.

'Yes?'

'Let's meet for dinner tonight. I'm not sure I want to brave grilled cheese,' he teased, the dimple on his left cheek showing as he tried not to laugh, 'and I definitely don't think I have the stomach for another curry.'

Cara feigned a hurt look. 'You really think my cooking's that bad?'

Shane gave a broad grin. 'So maybe now you know why I haven't married you.'

'Oh you . . .' Cara smiled and headed out the door.

OK, maybe sometimes complete honesty wasn't so great.

She hustled onto the train at Grand Canal Station, which was just a short walk from their apartment. While standing in the carriage, she tried to flatten down her hair, which had become inevitably frizzy from the bathroom humidity, while balancing all her work belongings in the process. Thankfully, Greygates was only three stops away, and she reached the office within ten minutes.

She pulled open the front door of the simple two-storey building that housed Octagon Design, trying to juggle her handbag and laptop case as well as the coffee she'd picked up on the way. She was dangerously close to losing the entire lot when suddenly a pair of hands shot out to grab her coffee and laptop case just as both were threatening to slip from her fingers.

'Cheers, Conor, sorry, I was close to losing the lot for a minute,' Cara said, exhaling a large breath. She looked up into the face of her boss, who was wearing his usual sardonic grin.

'Glad I could be of assistance. Might help if you realised you had only one pair of hands though.' Conor smiled.

'Yep, I guess it would.' She looked at her watch and winced. 'Sorry I'm late, I was just running a bit behind this morning.'

'Is there any other way to run in the morning?' he chuckled.

In his early forties, Conor Dempsey was handsome with striking blue eyes and sandy brown hair that was always worn slightly tousled.

Tall and broad-shouldered, he too had been born and bred in Greygates, but had spent his early twenties working in London before eventually returning to set up Octagon. While he was the consummate bachelor, with various women vying for his attention, he had never married, which always surprised Cara somewhat. Knowing him as well as she did, she'd never thought he quite fitted the playboy man-about-town image, no matter how much his lifestyle suggested otherwise.

'Well, I have to say, much of it is my own fault, I would have been out the door a good half hour ago only for Shane.' She scattered her bags and laptop case onto her desk, and Conor propped himself up on an unused side table directly across from her.

'Not a fight I hope.' Having known Cara long before she and Shane started going out, he was never shy about voicing his opinion on the relationship, in much the way a protective older brother would. A real straight talker, when you were in conversation with Conor Dempsey few subjects – personal or otherwise – were off limits.

It was just the two of them in the office, and even though business had been great since the company first opened its doors almost seven years earlier, Conor had no desire to expand and take on additional business, extra staff and thus additional commitment. He had seen too many other small-business owners crash and burn after doing so, burdened by extra debt and responsibilities, especially once the recession hit. Instead, he was happy to simply nurture and maintain Octagon's strong and long-standing relationship with their existing accounts, which usually kept them busy.

Conor paid Cara well, trusted in her and, in turn, she trusted him and worked her hardest for him and they had developed a close relationship that many would envy. She loved the job and felt herself very lucky to have a boss who actually appreciated her, as well as being able to consider him a friend at the same time.

'Ah no, nothing like that.' Cara paused for a moment as she thought again about the topic of her and Shane's conversation that morning. 'Conor, how come you never got married?'

'Don't you start, my mother is bad enough trying to get me married off as it is.' He jumped off the desk and rolled his eyes, and Cara smiled. She knew Conor's mum Greta, and thought it was lovely that he still was so close to his mother, even though he very definitely lived his own life in a gorgeous penthouse apartment not far from the office. Or perhaps it was that Conor's mother took care of him so well that there was no need (or room) for a permanent woman in his life?

'I suppose I just never found the right girl,' he said in reply, before looking at her closely. 'Why do you ask?'

'Well, Shane and I got on to the subject of weddings last night, and it sort of carried through to this morning. I feel stupid really. Somehow I had it in my head that Shane wasn't interested in that sort of thing, you know . . . marriage. Like he was satisfied with how things were between us and didn't need anything more. And given that you've never taken the plunge, I just thought that maybe you had felt that way at some point in life too.'

'Did Shane actually tell you that he didn't want to get married?'

Cara shook her head. 'No, he said he did.'

'Well then, what are you worried about?'

'I'm not worried; I just wondered how some people come to that decision, like, "Yes, I want to get married" or "No, it's definitely not for me".'

He nodded. 'Well, indeed it's not for everyone.'

'So it never interested you – not at all?' Cara pressed.

'Ah, it might have at one point, but I chalk that feeling up to being young and foolish,' Conor said. 'It's probably a good thing it didn't happen, or that it wasn't pursued at least. We probably would have just made each other miserable.'

Cara sat up, immediately interested. 'Who was she? Someone from when you were in London?'

'Ah, just a girl. That ship has sailed. Look, don't worry about Shane; I'm sure that when he's ready, he'll pop the question. He would be an eejit to let someone like you get away in any case. As for me, don't you worry, sweetheart – I might not want marriage, but you won't find me all alone in my old age either.'

Cara laughed and rolled her eyes. 'Yep, I can see you still

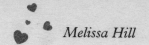

being able to pull them in when you're eighty, a bit like Jack Nicholson. You will be quite the Don Juan of the nursing-home scene, I bet.'

'I like the sound of that – I think, not sure about the Nicholson comparison. though, I'm not that old,' he joked, before turning his attention to the phone on his desk, which had just started ringing. 'Now get to work, you.'

'Yes, boss.'

The rest of the morning continued without challenge. Cara made her way through her work, fielded phone calls from clients, and essentially fell into her usual day-to-day work routine. It wasn't until one o'clock began to approach that her stomach started to make its usual protest that it was time for something other than what was on her to-do list.

This time, though, the rumbling of her stomach also reminded Cara that there was something she'd forgotten to do when she came in that morning.

As if on cue, the front door to the office flew open and in walked a familiar person. The very same person she had meant to phone earlier.

'Hey there sunshine,' her sister-in-law called out.

'Ah Kim, I completely forgot. I meant to call you earlier to apologise and—'

'Call me for what? So you could cancel on me?'

Cara looked guilty. 'Actually yes – sorry. I've got a lot more work on and—'

'Well tough, I'm here now, so get your stuff. I don't know about you but I'm starving.'

Kim ran her own cosmetics distribution business, supplying beauty salons and hotel spas the length and breadth of the country with her carefully chosen range of luxurious bath and body products.

A former model, she was ideal to front such a glamorous

business, but despite being involved in such an image-obsessed field, Kim loved her grub and, besides never missing a meal, was also one of those maddening women who could easily get away with carrying a few extra pounds.

Today she was dressed in head-to-toe Prada. Or was it Primark? Cara couldn't be sure. With Kim it could easily be either, and whether clad in designer or high street, she always looked fabulous. Her bouncy blonde locks reflected the office track lighting above and her peach complexion glowed with vitality, setting off her almond-shaped brown eyes. She was in her late thirties, almost a decade older than Cara, but at five foot eleven and in great shape, her sister-in-law could very easily outshine the considerably younger models who so often graced the pages of her company catalogues.

'Now, what would you say to a good burger?' she asked. 'That and some chips, I'm mad for chips.'

Cara shook her head. 'You know I hate you, don't you? Chips by the bucketload and still you can fit into those skinny pencil skirts.' Although Cara was reasonably slim, she had frustratingly wide hips and as such pencil skirts had never seen the inside of her wardrobe.

Kim shrugged and turned to Conor. 'Hey, Clooney, do you think you can run the show without her for an hour? Or will the whole place fall asunder if she's not here?' She knew Conor well and always jokingly referred to him, even to his face, as 'Clooney'; the comparison not just attributed to Conor's good looks, but also his perpetual bachelorhood.

'I think we might just survive,' Conor said. He looked at Cara. 'But if you're going for chips, bring me back some?'

'Bloody hell, I don't have much of a choice now do I? OK then,' she said, shaking her head, 'screw the diet for today; chips it is.'

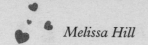

Gathering up her bag and coat, she said goodbye to Conor and walked through the door as Kim held it open for her.

'You're on a diet?' Kim enquired. 'Why?'

'Erm, because unlike some, I wasn't in line when they were handing out perfect genes.'

'Oh nonsense, you look gorgeous. But speaking of fitting into things,' her sister-in-law said, with a meaningful smile, 'I won't be fitting into pencil skirts for much longer.' Cara turned, her eyes widening. 'That's right, here we go again.' Kim laughed and pointed to her stomach.

'That's great news! When did you find out?' Cara smiled, going to embrace her.

Kim was a wonderful mother to Olivia and Lindsay, and she knew that the new Clancy baby too would find itself welcomed into a family full of love. Although she was a little surprised by the news; it was no secret that Kim had had very difficult births with her first two children – in fact with Lindsay she'd had such a terrible time of it, they'd both come close to dying.

'A couple of weeks ago. Besides my GP, you're the second to know. And your brother of course,' Kim added, grinning. 'I was feeling a little bit off lately, so last month I popped out at lunchtime and bought a test, and Bob's your uncle.' She winked. 'As you can probably tell, it wasn't exactly on the cards but what the hell . . .'

'It's really wonderful news. How far along are you?'

'About ten weeks. I suppose we really should wait a little while longer before we start telling people, but I'm feeling great and all's going well, so here's hoping.' Kim smiled. 'I suppose after the first one you get a bit blasé about the so-called rules. Anyway, we're telling the girls later today, so once they find out, there's no way we'll be able to keep it under wraps for much longer.'

Cara had to marvel at the laid-back way Kim talked about it all, but then again this was how her sister-in-law behaved about everything. Work, pregnancy, motherhood . . . Kim Clancy took it all in her stride and she truly seemed to have it all – a great husband and lovely family, as well as a busy and successful career.

'Forgive me for asking, but are you are at all worried about . . . you know, what happened before . . .' Cara wasn't sure how best to put it, but luckily Kim seemed to know exactly what she was referring to.

'You mean the messy bit at the end?' She looked sideways at Cara. 'Well, after the last time, Ben and I had a chat about it, and we decided that this time, we should think about heading all of that off at the pass.'

Cara frowned. 'I don't get you.'

'I'm going to plan a C-section for the delivery.'

'Oh.'

Kim looked at her hard. 'Don't tell me you're one of those? Too posh to push – natural is best and all that? I've been through the whole palaver twice and believe me there's nothing natural about it.'

'No, of course not. I think you're absolutely right to do what you think is best.' Notwithstanding that Cara didn't have the first notion about the realities of childbirth, she wouldn't dream of judging Kim for deciding to take a different approach. She was actually just surprised that she was so open about her plans, given that people generally kept these things quiet. As Kim had mentioned, people tended to be sniffy about the idea of planned C-sections and the whole 'too posh to push' attitude still prevailed.

'After what happened with Olivia, I probably should have arranged one with Lindsay, but of course it wasn't really the "done thing" back then,' Kim went on. 'Not that it is now either, and my doc took quite a bit of persuading from the outset, let me tell you,' she added and Cara smiled, struggling to imagine anyone trying to stand in the way of the force of nature that was Kim Clancy. 'Of course after fifteen hours of labour with Lindsay, I ended up having one anyway, so I think it's safe to say that I'm pretty much au fait with the pros and cons of both. Either way, my consultant's agreed and Ben and I are happy about it, so that's all that matters.'

'Absolutely.'

'Must admit it'll be a nice change too. This time there won't be any waiting around at the end, trying to figure out when it really is show time. The hospital will give me a date to go in, and all being well, I'll come out with Clancy number three, not feeling like I've done ten rounds with Freddy Krueger.'

Cara grimaced at the notion; she still remembered how ragged Kim had been after Lindsay's arrival five years before. 'Actually, when you describe it that way, it sounds like the right idea.'

'Of course it does. But you know yourself . . . wait for the fireworks and lectures to start once your mother finds out. I love Betty, but you and I both know she's a real traditionalist.'

That was true, Cara agreed. Irrespective of Kim's entirely rational reasoning, she could only imagine what her mother would say once she found out that her daughter-in-law was planning to intentionally bypass the labour ward.

But she also knew (and hoped) that any criticism Betty might level at Kim would simply roll off her. She was possibly the only woman Cara knew who truly didn't care a fig about what people thought about her and, not for the first time, she wished she had some of her sister-in-law's chutzpah.

Always calm and unruffled, Kim rarely seemed to have

a problem keeping day-to-day life in check, and never once complained about having to juggle a busy career with being a wife and mother. She hadn't even freaked out the time Lindsay used her satin Louboutins as a bathtime toy or when Olivia got chocolate ice cream on a white Gucci dress. Cara had been there at the time and Kim's response was classic. 'Bloody hell, that was the last of the ice cream.'

'So how's my brother taking the news?' Cara asked. 'Delighted I'm sure.'

'Yep, and secretly hoping this time his swimmers will figure out how to make it a boy.'

Cara laughed, knowing that the baby's gender would be the last thing on her brother's mind. Ben happened to be just as laid-back as his carefree, sophisticated wife. 'Nah really, he's over the moon, and like I said, we weren't trying or anything. But what the hell, what's one more? The more the merrier, and of course I'm not getting any younger either, so this is the last chance to produce a Clancy heir.'

'Well congratulations again, I'm so thrilled for you all, and I can't wait to meet my next niece or nephew in when . . . October?' Cara asked, trying to mentally calculate Kim's due date.

'Mid-November actually and thanks, but enough about us, what's happening with you?'

'Oh, just up to my eyeballs with work. Feeling a little behind, truth be told, but it's OK. Everything is good, nothing to complain about.'

'And how's the lovely Shane?' Kim smiled as they reached a nearby Eddie Rockets burger restaurant. The two women went inside, taking a seat at the counter with the lunch crowd.

'The same.' Cara smiled. She wasn't going to bring anything up about the night before, especially since there was nothing to worry about, but it was almost as if Kim could read her thoughts.

'What's that look for?' she asked, shrewdly narrowing her eyes. 'What's up?'

'Oh nothing bad,' Cara assured her. 'It's just . . . well, we had an interesting conversation this morning – about marriage.' She couldn't keep the smile from her face.

'Really? Tell me more. Although, with the way that you two go on, I would have thought that was decided a long time ago.'

Cara grabbed a menu and looked it over briefly before deciding to make it easy and just order whatever Kim was getting. The waitress behind the counter took a small pad and pencil from her apron.

'You ladies ready?' she asked.

Kim raised her eyebrows. 'Yep. I think I'll have the house burger, medium, with Swiss cheese, lettuce, tomato, pickles, onion, jalapeños, mustard, ketchup and mayo. And then a side of cheese fries with some bacon. With extra cheese. And a large Coke.' She looked up at the waitress and smiled. The girl raised her eyebrows, probably wondering where the hell Kim was going to fit it all. Then she turned to Cara. 'And yourself?'

'Ah, I think I'll just have the burger and a Coke. We can share the fries.'

'No we cannot,' Kim said quickly. She smiled at the waitress. 'Two portions please.'

The waitress took their menus and walked away to get the drinks. Cara laughed, turning to Kim. 'You know she hates your guts don't you? She's probably thinking "skinny bitch".'

Her sister-in-law waved a hand. 'Yeah, yeah, I'll come back when I've ballooned up and weigh fifteen stone. I'm sure that'll make her feel better. Anyway, we were talking about Shane?'

Cara briefly recapped what had happened the night before, as well as their conversation this morning. When she was finished, Kim shook her head. 'Well, I think it all sounds good, you both seem to be on the same page anyway.'

'I know, I can't believe how silly I felt after he told me all that this morning.'

'Well, I'd be willing to bet it will happen soon, a proposal I mean. You two have been together for a while now. But I'll say one thing – when Shane pops the question, do yourself a favour and just elope,' Kim said. Cara wondered why. From what she could remember of Kim and Ben's wedding, eight years ago, it was a big affair but nothing elaborate or ostentatious. Then again, she briefly recalled some . . . strife surrounding Betty and her level of interference in the build-up. While Cara knew her mother could be . . . persuasive at times, Betty had always been massively supportive of her and Cara knew she would want her very much involved in her own wedding plans.

'Oh, I could never do that, Kim! I'd have to have everyone there on the day,' Cara replied. 'I can never understand people who do that – head off to Vegas and get married on their own with nobody there to celebrate with them. What's the point if you can't share it with family and friends?'

At that moment their food arrived and both women tucked in, Kim wasting no time launching in to her cheese fries.

'OK then, but if a wedding is on the cards try and pick a date before I get whale-sized at least.'

'Yes, having seen you with the other two, I think dolphin-sized is more like it,' Cara replied drolly, 'especially since it appears you share a gene pool with the likes of Heidi Klum.'

'I wish!' Kim laughed. 'But in all seriousness,' she

continued, 'when it happens, the proposal I mean, just do what is right for the two of you. Trust me, you will get plenty of "advice" from everyone and anyone on the best way to do things, and remember that you don't have to take any of it. Know that whatever you choose, the people who love you and support you the most won't make the day about them, they'll make it about you and Shane, and show up to celebrate your special day regardless of what you decide to do. Just do what feels right for you. Ben and I did and we couldn't be happier today. Set the precedent early and go on to have a happy life.'

'Thanks, that's good advice.' Cara smiled at her. She really couldn't ask for a better sister-in-law. This is what sisterhood should really be like, she thought as her mind briefly turned to Heidi and Danielle. 'Course there isn't anything to plan, seeing as he hasn't asked me yet.'

Kim patted her hand. 'Just promise me that when he does, I'll be one of the first to know.'

'Goes without saying,' Cara said, thinking about how she had been the first in the family (besides Ben of course) to know Kim's big news. She turned her attention back to her food as Kim waved down the waitress again.

'Excuse me?' she asked. 'Can I get some more of these cheese fries?'

Cara's eyes widened. 'Seriously?'

'What?' Kim looked at her. 'I can't eat like this at business lunches so I need to make the most of it. It would scare off all my clients.'

Chapter 4

As Kim pulled away from dropping Cara off back at her office, she smiled fondly as she thought about the conversation with her sister-in-law. She hoped it all did work out between Cara and Shane, as she not only appreciated her relationship with Ben's sister and wanted her to be happy, but truly thought Cara and her lovely boyfriend made a good match.

She was also glad that her sister-in-law hadn't given her any grief about the decision she'd made regarding the baby's eventual delivery. Not that she'd expected her to; Cara was typically non-judgemental and open-minded about everything, but of course there was also the fact that she hadn't yet had a baby of her own.

And Kim knew from experience that it was certain to be fellow mums who had the most to say about anything to do with motherhood.

She also knew that once news of the planned delivery was open knowledge she was likely to get it with both barrels. However, Kim couldn't care less about what people thought of her decision, and she could never understand why people got on their high horses about planned caesareans. After all, pretty much all forms of delivery nowadays necessitated major medical intervention, so the 'Momtyrs', as Kim liked to call them, had nothing to be judgemental about.

Given that she'd experienced both sides of the coin, she

felt perfectly placed to be able to decide which option would be best for this baby and she wasn't leaving anything to chance.

Of course, many of her friends who'd gone down the same route (and swore by it) generally preferred not to be quite so upfront about the decision, but there was no question of that for Kim. Why should she have to hide or feel ashamed about a decision that she knew for sure would be the best thing for her family?

She would go in to the hospital on her prearranged delivery date, and be able to see her baby within hours. It would all be peaceful and efficient, and having a calm non-traumatised mother would give her newest son or daughter the best possible start in life.

Unlike poor Lindsay, who'd spent much of her first week being looked after by nursery staff because Kim had been in such a terrible state after the long and utterly excruciating labour.

Recovery from her eventual emergency C-section had been slow and very painful as the preceding hours of labour had already taken so much out of her. Three years before that, delivery with Olivia had also been drawn out and dangerous, and she recalled how she'd needed two separate blood transfusions afterwards.

Kim longed for the moment when she would be able to hold her newborn in her arms without crowds of medical staff frantically rushing around, terrifying all concerned. She remembered how frantic and upset Ben had been when she'd been rushed off to theatre with Lindsay and there was just no time for anyone to fill him in on what was happening. It had made for a horribly fraught experience, so much so that it took them both a few days to be able to get their heads around the arrival of the newest member of the family, never mind celebrate it.

Kim was determined that this time it would be different. She knew of course that there were risks involved, as in any surgery, but she was prepared to take those risks over the others she'd already experienced, any day.

Her thoughts turned to her beloved husband. Even after eight years of marriage, Ben still did it for her. She knew that she could be a handful, was never shy with her opinions, and always called it like she saw it.

However, she also knew that those parts of her personality were exactly why she and Ben worked so well together. While they were both laid-back about most things in their lives, Kim was forthright whereas Ben usually kept his counsel. They were a perfect balance and their happiness proved just how well they meshed.

This balance also overflowed to family life and their children. Olivia and Lindsay, eight and five respectively, complemented their lives. Olivia had shown up considerably shy of nine months after the wedding, and then three years later Lindsay had introduced herself.

Both were their mother's daughters in every imaginable way. While Ben was a handsome man with distinguished dark good looks that Mr Darcy would envy, both girls had inherited their mother's blonde locks and lanky, gazelle-like proportions. Ben regularly teased them that he would bemoan the day they reached their teens and would be surrounded by countless male admirers.

As Kim drove, she glanced at her watch, realising the girls would soon be getting home from school. She thought of the lovely news that she and Ben had to share with them, which was why they had both arranged to take the afternoon off and meet the girls when they arrived home.

Nearing the house, which was just on the very outskirts of the Greygates area, she saw that Ben was already there.

As one of the partners of a Dublin city centre accountancy practice, he often had the ability to come and go as he pleased.

She pulled in to the driveway and brought the car to a stop. Both girls tumbled from the SUV in front of her, backpacks and lunchboxes in hand. They waved wildly at their mother, excited that she, as well as their father, was apparently playing hookey.

Kim got out of her car and not a moment later she was surrounded by little arms that begged for a hug.

'Mummy, Mummy! You came home early too!' Olivia cried.

'Do you have a day off?' enquired Lindsay at the same time.

'Stop it,' Kim laughed as she held them both close. 'You both act as if you never see me!'

There was no denying that she'd worked hard over the years to build her business up from humble beginnings in the spare room of their house to the glossy offices Blissology now inhabited, but she felt she'd done it without compromising too much on family life. She'd set up the business while Olivia was still a toddler, and by the time Lindsay arrived, it was well established and thus didn't require as much of her attention.

It was only when Lindsay reached two and started going to a nearby crèche that the business really managed to hit its stride, becoming one of the biggest beauty distribution players in the Irish market, and Kim was proud of the fact that she'd managed to keep things going while still being there for her children. Of course none of it would have been possible without the support of Ben, who was very much a modern father and rowed in with the childcare whenever required.

So while the Clancy family enjoyed a good life/work balance, being self-employed still pretty much required significant personal commitment, and while Kim didn't mind playing hookey, it wasn't a regular occurrence.

'Is it a special occasion?' Olivia asked. Sure enough, their oldest daughter, who Kim always believed had a built-in intuitive ability, already knew something was up. It was as if she was sniffing the air for clues as to why both her parents would suddenly be home at two-thirty on a Thursday afternoon.

'Well, you might say that.' Ben smiled as he made his way over to greet his wife. He planted a light kiss on her cheek and looked knowingly into her eyes. He pulled her close quickly, his outstretched hand running gently over her midriff. Kim smiled at her husband and winked. 'Come on girls, let's get inside.' She passed her briefcase to Ben and reached out a hand to each of her girls. 'I'm famished. How does a round of banana splits sound?'

Later, over the promised banana splits, the girls looked at their parents expectantly.

'So you guys have something to tell us, don't you?' Olivia asked, narrowing her eyes suspiciously at Kim and Ben.

Kim was halfway convinced her eldest could read minds.

'What is it? What is it?' Lindsay piped up.

Kim and Ben exchanged a look.

'Well girls,' Ben started, 'Mummy and I have some exciting news.'

Kim smiled. 'Yes, well we all know we are a very lucky family, and it seems that we'll soon have another little person to share all of that luck with.'

'Another little person? You mean—' Olivia looked at Kim's tummy, understanding immediately.

Kim realised she was holding her breath. While it was good news, and likely to be received as such by willing recipients, with children you just never could tell. Olivia had been pretty young at the time of Lindsay's arrival, so this was really the first time both girls had the ability to digest what the addition of a third child to the household could mean.

Olivia spoke again. 'Is it going to be a girl or a boy?'

Kim exhaled; her oldest seemed to be handling this from an upfront and analytical place, as was her norm. That was good.

'Well, we aren't sure yet. We won't find that out for a while,' Kim replied gently. Digesting this, Olivia nodded.

'OK. Well, I'm fine with either,' she said, a small smile coming to her lips.

For her part, Lindsay looked curious about the idea, and clearly wanted to learn more about the impending arrival. 'How will it get here? Does the stork bring it? Or does it get left on the porch?' Her wide blue eyes were full of questions.

Ah, the innocence, thought Kim. She was about to speak when Olivia beat her to it.

'No silly, Mummy's going to get big and fat and then one day she just explodes. And poof, there's the baby.' She waved her arms around to illustrate the idea of an explosion.

Kim and Ben held back a snort of laughter at their eight-year-old's take on pregnancy. However, Lindsay looked terrified. Her mouth dropped open as she considered her mother's doom.

'Mummy, do you really explode?' Once again, Olivia had gotten the better of her little sister, and Kim was sure there would be nightmares tonight.

'No darling, I won't explode, not at all. But I will get

big and fat.' She laughed as she patted her still very flat tummy beneath her pencil skirt. She reached out to take Lindsay's hand. 'Everything will be OK,' she said with some conviction, thinking back to this morning's conversation with her obstetrician Dr Downey. She smiled at both her daughters.

'Well, I hope we get a boy this time,' Olivia said off-handedly. 'Then maybe Daddy won't be the odd one out any more.'

Kim snorted. It was totally like Olivia to offer her father a bone.

Ben smiled. 'Yes, things are a bit one-sided in this house aren't they?'

'Want a girl,' said Lindsay weakly. 'Want to be big sister.'

'Duh.' Olivia rolled her eyes. 'You'll be a big sister whether it's a girl *or* a boy. But remember, I'm still going to be the *biggest* sister.'

'Now, now, Olivia, you have to let Lindsay take on some of the responsibility too. Being a big sister is a *big* job after all,' Ben said seriously, looking at both of his daughters. 'I'm sure though between the two of you, you'll make a good team for Number Three.'

Both girls smiled winningly at their parents, and then Olivia decidedly offered up a high five to her sister. Grinning, Lindsay met it.

'What'll the baby's name be?' Lindsay asked and Kim and Ben looked at one another and shrugged.

'Well, we're not sure yet. It all depends on whether it is a girl or a boy. I guess we'll decide that when it gets here,' Kim told her.

It reminded her of how both girls had remained nameless for hours (or, in poor Lindsay's case, days) after the delivery, as Kim had been in such a bad state. This time would be

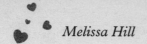

different though. If all went according to plan, she was determined that this baby would have a name within minutes of its arrival.

Names were important. With Olivia and Lindsay she was proud to say that both girls had lived up to their names' respective meanings.

Olivia was perceived to be a creative person with free-spirited and artistic tendencies as well as an avid, enquiring mind. Lindsay, on the other hand, was perceived as a contributor who was responsible, caring and reliable.

Kim was looking forward to choosing a name for the next, boy or girl, and ensuring that he or she fitted with whatever they decided to call them.

'Can I name the baby?' Lindsay asked. Olivia's eyebrows raised and a mischievous look formed in her eyes.

Ben looked amusedly at his wife and bit his lip.

'Well let's wait until the time comes, OK? It's a long way off yet but we'll definitely consider any ideas that you might have,' Kim replied in much the same voice that she'd use to negotiate a business deal.

'OK then,' Olivia said. 'But if it's a girl, I would like to enter the names of Hannah or Miley to consideration.'

Oh Christ, groaned Kim internally.

'But what if it's a boy?' Ben offered, obviously trying to move away from the thoughts of Hollywood pop stars.

'Justin!' Lindsay cried. 'Definitely, Justin.'

Kim snorted with laughter. 'I think I'm seeing a pattern here,' she said smiling at Ben. Her youngest was only five, and already she knew all about Justin bleedin' Bieber. Crikey, what would they be like when they were teenagers, if they knew this kind of stuff now?

'Well, that does it,' Ben said in a teasing voice. 'I think I know two little girls who watch far too much TV. It's the

History Channel for you two from now on.' He scooped them both up in his arms as they squealed with laughter.

'Great, next we'll be getting Caesar and Cleopatra . . .' Kim said archly.

Lindsay rushed forward and encircled Kim around her middle, as far as her little arms would go.

'Thank you Mummy,' she said, smiling.

'For what?' Kim asked, hugging her.

'For bringing us another baby. I don't care if you get fat.'

Kim hugged her daughter with all her might, tears shining in her eyes. *Remember this moment*, she cued herself.

No, she didn't care if she got fat either. She would balloon out to three hundred pounds if it meant she could feel this happy, for ever. She wouldn't trade any of this for the world. She had everything she needed, right under this roof and within these walls.

Chapter 5

By the time Cara was due to meet Shane for dinner, she was only beginning to shrug off the effects of the jalapeño burger and cheese fries at lunch.

Pregnant or not, she still didn't understand how Kim could put all that food away the way she did.

While Cara had never had any major problems with her weight, she still needed to make a conscious effort to work at it, religiously hauling her ass to the gym at least three times a week. Kim on the other hand stuffed her face, rarely worked out and still strutted around as glamorous and skinny as ever.

Freak of nature, definitely. Had to be genetics.

Cara checked the time on her watch. She was running late. She had meant to be at the restaurant – a lovely Mediterranean bistro called Stromboli in the city centre that was a favourite of theirs – by seven o'clock. It was now a quarter past and her taxi was still stuck in traffic.

She picked up her phone and typed a quick text message to Shane.

Sorry, almost there, traffic on the quays is hell, coming as fast as possible.

A moment later her phone pinged and she read his response.

Don't rush, I'm not going anywhere.

She smiled and let out a sigh of relief; thank goodness he was patient. While she would never have readily admitted to it, the truth was he ended up waiting for her a lot. Cara struggled with punctuality.

Her thoughts drifted back to their conversation earlier this morning and she vowed to herself that she would not bring the subject of marriage up again. Like Kim said, it would happen when the time was right, and she knew now that she had nothing to worry about; he'd assured her of that this morning.

Instead, she was going to be a sexy, confident, independent woman and was certainly not going to sit around wondering when her ring finger would find an accessory.

Moments later, the taxi zipped down a couple of side streets that landed her close to the restaurant entrance. Paying the driver, she reached into her bag for her lip gloss and, smoothing it on with the fingers of one hand, she fluffed her hair with the other.

She'd do.

She got out and walked into the restaurant, which was still full of an after-work crowd made up of well-heeled young professionals. Cara glanced around and tried to find Shane. She was sure that he was more than likely waiting in the bar area for her, so she scanned the occupants.

Spotting him, a smile jumped to her face and her heart leapt in her chest. The sight of him automatically sent a jolt of attraction and electricity through her core.

She strode across the hardwood floor, and the crowd almost seemed to part for her as she closed the distance between them. He held out a hand as she neared and she placed her palm in his.

'Hello gorgeous.' He smiled.

'I'm sorry I'm late, rush-hour traffic really can be a terror.'

49

'Don't worry about it, and I'm used to waiting for you. What are you having?' Shane got up from the barstool that he had been sitting on and offered it to her. The place really was packed.

She took a seat and considered the extensive wine list on the countertop. Normally, she was a red wine lover, but tonight was different.

'A Grey Goose dirty martini, extra dirty,' she said to the barman. Shane's eyebrows shot up in surprise. 'Extra dirty? What's gotten into you?'

'Just looking to mix it up a little, you know yourself.'

From the look on Shane's face, clearly he didn't. He smiled nervously and placed a protective hand on the back of Cara's stool.

The barman duly delivered her drink and she turned to Shane. 'To fun,' she said, clinking the edge of his gin and tonic.

'To the future,' he said, meeting her gaze. His look was surprisingly intense and Cara felt her heart give a deep thump in her chest. She took a sip of her drink and reminded herself once more: *sophisticated and sexy . . . no marriage talk.*

'So how was your day then?' she said, starting the conversation.

'The usual cut and thrust of the Irish accountancy world . . .'

'Right – how fascinating.' Cara feigned a yawn and Shane elbowed her.

They chatted happily until a waitress made her way over to let them know their table was ready.

Entering the dining area, they were led to a small alcove that housed one private table that looked out on to the rest of the room. It was surrounded by colourful stained-glass windows and the lights were dim to set the mood, setting off the rich mahogany of the tables and the colourful high backed banquette seating. It was a cosy space, and Cara knew from past experience that the amazing food served to enrich a diner's experience even more.

Shane stood behind Cara and pulled out her chair, allowing her to take a seat. She thanked him as he pushed the chair in and she moved the white cloth napkin from the tabletop on to her lap. He sat across from her and smiled.

He set his hands on the table but then back in his lap, before finally returning them to the table, as if he was unsure what to do with them. Cara noted the behaviour, and wondered what was wrong. He had seemed fine at the bar moments ago, and she didn't know what to make of the sudden fidgeting.

Oh shit . . .

'Everything all right?' she inquired nervously, still glancing at his hands. His fingers were now tapping the wood of the table, as if he was looking for a piano but would instead make do with pounding out a rhythm with whatever surface was provided.

'What?' he replied, bringing his attention back to Cara. He looked briefly at his fingers as if he had previously been unaware of what they had been doing. 'Oh sorry, I just need to order another drink.' He picked up his empty glass and his hand shook and rattled the leftover ice.

Cara was now seriously worried. First off, Shane was never jittery. Second, he was never impatient. And third, he wasn't a big drinker and certainly not some kind of addict who started to shake while he waited for his next fix.

'Shane, are you all right?' she asked, her internal radar screaming at her that something was up. Oh God, she *knew* she should never have mentioned that whole marriage thing this morning. Now he was spooked.

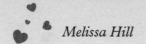

'Yes, why do you ask?' he said, offering up a smile that didn't quite reach his eyes.

'You're just acting sort of weird all of a sudden.' Cara glanced around at her fellow diners, looking for clues. She wondered if he had perhaps seen someone he knew but didn't want to meet, and that was what had set off the nervous behaviour.

'Really Cara, I'm fine, I'm just . . . I'm just hungry. I didn't get lunch today. Speaking of which, did you end up cancelling with Kim earlier? You mentioned this morning that you might.'

Her thoughts temporarily distracted, she shook her head. 'Actually, I did see her. I completely forgot that I was planning to cancel and she showed up at the office so we ended up going out anyway.' She smiled. 'I'm glad – it turns out she had some news.'

'Really? Tell me all.'

'Clancy baby number three is on the way. I'm the first in the family to know.'

Shane smiled and he looked like himself again. 'Well that's fantastic,' he said happily. 'I bet is Ben is over the moon.'

Cara nodded her head. 'They both are. I feel really chuffed that she told me first though. She really is like a sister to me.'

A waitress appeared to take their drinks. 'What can I get you?'

Shane picked up the wine list and pointed to his selection. 'Let's have a bottle of the Veuve Clicquot.'

She smiled. 'Good choice. I'll be right back.'

Cara looked at him, somewhat shocked at the champagne order but at the same time relieved. He couldn't be planning to break up with her if he was ordering champagne. Unless he was so desperate to be rid of her, he wanted to celebrate when it was over . . . 'What's with the champagne?' she asked suspiciously.

'Ah why not? We're a long time dead after all.'

Cara didn't understand. A second ago, Shane had looked like he couldn't wait to get out of here, now it seemed he was settling in for the night.

The waitress returned with an ice bucket, flutes and the bottle of champagne. She opened it and poured both Cara and Shane a glass. When she was finished, she looked at Shane. 'Would you like to order food now?'

Cara started to speak up but Shane shook his head. 'Let's have a glass of this first, and give us a few more moments.'

'Not a problem,' the waitress said, taking her leave.

So much for being hungry . . . Now Cara was thoroughly confused. 'So, seriously, what's the special occasion?' she inquired, holding up her glass of champagne and glancing at the bottle.

Across the table, Shane cleared his throat. He hadn't yet picked up his glass and he looked to be holding on to – no, clutching – the edge of the table. He pressed his lips together and seemed to be considering his next words.

Finally, he spoke. 'It's just, I . . .' Suddenly his words were cut off by a sharp cry from the other side of the restaurant, and their attention was immediately directed to where the sound came from. Across the room, a woman was crying what appeared to be happy tears as her dining companion, down on one knee at the side of the table, seemed to be sliding a diamond ring onto her left hand.

'Aww,' Cara said, smiling. She started to clap with the rest of the diners as the woman stood up and encircled her fiancé in her arms, covering his face with kisses. 'That's so sweet.' She turned her attention back to Shane. His pallor had changed to an even more ghostly shade, and the confident, calm smile that had graced his face earlier was gone. In truth, he looked like someone who was about to be sick at any moment.

Oh God, Cara thought, panicking. *He really is afraid of marriage.*

'Shane, are you all right?' she asked, all her fears from before suddenly returning. Regardless of what he'd said earlier about having no issues with marriage, no man should react that badly to someone else's engagement.

'Sorry, I just lost my train of thought there.' He shook his head as if hoping to shake off the memory of what had just taken place across the dining room.

'Talk about a cliché, huh?' Cara joked, indicating the couple and hoping to once again lighten the mood.

But Shane now looked positively green, and seemed to be having a hard time swallowing. He looked around as if he was trying to figure out where the nearest exit was.

Even more thoroughly confused at this point, Cara had no idea what to say next. She glanced at her glass of champagne and fought the urge to grab it and throw it back in one gulp. Searching her mind for a way to extricate them from this situation, she remembered that Shane had been about to make a toast.

'So,' she said with an easy-going smile, 'what were we about to toast to?'

Shane searched her face, and his eyes nervously moved back and forth in his head. 'Right . . . a toast, yes, right,' he stuttered, seemingly at a loss for words.

He stopped for a moment and cleared his throat again. 'Right, you know that, um . . .' Faltering, he looked down at his lap and seemed to be lost in thought for a moment. Then he grabbed his champagne glass in one hand and offered it up. 'Cheers to Ben and Kim and their soon-to-be new addition,' he said resolutely, smiling a weak smile. Cara didn't move to greet the gesture, so Shane leaned forward to clink her glass instead. Then he sat back in his chair and took a deep drink from the flute.

Cara sat across the table, feeling bewildered about what had just transpired.

Had he really bought a bottle of champagne worth nearly a hundred quid just to toast to family members who weren't even present at this dinner? she thought to herself. Not to mention that he'd only just learned the news about Kim and Ben's new baby. Cara felt a growing unease in the pit of her stomach and couldn't seem to organise her thoughts. All she knew was that something very important had happened – literally in the last few moments – that had greatly changed the tone of the evening.

For some reason, the relaxed mood from before they'd seen the other couple's proposal never returned, and Shane spent much of the meal in sullen silence. Cara was relieved when the bill was paid and they were finally able to leave.

Walking out on to the street, Shane seemed lost in another world and Cara hoped it wouldn't take long for them to find a taxi and just get home.

He turned to Cara suddenly. 'Actually, you go ahead. I need to go back to the office. I just realised I forgot something.'

Cara frowned at him. 'But it's after nine o'clock at night, Shane. Can't it wait till morning?'

'It really can't,' he insisted, signalling an oncoming taxi. 'Look, why don't you take this and go on home. I just need to go grab this . . . file and I'll be back in no time.'

Cara nodded glumly. Something was definitely wrong and she didn't know how to fix it; she just knew that for some reason Shane didn't want to come home with her. He wanted to be away from her. She cursed the newly engaged couple who had given rise to all the fears that she had thought she had put away. She had vowed not to mention the idea of marriage again tonight and, somehow, the notion had still followed her in to the restaurant by way of a third party. And now her boyfriend was looking to avoid her.

'All right,' she agreed lamely. 'If this file is so important, go ahead.' 'Hey,' Shane said, pulling her close and raising her chin so she would meet his gaze. 'I won't be long I promise, just go home and get settled, and I'll follow on shortly. Really, I promise I won't be long.' He kissed her, and there was something in it that made her anxiety ebb away a little.

'Shane, are we OK?' she couldn't help but ask. 'It's just that scene in there and the couple with the engagement . . . and then your mood and . . . just the way everything felt . . .' She blurted the words out, feeling all of the worries that had been piling up since last night suddenly cresting and overflowing around them.

'Hey, hey – what did I say this morning?'

'You said a lot of things . . .'

'And all of them were true. Look, I just had something on my mind tonight, that's all. Just go home and don't worry about a thing, OK? I'll see you soon.'

She nodded and got into the waiting taxi, not sure what else there was to say.

Later that night, Cara woke suddenly. She sat up in bed, turned to the alarm clock and looked at the time. 12:15 a.m. As her eyes adjusted to the darkness, she looked down at the other side of the bed. She reached a hand out: it was empty and cold. Shane was not beside her. She had left him hours ago at the restaurant and he still hadn't returned home.

Pushing aside the worries about their disastrous dinner earlier, she tried to figure out what had woken her up. She'd waited up for him as long as she could, but the events of the day had drained her and she had eventually fallen asleep.

Just then, Cara's phone chirped from the nightstand. She reached out to grab it, and fear entered her heart as she immediately had visions of the police calling telling her there had been an accident and that Shane was in the hospital.

'Oh God,' she breathed, preparing herself for the worst.

The screen came alive but it wasn't a call coming through. There was a lone text message. It was from Shane.

She swallowed hard. What if he wasn't coming home? What if he had decided that he didn't want to be with her . . . what if . . .?

She opened the message. It simply read

'Sorry to wake you. Meet me in the living room?'

The message was new and delivered a few seconds ago. Once again, confusion reigned. Shane was here in the apartment? But why was he texting her from their living room? She got out of bed and pulled her robe on.

Then suddenly, her senses, acute in the dark, were met with something unexpected.

A sweet, rich smell.

Cara began walking across the room and her bare feet came into contact with something on the floor. It was cold and velvety soft. Reaching to the wall to turn on the overhead light, she realised that the floor was covered in a trail of petals, rose petals. They led to the door.

A tentative smile rushed to her face, and something that felt like hope mixed with excitement bloomed in her heart. Her feet moved lightly across the room and she opened the door to find the hallway bathed in what seemed like soft candlelight.

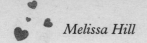

What the . . .?

She continued to follow the trail of rose petals down the hallway, past the kitchen and, finally, into the living room, where Shane stood. He had his back to her, and was looking out through the glass patio doors that showcased the night, lit only by the stars overhead.

'Shane? What are you doing? What's going on?' Cara asked hesitantly.

She knew he had heard her, but he began speaking without turning round.

'I knew I was doing something wrong in the restaurant earlier, you know. I wanted to do something special, but it went completely against who we are, as a couple. However, it is now officially a new day.'

She started to breathe easier. He seemed to be apologising for his strange behaviour earlier – mind you it was a slightly odd apology, but she appreciated it just the same.

'Shane, really, it's fine. I'm sure that when you saw that couple and after what we talked about this morning . . . I understand, there is a lot of pressure about the whole marriage thing, and it's all coming from me. I'm sorry, I should never have mentioned anything about it, and never would have, only for that stupid invitation . . .' She started to walk towards him.

Shane turned around then and met Cara's gaze. A smile was on his face, a truly genuine one. The kind she was used to.

'You really don't know, do you?' he said, chuckling a little.

'Know what?' She was at a loss. Her eyes were round as saucers as she tried to figure out what she had seemingly been missing.

Shane crossed the distance between them in three steps and pulled her into his arms. 'You make me so happy, you are my whole world, and I love you and I want you with me always. I don't want to share our special happy moments with a room full of strangers. I want this to be all about us. I was going to tell you all that in the restaurant tonight and then give you this . . .' He pulled a small black velvet box from the pocket of his jacket and sank to one knee in front of her.

Cara's breath caught in her throat and her heart started to beat wildly.

'But the time wasn't right, not then, and I wanted this moment to be special for you, for us, and I then realised that making a big show of it,' he continued, 'a big public proposal in some restaurant, wasn't right for us, and thankfully that bloke beat me to it and forced me into shutting up. I didn't want anything to ruin or spoil this moment.' He took a deep breath. 'Cara I love you, I have never loved anyone the way I love you. Please do me the honour of becoming my wife. Will you please make me the happiest man on the planet and marry me?'

Before Cara, still trying to recover from what he'd said, could say anything, he opened the ring box to reveal a perfect princess-cut diamond on a white gold band. Two smaller diamonds on either side of the bigger one also graced the band. It was simple, beautiful and classic. And it was perfect.

His eyes met Cara's as it finally dawned on her what was going on. He had been planning to propose in that restaurant . . . and of course – what was it she'd said at the time? Something about restaurant proposals being a cliché? She had taken everything that had happened and, thanks to her insecurities, had completely spun it out of context. She laughed at the silliness of the past few hours. When would she learn not to let her imagination run away with her?

'Oh my goodness . . .' she said, staring at the ring.

'You like it?'

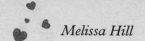

'Shane, it's beautiful, it's utterly perfect, I—'

'You haven't yet answered my question,' he reminded her gently and Cara shook her head, still somewhat numb from the surprise of it all.

'Yes, yes, yes!' Finally she flung herself into his arms and laughed while he placed the ring on her finger. They kissed deeply and passionately and all of Cara's insecurities and worries immediately left her mind. It was just them – her and Shane – and it would *always* be them; together, making their own way.

'Are you really surprised?' he asked, smiling. 'Are you happy?'

'Oh yes, very much so,' she grinned, staring at her hand and the beautiful diamond that twinkled in the candlelight.

'I thought you had figured it out, I really thought you did.' Shane kissed her again, this time on the forehead. 'After that guy beat me to the punch, I felt sick, I didn't know what to do or how to recover from it. And then when you said that it was all so clichéd, I almost had to rush to the loo to throw up.'

She laughed, remembering. 'I'm really sorry. I just thought that you'd been spooked, like you saw that proposal and felt pressured, especially after this morning.'

'Not a chance. To be honest, I've been planning this for a while. And when that wedding invite came yesterday, and we got to talking about it, it seemed like the right moment.'

She kissed him again, and without another word, Shane picked her up and dramatically carried her back to their bedroom, crossing the threshold with her as if she were already a bride.

'Then we're *definitely* going to that wedding,' Cara thought, realising she inadvertently had Audrey McCarthy to thank for what was the happiest moment of her life.

Chapter 6

The following morning, Cara hustled out her front door, phone in hand, punching her mother's number while at the same time sneaking a peek at her newly decorated ring finger. She was an engaged woman! She could hardly believe it. But of course her newly transformed state didn't work towards improving her timekeeping; if anything her and Shane's late-night, erm . . . celebrations meant that she'd be even later for work this morning. She prayed Conor would understand.

As per the norm, the phone in the Clancy household rang exactly once before Betty picked up; Cara was convinced that her mother carried the cordless handset around in her pocket from when she woke up in the morning to the time she went to bed at night.

'Hello? Cara? Is that you?'

Cara smiled. Her mother knew very well who it was. In Betty's eyes, caller ID was right up there with the discovery of electricity.

'Yes Mum, you know it's me, didn't it just come up on the display?' Cara said giddily.

'Why are you calling so early? Is everything all right? Are you OK? Oh my goodness, has there been an accident? Is Shane OK?'

Cara shook her head indulgently. In Betty Clancy's eyes, calling before ten o'clock in the morning meant that someone *must* have been in an car accident, fallen off a cliff or been run over by a lorry, and more than likely they weren't wearing clean underwear when it happened.

'Yes Mum, everything's fine. I just wanted to tell you that . . . well, something has happened . . . I have some news.' She grinned broadly.

'What's happened, Cara? Where are you, I'll send your father to go and get you. Just stay where you are, don't move and don't talk to anyone.'

Cara chuckled. There was absolutely nothing in her tone that would suggest an emergency, but her mother had no ability whatsoever to read people. Betty would definitely never have made it as a police investigator, she thought fondly.

'Mum, slow down for a minute. There's nothing to worry about, quite the opposite actually. I'm just ringing to tell you that Shane and I are engaged – he asked me to marry him last night!'

A scream of happiness erupted at the other end of the line, so loud that Cara had to hold the phone away from her ear. She smiled delightedly.

'Oh my goodness! Oh Cara, this is just brilliant news. Another wedding! I can hardly wait. Have you set a date yet? When are you going to go shopping for your dress? We can go today if you'd like. I presume you've taken the day off and . . . Oh where will we have it? I'll give Father O'Brien a call about booking the church, and a hotel of course. We'll need somewhere that could at least fit . . . oh I don't know . . . three hundred, I suppose? And get going on the guest list of course. Oh I think a spring wedding is always much nicer than the summer, don't you . . . ?'

'Mum, we haven't even considered any of that yet,' Cara said, laughing at her mother's excitable ramblings but at the

same time slightly taken aback. What was it she had she said
. . . church wedding? Three hundred people on the guest
list? Just because Heidi's marriage to Paul last year had been
a colossal, pompous affair didn't mean that she and Shane
wanted the same thing. The opposite in fact, she thought,
remembering how much of a bridezilla her little sister had
been. And given both her and Shane's reaction to Audrey
McCarthy's wedding invitation, she guessed he felt the same
way.

They'd both want something small and simple, nothing
overblown.

'The proposal only happened last night,' she replied,
laughing easily. 'We haven't had a chance to even think about
any of those things, let alone start planning anything.'

'Well, you have to start making plans soon. All the good
hotels in Dublin get taken up quickly, so we need to get a
date set and a deposit put down straight away,' Betty insisted.

'Mum, honestly, there's plenty of time,' Cara said, trying
to keep her voice casual, although inwardly she was a little
unnerved. She'd been so looking forward to sharing the news
with her mother, but hadn't anticipated that Betty would
actually be *that* excited about everything. 'And there's no
point in booking anything just yet, as Shane and I aren't
really sure what we want. As for three hundred guests . . .
I really don't think so. We were thinking along of the lines
of something smaller, something intimate.'

'But how small, Cara? Think about Shane's people alone
– all that fancy developer crowd, sure there must be hundreds
of them. Never mind the crew on our side, especially your
father's. The list of Clancy relations alone would probably
have over eighty on it. Really, I don't see how you can make
this wedding small. Not without excluding tonnes of people,'
she said matter-of-factly.

'But we don't even know all that many of Dad's family,' Cara protested nervously. True enough, outside of her uncle and a couple of her aunts and immediate cousins, she didn't know the bulk of the Clancy cohort, and she certainly didn't understand why she should have to invite all of them to her wedding.

As for Shane's side, well yes of course, by the nature of his father's business his parents were connected to many important people, but Cara didn't know those people, and it was very likely Shane didn't either. Therefore, why would they need to be invited?

'Really Mum, Shane and I haven't decided anything yet,' she repeated, trying to be diplomatic. 'But I really don't think some big affair is our style. We like the idea of keeping it nice and simple, and having just people we love and who are important to us there. We don't need lots of show.'

There was silence on the other end of the line and Cara's heart sank as she hoped she hadn't disappointed her mother.

'Really Mum, let's not worry about it just now,' she continued, 'there'll be lots of time to decide. Now is the time to celebrate. We can talk about everything on Sunday, at dinner?'

Betty routinely had the family over for Sunday dinner at the Clancy home in Greygates, so Cara figured this would be the perfect time to talk about it all. It would also be a great excuse for her and Shane to share their news with the rest of the family and celebrate.

'You know, that lovely church that Heidi got married in – Saint Joseph's – would be perfect, wouldn't it?' Betty said, as if Cara hadn't even spoken.

She'd hoped that her protestations might have bought her some time, but it seemed that her mother was determined to get her commitment to the aforementioned church wedding while on the phone, right now.

At the mention of her sister's nuptials the year before, she couldn't help but feel her hackles rise. 'Well, I'm not sure if Heidi and I have the same style or taste when it comes to things like this,' she managed to say tactfully. The very *last* thing she and Shane wanted was a wedding like Heidi and Paul's.

She remembered the ice swans that Heidi had insisted upon – to match the real swans she'd had Betty and Mick rent for the day as accessories on the pond on the grounds of the lavish, five-star hotel at which the wedding reception had been held. She recalled the flowers, which had cost her parents just shy of ten grand (ten grand!) that had decorated every surface at the church and the hotel, as well as a litany of other pointless embellishments that Heidi had insisted upon. It was utter craziness, and she knew that her parents were still paying for it.

'Well, I suppose I will have to go back to the bank with your father soon. We still have some of the equity release left from Heidi's, but we could always try for another top-up . . .'

'No Mum, no way,' Cara interjected vehemently, horrified at the very thought. 'Shane and I will be taking care of this ourselves – we don't want anyone else paying for anything to do with our wedding. It's not your responsibility—'

'What do you mean it's not my responsibility?' Betty gasped, as if the very notion was insulting. 'I am the mother of the bride. Your father and I are the parents of the bride. It's what we do.'

No, it's what Heidi brainwashed you into doing, Cara wanted to say, but she held her tongue.

'Honestly Mum, it's very generous of you to offer, and I

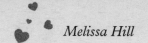

do appreciate it. But I just don't believe in going into all sorts of debt for one day, and I know Shane doesn't either, OK?'

'Oh Cara, you are just so practical, sometimes. All the time, actually. We're talking about your wedding, pet – your big day. Just understand that your father and I will do everything we can to make it wonderful. You just don't worry yourself about the costs, we'll sort something out.'

Cara felt tears in her eyes, unable to believe what she was hearing. Here her parents were, in their late fifties and nearing retirement, and still willing to go into more debt over their children's weddings. They were way too kind-hearted. But Cara knew that such generosity came with a price.

The family house Betty and Mick had been close to owning outright a couple of years ago was now, thanks to Heidi, another good ten years away from being paid for. And now her mother was talking about a third top-up? Well, maybe it didn't play on her sister's conscience, but there was no way Cara was going to drive her lovely parents – who'd ensured she'd never wanted for anything – into further debt in their advancing years

'Look, Mum, let's just talk about it all on Sunday over dinner. We still need to tell Shane's folks about the engagement – we're doing that tonight. So just hold off on anything until then, OK?'

'Of course, of course. And give the Richardsons my regards, won't you? I suppose this means we'll get to meet them soon – the lord and lady of the manor,' Betty added in the feigned haughty tone she used when referring to Shane's parents.

'Of course I will.'

It was true that the two sets of parents had never met, and Cara knew that privately Betty was foaming at the mouth to meet with the Richardsons. She guessed that would be happening soon. While she'd hoped to have introduced both couples before now, Shane's folks were so always so busy there had never seemed to be an opportunity.

'Anyway, congratulations again love, I am so happy for you,' Betty went on. She suddenly sounded teary and Cara felt her own eyes well up. 'You're going to be such a beautiful bride. Now, go on and have a great day,' she went on, before adding ominously, 'I have a few calls to make.'

'Well, you can make calls, but no deposits Mum, OK?' Cara had to laugh at her mother's irrepressible nature. 'Don't pay for anything and definitely don't make any big decisions without consulting us. Not yet.'

'Oh I really don't see why you are being so serious about it all, Cara. It's your wedding!'

'Mum, I know what it is. But you will talk to me before you start putting down deposits, yes? Promise?'

Again, silence from the other end of the line and Cara knew her reticence had put a spanner in the works as Betty had no doubt decided on having the whole shebang organised by five o'clock that afternoon.

'I'm serious Mum,' she scolded. 'If you book anything, if you place any money on anything wedding-related, Shane and I will . . .' Cara quickly considered what could be the worst thing they could do and yesterday's conversation with Kim popped into her head. 'Shane and I will elope to Las Vegas some time without telling anyone,' she finished wickedly.

There was a sharp intake of breath.

Trump card! Cara grinned, knowing she'd hit the jackpot. Nothing would horrify her mother more than her daughter eloping without her, not to mention the idea of her eloping and being walked down the aisle to Elvis singing 'Love Me Tender.'

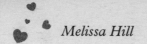

'Oh Cara, you wouldn't . . .!' Betty cried.

'You know I would. Married by Elvis in the Little Chapel of Love. Who knows, maybe we could even do a drive-thru wedding. Can you imagine it?' she teased, unable to resist. She heard her mother breathing hard. Finally, Betty spoke. 'Fine, fine,' she conceded.

Cara breathed a sigh of relief. She might have won the battle, but she knew she hadn't won the war.

As she and her mother said their goodbyes, she wondered how she was going to get out of a huge wedding at St Joseph's, in a big Cinderella dress (the type her mother favoured) and indeed have to face the prospect of mingling with three hundred-odd people she didn't even know. While she was sure that type of thing was fine for some people, she knew by the way her stomach felt at that moment that it was certainly not what she and Shane wanted for themselves.

She looked again at the engagement ring on her finger and went back over her conversation with her mother.

She wondered what Shane's parents would say this evening. Well, at least they were the parents of the groom so technically, weren't supposed to get involved in any of the arrangements. They were just supposed to show up.

Cara closed her eyes briefly and tried to focus her thoughts. Betty knew her so well, so surely she would appreciate that she wasn't Heidi and she wanted to do things differently. They had always wanted different things, had always been so different in every way, so why would her mother think that Cara would want to emulate her younger sister's elaborate nuptials?

She shook the thoughts from her mind and tried to regain some of her earlier positivity. Of course, this was about her and Shane and it would only be about what they wanted.

Cara tried to picture herself in the big Cinderella dress at the front of a church along with three hundred people that she didn't know watching her and Shane get married. But she couldn't see it. It didn't fit, didn't mesh with who she and Shane were as a couple. She tried to picture what did fit, what her idea of the perfect wedding was, and she realised her view was foggy and undefined.

A small wedding, definitely, but where? And who to invite? Her instincts said just family and friends, but maybe her mother had a point, and Shane would want to invite lots of his family's friends and acquaintances. Last night, after he proposed, they hadn't discussed the technicalities and specifics of the wedding, only the idea of marriage itself and how happy they were about it all.

Her conversation with her mother still fresh in her mind, Cara thought of all the things that needed to be considered, never mind organised, and felt a flutter of panic. She bit her lip, trying to quell the faint anxiety that now coursed through her veins.

If this was supposed to be such a wonderful time, then why did she suddenly feel so panicked?

Chapter 7

'Late as usual,' Shane scolded good-naturedly as later that evening after work, Cara rushed through the courtyard entrance to the restaurant. They were meeting Shane's parents for dinner, and while the reservation was for seven o'clock, it was now five after.

'I'm sorry, I'm sorry . . . You know me,' Cara said, wincing, as they made their way inside. While she usually didn't worry so much about being five minutes late for a dinner reservation, this was L'Ecrivain, one of Dublin's most upmarket restaurants, and it was after all Shane's parents they were meeting. And she figured if the Richardsons were willing to shell out for a Michelin-starred dinner on their behalf, the least she could do was get there on time.

'No big deal. Don't worry, they're waiting downstairs at the bar, I told them you were just stuck in traffic,' Shane reassured her.

His relaxed expression immediately put Cara at ease. All day, she'd struggled to shake off the anxiety that had reared its head during the phone call with her mother. Betty's initial reaction to her news had opened up a new can of worms that she hadn't considered: other people's opinions about what she and Shane should do for their wedding.

'Do I look all right?' she asked nervously. Before leaving Octagon earlier, she'd changed out of her work clothes and into a pretty patterned tea dress and heels, much to Conor's amusement.

'Very demure,' her boss had teased. 'Eminently suitable for meeting the in-laws.'

'Smart-ass. It's not my first time meeting them, you know,' she'd retorted, annoyed that Conor seemed determined to take the mickey out of her, when he knew full well how nervous she often was around Shane's parents.

Although he'd been lovely when she'd told him the good news.

'Congratulations. Lucky guy. I hope he makes you very happy,' Conor had said simply when Cara had shown him her diamond, and she wished that everyone's reaction could be so straightforward.

'You look fantastic,' Shane told her now. 'You're glowing. And actually, I think my parents are excited too. It's like they sense something is up.'

She smiled and took a deep breath. Although they could be quite intimidating, she had always gotten along well with Shane's parents, Lauren and Gene Richardson. Even though they were somewhat pretentious and obsessed with money and status, Cara didn't begrudge them. After all, they had raised Shane to be a kind and generous man, so they had to have done something right.

And while she didn't share some of their ideas and opinions, they had welcomed her from day one, and didn't turn their noses up at her working-class background. That meant something.

Cara and Shane entered the restaurant and headed directly for the wine bar, a beautiful space in the middle of which sat a grand piano, whereupon a gracious member of the bar staff immediately offered them a glass of champagne.

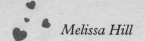

Lauren and Gene were seated at a high table, a glass of champagne already in front of each of them.

Shane's mother, always impeccably put together, looked considerably younger than her years, and not a single strand of grey hair could be found anywhere in her elegant, deep chestnut coiffed hair. Her face was without lines, which Cara attributed to the skin caviar that she applied religiously to her face each day, and which also happened to cost hundreds per ounce. She also made sure to keep herself in good shape through twice daily personal training sessions and an on-staff yoga instructor.

Gene was the quintessential distinguished gentleman, with fair good looks that he had bestowed upon his son. He had the posture of an aristocrat and always spoke well, with a heavy and rather grandiose accent.

'Ah, there you are, my dear!' Gene smiled as he reached forward to welcome Cara. She kissed him on both cheeks.

'Good to see you Gene,' she replied. It had taken a while, but now she felt comfortable using their first names when addressing them. 'Lauren, you look beautiful.'

Dressed in head to toe Chanel, Lauren Richardson welcomed Cara into a gentle hug, but Cara immediately worried about 'wrinkling' her.

'So do you,' said Lauren quietly. As was the norm, Shane's parents consistently spoke in measured tones, rarely raised their voices and were quick to consider appearances before ever showing too much emotion.

Soon afterwards, the foursome were led upstairs and shown to one of the best tables in the house. Cara was always surprised at who her future in-laws knew and while she didn't aspire to climb the social ladder, she still felt a little starstruck when she had the opportunity to be introduced to well-known Irish politicians or TV personalities, just because they happened to want to say hello to Shane's parents.

'I'm so sorry I'm late. The traffic was absolute murder,' Cara apologised. Both Lauren and Gene settled back into their seats, placing their napkins on their laps as Cara jostled to place her handbag under the table and situate herself in her chair. She noted their calm exteriors and immediately tried to mirror them. She always felt so brash when she was around his parents. They were such a departure from her own family who, like her, all tended to be disorganised and boisterous.

'Don't give it a second thought, dear,' Lauren reassured her as she picked up the cocktail already waiting on the table, taking a delicate sip. 'Gene took the liberty of ordering pre-dinner cocktails. I hope you don't mind.'

As if on cue, a gin and tonic appeared in front of Cara and, while she wasn't particularly partial to gin, she didn't want to tell Gene (again) that it wasn't one of her favourites. She took a small sip.

'Thank you,' she smiled politely, trying not to grimace at the sharp taste of the alcohol.

'You just missed Bono. If you'd arrived just a few minutes earlier, we would have been happy to introduce you,' Lauren commented.

Bono? Did she seriously mean . . . Cara looked at Shane, who, well used to his parents' name-dropping, just smiled and surreptitiously rolled his eyes.

'Oh, it's too bad I missed him,' she replied politely, although admittedly she wasn't a fan.

A brief bout of silence ensued and Cara shifted in her seat. Lauren and Gene sat back in their chairs as a very pleasant waiter offered them a basket filled with a mouth-watering selection of freshly baked bread.

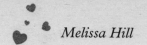

Cara lifted up a hand to point out the Guinness bread, which looked particularly tempting. As she did, she saw Lauren's eyes dart to the ring sparkling vividly beneath the overhead lighting.

'Oh,' Lauren smiled. 'What a beautiful ring.'

Cara swallowed hard, and looked quickly at Shane. 'Oh. Thank you.' She wasn't sure what to say now. Was he going to announce it or . . .?

Thankfully, Shane took his cue. When the waiter had disappeared, he reached forward and took Cara's hand in his. 'Mother, trust you to notice. Always the magpie.' He grinned and looked from one parent to the other. 'Actually, Cara and I have some news.' He smiled at Cara. 'I have asked Cara to marry me and much to my delight, she has accepted.'

There was a brief silence, and Cara noticed Gene and Lauren glance quickly at one another before eventually Gene spoke.

'This is wonderful news!' he boomed. 'Well done, son. Cara, welcome to the family.'

Lauren smiled and patted her hand. 'Congratulations dear.'

Immediately, Cara felt herself relax. Perfect. Just congratulations and welcome to the family. Exactly the role of the groom's side. No pressure and no suggestions about churches, the guest list, or how things should or shouldn't be done.

'Shane, you have excellent taste,' Lauren cooed, examining the ring more closely. So very stylish and just enough for the moment. You can always upgrade to something bigger in the future of course.'

OK. So much for 'no suggestions.'

'I think it's perfect. I couldn't have chosen better myself,'

Cara said, smiling at Shane in case he was deflated by the side (or was it direct?) swipe at the size of the diamond.

'So,' Lauren continued. She reached for her bag and extracted a Louis Vuitton datebook. She began flipping pages, examining the months. 'What dates are you considering? I think late autumn would be perfect, and it would really match your colouring, Cara.'

'October would be good actually,' Gene agreed. 'I'll have a word with Patrick Jones from the Club. I heard recently that the Williams' girl has just got engaged and we don't want to be beaten to the punch.'

Cara opened and closed her mouth, at a loss for words. She seriously hoped he wasn't talking about the K-Club, of which Shane's parents were members. It was a lovely spot but way too lavish and upmarket for them. Seeing his fiancée's look of concern, Shane spoke up.

'Mother, Father, that won't be necessary. We haven't quite decided what we are going to do yet, but I don't think the Club is in our plans.'

His parents stared at him blankly, and Cara finally found her voice and stepped in. 'Yes, as I told my mother this morning, we think that we want to keep things small.'

Lauren and Gene Richardson regarded their son and future daughter-in-law with puzzled expressions, seemingly trying to digest this.

Then all of a sudden, Shane's mother smiled fondly, as if she'd figured out just why they wanted a small wedding.

'Oh Cara, dear, really, please don't worry – of course Gene and I will take care of everything. I completely appreciate that you wouldn't want your parents to worry about paying for your wedding. We have the means; we will take care of *everything*.'

'No Lauren, that's really not it,' Cara replied, somewhat

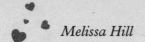

affronted. 'Affordability has nothing to do with it. Honestly, Shane and I just want to keep it small, we just want our loved ones and close friends there . . .' She looked to Shane, who nodded in an agreement.

But, seemingly unable to digest this, Lauren immediately jumped to another –very different – conclusion as to why anyone would want a small wedding. She looked at Cara's half-finished gin and tonic. 'Well Cara, if my suspicions are correct, I'm not entirely sure it's appropriate for you to be drinking alcohol—'

Cara flushed bright red. 'That's not . . .'

'Mother!' Shane chided sternly. 'Cara is *not* pregnant. And really, money is not the issue either. We both feel that we want a small affair and a showy wedding is just not our style. End of story.'

Cara breathed a sigh of relief. Thank goodness Shane was here to back her up. She didn't feel as defenceless as when she had spoken to her mother.

However, the expressions on Lauren and Gene's faces suggested that the subject was certainly far from closed.

'Shane, I simply do not understand what you are saying. A small wedding? However would we manage that? I can think of at least two hundred people who need to be on the guest list,' Gene persisted. 'And that doesn't even get into business associates and other acquaintances. When I think of all of the weddings that we've attended over the years . . . it is only good etiquette that we return that invitation.'

'Absolutely. It is required,' Lauren put in haughtily.

'No Mother, it is not required,' Shane replied, his tone firm. Rarely did he lose his temper, but Cara could tell that he was exasperated with his parents' obsession with society requirements. 'Cara and I wouldn't know those people if we fell over them on the street. And I'm willing to bet that you

The Guest List

barely know them yourselves. Therefore, they do not need to be involved in this.'

Cara stole a glance across the table. Both his parents were stony-faced. Lauren started to shake her head. 'I don't think you understand, Shane. We are very happy for you both. We want you to have everything you dreamed about on your special day. But understand that as our only son and heir to the business, this wedding is about us just as much as it is about you,' she finished, eyeing them both directly.

Gene nodded in agreement. 'Yes. Shane, your mother is absolutely right. Don't forget that this wedding will also be about your mother and me welcoming Cara as our daughter into our family. Some silly *little* ceremony is not going to cut it. You simply do not have a choice in the matter. The social order demands that this wedding represent our standing,' he said officiously.

Cara couldn't believe what she was hearing. Social order demands? *Their* standing? No choice? What the bloody hell was going on?

Shane snorted his disagreement. 'Social order? In this country? You mean the back-scratching and the palm-greasing that all your business buddies in the golden circle get up to? Social order my foot. Cara and I want nothing to do with any of that bullshit. We're going to get married the way *we* want to. End of story.'

If Cara could have crawled under that table at that moment, she would have. Instead, she sat there frozen. Never had she heard Shane speak that way to his parents' faces. He might as well have stood up and slapped them.

'Shane Richardson, I have never—' Lauren fanned herself with her datebook as if she was in danger of fainting and, unless Cara was mistaken, she was starting to tear up. This

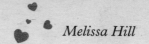

was a shock – she hadn't been aware that Shane's mother had tear ducts. 'How can you be so selfish?' Lauren gasped.

'Selfish? Me? Mother, are you listening to yourself? We've told you three if not four times what we want and you are dismissing it. You just said our wedding is about you! It's certainly not Cara and me who are being selfish. We have thanked you for your generous offer to pay, but we have declined. That should be the end of it.'

Cara looked around and noticed that their table was getting curious looks from nearby diners. This was turning into a disaster and she realised quickly that she needed to try and smooth the waters.

'Lauren, Gene, we really appreciate your generosity, but honestly, we've both been to many large weddings over the years, and we're very sure it's not what we want. We really would prefer a low-key affair,' Cara said, smiling. 'I understand your confusion – my mother was the same this morning when I outlined our plans to her. Shane and I really could not justify someone going into debt because of our wedding.'

Lauren sniffed. 'My dear, we would not be going into *debt*. Maybe your parents would have to do so, but I assure you we would not. We are doing this because we love you and care about you, out of the goodness of our hearts, and you are throwing this generosity in our faces.'

Cara's anger flared, first at the cheap shot against her family, and then for Lauren's attempt at making herself a martyr. How did she and Shane suddenly become the bad guys in this situation?

Gene threw his napkin down on the table and stood up. He extracted a hundred-euro note from his wallet and threw it on the table.

'Oh for God's sakes, Father—' Shane began.

'I have completely lost my appetite. Lauren, let's go,' Gene said sharply. 'I'll make my apologies on the way out. I'm sure they'll understand,' he continued, referring to the restaurant's proprietors, who were evidently friends. Then he turned his attention back to Cara and Shane. 'Let me just say I have never been more offended. Son, please know that while we are very happy for you, we certainly are *not* happy with your behaviour this evening.'

Lauren too stood up, and without a word followed her husband downstairs, leaving Cara and Shane staring at each other in shocked silence.

Chapter 8

It was Sunday morning and Heidi could barely contain her excitement. She just couldn't wait to get to her mother and father's house, make her big announcement and allow the showering of love and praise to begin.

She had struggled to keep her news to herself for the past few days, and had to elbow Paul when he'd almost let it slip on the phone to his own mother the other day.

There would no 'letting slip' this news, especially not when Heidi wasn't there in person to see the look on people's faces.

But now, it was finally time to face her family and she just couldn't wait to get in the car and drive the short distance across town to the Clancy house.

Paul was being just fantastic since he'd learned the good news. He'd already insisted on going to get the brakes checked on the jeep, as well as an oil change, engine tune, and four new tyres. He insisted that they couldn't be too careful if Heidi was going to be in the jeep, whether driving it or as a passenger.

Now, reapplying her Armani make-up to give her skin a dewy 'glowing' sheen, Heidi straightened her clothes and headed out front, where Paul was already waiting in the jeep.

Seeing her approach, Heidi's husband dutifully jumped out and rushed to her side. While she was only just over six weeks gone, she had already mastered the art of the pregnant waddle, and whenever she moved, she made sure to place a protective hand over her non-existent bump, shielding her unborn child from invisible hazards that could potentially pop up from anywhere.

Paul put an arm around his wife and helped her walk down the steps of their front porch. 'How are you feeling, sweetheart?' he asked. 'Everything OK with you and the little one?'

Heidi raised her chin and nodded quickly. 'Fine. But Paul, I didn't appreciate you leaving the breakfast dishes out this morning for me to deal with. I can't bend down to the dishwasher, honey. I can't lift anything, and I shouldn't be moving around so much anyway.'

Heidi settled herself in the car. She wondered what her mother's reaction would be like, and imagined how excited all of her family would be when she told them. While it was true that her child wouldn't be the first Clancy grandchild – Ben had beaten her to that, she thought sourly – it would be the first borne by one of the Clancy girls, which made a huge difference.

'Here we are, love,' Paul cooed a few minutes later, pulling up outside the house. 'Are you ready?'

Heidi looked up at her parents' house. It was a simple, unassuming three-bed semi-detached with a garage conversion. It was the home they'd all grown up in, the only house her parents had ever owned.

She did think that Betty and Mick could do with modernising the place, and had offered many times to share the benefit of her natural flair for interior design, but it seemed they were happy enough with the way it was. Well, she would definitely have to instruct them on proper baby-proofing procedures. Too many sharp edges in this house, not to mention, steep, steep stairs. There was no way her baby was going to be under that roof, until Betty and Mick had every electrical outlet secured and every edge on every table covered with those sponge-like protectors they sold in stores.

'I'm ready,' she told Paul, who duly hurried round the car and opened the door for her. Heidi extended a hand for assistance as if she was dismounting on to the red carpet for the Academy Awards. Paul gingerly helped her, handling her as if she was a delicate, antique glass vase.

'Did you remember to use the hand sanitiser after the steering wheel? Who knows where some dirty mechanic's hands have been,' she said grudgingly as she looked at her own hand, almost as if she expected it to be crawling with germs. 'I can't be getting sick, you know.'

'Yes, yes, of course I used the hand sanitiser,' Paul confirmed. He patted her gently on the arm. 'No need to be nervous, honey. This is going to be fun.'

Heidi looked at him. She *was* nervous. She exhaled a breath she didn't even know she'd been holding, and smiled at her husband, all at once grateful for having him. He knew her so well and understood her better than anyone else.

Taking tentative steps up the pathway to her parents' house, she could already hear everyone inside, and felt gratified that she'd scheduled them to be half an hour late so that she and Paul would be the last to arrive. This way, her grand entrance would be witnessed by all of them.

As they reached the front door, Heidi took a moment to smooth down her shirt and flick back her hair. She wondered if her family would just *know*. She was sure that she was glowing, as if she was radiating pregnancy. Almost like she was a beacon of childbearing beauty. She felt like Eileithyia, the Greek goddess of childbirth. She was a *vessel*.

Paul knocked briefly before pushing open the front door,

which had been left unlocked for the visitors. Heidi moved slowly, almost forgetting to waddle, but then she remembered herself as she entered her parents' living room.

Yes, everyone else was already there – her mother, father, Cara and Shane, and Ben and Kim and her little nieces. Much to her dismay her parents didn't seem to notice her entrance – her mother was too busy hugging Cara and then Shane before buzzing around Kim, and her father was shaking Shane's hand and then her brother's, while patting both men on the back. Typical – somehow Cara always managed to steal the limelight. It had been the same growing up and despite being the baby of the family, Heidi had always instinctively known that her elder sister had always been her parents' favourite. Cara was the one who'd always done well in school, at sports and then eventually at university. Heidi hadn't bothered going to uni; by then she'd long since given up trying to keep pace with Cara's lengthy list of achievements. Her parents had done their best to make up for such obvious favouritism by showering her with affection, but there was still no denying that she would always be second to their precious Cara. And that hurt.

But this time, Heidi had managed to do something Cara hadn't yet managed to do: provide her parents with a Clancy grandchild.

There was palpable excitement in the room, and Heidi couldn't figure out why. Was it possible that some of them already knew about her news? But that was impossible – she hadn't said a word since finding out, and Paul knew he was sworn to secrecy. Unless something had slipped out . . . She glanced at her husband, but he too was taking in the scene with a look of confusion on his face. No, he wouldn't have slipped. Besides, he rarely spoke on the phone to her family. Unless someone called the house and

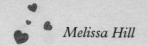

he picked up, Paul's interaction with her family was usually confined to events like this.

She continued to take in the scene in front of her with some confusion. They all looked so cheery, jubilant almost. How could they know?

But wait – no - there was something wrong with all of this, Heidi realised then. They hadn't yet said hello to her. None of them were even looking in her direction. They hadn't even *acknowledged* her presence yet. In fact she didn't think they'd even noticed her arrival.

'Ahem,' she coughed.

Not a single person turned in her direction.

'AHEM!'

Still nothing.

'*Excuse* me!' she called out finally, at the top of her lungs. The chatter across the room subsided and, finally, some of them noticed she was there.

'Heidi, hello. Sorry, I didn't see you come in.' Kim grinned. 'So much going on here. How are you?'

'Hi.' Heidi coolly returned her sister-in-law's greeting.

'Hello there!' Betty rushed forward and encircled her youngest daughter in a fond embrace that Heidi guessed was way too rough. She would need to tell them all soon. She couldn't be jostled about like this; it wasn't good for the baby.

'Mum, don't,' she said, trying to back away from her mother.

Betty frowned. 'What's the matter pet?

'Well . . .' Heidi paused dramatically and smiled. 'Seeing as you're all here, I have something to—'

'Aunt Heidi, Aunt Heidi,' her niece Olivia sang out, 'Aunt Cara's getting married and Mummy is going to have another baby!' The little girl cheered as she jumped up and down.

Heidi almost choked. Cara, married? And what was that about . . . a baby?

'I'm sorry sweetie?' she replied hoarsely, pretending she hadn't heard.

'Oh Liv, let your aunt get in the door first,' Kim chided. 'Sorry Heidi, no secrets with this one!' she laughed, and Heidi glared at her sister-in-law.

'It is indeed a double celebration!' Betty exclaimed. 'Yes, Cara and Shane are engaged.' She beamed at Cara. 'I know you wanted to tell everyone face to face yourself but . . . love, show Heidi your ring!'

Cara smiled shyly and extended her left hand towards Heidi.

Sure enough, there was a sparkling diamond ring on the third finger of her left hand. A nice ring too, she realised, breaking out in a mild sweat.

'It happened the other night Heidi, and yes, Shane and I are engaged. I would have phoned but I thought it would be nicer to tell everyone together in person today.'

'Isn't it great news?' her dad urged when Heidi remained silent. 'And then another Clancy grandchild on the way too,' Mick added, shaking his head. 'I just can't believe it.'

Heidi was about to start crying. Her shoulders started to shake and she tried to fight back a sob. This was supposed to be her day, it was supposed be all about *her* big news.

For once.

She glanced across the room at her sister-in-law. Kim looked perfectly relaxed and carefree, tickling Lindsay and tossing the little girl up and down in exaggerated jumps. She didn't seem pregnant at all, and if she was she certainly wasn't being careful enough.

'You're pregnant again?' she asked Kim in a small voice. She had had no idea Kim and Ben were hoping to add to

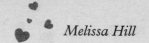

their family. If she'd had known that, then of course she'd have made sure she and Paul got there first . . .

Kim grinned. 'I know, a bit of a surprise for us too, to be honest. But it's great news, and I'm feeling fine so far – touch wood.'

'No fear of you from what I saw over lunch the other day!' Cara laughed. 'Already she's using the old eating for two excuse.'

Heidi was so disappointed she could barely move. None of them cared about her, or her news. They only cared about Cara and Kim. What's worse is that they had all obviously been talking to each other about everything that was going on before today. Cara seemed to know all about Kim's pregnancy and knowing her sister, Kim would have been the first person she told about her engagement. Heidi was wounded afresh. The two of them were thick as thieves and rarely included her in their outings. Of course they had so much in common too didn't they? Both career-obsessed and selfish to the last.

Damn. Now, Heidi was sorry she hadn't phoned up her mum and dad to tell them about her pregnancy immediately after she'd found out.

She looked at Cara, who had the usual self-satisfied expression on her face; she looked thrilled to be the centre of attention as always.

Heidi felt ill. Now the day was completely tarnished. None of this was turning out like she planned, far from it.

'Heidi? Are you going to congratulate Cara and Kim?' her father asked, having noticed that she'd barely uttered a word.

No, she damn well wasn't. Not at least until she got some congratulations sent her way first.

'Actually, I have some news myself,' she said, raising her

chin once again and trying to regain her posture. She looked at Paul. Yes, she would include him in the announcement. It was more than she could say about the other women in the family, who as usual had made it all about them alone. 'Rather, *Paul* and I have some news.'

Her husband smiled, and gently put a supportive arm around her shoulders.

'Oh. What is it?' her mother asked, pausing a little.

'We are going to have a baby. Our *first* baby,' she reinforced, as if anyone had questioned whether this was their first or fourteenth.

'Oh my goodness! Oh Heidi!' Betty rushed forward once again and threw her arms around her youngest daughter, pulling Paul into her embrace at the same time. 'Oh I can't believe this. So much good news in this family these days! We are all so lucky!'

Heidi pushed away. 'Please Mum, you have to be careful, you can't be so rough with me.'

'Oh for heaven's sakes sweetheart,' Betty laughed happily. 'I think I know what you can and cannot do when you are pregnant.' She enveloped her daughter in another hug.

'Yes I know it can feel bit like that, especially with your first, but really, you're not breakable,' Kim added, and Heidi looked daggers at her.

'I'm six weeks, Kim. The early days are especially delicate,' she informed her.

Kim waved a hand. 'Seriously, don't stress about it. Most women wouldn't even know at this stage, and babies are hardy.'

'Kim's right, love,' Betty agreed. 'Women have been having babies for thousands of years, there's no need to be fragile.'

Heidi reminded herself that this sort of attitude was exactly what you'd expect from Kim. She breathed a sigh of relief when Paul stepped forward to take a protective stance in front of his wife. 'Well Kim,' he said, 'Heidi and I are taking a different approach. We'd rather she took things easy and I'll do my best to make sure she does.'

Kim chuckled. 'Oh, right. Ben!' she called out to her husband, laughing, 'you're on piggyback duty for the next few months.'

Heidi's brother joined in with the laughter and she glared at him too. She couldn't believe that Ben bought into Kim's carelessness. What kind of a mother was she?

'It's great news Heidi, congratulations. We're thrilled for you,' Cara put in then, evidently trying to break the tension. Her attention diverted momentarily from Kim, Heidi was momentarily grateful for the fact that it had been Cara to make the concession and congratulate her first.

She raised a small smile. 'Yes, congratulations to you too, and you Shane. But weddings are a lot of work you know, you have so much planning to do. Still,' she added with a sigh, 'at least you can spread the plans out over a year or so, and can set your own schedule. You can't do that with a baby; you only have so much time.'

'Oh, there's not that much to it, really,' Kim laughed airily. 'You just buy a six-pack of Babygros a week or two before, then sit back and wait for it all to kick off. Although, some people can even schedule it these days,' she said, looking knowingly at her husband, who winked.

Heidi stared at Kim in horror. 'Childbirth is a beautiful and natural thing. You don't *schedule* a baby!'

'Well, try it once and see how you get on. Maybe afterwards you'll be singing a different tune,' her brother said shortly, and she remembered again that Kim had supposedly had difficult births with her first two.

Drama queen.

She shook her head, trying to wrap her thoughts around all that was happening. It wasn't fair, why did Cara have to get engaged? And why did Kim need a third baby? They had ruined everything for her. And to make it worse, neither of them was acting like her pregnancy was a big deal.

She turned her attention back to her family. Her mother and Kim had already gone back to buzzing over Cara's ring. 'Now, about this wedding, Cara,' her mother was saying. 'What did your parents say, Shane? I'm sure they must be thrilled!' Heidi noticed that at this, Cara looked slightly green around the gills.

Well don't demand the spotlight if you can't handle the attention.

Heidi knew that *she* could handle it, but no one was paying her the slightest bit of notice.

'Let's get dinner organised first and then we can chat all about it,' Betty continued, beckoning to Cara and Kim as she headed out of the room. Then she turned her attention to Heidi. 'You too, love; all hands on deck in the kitchen.'

Heidi stared at her mother in absolute horror. Did they really expect her to help out? In a steaming hot kitchen, carrying heavy plates and helping with dinner? She needed to relax!

'Although, you might want to grab an apron, pet,' Betty continued, 'you don't want to mess up that pretty top.'

'Mum, I can't do that; I need to stay off my feet.'

Her mother looked at her, confused. 'Are you not feeling well?'

Heidi answered too quickly. 'No, I feel fine, but I am *pregnant*!'

Out of the corner of her eye she saw Kim exchange an amused glance with Cara. 'Well, the baby's got to eat too,'

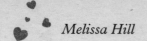

her sister-in-law said. 'And aren't you starving? I know I am.'

Ben chuckled. 'Yeah Paul, now is definitely the time to put locks on the cupboards. If my little sis is anything like Kim she'll eat you out of house and home.'

Heidi felt like crying. This was horrible. Not only had her big news been trumped by everyone else's, but her family were acting as if having a baby was no big deal; almost as if you could continue to go on and lead a normal life while you were pregnant.

They were even making her do work, for goodness' sake! Cooking in the kitchen like some kind of slave.

This was turning out to be the worst day ever.

Chapter 9

On Monday morning Cara sat at her desk, outlining to Conor all that had happened over the weekend, and how her and Shane's plans for a small, fuss-free wedding were being very quickly hijacked from all directions.

'Sounds like you're really getting it from both sides,' he said sympathetically. 'Have you heard from Shane's parents since?' He was perched on the corner of her desk with a cup of coffee in hand.

'No, not a word. Shane tried calling his father yesterday, but it went straight to voicemail. I'm not sure what to do. I thought this was supposed to be a happy time.' Cara placed her head in her hands and massaged her temples. 'The only ones who haven't given us any grief are Kim and Ben. Even Heidi could barely bring herself to congratulate us yesterday at dinner . . .'

'Well, if you're describing the scene accurately, it sounds to me like both your and Kim's announcements somewhat overshadowed your little sister's news. Talk about bad timing.'

Cara shrugged and sat back in her chair. 'Well, that is true; she did seem a bit deflated. But we're all thrilled for her and Paul, and I think we made that clear. She doesn't have to give me the cold shoulder, just because I happened to have a little bit of news too. But that's Heidi for you.'

Conor smiled and shook his head. 'Women – ye can be such catty creatures. And from what you tell me about your

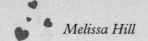

sister, she subscribes to the belief that the sun and moon and stars revolve entirely around her precious backside.'

Cara chuckled guiltily. 'Oh stop it, she's not that bad.' Although it did indeed describe Heidi to a T, but still she felt duty-bound to defend her sister. 'As for the wedding, I just don't know what we're going to do. Shane is being steadfast, insisting that we are going to do whatever the hell we want, but it doesn't feel right – not when everyone seems dead set against a small wedding.' She shook her head in frustration. 'Everyone has an opinion; everyone thinks we should do things this way and that. Honestly Conor, my head is spinning.'

'Then don't take the advice,' her boss said. 'And if someone feels the need to tell you what they believe you need to do, simply smile politely, nod and tell them to feck off.'

Cara smiled at the notion. She knew Conor was right, but at the same time she also knew that he had no idea what it was like to be in this situation. She wasn't a confrontational person and she felt at a loss as to how to control the wedding tsunami that she felt was starting to brew around her.

'You know, you really aren't in the position to be giving this kind of advice, seeing that you've never been engaged or married yourself,' she teased.

'You're probably right, what would a consummate bachelor know about weddings?' Conor stood up and patted Cara on the shoulder. 'Really though, I do have one piece of advice for you and I think it's quite important.'

Cara rolled her eyes. 'Let me take notes, I'll add it to the list.'

'Ah don't be so dramatic. But honestly, even if you don't take anyone's else advice, just keep this in mind. Remember, whoever holds the purse strings for the wedding has the control. Don't accept a cent from anyone else if possible.

Then you and Shane will be the only ones calling the shots. All the decisions will be yours and the rest of them will just have to go along with it.'

It was the best piece of advice Cara had received yet.

She nodded and ran a hand through her hair. 'You're right and in fairness, I'm probably getting my knickers in a twist over nothing. I just didn't expect so many people to want to stick their oar in. It is only one day after all. Why so much fuss and drama?'

Conor shrugged. 'Heck if I know. But now do you understand why I never bothered with all this palaver? Too much stress babe, way too much.'

Cara smiled, already feeling a whole lot better. Conor was like that, always able to calm her down and get her to focus on the important things in life. He was like that with everything, so easy-going and laid-back. Nothing fazed him.

So maybe she should try and be more like that about the wedding. Let nothing faze her. Let people say what they wanted.

She was meeting the girls tonight – a group of old friends who, now that most were married and some had kids, rarely got to see one another. But when news of Cara's engagement broke they'd arranged to meet up for a celebration. No doubt it would be an early night but it was bound to be good fun.

Exactly what Cara needed.

'There she is! Cara! Over here!'

Later that same evening as she walked into O'Shea's, a popular Greygates pub, Cara looked in the direction of the voice of her best friend, Maria.

'Hey!' she grinned, as she made her way across the room to where Maria and her other friends, Lilly and Samantha, sat.

As she approached the table Samantha started to bounce around in her seat. 'Oh come on, come on. I want to see. Show us the sparkler!'

Samantha reached forward and grabbed Cara's hand, pulling her close. Caught by the unexpected action, Cara almost tripped on the thick carpeting under her feet but she had to smile at her friend's enthusiasm.

'Oh it's just gorgeous!' Lilly gushed, brushing her straightened dark hair over her shoulder so she could take a better look. 'Congrats Cara – Shane has amazing taste.'

Cara pulled her hand back as she took her seat. 'Sorry I'm late . . .'

'Well I see you haven't changed much!' Maria laughed. 'Besides, I'm sure you've loads going on at the moment with all the wedding plans.'

Cara smiled a non-committal smile.

'Well, seeing as we're celebrating, we took the liberty of ordering champagne in your honour,' Lilly said, pouring her a glass.

The four women toasted and Cara sat back in her chair, already feeling more relaxed than she had in days.

Yes, this is going to be a fun night, she thought.

After taking a sip of champagne, Samantha placed her glass back on the table and locked her blue eyes on Cara in a steely gaze. 'So tell us – what have you organised so far?'

'For the wedding you mean?' Cara furrowed her brow. By her count, it was only Monday. She had been engaged now for approximately . . . five days. 'Well, it only all happened last week, so outside of telling our families and what not . . .' She shrugged.

The three women looked at Cara with confusion.

'What do you mean? Surely you've set a date though?' Lilly frowned.

'Well, no, not—'

'Cara, honestly, that's the first thing you should do, and you need to do it ASAP,' Lilly informed her knowledgeably. 'I picked the date within forty-eight hours of Simon asking me. There's tough competition for dates now, you have to remember that.'

'Yes, really Cara, you need to be on top of this,' Samantha agreed, nodding sagely. 'You have to get the deposit down, before all of the good hotels fill up.'

'Definitely,' Maria chimed in. 'When Brian and I went looking, I almost went bonkers when I found out that Powerscourt was booked out for nearly two years in advance! But of course we were blessed because of that cancellation . . .'

Cara placed her glass on the table and tried to quell the rising tide of anxiety that was threatening to strangle her. This is what she had hoped to avoid tonight, all the stress and lecturing. Why did everyone feel the need to bestow their unsolicited wedding advice upon her?

'Really girls, I appreciate the advice but it's grand,' she said with a tight smile. 'At the moment, Shane and I are just enjoying being newly engaged. As for the wedding, there's no panic. All that will fall into place.'

But Lilly was shaking her head in disagreement.

'Well OK then, if you don't want to take charge, you probably should call the woman who did my wedding, do you remember how great she was? Let me get her number for you.'

Cara thought back. From what she could recall of Lilly's wedding planner she was a bossy old biddy who had spent the day barking orders at everyone including Lilly and her hapless groom.

Ah, that would be a definite no, she muttered silently, as she watched Lilly scroll through her BlackBerry contacts.

'Thanks, but really that's not necessary,' she told her. 'We probably aren't going to go in for anything so elaborate. Don't get me wrong,' she added quickly, as her friend's face dropped, 'your wedding was amazing – it really was, but Shane and I are thinking small.' She hoped they'd all get the message and leave it at that.

Lilly looked up from her BlackBerry. 'Regardless, you'll still need a wedding planner, someone to keep you on track with all the admin. Plus, they know how to get the right appointments; you can't get into certain bridal stores under your own steam, particularly in London.'

'It's okay Lil, really it is. Like I said, I'm not sure if your planner is really our style, and I certainly won't be going for Vera Wang or anything.' Cara was trying her utmost to keep her cool, but every conversation about this wedding was one that seemed to be debatable. She was trying to say 'no thanks' politely, because really, she would rather cut her own arm off than even consider contracting a wedding planner who would be better suited as a drill sergeant.

'But Cara,' Samantha argued. 'Lilly's wedding planner was just amazing, the best! You'd be lucky to get her, I tried to book her for ours, but she was fully committed at the time. I was so upset.'

Cara pursed her lips. 'She might be the best, but really, I am just not interested in having her for my wedding.'

'I don't see why you don't want to use her,' Lilly replied tartly. 'She's the best in the country by a mile, and in constant demand. You can't argue with that type of success.'

Cara felt her blood pressure rising. Again, it was all about everyone else's opinions! She almost wanted to scream that this wedding was not about 'the best' or 'the most in demand' – it was about her and Shane!

'Like I said, I just don't think that sort of thing is for us.'

She hoped her tone would indicate this subject was closed for further discussion.

'Well then what sort of thing exactly *are* you planning on doing?' Maria asked. 'You don't seem to have any plans at all yet.'

'Yes, have you chosen your bridesmaids? Oh your sisters I suppose . . .'

Cara tried to tune out the constant questioning and looked around the pub, plotting her means for escape. She felt like she was suffocating, and if she didn't get out of here soon, she was bound to go crazy. She turned her attention back to the table and her friends, but felt herself straining to make eye contact.

'Look guys, can we talk about something else? I'm actually already kind of tired of discussing weddings. Nobody can talk about anything else since we got engaged. It's really stressing me out.'

There was a brief silence, and all three of her friends looked at one another. Good, Cara thought, relieved, she must have finally gotten through to them.

'Is everything OK?' Lilly asked then, and at her friend's suddenly sympathetic tone, Cara exhaled. 'Yes. I mean . . . no, it's not, I'm really just not sure . . . it's all so confusing . . .' To her horror, all of a sudden she felt herself starting to choke up.

She really didn't want to start crying in public, but Lilly's kindness seemed to have set her off. 'I don't know; it's just been so overwhelming. I mean, my mum has her heart set on a big white church wedding and then Shane's parents went nuts on us the other night, and called us selfish because we didn't want them to pay for the whole thing and then—'

Samantha interrupted her. 'I'm sure it must be a lot of pressure. Is everything OK with you and Shane?'

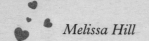

She looked up, confused by the sudden change in direction. 'What? Yes, of course, everything is fine with Shane. I don't see what—'

'Cos you know, you don't have to go through with this, not if you don't want to,' her friend continued, as if she had zeroed in on the reason behind Cara's delay in getting started on the planning. As if Cara had some psychological wall constructed against the wedding plans because in reality she just didn't want to marry Shane.

She shook her head, mystified. 'Of course not. Everything is fine there – it is our families, they are bonkers and—'

'Cara, really there is nothing to be ashamed about,' Lilly chimed in. 'I was the same; during the planning I had a notion to scrap the whole lot, including Peter, that's how stressed I got by it all. Everything gets so big, and so out of control that you just want to call the whole thing off.'

'Yes Cara, if you really feel that way, you don't have to get married, much better to call it off now than suffer through a divorce later,' Maria agreed sagely.

'No, really, that's not it at all!' Cara tried to keep her voice even but she felt like screaming. What the hell was wrong with them? 'Everything is fine between Shane and me. We've only been engaged a couple of days, but frankly everyone in our lives is stressing me the hell out because of situations like this! Honestly, I walked in here tonight hoping for a bit of a laugh with the three of you, and instead I'm faced with the Spanish Inquisition over wedding planners and dates and – lots of other bloody nonsense when at this stage, I'm thinking that the best course of action would be to run away and get it over and done with!'

Samantha, Maria and Lilly stared at Cara in shocked silence.

'Would you do that – honestly?' Lilly asked, her voice

barely above a whisper. She was looking at Cara as though she had just suggested murdering someone.

'I don't know, maybe. I mean, all I want to do at the moment is enjoy being engaged, rather than have to plan a huge event with military precision. Samantha, I am not the super-planner that you are, and Lilly, I am not interested in a wedding so big that I barely know any of my guests. I don't want Powerscourt or a Vera Wang dress.' Realising she might have insulted her friend, she added, 'Think about it – with my hips?' and Lilly smiled.

Samantha reached across the table and took Cara's hand. 'We're sorry, we didn't mean to get so crazy. It's just, you know, that's what you do when a friend gets engaged. You helped us so much for our weddings that of course we want to help you with yours.'

'Sam, that's really kind of you, honestly and I appreciate it, but really I'm just not sure if what you guys did for your weddings is right for me and Shane.'

'Well, it's completely your decision,' Samantha conceded.

'I know, but I am afraid there are a few people who don't subscribe to that belief at the moment.'

The three women regarded her silently for a moment, and she guessed that they'd realised they were not only guilty of inflicting their respective opinions, but were no doubt recalling their own experiences back when planning their own weddings.

'You know my wedding planner?' Lilly said suddenly.

Cara looked up, worried her friend was about to embark on another string of well-meaning 'advice.'

'Well, she was a complete bitch.' She rolled her eyes. 'Honestly, I was scared shitless of her. I put on a pound – a single *pound* the week of the wedding and she made me do a round on the treadmill on the morning of the

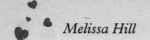

ceremony. Wouldn't let me eat anything other than a banana for breakfast and there I was gagging for a fry-up. 'Oul wagon.'

The four women burst out laughing and for the first time that evening, Cara felt that her friends were finally getting it.

Well, if nothing else, it was a start.

Chapter 10

Heidi was beside herself with excitement. She was on her way to Holles Street Maternity Hospital for her very first prenatal appointment.

Now eight weeks pregnant, she hadn't initially been sure what hospital to choose in which to have her baby, or whether she should attend as a public or private patient. Her GP had outlined the options, and while she was naturally inclined to choose a private hospital over a public one, something Kim had said recently had made up her mind for her.

That day at her parents' house when Heidi had announced the pregnancy (and discovered that she wasn't the only one with such news), her sister-in-law had let slip that she was attending a private hospital, because she 'could be in and out of prenatal consultations within minutes, and back at her desk in quick time', whereas it seemed the public waiting time was considerably longer.

'Going public was fine for the first time with Olivia when Blissology was just in the early stages and wasn't so busy, but I just couldn't afford to be waiting around with Lindsay,' she'd said.

Heidi had been horrified. To think that Kim thought so little of her baby that she wouldn't give the necessary time away from her precious business for a prenatal appointment? How incredibly selfish.

That had made Heidi's mind up there and then. While

she was of course aware of all the horror stories about long waits and overcrowded hospitals throughout the Irish health service, she'd actually been quite taken aback at the efficiency of the hospital when she'd phoned a week or so ago to make an appointment.

At eight-thirty a.m., the slot they'd given her was a little earlier than she'd have liked, especially as Heidi enjoyed her lie-ins and needed even more rest now that she was two months gone, but at the same time she was prepared to make whatever sacrifices were required for her baby.

Paul had an early meeting this same morning and so wouldn't be able to accompany her to the appointment. He couldn't cancel, he'd told her, especially when she'd only told him about the visit a few days before. To be honest, it had slipped Heidi's mind, as she'd been spending much of her time going around the shops looking for baby clothes.

At first, she'd been outraged about Paul missing such an important milestone, but at the same time, she conceded, maybe it was for the best, at least for the first visit. Paul would no doubt spend the entire appointment asking questions like was it OK for Heidi to drive and do housework and such nonsense, when of course it wasn't OK.

He'd dropped her off at the hospital on his way to the office earlier that morning and had promised to meet her for lunch and see how it had all gone.

Heidi figured she'd spend a good hour chatting to the doctor about the various aspects of her pregnancy, and outlining the details of her birth plan, before heading on to Grafton Street for a spot of shopping afterwards.

It would be good if she could get some good clear ultrasound scan shots of her baby, but the receptionist had advised over the phone that a scan wasn't always standard on a first appointment. Heidi smiled. She was sure she could sweet-talk the doctor into giving her an ultrasound. It would be simply amazing to be able to show the first pictures of her baby to everyone. Maybe when they saw in black and white how tiny and fragile it was, they might start giving her pregnancy the respect it deserved.

Hefting her handbag high on her shoulder, Heidi pushed open the main door of the hospital and, following the signs, made her way to the prenatal reception area. She was hoping they had some up-to-date magazines in the waiting room; she hadn't yet had a chance to pick up the latest copy of *Vogue* and was looking forward to flicking through the fashion pages while she waited.

Approaching the reception desk, she announced her arrival to the pleasant-looking lady there.

'The waiting area is just through there,' the woman said, having taken her details, and Heidi marvelled again at the politeness and efficiency of the public health system.

Really, why would anyone consider spending a fortune on private consultant obstetrician care, when the very same services were available here for free? Especially when that very same fortune would be better spent on day spas or chic maternity clothes?

Smiling, Heidi reached into her handbag and pulled out a sheet of paper. She handed it to the receptionist.

'What's this?' the woman asked, giving her a puzzled look.

'My birth plan,' Heidi replied easily. 'I presume you'll be needing a copy for when the time comes.'

The woman didn't say anything for a moment; she just read through the list, and Heidi guessed she was impressed at the level of detail and planning that had gone into each request. Indeed she'd put a lot of thought into the birth plan; the background music (Debussy), the specific aroma and brand of scented candle (NEOM Lemon and Watergrass),

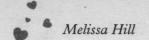

how many people should attend the delivery, what Paul's role should be and so on.

'Well, this is . . . interesting,' the woman replied eventually. 'First baby?' she asked, and Heidi nodded proudly.

'Just so you know, it's probably not a good idea to rely too much on these,' the other woman continued, in a kindly tone. 'Things can change very quickly in the labour ward, and our midwives are very experienced.'

'Oh I'm sure they are. But like the books say, in order for the needs of the mother to be best served, it's important that everyone knows what's required of them.'

'Of course,' the receptionist said, and was it Heidi's imagination or was she looking at her strangely? 'As I said, just head on down the hallway.'

Smiling, Heidi followed her directions and pushed open the door of the waiting room.

Only to be met with the sight from hell.

She didn't think she had ever seen so many people crammed into such a tiny space, ever! And never mind magazines – much to her horror Heidi quickly realised that there were no *seats* available. And all these children screaming and running around . . . The noise and chatter was deafening.

But why on earth were all these pregnant women here already, clearly way in advance of their appointments?

Heidi took deep breaths, trying to control her breathing. Thank goodness she had an early consultation and wouldn't have to wait around too long in the midst of all this . . . chaos.

Wiping her brow, Heidi hesitated a little before approaching a heavily pregnant woman standing close by. *Standing!*

She looked daggers at a man sitting nearby. Who did he think he was, taking up a seat when there were so many people – like Heidi – desperately in need of one?

'Excuse me,' she said to the heavily pregnant woman. 'I

was wondering, what time does the clinic start? Can you believe this crowd? What time is your appointment? I have an eight-thirty so at least I won't be waiting long but—'

'First time here, yeah?' the woman said, smirking a little, and Heidi nodded seriously.

'Yes, and I'm really not sure why everyone has to be here so early—'

'Well sorry to break it to you sweetheart, but we *all* have that eight-thirty appointment.' She nodded at the crowds. 'Might as well get comfortable for the next few hours. It's first come, first served around here.'

Kim was at her desk reviewing a proof for Blissology's latest catalogue when the phone rang. She hit the speaker button without looking as she flipped over a page, turning her attention to a photo spread showcasing their best-selling seaweed bath soak.

'Yes?'

'I have a call for you,' Simone, her assistant, said crisply. 'Your sister-in-law is on line two.'

'Cara? Great, put her through.'

'No,' said Simone hesitantly. 'It's Heidi actually.'

Kim frowned. 'Heidi? Seriously?' she repeated, somewhat incredulous. She could count on one hand the number of times Ben's youngest sister had called her, whether at her office or at home. They had a very different relationship to the one she had with Cara; they weren't exactly good friends or even the slightest bit close as Heidi seemed to have taken a dislike to her from day one. Kim's internal radar bleeped as she wondered what this was about. Whatever it was, she was sure it couldn't be anything good.

'Shall I take a message? Tell her you're in a meeting maybe?' Simone prompted.

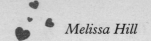

Better not, thought Kim. If there was one thing Heidi hated, it was being dismissed, or ignored.

'No, no, it's fine Simone, thanks. Put her through.'

'No problem.'

Kim took a deep breath and steeled herself before she picked up the line.

'Hello there, Heidi. How are you?' she asked breezily, quickly switching off the speakerphone button.

'That is quite a question Kim,' the other woman snapped. 'You should know all too well how I am, especially after your little stunt!'

Kim rolled her eyes and rubbed her forehead. OK, so nothing new here, she groaned inwardly. Heidi had her knickers in a twist. About what she wasn't entirely sure . . .

'Heidi, I have no idea what you are talking about. What stunt?' she asked. Was she still cheesed off about her big announcement being usurped that time by news of Cara's engagement? Not to mention the news about her own pregnancy, Kim recalled, grimacing.

That day at Betty and Mick's Kim could tell on the spot that Heidi had been livid that her news had been overshadowed, albeit unintentionally, by the rest of the family activity. While Kim believed everyone's news was something that should be received with joy and celebrated accordingly, knowing how Heidi's mind often worked she suspected that the younger girl believed she and Cara had planned it all out of spite.

But that was a couple of weeks ago so what . . .?

'Oh, you know very well what I'm talking about,' Heidi hissed. 'Telling me to go public for my prenatal appointment, as if it was no big deal! You did it on purpose, didn't you?'

Kim was well and truly flummoxed. 'Did what on purpose? And I certainly don't remember telling you to go public,

Heidi. I merely pointed out that I found it fine on my first pregnancy, but that my needs had changed for my second, and again for this one. Why . . .?'

But then, guessing what must have happened, Kim grimaced. Had her sister-in-law gone along to an appointment in one of the public hospitals recently? Oh dear. Poor delicate little Heidi was definitely not cut out for the inevitable three-hour wait amongst the hoi polloi. Given all her airs and graces, she truly was the last woman on earth Kim could envision going public. So what in the world had possessed her?

'It was like something out of a third-world country, Kim. Honestly, how could anyone say that it's no big deal? We were treated like herds of cattle, and there was nowhere to sit, and no magazines to read or anything, to say nothing of all the noise. Just by sitting there I was endangering my baby. All of that kind of stress is not good for anyone. I shouldn't have to be telling you all this!'

Kim held the phone back from her ear as Heidi's voice increased in decibels. She was sure that the girl would be able to break glass soon if her voice got much higher.

She shook her head. She'd forgotten how spoilt her husband's little sister could be, and how immune she was from the realities of day-to-day life for most people. In fact, Kim would have thought she would have been the first in the door of Dublin's more exclusive and expensive private maternity hospital.

However, at least Heidi had a choice as to whether to go public or private during her pregnancy. Many women didn't and they just had to make do with the services that were provided – magazines or otherwise. Trying to imagine her snobbish sister-in-law standing in the midst of all the bored and impatient women from all walks of life in the waiting room, she couldn't help but smile. She guessed that it was probably private all the way for Princess Heidi from now on.

Still, Heidi sounded very close to tears on the other end of the line and Kim softened a little. While they might not be close, she would never have done anything to purposely to upset Heidi.

'Heidi, I can assure you I did not urge you to go public – I merely outlined the options available to you that day at your mum and dad's. Like I said, it was fine for me the first time round, but as that was over eight years ago, I have no idea what it's like in the public system now. For what it's worth, I can give you the number of the obstetrician I'm using. She's great and is based out of—'

'Oh it's all you, you, you isn't it Kim? Same that day at the dinner – it had to be all about you and Cara's engagement. I had one shot – *one shot* – to tell everyone my wonderful news, and the two of you had to go and ruin everything—'

'Now hold on a minute; that is not fair. No one tried to ruin anything for you, Heidi. Cara had just got engaged and she walked in with a brand new diamond to show us all, and celebrate with her and Shane. You should be happy for her. She wasn't trying to steal your thunder and nor was I. Rather, I think that all of our news that day was something to be happy about – is still something to be happy about,' Kim said her voice taking on a harder edge. Seeing as her original attempt at trying to stroke Heidi's sensitive ego had failed, she was now all business.

Heidi breathed heavily into the phone. 'And then, all this nonsense about helping with dinner, and acting like all of it is no big deal, when you know I was in a delicate condition.'

'Really Heidi, if I recall you were barely a few weeks

pregnant then, so of course it was fine for you to help out with the housework – still is.' Kim couldn't believe what she was hearing. 'Nor was I trying to imply that your pregnancy was not a big deal. You and I simply have different viewpoints in that regard, and just as you are entitled to do as you want with your pregnancy, I should be afforded the same privilege.'

'No Kim, you purposely downplay everything and I know you do it just to try and make me feel silly for wanting to be careful. You do it so everyone thinks I'm a drama queen.'

Kim's eyes widened at this and she thought that actually her sister-in-law didn't need any support whatsoever in the drama department.

'I do no such thing. Everyone is different and if you are offended by my opinions, then that is your issue. To be truthful, I couldn't care less if you have your baby while standing on your head in the bathtub—'

'Exactly, you don't care. You don't give a rat's ass about anyone other than yourself. You don't care about me at all.'

Kim was speechless. Her sister-in-law was completely off her rocker.

'Heidi,' she said slowly, the way she would if she were speaking to a toddler. 'Of course I care about you; you are a part of my family. All I was saying is that your decisions are your own. While I don't particularly go in for the belief that you need to spend nine months of your life while pregnant on bed rest, if that pregnancy is perfectly healthy, that is *my* opinion. Maybe it's different because I have been through the whole thing twice before—'

'And you think that makes you special, huh? Because you have done it before, the big expert.'

Kim could see that there would be no winning this conversation. Not if Heidi insisted on taking every comment she

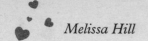

made completely out of context. The woman was simply determined to play the victim.

Kim sighed heavily. 'Look Heidi, I really don't have time for this just now. I have a lot of work to do and a brochure to sign off on, so I simply cannot get into this discussion with you at the moment.'

'Oh yes, so high and mighty, aren't you Kim? With your big *company* and your *responsibilities*. Well I have no problem being a stay-at-home mother even though I know you working women look down on us and sneer because we care enough to be around to raise our children, instead of playing the big businesswoman.'

Kim was trying desperately to keep her temper from exploding.

'Heidi, to my knowledge, you are not a stay-at-home mother as you don't yet have a child to take care of. You are simply pregnant. Again, if you don't want to work, fine, that's your choice and I'm not arguing with you, and certainly not sneering about it. What you do or do not do every day is between you and your husband . . .'

Kim sat back in her chair and looked at the time impatiently. This foolishness had gone on long enough. She had copy to proof.

Kim knew she would pay for this later, but she also knew that there was no other way to get out of this conversation. Looking regretfully at the phone, she secretly wished that she had told Simone to send it to voicemail.

Oh well, hindsight was twenty-twenty, she thought, her finger hovering over the disconnect button.

Heidi was still continuing her tirade on the other end of the line, and Kim figured it would take her a while to figure out that she had hung up. Quietly, she disconnected and placed the phone back on the receiver, then sat back in her chair, exhausted by the conversation. She knew that this situation with Heidi would only get worse before it got better. Especially as she seemed to view their mutual pregnancies as some kind of competitive situation.

Her sister-in-law's air of self-righteousness really was silly though. After all, she was pregnant, not dying. And for all her protestations, she wasn't some kind of delicate flower either.

Kim stood up and walked to her door. She wanted to tell Simone that any more calls from Heidi were to be screened. No doubt her sister-in-law was sitting at home right now planning her next line of attack.

She shook her head. Why did happy life events in the Clancy family always have to be wrapped up in so much drama?

Chapter 11

It was over two weeks since Cara and Shane had broken the news of their engagement to the Richardsons, and since then, the two couples had been in relative gridlock. Shane would call his parents and automatically be sent to voicemail. He would leave a message, and neither Lauren nor Gene would call him back.

Sitting at the dressing table in her bedroom applying make-up, Cara put her chin in her hand. She wouldn't say so to Shane, but the truth was she was feeling very angry with his parents now. While they went about in a snit, she knew that Shane's feelings continued to be hurt with each and every unreturned phone call.

Who was acting selfish? she thought to herself. At least she knew she wasn't marrying some spoilt child, which was exactly how his parents were acting. She had found that recently it was hard to keep some of these feelings to herself, and she had told as much in confidence to Kim.

However, at the same time, she didn't know exactly what her role was just yet. Until a few weeks ago, she had just been their son's girlfriend; now she was their future daughter-in-law and soon to be part of the family. Therefore, wasn't it fair that she also got to express her opinion on how ridiculous they were acting? Especially since they were making what was supposed to be a happy time in the life of their son very stressful.

She thought about the relationship Shane had with his parents. They had always been close, especially since he was their only son, their only child. She tried to put herself in their shoes. Yes, of course, they only got one shot at a child's wedding and she was sure that they wanted to highlight what they believed was important, namely showing off their son and his bride and impressing their business buddies with their good taste. She worked to convince herself that his parents merely had good intentions, but every time she tried, she came up short.

She shook her head in frustration and picked up her mascara wand, ready to apply it to her eyelashes. True enough, parents usually wanted to be a part of the wedding planning, but it really wasn't their role. And Lauren and Gene were parents of the *groom*, not the bride.

Cara jerked her chin out. 'Well, if they wanted to plan a wedding so bloody much, they should have tried for a girl after Shane,' she muttered under her breath.

'What was that, love?' Shane asked, entering the bedroom. He was adjusting a light blue tie around his neck, and straightening his grey suit jacket.

'Ah nothing, just talking to myself.' She looked up at him. 'Well, well, don't you look dashing? I must admit Richardson, you do clean up well.'

They were getting ready to go to the McCarthy–Bourke wedding they'd been invited to three weeks before; the invite that had essentially sparked off their own engagement.

'Do you think the bride will approve?' Shane smirked. 'Or should I bring a change of clothes in case I don't live up to her expectations? You don't suppose they will have someone at the door checking the clothes labels?'

'You never know. I suppose I better make sure I have clean underwear on,' Cara giggled.

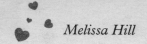

'Ready to go?'

'Can't wait,' Cara groaned, getting up.

'Ah don't be like that.' Shane slung an arm around her shoulder. 'If nothing else, it should give us a few ideas.'

It didn't take Cara and Shane long to realise that the word 'decadent' would have been an understatement if used to describe the white satin and organza-covered, swan and ice-sculptured, rose-laden extravaganza that was Audrey McCarthy's wedding.

'Man, this place looks like Versace threw up on it,' Shane whispered as they made their way to their seats in the hotel garden under a luscious tulle-covered canopy that served as Audrey and Joseph's personal wedding chapel. At a guess, the place housed at least four hundred guests.

'Hush!' Cara laughed as she kept an eye out for anyone else she might know.

'Ten quid says she arrives in a horse-drawn carriage,' Shane snickered.

They found some free seats near the aisle, about halfway from the front of the 'chapel'. Still, even from this vantage point, Cara reckoned a pair of binoculars would have come in handy.

'It'll be amazing if we see anything from here,' Shane pointed out, rolling his eyes.

'Oh, I'm sure Audrey would have accounted for that,' Cara chided forebodingly.

As they sat, Shane busied himself by looking through the programme for the ceremony, but Cara was far more interested in looking around at the other guests. Shockingly enough, she couldn't count a single one who had not followed the rules stated on the invitation. No female had dared wear white, or indeed anything from Karen Millen or Coast. Cara herself had sought out an oft-worn purple dress that channelled Diane Von Furstenberg but was actually from Dunnes Stores. The invite had mentioned nothing about boycotting Dunnes.

'She must have some very loyal friends,' she pointed out. 'I wouldn't have been surprised if someone showed up in white out of spite.'

'More like the girl knows a thing or two about bullying,' Shane countered. Cara nodded in agreement. Shane had never met Audrey, but from what she remembered of her, he was right. Her college friend had always been . . . forthright in her opinions, to say the least.

A string quartet began to play at the front of the chapel, and the groom and his best man entered through the side. Although both were resplendent in what had to be Armani morning coats, Cara took note of the fact that, as handsome as the men looked, both – but especially the groom – looked absolutely miserable.

'What's yer man's name again?' Shane asked as he flipped through the programme. 'The groom I mean.'

'Does it really matter?' Cara asked. Clearly this ceremony was all about the bride.

'Ah. Joseph Bourke,' her fiancé confirmed. He shook his head. 'Poor bastard.'

Cara had already moved on from wondering about the groom and instead was taking in the show. As expected, the mothers were escorted in first, and then the bridesmaids arrived. Each woman had on a beautiful cerise pink gown, each fit to their specific body shape in a simple unfussy style that flattered their very different figures individually.

Cara had to give Audrey credit; at least she hadn't set out to find the worst monstrosity known to the world of bridesmaids to force upon her attendants, just to make herself look

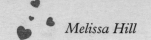

better. Why didn't most brides understand that no one would usurp their special day – that all brides were beautiful?

Cara recognised a few other faces from her college days, but couldn't place the names; it had been several years after all, and if not for this wedding invite, she probably wouldn't have crossed paths with Audrey ever again.

Suddenly, the music rose to a crescendo, heralding the bride's arrival. From the back of the chapel, a chorus of oohs and ahhs echoed, and Cara tried to look back past the standing crowd to see what was happening outside.

As if guessing that this was exactly what the crowd would be thinking in unison at that particular moment, two large plasma screen TVs flickered on at the front of the room. The bride had made sure every single person there would witness her arrival.

But not only was she in a horse-drawn carriage as Shane predicted, her chariot was made of glass, just like Cinderella's.

'Holy shit,' Shane muttered.

'Shh!' Cara elbowed him as she took in the spectacle before her. Well . . . the big screens *were* handy, she had to admit.

'I bet she's wearing glass slippers too. Of all the ridiculous, little-girl princess nonsense—' Shane whispered, only to be shushed by a woman the next row over.

At that moment a man, presumably Audrey's father, exited from the glass carriage. He was about Cara's dad's age and if the expression on his face was any indication of his mood, he was completely shell-shocked by everything that was happening.

'Look at that poor bloke,' whispered Shane. 'He's probably just been handed the bill for all this.'

Cara had to hold back giggles. 'Will you stop it! You are so bad.'

A collective gasp echoed through the crowd as Audrey exited the carriage with the help of her father. A vision in layers upon layers of white satin and tulle, her dress alone must have cost the annual GDP of some small country.

Upon first glance Audrey's smile looked radiant, but Cara could see her eyes darting wildly around the room, taking in every person, every flower, every strand of fairy lights.

As Audrey made her way up the aisle one graceful step at a time, Cara noted that her smile, up close, seemed more tense than radiant, and while there was no denying that she was beautiful, you could also tell she was making a mental checklist of what she didn't approve of, what was wrong, and what someone would get thoroughly chewed out for later.

To Cara's untrained eye, everything looked perfect. Extravagant, but perfect. Why on earth should the bride look so tense on her wedding day?

Although, maybe she was being harsh. Maybe Audrey was simply nervous, suffering from a bout of stage fright. Cara scolded herself for being overly judgemental. Audrey was more than likely overwhelmed with everything that was happening. What bride wouldn't be?

Audrey passed where Cara and Shane were sitting and Cara had to admit that the dress was beautiful, as was the cathedral-length veil that followed her down the aisle. She tried to envision herself in a dress like that, tried to put herself in Audrey's shoes. What did it feel like exactly? To have the eyes of hundreds of people on you all at once, studying you, judging you, making comparisons?

She gulped.

The ceremony progressed as normal from there, and all was perfectly choreographed. From the beautiful reading by the bride's tearful sister, to the lighting of the unity candle by both mothers. This was an open declaration of love and commitment and indeed, both families were equally highlighted and included.

When the marriage ceremony was over, cocktails were quickly served and Cara and Shane made their way out to the allotted space where waiters passed canapés and carried silver trays of Dom Perignon. Cara took in every detail, making mental notes about possible ideas for their own wedding.

'It was a nice ceremony, wasn't it?' she inquired, interested to gauge Shane's train of thought.

'I suppose. Wasn't it fairly standard though – apart from all the pomp at the beginning?'

'Oh, I don't know, I thought it was lovely, you know, involving both of the families like that, the mothers, the sisters, making sure everyone felt included.'

As if he intuitively caught her vibe and what she was thinking, Shane softened his tone. 'Are you wondering if a big splash might be a better alternative to the intimate do we were considering after all?' he asked mildly.

She bit her lip and studied his face. 'Would it be terrible if I *was* thinking that?'

Shane pressed his lips together and shook his head as he lowered his eyes to examine his glass of champagne.

'Of course not. Look, regardless of what we decide I am going to be the happiest man in the world because I am marrying you, OK? So whether you want something huge or something small, really, I'll be happy to go along with it.'

She smiled at him. 'I'm not saying I want this, the glass carriage or anything like that, not at all. I don't know, I just suppose I was looking at the families, and no one is fighting and it seems like . . . it's sort of hard to explain . . . yes, there must have been a lot of organising beforehand but, on the day, it seems that everything just works out.' She lowered her eyes demurely. 'I'm sorry, maybe I'm just being silly.' Afraid to meet his gaze, she took a sip of champagne. 'Don't mind me.'

Shane took a step to close the distance between them. He brought his hand to her chin and raised her eyes to meet his. 'You are not silly. And of course I would rather you talked to me about all of this. Like I said, I don't care if there are ten or ten thousand names on the guest list, or you are wearing a million-euro dress or a flour sack. At the end of it all, you will be my wife and that is all that matters to me. That's all that counts.'

He leaned down to kiss her and Cara felt her heart soar. She was so lucky to have someone like Shane who just understood her inside and out. She returned his kiss and hugged him close. Then a high-pitched voice interrupted them.

'Cara Clancy! I'm so glad you came!'

Cara turned away from Shane to be met with the vision in white herself.

'Haha, look, look at me, I'm now Mrs McCarthy-Bourke!' Audrey giggled coquettishly. 'And you must meet my *husband*!' Following close behind, somewhat reluctantly as he pulled at the bow tie around his neck, was the hapless groom. 'Cara, this is Joseph – Joseph, my old college friend, Cara.' She glanced pointedly at Shane. 'And I'm sorry, but I don't think I know your "plus one".'

Oops, they'd forgotten about *that* rule. Cara smiled broadly. 'Joseph, so nice to meet you, and huge congratulations to you both. This is my fiancé, Shane.' She put her arm through Shane's as he reached forward to offer congratulations and shake the groom's hand.

'Fiancé?' Audrey echoed, her eyes wide. 'I didn't know you were engaged.'

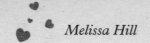

'Yes, it happened just a few weeks ago actually, and we are . . .'

But Audrey's gaze darted away from Cara's face, and her expression soured. 'I'm sorry?' she replied absently.

'I said, it just happened a few weeks ago, right round the time we received your invitation actually and . . .'

Again, Audrey's gaze drifted over Cara's head, looking far beyond them. 'Dammit,' she muttered darkly.

'Is everything all right?'

Audrey's face was tense, but her mouth suddenly broke out into a huge smile that didn't reach her eyes. 'Yes, of course! It's just . . . something that needs to be dealt with, a catering issue. Sorry, can you hold on for one second please?' She held up a finger to Cara and before Cara could answer, thrust her bouquet at Joseph and hurried away.

Cara and Shane looked at each other and watched as Audrey made a beeline for a waiter who was clearly struggling to balance a tray of champagne. From twenty feet away, they heard her berate the young man, who couldn't have been more than seventeen years old.

'Where is your supervisor?' she hissed. 'I told the caterer I wanted properly trained waiting staff, not a bunch of bumbling know-nothings who would be better off in some student pub. I want you off the floor now. Off! Immediately!'

For a brief moment Cara worried that the beautiful bride might actually cause physical damage to the guy, or at least throw the tray of champagne flutes at him.

Shane looked at her and raised an eyebrow. 'So, um Joseph, lovely wedding. Really fantastic,' he said to the groom. 'You must be over the moon.'

Joseph's voice was flat. 'Yes of course, lovely being surrounded by so many people, so many people we know and you know – don't know. Lots of planning went into this, and Audrey did a bang-up job, really, she did. Looking forward to the honeymoon – and Jesus bloody Christ what do you have to do to get a drink around here?' he snapped.

Shane stepped in, clearly understanding that this 'Wedding Wonderland' was making the groom walk a very thin line between sanity and the opposite.

'What are you drinking, mate?'

'JD, neat. I know they have it, they better have it. Make it a double, a treble even.'

'Done. Be right back.' Shane walked off in the direction of the bar, leaving Cara by herself with an increasingly jittery groom. She looked over her shoulder, realising Audrey had now gone off somewhere else. She was unsure if that was a blessing or a curse.

'So, the honeymoon next. I'll bet you can't wait. Where are you off to?' she asked amiably.

Joseph wouldn't meet her gaze. 'Malaysia, some godforsaken place in the middle of the jungle. Not that I picked it. Not that I picked *anything*, not this, not any of it. Nope, no say whatsoever.' He fidgeted again with his bow tie. 'Jesus Christ, where's that drink, I'm sweating bullets here . . .'

Cara looked around, hoping that Shane would come back soon. Preferably with something strong for her, too. 'I'm sure he won't be long.'

'I mean come on, all of this nonsense, this bullshit for one day. And would you look at those stupid, bloody flowers. All those damn flowers.'

Cara bit her lip. Was there some form of etiquette she was supposed to be following? She didn't know this man, he was clearly distressed, but then again, had he not just got married thirty minutes before?

'But really Joseph, the flowers are stunning – everything is lovely. It's all just beautiful really.'

'Yeah, yeah, beautiful. Nearly two hundred grand's worth of beautiful. Two hundred grand . . . And it's not as if we're getting away with anything either. Her parents only could go in for fifty grand, same as mine, they had to sell one of the cars, remortgage their house and what have you – my parents aren't millionaires, you know. Us now, me and Audrey – one hundred grand in debt. One hundred thousand euro. Dear sweet Jesus,' Joseph croaked as if the reality had just hit him. Cara was worried he was close to tears. Again, she looked around for Audrey or Shane. No sign of either of them. 'And for what?' Joseph continued. 'A pair of fucking ice swans? Some fancy canapés and a dress she's going to wear just once?' His eyes rolled wildly in his head.

Shane really needed to get back with that whiskey.

'But Joseph, everyone is so happy at the moment,' Cara continued politely, hoping to make him feel better although inwardly she was staggered by the sums. 'It's a wonderful day, you could really feel the love in the room, the ceremony was so beautiful and—'

Joseph snorted. 'Feel the love? My parents are barely speaking to me. And her mother, that *cow*, stupid woman sticking her oar into *everything* – and you saw her up there crying – pretending everything is hunky-dory. I swear, if I never see any of them again . . .'

Cara automatically took a step back. Joseph's frustration had quickly turned to anger. 'You know, I've always had a great relationship with my parents, but my dad wanted to retire soon . . .' He shook his head regretfully. 'They're just ordinary hardworking people, I shouldn't have dragged them into paying for this mess, but Audrey was determined, she just had to have it like this. If I had my way, I would have taken off and got married on a beach, just the two of us, that sort of thing but no way . . . Not possible. Audrey had a vision – she's been dreaming of this for most of her life and for what? All this nonsense?' He glared at Cara, as if she was personally responsible. 'Why don't they take little girls aside and tell them that the quickest way to ruin happy ever after is to perpetuate the ridiculousness that they need to be a princess on their wedding day?'

Thankfully, at that moment Shane returned. 'Here's your drink, man.' He thrust into Joseph's hand a glass of whiskey, which the groom quickly threw back in one gulp. Eyes closed, he momentarily relaxed as the alcohol burned its way down to his stomach.

Shane regarded Cara with a quizzical expression. He opened his mouth briefly, as if to ask about what had just transpired, but Cara shook her head, warning him to keep quiet.

Joseph took a deep breath and opened his eyes groggily. Cara wondered just how many bourbons the groom had imbibed prior to the ceremony.

'See these glasses?' he said, staring at the empty tumbler. 'This is called an "upcharge". We could have had regular glasses, the kind that you drink from in any hotel or bar in Ireland. But no, we had to have Baccarat crystal rocks glasses. Do you know what a Baccarat fucking crystal rocks glass looks like?' He shoved the glass up against Cara's face. '*This* is what a Baccarat fucking crystal rocks glass looks like, and guess how much it costs to have them here today? Go on, guess!'

'Umm, no idea,' Cara replied truthfully, but then decided she'd better play along. Surely fancy glasses wouldn't cost that much more than regular ones. 'Maybe a couple of quid extra per glass?'

The groom laughed uproariously and Cara locked eyes with Shane. It was time to leave.

'A couple of quid! Ha! *Nothing* at this godforsaken sideshow cost a couple of quid. Try an extra *twenty* quid per glass. Per glass! For crystal that no one bloody cares about! And for that princely sum, you are only permitted to *drink* from it, you don't even get to keep it.' He stared in wonderment at the glass. 'I don't even own these – twenty quid a pop and I don't even own them, I'm just renting them for a couple of hours. Can you believe it?' His face grew red and he looked again at the scene around him as if he was a drowning man. 'I heard correct earlier, you two are engaged yes? Getting married?' Cara and Shane nodded their heads meekly.

'And I take it you want to stay married?'

'Well of course,' Cara replied uncomfortably.

'Then do yourselves a favour. Skip all this bullshit, this nonsense. I don't know how we're ever going to able to pay all this off. I was made redundant a couple of months ago, but so much was already arranged and Audrey was insistent—' Joseph put his face in his hands as if he was about to start sobbing and Cara looked uncomfortably at Shane, at a loss what to do.

'Mate, do you want to sit down for a while? Can I get anyone, do anything for you?' Shane placed a hand on the groom's shoulder.

'Well yes, you can do something for me, actually.'

'Sure, just name it. Anything.'

'Tell me which way the fucking bar is.'

Cara swallowed hard. With the way Joseph was drinking, the night was destined to end badly. And she knew that she didn't want to be around to witness the inevitable carnage. Poor Audrey and Joseph. He'd recently lost his job? She looked around at the lavish spread, the unmistakable expense of it all. Why go through with all of this if ultimately they couldn't afford it?

'Erm, it's that way,' Shane said quietly, pointing in the direction of the bar.

'Thanks and hey, thanks for listening,' Joseph said, patting Cara on the shoulder. 'Congratulations on your engagement and all that, much luck to you. May you find a lifetime of happiness and all that bullshit,' Joseph hiccupped. 'I need to get a drink and find my blushing bride. Hah! Audrey blushing. You saw her earlier; she's more likely to shoot daggers at you—' He took a deep breath. 'Anyway, thanks for the drink, and cheers.' The groom raised his glass once again in their direction as he stumbled off.

Shane turned and looked at Cara, his hands in his pockets. 'So, shall I go and look for their wedding planner so we can put our deposit down?'

She shook her head, still slightly shell-shocked by the horrible reality behind Audrey and Joseph's supposed Big Day.

She grabbed his hand. 'No, let's just get the hell out of here. I think we need to talk.'

Chapter 12

They were both quiet during the taxi journey home from the wedding, each lost in their own thoughts.

'You know you shouldn't let all that bother you,' Shane said eventually. 'Our wedding doesn't have to be like that.'

'Maybe you get that and I get that, but I am afraid no one else seems to.'

'What do you mean?'

'Well there's your parents still not speaking to us for one. And despite what I said, I've already had to get Mum to cancel the church booking.' She had been flabbergasted to learn that Betty had gone ahead and booked her precious St Joseph's church for April of the following year, 'just in case'. While it was lovely that her mother was so excited about her wedding and determined to throw herself into the planning of it, the level of Betty's determination was disconcerting. 'To think we haven't even set a bloody date yet.' Cara kneaded her forehead. 'And then a while back, when I was out with the girls that time, they just jumped all over me about the wedding plans, same as what everyone has been doing lately, asking questions, offering opinions, telling me what to do. Honestly, I feel like I'm being smothered.'

Yet unlike Cara, Shane seemed to be taking all these intrusions in his stride. 'Look, nobody else's opinions matter, just ours.'

But Cara said nothing, realising that he just didn't understand how stressful it was all becoming, for her at least.

When they reached the apartment and went inside, he threw his jacket on the sofa and sighed.

'And this is supposed to be the happy time,' he said wryly. 'The easy bit, before all the chaos starts.'

Cara reached forward and put her arms around him. 'Look, I am happy, I'm happy with you, I love you. But you heard Joseph earlier, about all that family strife and how he'd probably never speak to his in-laws again. Already everyone has the same sort of expectations for us, and how we should do things. It's like we have to follow certain rules or we're doing something wrong, or being . . . weird or something. Crikey Shane, if I learned anything today it's that a big affair is a million miles from what I want. I don't want a wedding planner or Baccarat crystal glasses and I certainly don't want half the country on the guest list. I keep thinking about poor Joseph and imagining you the same way – ragged and bitter on what's supposed to be the happiest day of your life. I just – oh, I just don't know.' She rubbed her temples.

'OK, let's look at it this way,' Shane said gently. 'Let's stop thinking about the negative stuff and all the things we don't want. What *do* we want? What do you want? Really, be honest, what do you envision for your wedding day?'

'Well, other than what we said before about it being small and—'

'No I mean what do you envision now, this minute? What's your instinct?'

Cara closed her eyes and tried to put all the recent chaos out of her head, and simply imagine her and Shane's wedding day and what would suit them best.

She breathed deeply and very easily began to conjure a

scene in her mind. She pictured herself in a simple white satin sheath, the kind that would drape easily over her curves without requiring corsets or crinoline. Instead of heels torturing her feet, she pictured herself in flats, or perhaps barefoot, with her hair down and a simple veil pinned effortlessly at the crown of her head. The veil would catch a light breeze as she walked up the aisle towards Shane.

And there was Shane, waiting for her, his skin tanned and golden, the picture of health and vitality rather than the white-faced bag of nerves that was Joseph Bourke, a tender smile lighting up his face as she approached.

Cara expanded the scene in her mind. She thought about the guests, the people she wanted to share the moment with, and realised she knew every face, and only the people who mattered were present. Her beloved parents, her sisters, good friends . . . she cared about them all and there wasn't a stranger amongst them.

Then out of nowhere she imagined herself tasting salt in the air and hearing waves crash upon the shore. The air was warm and a setting sun was casting brilliant hues of red and orange upon the turquoise of the ocean. She could smell the scent of frangipani in the breeze.

Cara felt a smile find its way to her lips.

'What are you thinking about?' Shane whispered, taking her hands gently.

She was smiling broadly, still lost in the vision. 'No Cinderella dresses or tuxedos, just you and me calm and relaxed, surrounded by our family and everyone we love. I know all the faces, and so do you.'

'Liking the sound of it so far. What else?'

'A beach,' she smiled, her eyes still closed. 'Somewhere warm and beautiful. It's sunset, and the waves are rolling in, and it's just . . . it's just beautiful, magical almost. It's perfect.'

She opened her eyes and met Shane's gaze. He was smiling too.

'You know, that's the most at ease you've looked in weeks.'

'I know.' As she began to feel the weight of all her previous anxiety lifting, Shane spoke again.

'Let's do it,' he said matter-of-factly.

Her eyes flew open. 'What?'

'A beach wedding. Somewhere warm, sand under our feet, at sunset, on a tropical island. The whole shebang. Let's do it.'

She stared at Shane, her heart racing. It did sound perfect, and what's more it sounded *right*, but . . .

'What would everyone think?'

'Who cares?' he said, shaking his head. 'Who cares what anyone thinks? How many times have we said that this is about me and you. This is *our* day and it should be all about what we want. So let's make the dream a reality, and if someone doesn't like it, they can bugger off.'

Cara smiled, remembering that Conor had given her pretty much the same advice a while back. 'Conor said something similar actually,' she laughed.

'Well, then the man talks sense – for once. What do you think?'

She visualised the scene on the beach again. She pictured herself holding a small bouquet of orchids or something simple and beautiful. She could almost feel the warm air on her skin, taste the salt spray on her tongue. She was sold.

'OK then yes, let's do it!' she said excitedly. 'Let's have a beach wedding.' She threw her arms around his neck and kissed him. 'With just our families and a handful of friends.'

'And let's do it soon,' Shane laughed. 'Before anyone has the chance to change our minds.'

Chapter 13

The moment the phone rang in her Palm Beach condo on the other side of the Atlantic, Danielle Clancy had a dark premonition. She couldn't quite put her finger on it, but a sense of unease suddenly crept in.

She placed her hand on the phone and left it there for a moment, refusing to even look at the caller ID. Something was up, she just knew it.

She hastily grabbed the phone and found herself swallowing hard before she said, 'Hello?'

'Danielle? Hi, it's Cara.'

She exhaled a little. Cara. Only Cara. Nothing to worry about, nothing to be upset about. Where had the spike in intuitive energy come from a moment earlier? Cara was on the other side of the ocean. Nothing to be worried about, Danielle reassured herself. Simple sister-to-sister chat. Nothing more than that.

Except she and Cara didn't really do 'sister-to-sister' chats.

'Hey there . . . Cara, how are you doing?' she drawled hesitantly.

'Gosh, Danielle, I can't believe that's you, you sound a hundred per cent American. No hint of an Irish accent at all!' Cara laughed.

'Well, I have lived here for quite a long time now,' Danielle reminded her.

It had been a very long time since she'd left Ireland – a

lifetime, for all intents and purposes. Sure Danielle had been back across the Atlantic a few times over the years, but she didn't make a habit of it. Truthfully, most of the time, she preferred to sneak in and out of Europe without her family knowing anything about it.

'I know. I can't even remember the last time you were home,' Cara continued. 'So how is everything? What's been happening with you? How is Zack?'

Holding her breath, Danielle wished that Cara would skip the small talk and just say what she needed to say. She knew there was a purpose to this phone call and she could hazard a guess it had something to do with what was happening back home.

Danielle didn't really have a chatty relationship with her sisters. Heidi and Cara were both so much younger than her for starters, and the fact that she had been away from home for so long meant it was hard to simply chit-chat on the phone without feeling like she was talking to a stranger.

'Well, things are good Cara, really. Business is good, Zack is good, life is good.'

And that about summed it up really, Danielle thought, smiling.

'Fantastic. We'd really love to meet Zack, you know – you've been with him for what, five years now? What a mystery man he is. Any wedding bells in the future for you two?'

'Oh, I'm not sure if that's right for either of us just now, we are quite comfortable as we are,' Danielle replied uncomfortably. 'So really Cara, what's going on? What can I do for you?' She felt a bit mean for turning her tone businesslike, the voice she used when brokering a real estate deal at work, but her mounting anxiety was becoming a little too much to bear.

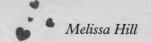

'Well, I wasn't sure if Mum had called you yet . . .'

Danielle's breath caught. Oh no, was it her dad? Was there something wrong with him? Danielle adored Mick; he was the only one in the family who understood her, and the only one who'd stood up for her and considered her feelings back then . . .

'No, she hasn't,' she interrupted quickly, her heart racing, wishing Cara would just get the news over and done with.

'Oh, well, right. Well, I didn't think she had rung you about it, but I just wanted to check.'

'Rung me about what?' Danielle was getting seriously agitated. She hated to have her aura poisoned by negative thoughts, which funnily enough is what any contact with her family usually provoked.

'Well, I have some news,' Cara sang happily. 'I'm engaged!'

Engaged . . . Automatically, Danielle felt herself exhale. There was no bad news, nothing to get upset about. Cara was getting married to . . . yes, Shane. That was his name, she thought. Her sister was getting married to Shane, which probably meant some big affair back home. She recalled that his parents were big cheeses of some kind.

Then she felt her anxiety rise once again. Cara would probably want her there, like Heidi had wanted her for her wedding a year before. But of course, that couldn't happen. Danielle had promptly brushed the invitation off with a long, confusing saga about work commitments. And like it or not, there was no way she would be able to attend this wedding either.

She quickly struggled to think of an excuse to have ready before Cara got the chance to ask. 'Well, congratulations,' she said, meaning it and feeling some of her normal control and confidence reassert itself. Of course she could manage this. Nothing to worry about here. 'So I guess the wedding plans are well under way then? Mum in the middle of it all again, I suppose, bossing everyone around and foisting her ideas on you,' she added, trying to keep some of the bitterness out of her voice.

Deflect the conversation, keep Cara talking, signal in advance how busy you are, then she might not ask you to be a bridesmaid, she mentored herself.

'You know her too well!' Cara laughed. 'Truthfully, she has been a little bit . . . bossy,' she added reluctantly, and Danielle recalled how close Betty and Cara were. Clearly her mother's true colours were showing through now though. 'I've never seen this side to her before. Talking about this dress and that centrepiece, and who would look best in whichever colour . . . it's all a bit crazy.'

Danielle couldn't help but smile. To be fair, Cara was great. There was no pretentiousness with her (compared to the dreadful Heidi) and she supposed, in another life, it would have been nice to have had a closer relationship with her, but so much time had passed . . .

'So have you set a date?' she asked, wheedling. 'I'm assuming . . . Shane just asked you . . .' Danielle winced, sorely hoping she'd remembered Cara's boyfriend's name correctly.

'Yes, he proposed a couple of weeks ago. I'm actually really surprised Mum didn't call you,' Cara said, and a touch of regret entered her voice. 'I would have myself otherwise . . .'

Well, I'm not surprised in the least, Danielle thought sourly.

'I guess she just forgot about it in the midst of all the celebrations—'

'But didn't she call about you Heidi's engagement that time?' Cara pressed. 'Oh and speaking of Heidi, I'm sure that if Mum didn't phone about me, she hardly phoned about that either. Our little sister has a baby on the way, can you believe it? Heidi as a mum. I don't know about you but she's been the baby herself in the family for so long I find it hard to imagine,' she added conversationally. 'And so is Kim for that matter, pregnant I mean. So there you go; all the news.'

Despite herself, Danielle felt wounded. *A wedding and two babies, and not a single phone call?* Wow, it was pretty obvious where she stood in the family dynamic.

'Sounds like you've all been very busy,' she said, injecting some enthusiasm into her tone. She supposed she should feel upset about her disintegrated relationship with her family, and the fact that she was clearly the black sheep of the bunch, barely even deserving of a phone call these days, but in all honesty, she wasn't upset at all. In a way, she was relieved. Happy even. If they couldn't be bothered to tell her this kind of news then surely no one would expect her to be an active participant in what was happening. Which was why she felt confident about her next question. 'So when's the big day, *your* big day I mean?'

'Actually, that's what I wanted to talk to you about,' Cara said, sounding excited. 'We haven't set a date or anything and actually you're the first person I've spoken to about this, because I'm kinda nervous about how everyone will react when we tell them. You see, it hasn't been easy lately. Not at all.'

'Spoken to about what?' Danielle asked, intrigued even as her instincts were urging her to back away and just stay out of it, whatever it was. However, she couldn't help but wonder what role she could possibly play in all of this, and was even more curious as to why Cara would be turning to her, instead of Betty or indeed Kim. Over the years she'd always got the impression Ben's wife and Cara were close.

'Well, like you said, Mum is all set on the notion of a big traditional white wedding along the lines of Heidi's; the church, humongous dress, a guest list in the hundreds, you know yourself. And really Shane and I aren't interested in any of that. What's more, his parents are barely speaking to us – strike that, they aren't talking to us *at all* because when we told them about our engagement, they immediately offered to pay for the wedding because they wanted to invite all of their society friends and have their own version of a shindig.' She sighed deeply. 'So it's all a bit mad really. But at the end of the day, Shane and I realise now that we just want a small wedding, something intimate with just family and close friends. You know, the people we love.'

Danielle still wasn't sure how any of this could possibly involve her. 'So, if you want a small wedding just have a small wedding, sweetheart,' she advised warmly. She quite liked the notion that Cara had sought her out for advice and that things weren't always so rosy with Betty.

'Well, that's just the thing,' Cara said. 'We don't know how we could possibly make that happen without loads more interference, and people trying to take control. So we've decided that we should look away from Ireland and just take off, preferably somewhere warm, and have a beach wedding.'

Danielle paused, as she immediately began to see the pieces fall into place. She knew where people usually had beach weddings – on paradise islands like Barbados, St Lucia, Antigua, all of which were practically in her backyard.

Cara continued. 'So we've picked up some brochures and information on various locations that might be suitable, but I was wondering if maybe you could give me a little insight as we've never been to any of these places, and really, it seems like you've been *everywhere*.'

Danielle breathed deeply. OK, that sounded harmless

enough. Cara was just looking for travel advice. She could do travel advice.

'Well,' she said lightly, hoping that she could manipulate the conversation a little. 'Where were you thinking? Barcelona? Sicily? Lake Garda? Maybe Capri?' Best to try and keep them on that side of the pond, definitely.

'Oh!' Cara exclaimed, as if she hadn't thought of those places before. 'Well, actually, we were thinking somewhere tropical. For a real beach wedding—'

'Yes, but there are beaches in France and Italy too.'

'Yes, I suppose there are,' Cara agreed. 'But we're thinking October, and the weather isn't great in the Med round then. Actually, we have our hearts set on the Caribbean to be honest. White sands, turquoise waters . . . the whole paradise island thing; what do you think?'

Danielle felt her heart race. The last thing she wanted was her entire family coming over in this direction. Most of the Caribbean islands were barely a couple of hours' plane ride away. If they were all here, she would *have* to see them, Betty too. And that would be a recipe for disaster.

She had to think fast.

'I get your thinking but I doubt there's any way Mum will go for that. I take it she's still never been abroad? Actually, are you sure she even has a passport?' she added jokingly. She bit her lip, hating having to play on Cara's insecurities, but desperate times called for desperate measures.

She heard Cara sigh heavily. 'To be honest, I never really considered that . . .' The poor thing's voice was barely above a whisper, and Danielle knew that whether she liked it or not, she was being sucked further into this. She knew she needed to change Cara's mind, and try and prevent her from getting married in this part of the world, but she couldn't bring herself to hurt her feelings either. Cara had never done anything wrong and she wouldn't remember all that had gone on between Danielle and Betty back then.

Still Danielle's fight or flight response was winning out.

'And what about Heidi?' she pointed out. 'As she's pregnant, she might not want to fly, nor Kim for that matter. And if they didn't want to go all the way to the Caribbean, then have you considered that you and . . . Shane might have nobody at all at your wedding?'

'Well, you'd come, surely?' Cara said in a small voice.

Oh shit. How to answer that?

Danielle tried to dodge the point-blank question. 'That's not really the point I'm trying to make, Cara. You said that it was important that the people who matter most are there to share the day with you – Mum and Dad and the rest of the family of course. So, at least if you get married back home, they would definitely be there, no questions asked.'

She hoped that alluding to the fact that herself and Cara were not all that close might hit home a little.

'Besides, how do you even begin to plan a wedding from an ocean away? Oh, I'm sure all the brochures look great and they say they have wedding planners on site, and all of that stuff, but have either of you actually ever been to the Caribbean, Cara? Really, it's horrible. Humid as hell, bugs everywhere . . . plus too many damn tourists.'

'But you go there all the time, don't you? I think the last time we spoke, you and Zack had just come back from St Lucia and you said it was amazing. That you couldn't wait to go back, and that you were even considering buying property there. We have a brochure here for St Lucia . . . we could maybe do it there?' Cara suggested hopefully.

It was true, Danielle did love St Lucia. But she loved it with Zack, or on her own. Not with the Irish crew in tow.

She couldn't even begin to imagine that brood in her vacation paradise.

'Well, St Lucia is one of the more expensive islands. I mean, yes, it's lovely, but it is *very* expensive. I'm not sure if you could afford it if you are trying to keep prices reasonable. Dominican Republic is cheap, so is Jamaica, but unfortunately you can't leave the resorts without seeing armed soldiers everywhere. Not the most romantic backdrop for a wedding.'

Cara sighed again, and when she finally spoke her voice was thick, as if she was trying to hold back tears. 'I'm sorry, maybe you're right. I just thought . . . I just hoped that maybe I could get some advice from someone who wasn't so invested in all of this – someone objective – but this is just turning into a nightmare.' She breathed heavily. 'I'm just trying to do something that will be good for me and Shane, while also involving the people I love most, my family. But I don't want to disappoint Mum and Dad either. I just don't see how I'm going to make anyone happy. There are so many roadblocks. And it just seems that every possible solution I consider turns out to be a dead end and now I feel like an idiot for considering this too. Sorry to rant by the way, I'll let you go.'

Danielle felt terrible. She was being a complete cow in her attempt at self-preservation, and completely discounting poor Cara's feelings. 'Cara, I'm sorry. I probably shouldn't have been so blunt. St Lucia is really lovely, it's a beautiful place and you know, maybe it might be affordable after all. Now, I can't make any promises, but I know some people who run resorts on the island, and maybe I could, you know, maybe put you in touch with a couple of them, see if you can't get some specials? I mean, again, no promises.'

At this, Cara's mood changed immediately and Danielle

could almost feel her excitement surge through the phone. 'Oh Danielle, would you really? Oh that would be wonderful! I would so appreciate it. As I said, we really just want something simple for our wedding, it doesn't have to be anything crazy. Just somewhere warm, some white sand and a pretty spot on the beach.' She laughed. 'I honestly think everyone will be excited once they hear about what we have planned – it'll be like a big family holiday after all!'

Danielle nodded and looked towards her patio windows. The hot Florida sun was high over the ocean – her ocean. That's how she had thought of it since buying this wonderful beachfront property in Fort Lauderdale almost fifteen years ago.

Sure, she could put Cara in touch with some people on the island, people who might know the best resort in which to host a wedding. No big deal, right? It didn't mean it was a *done* deal. Plus, she was banking on the fact that her mother would explode in a fit of rage at the prospect of her favourite daughter, her precious Cara, getting married on some beach in a foreign country.

'Oh Danielle, it would just be perfect,' Cara enthused. 'And it would be so close for you too. And the perfect excuse for us all get to meet Zack too!'

Danielle's eyes widened. *Zack, meeting her family? That was so not gonna happen.* No, absolutely not.

'Let's take it one step at a time, shall we?' she said, trying to keep her voice even.

'Oh yes, yes, of course. Danielle, thank you so much for your help. I can't even tell you how much I appreciate you putting me in touch with the people you know.'

'I'll email you the information later, OK?'

'Today?'

'Sure.'

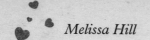

Melissa Hill

'Oh, fantastic,' Cara gushed happily. 'Thank you so much. I feel so positive now that things will just all work out – and as soon as I know anything, I'll be sure to let you know. And I can't wait to see you either! It's been way too long.'

'Erm . . . yes, of course.'

The two said their goodbyes, and afterwards Danielle put the phone down gently, as if it was a time bomb.

Holy crap, what can of worms had that just opened?

Chapter 14

Cara and Shane were sifting through the pile of brochures for St Lucia. The island looked truly magnificent, and she could easily picture her wedding day, on soft smooth sand looking towards the perfect horizon, while palm trees lined the still shores, the sea breeze blowing and the movement of the waves as they said 'I do'. All on a paradise tropical island with the soaring volcanic Pitons and rainforest as background.

'It looks incredible doesn't it?' Shane said excitedly as he shuffled through the brochure for the Paradise Oasis resort, their preferred venue out of the options Danielle had sent them. 'So should we just go ahead and book it all? Put our deposit down and then tell everyone? Or tell everyone and then put our deposit down afterwards?'

It looked so wonderful and seemed so perfect in theory, but at the same time Cara couldn't help but feel nervous about the prospect of telling her mum and dad, her mother in particular, that this was what she and Shane were planning on doing. She knew how desperate Betty was for a traditional ceremony, and so far had been successful in her attempts at dodging any talk about the wedding, and coming up with excuses to avoid discussions surrounding potential churches and timings.

But Cara still couldn't believe how straightforward it all seemed once, as promised, Danielle sent through her contacts for resorts on the island.

She was beginning to worry that Danielle truly did think that her and Shane's plans for a beach wedding were a big mistake, when all of a sudden the email arrived in her inbox.

She had to admit that while she wasn't especially close to her older sister, she sort of looked up to her in any case. Her life in Florida always sounded so glamorous and she admired her free-thinking spirit, maturity and independence as well as envying the fact that Danielle remained largely oblivious to day-to-day Clancy family drama; from Heidi's tantrums to Mick's aches and pains, not to mention Betty's interference.

Cara had few childhood memories of Danielle before she moved out. And if she was being honest, most of the memories she did have were based on pictures from photo albums kept at home at her parents' house. She had perused these mainly on her own, as Betty always seemed hesitant to talk about her. There was no denying that there had been some big falling-out between those two, but Cara had never been able to figure out the reason for it.

While Danielle did come home for visits every few years, it wasn't as if there was a big homecoming celebration. But given that there was undeniable tension between her mother and Danielle, Cara now wondered what it would be like at the wedding.

Surely Betty and Danielle could put aside whatever long-held differences they might have for her special day?

No, she couldn't go down that road, couldn't start wondering about things she just couldn't control. Cara looked at her fiancé sitting across the dining room table from her and decided that they should just take the bull by the horns and get it done. Once they'd drawn up the guest list and broken the news to the few people on it, it would be time to plan the trip as well as the ceremony. Even though a beach wedding would make things simpler, there was lots to be done and she knew that she'd better get cracking.

'I think we just go ahead and book it,' she said confidently. 'Then it's done and we can't be swayed by anyone else. Yes, let's do it.'

'Great. And definitely September then?' Shane queried. September was one of the most affordable months in the brochure, and it also gave them a good four months to plan everything.

'I think it sounds perfect. You don't think we will have any issues, with the weather or anything?' September was apparently smack bang in the middle of the Atlantic hurricane season and possibly one of the reasons they were being offered such a fantastic deal on the package.

'I don't think that any of us can predict that. Unless you'd feel better waiting until after the season is over?' Shane asked. 'Trouble is, we're working with a tight enough window as it is, because of Heidi and Kim.'

Cara shook her head determinedly. 'No, you're right, I'm not going to worry about it. Like you said, you can't control everything. Besides, I definitely don't want to drag everything all out to next year,' she said resolutely.

'Good. Shall we go ahead with the booking then?' Shane asked.

Cara clapped her hands together excitedly. 'Yes, let's do it.'

Moments later, Shane got off the phone with the resort. He'd given his credit card number for the deposit, and then dutifully faxed the signed booking contract, promising to put the hard copy in the post later.

When it was all done, Cara let out a huge sigh of relief.

It was all confirmed. She and Shane were officially going to be married on the island of St Lucia in four months and counting!

Cara threw her arms around her husband-to-be, who was equally jubilant.

The plans were set in motion, and there was no going back. It would be smooth sailing from now on, she just knew it.

Now all she had to do was tell the guests.

However, the following Monday evening Cara was not feeling so positive. In fact, she was downright nervous as she and Shane climbed the front steps to her parents' home. Having finalised the booking over the weekend, they were going to tell Betty and Mick the news today. They had come prepared with a selection of information on St Lucia, leaflets and brochures with pictures of the resort where the wedding would be held, and finally the booking confirmation for their flights, which Cara and Shane had also booked recently.

'Cara just breathe, everything is going to be fine,' said Shane encouragingly. 'What's not to like about this? Everyone's getting a holiday to somewhere exotic, somewhere they have never been. It will be fine.'

But Cara wasn't so sure. Shane came from a worldly family after all, and while Lauren and Gene were still acting like silly children at the moment, they were bound to be much more open to travelling to exotic destinations. Whereas the furthest Betty and Mick had been was across the Irish Sea to visit family in the UK.

'Cara, I'm serious, relax. Everything will be fine.'

She nodded and took a deep breath as she went through the front door, to be immediately met with the smell of her mother's shepherd's pie. Of course. She smiled at how wonderfully predictable Betty was. It was a Monday and Monday had been shepherd's pie night for as long as Cara could remember.

'Hello?' she called out. 'Mum, Dad?'

Shane followed Cara into the house and Betty appeared in the doorway of the kitchen, wiping her hands with a dishtowel.

'Oh. Cara love. And Shane. What are you two doing here?' She rushed forward to kiss her daughter on the cheek. 'I'm a mess. Just in the middle of making dinner. Why didn't you tell me you were coming over, I'd have made more – although of course I'll be able to stretch it out, put on a few more vegetables,' she babbled. 'I hope you haven't eaten yet.'

Cara smiled at the warm familiarity. No, she and Shane hadn't eaten, and even if they had, her mother would still have encouraged them to have at least two helpings.

'Where's Dad?' Cara asked as she followed her mother into the kitchen.

'Oh he's out the back somewhere – skulking around in the shed and trying to avoid any housework as usual. Shane, will you run out and get him? Cara, grab that spoon for me, will you?'

Cara dutifully did as she was told, giving the brochures and tickets a tentative glance as she placed all the documents in a neat stack on the countertop. Shane gave her a little wink as he retreated to the backyard to find Mick.

'So how's everything?' her mother asked companionably.

'Good – great, actually. We've made a decision about the wedding plans, that's why we're here actually, to let you know what we're going to—'

'Ah great! It's nice to hear you're finally making some decisions, you know you've been driving us all batty with your indecision. So when's the date? Oh and while Shane is outside,' she said conspiratorially, 'have you made things up with his parents yet? Terrible carry-on really. They shouldn't be going on like that; after all it's your big day.

And to my mind, if they continue on sulking like this they are going to miss out on all the fun,' Betty said, her tone full of reproach.

Cara swallowed. Things still hadn't thawed between them and the Richardsons. 'I'm afraid not, but I'm sure they'll come round eventually.' She certainly hoped so.

'Well you shouldn't let these things draw out for too long, Cara. It will only make it worse. His parents might be big-shot society types but they'll soon find out the Clancys can throw quite the party ourselves, eh?' Betty winked at her daughter and Cara felt a lump of apprehension grow in her stomach. She needed to just spit the news out and get it over with.

'About that Mum . . . Shane and I have been brainstorming over the last while, and now we know exactly what we want.'

'That's great pet! I hope you're thinking St Joseph's because they have that wonderful balcony with the pipe organ, and of course it can fit at least three hundred easily, if not three fifty. And Father O'Brien is such a lovely priest, very modern and everything, he will do such a lovely ceremony.'

'Well no . . .'

'Ah, don't tell me you're going for St Mary's? Really, it's so dark in there; all the photos would come out terrible. And speaking of photos, I found a great photographer for you. You know my friend Noreen from bridge class? Well her son is a professional photographer apparently. We can set up a meeting, go through his portfolio and see what you think. We'd probably get a good quote too, considering.'

Cara was about to speak when the back door opened and Shane and Mick walked through. As usual, Mick greeted his daughter with a warm hug and a kiss.

'So I hear you're getting to grips with the wedding plans then?' he said happily. 'I guess I should break out the chequebook so. Go on then, how much is this all going to cost me?' Her father was smiling and jovial about the prospect of writing wedding cheques, but behind the façade, Cara thought she saw some trepidation too. Her heart swelled up with pride that this wedding was, in fact, going to cost her parents nothing at all. The opposite actually, as this time they would in fact be benefiting, given that she and Shane were taking care of the cost of their travel and hotel stay.

With that thought in the forefront of her mind, she spoke with confidence. 'Actually Dad, that's where the good news comes in. The wedding is going to cost you nothing. Not a single penny.' She looked at Shane and he smiled, coming up behind her to put his arm around her shoulder.

'What's all this?' her father said with confusion. 'What do you mean it won't cost us anything? Did ye win the lotto or something?' he laughed.

Betty looked from Cara to Shane and back again. 'Oh no, the wedding is off is that it?' she asked, her tone frantic. 'Do you want to be one of those trendy, new age couples who just live together their whole lives? And have a gaggle of illegitimate children all with silly hyphenated surnames? Oh God Mick, talk some sense into your daughter . . .'

'Mum!' Cara laughed. 'It's nothing like that, really.'

'Of course we're getting married,' Shane reassured Betty. 'Don't worry about that. We're going to do things in a slightly different way, that's all.'

Both of her parents wore blank expressions, but seemed calmer knowing that the prospect of a big day out had not been taken off the table.

'Well? What are these grand plans then? And why isn't it

going to cost me anything?' said Mick, his tone still suspicious.

Cara knew it was now or never. She cleared her throat and blurted it out all at once, desperate to share her excitement with them. 'Because we're going to have the wedding in St Lucia!'

The blank expressions remained. Mick and Betty regarded their daughter as if she was speaking a strange language.

'St Lucia's? Where's that? I don't think I've heard of it before,' Betty said frowning. 'Is it Catholic?'

'No Mum, I'm not talking about a church,' Cara explained happily. 'The island, St Lucia. In the Caribbean. We're going to have a beach wedding!' She smiled, although her enthusiasm was shaken somewhat as her parents continued to look at her as if she was an alien.

'Shane?' her father asked, turning to him, bemused. 'What's all this about?'

'Like Cara said Mick,' Shane spoke in a measured tone, as if he was explaining something to a small child. 'Cara and I have decided to have a beach wedding. On the Caribbean island of St Lucia. It is our intention, our *preference*, to only have family and close friends at this ceremony. We are not interested in a church wedding, nor are we interested in having a bunch of people that we do not know there. Furthermore, we are not interested in going into debt, or having someone else go into debt over the financing of our wedding day. We are going to have a beautiful ceremony on a beach in St Lucia, and we are flying both families out there and paying for everything. That is what we are doing.' Shane smiled pleasantly, but Cara could tell he still meant business. She tried to feed off of his no-nonsense attitude.

'Oh you're just going to love it! We brought all the information and photos for you both to look at and everything.

Danielle helped us find the most beautiful resort. It's absolutely stunning and it will be so perfect – look.' She hustled over to the countertop and thrust the brochures that she had brought into her mother's hand.

However, Betty seemed to have only heard the mention of the name Danielle.

'Danielle?' she repeated, her forehead wrinkling. 'You went to *Danielle* to plan your wedding? What on earth could *she* possibly know about weddings? And why would you go to her and not me, Cara?' Betty added, sounding hurt.

'Why don't we just all sit down and we can go through everything together?' encouraged Shane. 'We should have a cuppa while we do so.' He filled the kettle with water and switched it on. Over her parents' heads Cara met his eye and gave him a worried look.

Shane led Betty and Mick to the kitchen table, where he got them firmly planted in their seats. Her mother stared with distaste at the pamphlets that Cara was doing her best to spread in front of them, as if she was systematically covering their table with rubbish. The confused expressions had not left their faces.

'I'll tell you what happened. Remember I was telling you about that wedding we were invited to, my old friend Audrey's? Well, we went at the weekend, and it was just awful, horrible really. The families were miserable, the groom was drunk and upset and the bride . . . well she was insane, wasn't she Shane?' She looked to her fiancé, who nodded in agreement. 'They're up to their necks in debt over it and Shane and I know that's not what we want for our wedding. So we started thinking about what we did want, and this is exactly it. A lovely, intimate beach wedding in a beautiful destination and a small selection of guests and a simple ceremony that will allow us to celebrate with the people we love. And even better – we can all have a holiday afterwards and soak up the sun while we celebrate.' Cara smiled happily, trying to encourage her parents to share in her excitement. 'Like I said, I called Danielle and she put me in touch with a contact of hers who gave us a really fantastic rate on a wedding package in this resort. We are getting married in September. September twelfth.'

'So is Danielle going to be there then?' Betty asked cagily.

'Well, yes, of course, I'm sure she will be, especially when the Caribbean is so close for her. Why wouldn't she be?'

Betty shook her head, and Cara was about to press on, wondering exactly what the problem was with having her older sister at her wedding, when Mick jumped in.

'Well whatever about Danielle, we can't go, Cara. Sure we don't even have passports. How long is the flight to that place anyway? St Lucia – sounds expensive; I'm not sure we can afford to go swanning off somewhere like that.'

Cara's face fell. So this was how they were going to play it, she thought, feeling wounded. Just a moment ago her father had been ready to write them a blank cheque for a wedding there and then. But now they couldn't afford plane tickets to cross the Atlantic? She looked again at Shane, who seemed to read her thoughts.

'Well Mick, like we already said, this won't cost you a thing,' he said, putting mugs of tea in front of his future in-laws. 'As for the passports, there's plenty of time to get them sorted before we leave. With regard to the plane tickets, well, that's already taken care of. Here are your booking confirmations, so really, you don't have to do a thing,' he continued matter-of-factly, pointing out the airline information. 'All you will have to do is pack your bags. Easy as that.'

Mick was considering his future son-in-law, looking for a point to argue, when Betty chimed in.

'September, you said – but that's only four months away! However do you plan a wedding in only four months? There's no way we'll be able to get your dress made in that short a time. Why, it took at least nine for Heidi's.' She looked completely perplexed. 'Although how you are supposed to navigate a great big gown on some beach is beyond me . . .'

Cara shook her head. 'Don't worry, I'm not having a dress that is anything like a great big gown, Mum. That's not my style. And it's not going to take any length of time to organise a suitable dress either. I can always get one off the rack. Not to mention that I wouldn't wear a big Cinderella dress in that heat in any case.'

Mick saw his opening. 'The heat? What do you mean – heat? Now, you know I don't take the heat well. It's bad for my arthritis.'

'And the bugs, what about the bugs?' Betty chimed in. 'Swarms of insects, and mosquitoes in places like that, we'd be eaten alive out there, probably all come back with typhoid or malaria or that kind of thing.' She was beside herself with consternation. 'Which reminds me, what vaccinations will we to have to get? And what type of food do you get in these places? You know I don't like strange food. We might all end up with food poisoning . . . can you even drink the water?'

'Mum, the food will be perfectly lovely and the water is fine,' Cara said, feeling the beginnings of a headache beneath her temple.

'Ah this is madness, Cara. Why can't we just stay here? That way no one will die from dengue fever or diphtheria. Plus, we will have food that everyone is going to like. No one will have to try anything new and no one will get sick from lack of proper sanitation.'

'Oh Dad, for goodness sakes, St Lucia is not a third-world country. It's one of the premier islands in the Caribbean. The place is a playground for celebrities – it's like the French Riviera of that part of the world!'

Mick was unimpressed. 'Yes, so you say, but you've never been there, have you? Fancy brochures are all very fine and well but really, you have no idea what you are getting into.'

'Well, neither have you. You've barely been outside of Ireland,' Cara retorted bluntly.

'I bet you can't even drink the water without spending the rest of the day on the loo.'

'So drink bottled water then.' She hated this. Why were they being so difficult?

'Cara . . .' Shane put in gently, evidently sensing her distress and trying to calm things down. 'Mick, honestly, it's a luxury resort. There won't be any problems.'

'Chances are they won't even speak English out there,' her mother went on as if Shane hadn't spoken. 'How are we supposed to communicate?'

Cara wanted to cry.

'I can't believe you're subjecting us to foreign travel,' Betty continued with a scowl. 'And only having family, you say. What will our friends think? Shane, what will your parents think? It's embarrassing, shameful it is. Running away, leaving the country like you purposely do not want anyone to be around. You are going to be insulting a lot of people. Especially you, Shane, seeing as your family is so well connected. We thought the guest list would be a mile long. And just think, your poor mother will be devastated,' she bemoaned. 'Her only son. Getting married on some desert island.'

Shane shook his head. 'My parents have nothing to do with the matter at hand. It's not their decision. They will either go along with our wishes, and attend the wedding with smiles on their faces, or . . .' he paused ominously, 'they can sit at home and watch it on DVD when we return. I suppose you both have that option as well. We have already paid the deposit. This is happening.'

Cara winced at his bluntness, but there it was. End of discussion. Shane had delivered the necessary ultimatum. Take it or leave it.

She was about to open her mouth to speak, but Shane caught her eye and shook his head ever so slightly. No more talking on their end; important to make it clear that this wasn't a subject for negotiation. Mick and Betty were going to come to their own acceptance on it and stop acting like children, or they would miss out.

Her parents locked gazes and Cara knew that they were communicating non-verbally, the way couples did who had spent years together and who knew each other inside and out. It was killing her that her parents seemed so set against their plans, but what could she do? This was what she and Shane wanted.

Finally Betty spoke. 'So, you really are leaving us no options . . . I hope you know we're very upset with you,' she said sternly.

'Mum, that is your right,' Cara replied, tears in her eyes. 'But try and understand that this is what Shane and I want and this is what we are doing. With or without you,' she added defiantly, although inside her heart was breaking. She couldn't imagine not having her parents at her wedding, and desperately hoped that they'd come round. 'But it would upset me terribly if you weren't there,' she added softly, meeting Betty's gaze. 'This is a big deal and it would mean a lot to both of us if you would just respect our decision and be happy for us.'

'Well, of course we are happy for you, but I just don't know why you have to go to such lengths to get married,' Mick said. 'For God's sake, Heidi didn't get up to such nonsense.' Cara noted that, although he was still complaining, his voice had lost its original bluster.

'No, Dad, Heidi got up to her own brand of nonsense, which you are still paying for. That is exactly what we don't want. Heidi and I are very different.'

'You know she's not going to be happy about this either,' Betty said, and then her eyes widened, remembering. 'The baby! How is Heidi supposed to travel with the baby on the way?'

'I've already thought of that Mum, it's only four months away, and it will be entirely safe for her to travel. Kim, too.'

Betty harrumphed and shook her head. 'I don't know what has got into you, Cara.' She looked at her husband. 'Mick, it's like I don't know this daughter of ours all of a sudden. Go and have your island wedding. We'll be there of course, but we won't like it, just so you know in advance.'

The rest of the evening progressed uncomfortably, with the dinner table conversation consisting primarily of sporadic complaints. Complaints about the length of the plane journey, the time difference, the various diseases they'd be exposed to, as well as the notion of getting sand in uncomfortable places. Cara and Shane tried their utmost to deflect each comment good-naturedly and tried not to let the whining affect them.

But by the time they left for home, Cara had a splitting headache and was ready to crawl into bed.

'Right. One set down and one to go,' Shane said tightly, on the drive back to their apartment.

Cara groaned, not only at the thought of telling Shane's parents but also at having to initiate conversation with people who had been doing their best to ignore them for several weeks.

Shane put his arm around his beleaguered wife-to-be. 'Look on the bright side though, at least my parents have passports.'

Chapter 15

Betty couldn't concentrate. No matter what she tried to do, her thoughts kept drifting back to Cara. Cara and her beach wedding. Cara and her need to rush them all off to some foreign country where they would all probably get sick and die of some strange tropical disease or, at the very least, all get food poisoning from eating something only fit for the natives. Why did her daughter have to be so complicated?

Betty stood at the sink aimlessly washing a dish that had been used at dinner. Even though Cara and Shane had only been gone for just over half an hour, Betty was already obsessing over this new idea for their wedding. Thinking back on it, despite all her posturing and her demands Heidi's wedding had been so easy, Betty thought.

She understood that her daughters were very different and were entitled to believe and do what they wanted with their lives, but she had worked so hard to make sure that her children followed a certain path, did things a certain way – the right way. While some might call her controlling, she simply believed it was her right as a mother to have certain expectations met by her children. She had done the same for her own parents – now it was time for her children to deliver the same to her.

When Heidi got married, the entire process had in a way been effortless, as Heidi had clearly loved all of the attention that came with a big wedding. While Betty knew that her youngest did have certain flaws, namely a certain penchant for playing the damsel in distress, it also could be said that Heidi was the last person who would ever butt heads with another party who was simply looking to shower her with love and attention.

Which is exactly what she and Mick were trying to do with Cara. But no. She wouldn't have it. Flat out refused their generosity, saying that she and Shane would pay for all of it themselves. Although, it wasn't as if she and Mick could necessarily afford another wedding either, Betty admitted. Not when they were still trying to pay off the outlay for Heidi's do, and then not to mention Mick wanting to retire soon. She wrestled with the reality of the situation.

She thought about the credit card statement she had received in the post the previous day, as well as the other card that was almost up to its limit. Then there was the second mortgage. Betty hated thinking about that, and still felt slightly nauseated every month when they went to pay it. If they ran up another big wedding bill, Mick would probably have to put off the idea of retirement for another few years at the very least. Truthfully, she might have to consider going back to work herself, at least part-time.

But notwithstanding this, she and Mick would never have denied Cara a big wedding. And they could get round the financial aspect if needs be. They could ask for an increase on their overdraft, and of course Betty had a bit of nice jewellery that she could sell. She would sacrifice, *they* would sacrifice whatever necessary, especially for their daughter. After all, didn't every girl want a big white wedding?

Apparently not, Betty thought. Not Cara. No going into debt over the Big Day, no fuss, nothing special. There was no denying that Cara had always been very practical and so smart, compared to Heidi who was a bit ditzy, and then Danielle, who was a completely different ball game. But that was really beside the point. Betty *wanted* Cara to have a big wedding. She loved everything that went along with it – the idea of showing off her beautiful daughter and throwing a big party with tonnes of guests to celebrate. But now she was being denied that too. It was hurtful because she and Cara had always been so close, and while she knew she shouldn't admit it (and would never do so out loud), she couldn't deny that Cara was also her favourite.

A wedding. In a foreign country. Hours and hours away. A celebration that was essentially being whittled away to nothing. A bare bones ceremony, no big dress and wedding cake, only a few guests.

That didn't sound like a wedding at all, thought Betty. Imagine the sand that would be getting in their eyes and their shoes? But hadn't Cara said something about wanting to go barefoot, like some kind of peasant . . .?

Cara and Shane could travel where they wanted for their honeymoon. If only she could convince them to have the ceremony here in Ireland.

Betty put her hands in the soapy water and felt around for another dish. Finding one, she brought it out of the water and took out her frustration on it, scrubbing it mercilessly.

She had to come up with a plan. True, Cara and Shane had said that they had already put down their deposit. That was going to be hard to combat. But really, what was a deposit in the scheme of things? How much could they have possibly spent?

Betty remembered the plane tickets and Shane's promise to also pay for the passports application, which was very generous of them really. But that was Cara, generous to a fault.

She hated feeling negative about what should be a happy time in her daughter's life, and she supposed that if she just went along with it, it would be relative smooth sailing. But wasn't she denying her instincts by doing that? Betty felt certain that deep down Cara didn't really want a beach wedding and would be disappointed by it in the end. No, a big white wedding here in Ireland and lots of fuss was more her daughter's style – and more to the point, it was what she deserved. Knowing Cara, she'd only come up with this notion because she didn't want to put herself and Mick to more expense.

Well, Betty couldn't allow that, wouldn't allow her beloved daughter to sacrifice her big day. She just needed to convince her that it was fine to have the wedding here and that she and her father wouldn't be overstretching themselves.

Perhaps then this mad notion of a foreign wedding would fade into the distance.

But she needed a support mechanism too, Betty realised. She needed someone else to help her try and talk some sense into Cara.

Immediately her thoughts moved to Shane's parents. They were already annoyed at the couple, so this news was likely to infuriate them. Especially with them being so posh and uppity. They were more than likely well-travelled and probably knew all about the Caribbean, but they would hardly want their only son to be married in some teeny ceremony on a public beach in front of all the natives. What parents would?

However, Betty quickly faced a snag there. She had never met Shane's parents, not yet at least. But wasn't this situation emergency enough to track down their phone number and get them on her side?

But what if they didn't immediately see her side?

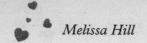

No, she thought, *of course they would.*

But what if they didn't? Furthermore, what if they had an idea that she disagreed with? Then Betty would be fighting against two separate parties with the possibility of competing against his parents. That wouldn't do . . .

Betty quickly crossed the Richardsons off her list. There were too many variables when it came to his parents because her knowledge of the family was limited. If she could meet them first, maybe she would have more leverage? Maybe she could innocently get Cara to set up a time for both families to meet some time soon (in the guise of celebrating the engagement maybe?); then she could possibly gauge their feelings about all of this and unite with them to get this nonsense stopped.

That was a Plan B, Betty decided. Problem was, it certainly didn't help her today. She needed to think in the short term.

So what was Plan A?

She could turn to Kim . . .

No, that wouldn't work either, she thought. Kim wouldn't be able to read between the lines and would no doubt stand by Cara's decision, seeing that the girl was so contrary about everything herself. Her daughter-in-law certainly had her own strong opinions, ones that Betty consistently found herself disagreeing with.

She withdrew her hands from the soapy water, realising that she was all out of dirty dishes. She wiped the countertop and put away the remaining dinner accoutrements. Looking around, she saw that her kitchen was sparkling. Usually, that was enough to set her mind at ease. But not tonight. Not with everything that had happened.

She crossed the kitchen and took a seat at the table. The brochures and pictures of the resort in St Lucia were still spread across the surface and absently, Betty flipped through them once again.

It was true that all the pictures were very pretty and the resort itself was unlike anything that Betty had ever seen before. Certainly she had never been to a place like this. If it were for any other reason maybe she would be in the position where she would entertain the idea. But who ever heard of a beach wedding? She thought of the term as something very foreign and uncomfortable – for people who were eloping or had something to be ashamed of, perhaps. It just wasn't done, not in her world, not something that was common in the way of life that she was used to. And definitely not something she understood.

Of course, Betty thought darkly, she knew exactly who was to blame. This would have never been an option for Cara if it weren't for Danielle's meddling. Betty guessed that her oldest daughter was just doing this to spite her, planting ideas in Cara's head, drawing her away from home.

She loved Danielle, of course she did, but she just didn't understand her firstborn. It had always been that way, ever since she had been a small child.

She had always been so outgoing, adventurous, and so rebellious too. If there was strife to be had, certainly it would be Danielle who would land in it – usually head first. Betty had never understood how she had produced a daughter who was just her opposite in every way . . .

She closed her eyes and rubbed her temples. When she reopened them she pushed the St Lucia brochures aside.

She knew that Danielle was a grown woman now, with a good career and all the trappings that went with it. She had a jet-setting lifestyle and a wealthy boyfriend who was clearly committed to her. But why, after supposedly five years together, had she never introduced them to that boyfriend of hers? Why did she feel like family visits were optional? And *why* couldn't she ever just do what Betty wanted her to do?

Betty felt her blood pressure rising and realised that this was the root of all of her frustration. Danielle had never followed the rules and had always tried to go her own way, even if it was the wrong way. And now Cara was trying to do the same. Running across the ocean, away from the friends and family members who had surrounded and supported her for her entire life.

Betty didn't like thinking about the reason Danielle had left, nor the part she herself may have played in it. But she did know one thing for sure; she wasn't going to make the same mistakes and risk losing Cara.

Which is why she couldn't allow her older daughter to get too tied up in arranging this wedding. Where Danielle was concerned, chaos reigned.

Betty frowned. She needed to show a united front against this beach wedding, preferably with someone who would be as upset by the idea as she was. When she realised the answer, she shook her head, wondering why she hadn't thought of it before now.

Heidi.

Of course Heidi would throw a fit. Heidi could always be depended on to throw a fit, especially when she didn't agree with whatever someone else was doing.

Betty thought with confidence that Heidi was sure not to agree with Cara's idea for the wedding. Especially now that she was pregnant.

She knew that her youngest was being slightly overdramatic with some of the nonsense that she was spouting about what you could and could not do while expecting. After all, Betty had been through it all before and realised that there were a lot of superstitions out there, especially amongst some first-time mothers and the crazy, new age doctors who seemed to put all kinds of nonsense into the heads of pregnant women. Telling them they couldn't eat cheese and fish and all that rubbish. These days there were so many dos and don'ts it was making women afraid of their own shadows.

As far as Betty was concerned, most of these so called 'fears' were completely unfounded, but at the same time that didn't mean that she couldn't play on some of them. Cara might think she had her heart set on this beach wedding, but the more people who came out of the woodwork to complain about it, the more likely she was to reconsider and think about having a traditional church wedding here in Ireland instead.

Betty smiled again. All was not lost. She shouldn't have got so upset earlier; this could be solved and she was sure she could eventually get Cara to see sense. But the first step was calling Heidi.

She picked up the phone and dialled.

On the fourth ring, Heidi answered. 'Hello?'

Her voice seemed a little groggy, as if she had been sleeping.

'Heidi darling, it's Mum. Did I wake you up?'

'Oh, I was just resting my eyes. I am just so tired lately,' Heidi gasped.

'Perfectly normal, really it is, all those excess hormones and what not,' Betty cooed. 'With the changes your body is going through, sleep is the best way to deal with them.' She shook her head, thinking of her own pregnancies where she had worked almost up until the day she had given birth. There had been no lying around, and no 'resting her eyes' for Betty. Not when she and Mick had bills to pay and mouths to feed.

'So I'm actually phoning with a bit of news about your sister. Turns out Cara has set a date for her wedding. It's the middle of September, the twelfth to be exact.'

There was a brief silence on the other end before finally Heidi spoke. 'But I'll be in my last trimester . . . Couldn't she have at least waited until after I have the baby?'

'Yes, you will be. Just shy of seven months if I'm doing the sums correctly?'

'That's right,' Heidi said. Betty could tell that her daughter was smiling; she knew Heidi loved it when people paid attention to the intricate details.

'Yes, she surprised your father and me with the news of the date tonight. And not only that,' Betty paused, 'turns out we are all going to have to start stocking up on suncream, because the wedding is going to be in St Lucia. The Caribbean,' she added helpfully.

There was a very long silence at the end of the line, but Betty knew that if she was calling it right, that silence wouldn't last for much longer.

'Heidi, pet? Are you there?' she asked innocently.

'They . . . are . . . doing . . . WHAT?' Heidi said, enunciating each word slowly and carefully.

Bingo, Betty thought, wincing at her daughter's tone.

'Yes, St Lucia. Out on the beach apparently. In front of all and sundry.'

'But *I* can't go to St Lucia!' Heidi wailed. 'I won't be allowed to fly! Why is Cara doing this? Mum, I really hope you told her that when you are pregnant you cannot fly. And I hope you told her that this was a crazy idea!'

'Well, I told her that you were probably going to have some issues with it, yes. But she and Shane were both resolute that this is what they wanted.'

Heidi breathed heavily down the phone. 'I really can't

believe this . . . Mum, I'm sorry,' she gasped. 'I have to go. All this stress isn't good for the baby, so I'd better hang up soon before my blood pressure gets any higher.' She groaned. 'A beach wedding? Of all the selfish . . . well, Cara will just have to get this ridiculous idea out of her head quick smart.'

Betty barely had the chance to say goodbye before the line went dead.

She stared at the mouthpiece. Her youngest was a real piece of dynamite, with an incredibly short fuse. Betty knew that Heidi could certainly be depended on to make Cara see sense, and realise that it would be better to keep the wedding close to home.

After all, this was supposed to be a happy time. And what kind of bride-to-be would want their entire family up in arms?

Chapter 16

Heidi paced the room, seething. Before her mother's phone call, she had been sitting on the sofa with her feet up and relaxing in front of the TV, enjoying – and dozing off in front of – a rerun of *Desperate Housewives*. But now she was a million miles from relaxed.

She knew that she shouldn't be getting so worked up about her sister's wedding, not in her condition. But really, she'd already had quite enough of Cara lately, what with stealing her thunder with her engagement, and now with her stupid beach wedding. The fact was that Cara had been stealing Heidi's thunder all her life.

Not that she was so worried about Cara usurping her own wedding celebrations. After all, she knew well that no other wedding could possibly live up to the extravaganza she and Paul had thrown last year.

No, this wasn't about the wedding, beach or otherwise. What really bothered her was that Cara wasn't considering her feelings *at all*. It was as if her sister didn't care about whether or not she could travel, hadn't considered it even.

Same old same old. Didn't *anyone* in this family give a toss about her feelings?

Heidi hadn't envisioned having to go a wedding close to seven months pregnant, let alone one in a hot, humid climate. She was likely to be sweating and uncomfortable, and no one liked sweating and uncomfortable pregnant women. No, they liked glowing, cute and tidy pregnant women, which is what she was likely to be if the wedding was held here.

She'd anticipated that it would take Cara and Shane a lot longer than four months to arrange their big day, especially when there was just so much to think about. Whoever heard of anyone getting engaged and married in the same year – what was the point of that, when much of the fun was getting everything organised and making sure everyone else was involved?

But that was bloody Cara, wasn't it? Sensible to the last. Swanning off to a place that she'd never even been to and having people she'd never even met arrange her own wedding. How could a complete stranger possibly understand how important it was that everything needed to be perfect?

Heidi remembered having to phone her wedding cake designer at least fifteen times to confirm her preferences before he finished the cake, and as for the dress designer – well, she was practically Heidi's best friend by the end of it. Or used to be, at least.

Imagine having to lug a beautiful wedding dress all the way across the globe to get married on a dirty beach. Ugh, Heidi couldn't imagine anything more disgusting.

She tried to imagine herself standing on such a beach seven months pregnant. Heidi did not want damp armpits and a shiny face to be recorded for posterity.

Also there was no question that she could embark on such a long plane ride at that stage of her pregnancy – how could anyone be expected to do that? No, Heidi decided, there was just no way she was dragging herself halfway across the world for some tacky wedding. Cara and Shane would just have to get married here in Ireland. End of story.

Heidi grabbed the phone again and fought the urge to throw it against the wall.

Instead she grabbed the handset in a steely grip and dialled her sister's phone number.

It rang several times but then, just as Heidi felt sure she was about to be sent to voicemail, Cara answered.

'Hello?'

Heidi paused, interested. There was no denying the weariness in Cara's voice. She sounded as if she was exhausted. This perked her up no end; it meant that she would have the advantage.

'Cara. It's Heidi here. I just spoke to Mum and she told me about your ridiculous plan to get married in St Lucia. You have no idea how upsetting this is.'

She was met with silence. Not a word. Heidi couldn't even hear her sister breathing on the other end of the line, and she wondered if they might have been cut off.

'Cara, are you there?'

She heard Cara inhale deeply. 'Yes Heidi, I am here and you have no idea how not in the mood I am for this just now.'

Heidi was taken aback. 'Excuse me?'

'You heard me,' Cara said dryly. 'I am not going to listen to you complain about my decisions.'

'But you haven't even taken a moment to listen to what I'm going to say!' Heidi cried.

'No, I haven't but it's not as if I need a crystal ball to know what you are calling about. The wedding will be in St Lucia in September, Heidi, a good two months-odd before your due date.'

She sighed, and Heidi noticed how defeated she sounded. Why? Had someone else complained about it too?

'I would love to have you there,' Cara went on, 'and as far as I know flying shouldn't be a problem, but if you have to get special permission from your doctor to travel or feel that it is unsafe or whatever, then that's your choice. But Shane and I have made our decision and this is not a subject that is up for discussion. And you can call Mum back and tell her the same. I'm not going to be bossed around,' Cara stated confidently.

Heidi bit her lip. She hadn't even been granted the opportunity to air her grievances. Cara had seemed to know exactly what had been on her mind. And still she didn't care . . .

'Now if you will excuse me Heidi, I have had a very long day and quite frankly, I can't deal with any more family drama just now. I hope you have a good night.'

The line went dead and Heidi stared at the receiver as if it had suddenly grown legs. She couldn't believe it. Her own sister had hung up on her!

'Paul?' she called out, throwing herself back upon the cushions. She didn't like the way people were treating her lately, and as usual she wasn't being taken seriously.

Moments later her husband rushed into the room, breathless.

'Yes? What is it, sweetheart? Are you OK?' He dropped to the side of the sofa. Her eyes filled with tears. 'Cara just hung up on me,' she told him.

Paul rushed to put his arms around her. 'Why would she do that?' he cooed.

'I don't know. But listen to what else is new. Did you know she scheduled her wedding for September? In St Lucia?'

Paul quickly did the maths in his head and realised his poor wife would be in full bloom in September. He frowned.

'What is Cara thinking? Ah no, I'm sure she just forgot. And when she realises I'm sure she'll change it for you—'

'No, that's just the point; she said that she wouldn't change anything. That we didn't have to like it, and it was our choice whether we went to the wedding or not—'

'So then we just won't go if you don't want to,' he said, and she was once again grateful to have him in her corner.

The only one who ever seemed to be. She shook her head. 'But if we don't go then I'll be the one left out – again. And especially so close to the baby's due date and everything. My entire family will all be over there concentrating on Cara's wedding and I'll be left here on my own. What if the baby comes early and everybody misses it?'

'That early? Hardly. But sure if it does happen, they can just see the baby when they get back can't they?'

'Not the baby, Paul, the birth! I don't want to go into labour when there's nobody else around to—' She crossed her arms. 'Oh you just don't get it.'

At least his wife was right about that much, Paul thought. He didn't understand many of the complexities of the female mind. Especially the *pregnant* female mind. He supposed it was because of all the hormones that were running rampant. Maybe he could just change the subject.

'Would you like a cup of tea?' he offered.

'I can't drink tea, Paul. It's *caffeinated*, you know that. It will be bad for the baby. Maybe just some warm milk instead? And some of those shortbread cookies,' she added, feeling a little bit better. Paul always made her feel better.

But not long after he left the room to get her snack, Heidi began to feel powerless once again.

It was clear that Cara did not care whether she was at the wedding or not. Hell, was she even planning on asking her to be bridesmaid?

Of all the insults, Heidi thought. *I asked her to be bridesmaid.*

Her initial worries about St Lucia temporarily forgotten, Heidi quickly turned her attention to what colour bridesmaid dress a woman seven months pregnant would look best in – all the while wounded about not yet being asked.

Chapter 17

'Oh my goodness! I think that's a fantastic idea!' Kim cheered.

Cara breathed a sigh of relief into the phone. 'Really? You honestly think so?' She was feeling quite tired of all the negativity and complaints by now, and Kim's positive attitude immediately buoyed her spirits. 'And you'll all come?' she asked hopefully.

'Of course we will. We wouldn't miss it for the world!' Her sister-in-law laughed. 'Why wouldn't we come? Ah, here we go,' she added, immediately wise to the fact that there was something else in the mix. 'What's the problem then, who's giving you grief?'

'Ah, it's nothing really.'

'Tell me,' Kim insisted.

Cara sighed. 'Well, Mum and Dad were less than pleased last night, which was a bit upsetting. And then Heidi phoned afterwards in a fit about the timing. We still haven't told Shane's parents, but I am really not anticipating good things. Especially since they aren't even speaking to us at the moment.'

'Oh feck it, ignore them all. This isn't about them. If you want to have your wedding in St Lucia, then have it. And if the others can't respect your wishes, don't bother with them. They are the ones who will miss out,' Kim said encouragingly.

'But why do they have to protest so much? I mean, why

do they have to make me feel so terrible for doing what we want for our wedding? Especially when Mum is usually so supportive . . .'

Kim shook her head. Cara sounded truly upset and she inwardly cursed her husband's family for their idiocy. Why did people have to put the ones they loved through so much strife?

'Look, when you do something different than what is considered normal, some people who might only be thinking about themselves are going to get their noses bent out of joint. They will come around, or they will be excluded. You'll see.'

'But I don't want to exclude anyone—'

'I know you don't, but in order for this to work, you are going to have to ensure that they realise this is simply not their decision. If they see you sticking to your guns, and not giving in, they will realise they have two choices – they can either support you or they can be left out of the fun entirely.'

Cara knew Kim was right and that in order for their plans in St Lucia to happen, she would just have to develop a tougher skin. She wished she had some of Kim's chutzpah. While she didn't consider herself a shrinking violet, she also hated confrontation.

'So, anyway, on to happier topics. Tell me all that you've planned. Is there anything I can do to help?'

Cara smiled. She was lucky to have Kim and she secretly applauded her brother again for bringing her into her life. 'Not much to do really from a logistics standpoint on the wedding side – the resort has a lovely wedding planner who's going to arrange everything. All we have to do is turn up on the day. But I do have to go dress shopping soon and I think I'd appreciate a bit of help on that one. I just want something simple. Hey, though, while I think of it, quick question. You aren't going to have any problems travelling or being able to get on a plane are you?'

'What are you saying; you think my ass is going to get so big they won't let me on?' Kim laughed.

'No, like isn't there some sort of rule about travelling when pregnant?'

Kim laughed loudly. 'Of course not. Well I suppose if you are very close to due date or have a high-risk pregnancy, some doctors will advise against flying – something to do with the cabin pressure – but really, I was able to travel easily when carrying both of the girls and in September my due date will still be ages away anyway—' Then she groaned. 'Oh please, let me guess, Heidi is saying she can't fly? I should have guessed that would be an excuse. The same one seems to think it isn't safe to *walk*.'

Cara hid a smile. 'I know she's a little over the top about the pregnancy, but at the same time I'm completely inexperienced in all of this stuff, and I certainly don't want to make someone do anything that might put their unborn baby at risk.'

'No baby is going to be at risk, don't worry about that. I'll tell Heidi as much the next time I see her.'

'Oh, don't say anything on my behalf. I just wasn't sure of the specifics,' Cara said.

'Cara, you see there, that's your problem. You are too damn nice. Heidi is a little drama queen and you know it.'

'Maybe.'

'No maybe about it. Anyway, dress shopping then? When are we going?' Kim continued, turning Cara's attention to happier subjects.

'So you'll come with me?'

'Of course I will. Dress shopping is one of the best bits of wedding planning – it'll be great fun.'

'Well, I suppose I might as well ask you then, I would really love it if you would be a bridesmaid, Kim. Would you?'

Her sister-in-law squealed like a schoolgirl. 'I'd be honoured, thank you for asking me. As long as you don't mind me dragging my big butt down the beach in front of you, of course. I've never been a bridesmaid before, and while I know I'm getting a bit old for taffeta, I'll still wear whatever you pick out, no matter how horrendous and ghastly, without uttering a single complaint.'

Cara's heart soared. Why couldn't all of her family behave this way?

'Thanks Kim. Not just for being my bridesmaid but for making all of this so easy. I really appreciate it. I just want to make sure you know that.'

'No worries honey, that's what I'm here for. A sounding board when the rest of our nutty family is driving you mad.'

A few moments later they said their goodbyes. Kim was happy that she could be there for Cara, but she found herself wildly disappointed in her in-laws. It was awful of them to make Cara feel miserable about her decision; it wasn't their role and it was very unfair.

She thought of several choice words that she had on the subject, to be directed at her mother-in-law, as well as Heidi. Kim pressed her lips together. She certainly wasn't going to stand back and watch Cara get bullied. She made a silent oath to herself that she would be in Cara's corner, and have her back no matter what craziness the family decided to throw at her.

She walked into the kitchen to find Ben making chocolate milk for Olivia and Lindsay. It was close to nine o'clock, way past the girls' bedtime, but no big deal. 'Oh good! Chocolate before bedtime, nice job Daddy,' she laughed dryly. 'And be sure to make it extra chocolatey for good measure. I won't be happy unless these two are bouncing off the walls . . .' She idly wondered what oh-so-proper Heidi would have to say about feeding the girls chocolate and caffeine on a school night.

Ben laughed. 'Well, I thought it would be a nice treat for our two little girls.'

'And your lovely wife too I hope?' Kim smiled and put her arm around him. Then she turned to her daughters who were sitting watching TV.

'So guess what, girls? Aunt Cara is getting married in a tropical paradise far, far away.'

Olivia's eyes got wide and Kim knew that her daughter's imagination didn't need much to run wild. 'A tropical paradise? Are we going? Will there be monkeys?' she asked quickly.

Kim was unsure where the monkey question had come from but figured it was an interesting one. 'Of course we are. Do you think I would miss out on Auntie's special day? And for the record, I think the inclusion of monkeys is a fantastic idea. I'll mention it to the bride.'

'Is Number Three coming too?' Lindsay asked, referring to the name they had given their unborn sibling.

'Well I suppose he or she will have to – they will still be in Mummy's tummy.'

The girls looked at each other with self-satisfied smiles, knowing that they had a tropical island to look forward to in their future. A trip that involved their parents, and possibly monkeys, and that Number Three would also be a part of it.

Kim turned to Ben and smiled.

'I just wanted to say, thanks for being normal.'

He raised an eyebrow at his wife. 'What's that supposed to mean? And monkeys? Where exactly is this wedding?'

'St Lucia, and what I meant was, don't give your sister any grief about the wedding, OK?'

'Why would I do that?'

'I wasn't saying that you would, but no teasing her or anything, OK? From what I hear, she's had a rough time about it already from your mum and dad, and Heidi.'

Ben rolled his eyes. 'You know my thoughts on all that.'

Indeed she did. Ben stayed well out of his family's affairs, knowing that involving himself was pointless and would only cause headaches.

A moment passed and Ben looked at Kim. 'St Lucia, huh? Well that's interesting,' he said mildly.

'Why's that?' she asked, noticing the change in his tone.

'That's over in Danielle's neck of the woods, isn't it? I wonder if she will be there.'

Kim thought back to her conversation with Cara and remembered that Cara had indeed said something about Danielle helping her with the initial arrangements.

'Now that you mention it, Cara did say that she recently spoke to your sister, and it was Danielle who actually helped her find the resort.'

Ben looked surprised. 'Wow. I find the idea of Danielle assisting on a project that would bring all of us closer to where she lives very surprising. She really hasn't had anything to do with us in ages.'

Kim had to admit that she didn't know much about her oldest sister-in-law, only having met her once or twice at best. Of course there was an oddball in practically every Irish family, and it seemed Danielle was the obligatory black sheep in the Clancy household.

Ben never really spoke about her and Kim knew that it was a sore subject for Betty and not really to be discussed in her presence, so she couldn't help but be curious about her. Reading between the lines, Kim got the impression that Danielle was a somewhat fragile soul. Given Betty's overbearing ways, she couldn't help but feel a little sorry for her.

'You always make her out to be sort of . . . unhinged or something.' While Ben might have worked actively to stay out of the drama that his family had the ability to perpetuate, he too seemed somewhat judgemental about his older sister.

'Nah, I don't mean to be like that; it's just that Danielle's just never made that much of an effort – especially since she moved abroad. If she shows up at Cara's wedding, I'll be surprised. Remember she didn't come to ours – or Heidi's.'

Kim remembered. She also remembered that Betty hadn't seemed to mind her oldest daughter's absence. That had been a bit off form, considering how involved Betty was in all of her children's lives.

'Well, we'll definitely be close to where she lives, that's for sure. Isn't she based in the Fort Lauderdale area?'

'So I believe,' Ben said. 'Nobody's ever been over to visit her, and she hasn't exactly been forthcoming with invitations either, if you know what I mean.'

'Well if she is so close, I'm sure she will be at the wedding. I mean, St Lucia's practically next door, isn't it?'

'Pretty much. I just hope Cara knows what she is getting herself into – not just with the wedding.' Ben pursed his lips. 'Because the only thing worse than my mother on her own is my mother within a ten-foot radius of Danielle.'

Chapter 18

Danielle paced the length of her living room. She had just opened her email to find a message from Cara. Apparently everything in St Lucia was now booked and ready to go.

She fidgeted with her hands. If it wasn't for her offer to put Cara in touch with her contact at the resort, none of this would be happening right now. She was ultimately the one who had set this in motion, the one who had effectively signed her own death certificate, so to speak – by giving way to the opportunity to have her family – Betty – close by. It gave her a sick feeling in her stomach. It was like a freight train plunging ahead and she was powerless to stop it.

She opened her patio doors and walked out onto the sun porch. Taking a seat on the chaise longue, she watched the tide roll in and out, lost in her thoughts.

She could handle this, she reassured herself. After all, she had been away from them for so long now, and had made too much of herself to allow some simple, little family wedding crumble everything that she had worked so hard at building.

She could control this. Right?

September twelfth. Only four months away. Four months to figure out how she was going to keep Zack away from her family. Four months to figure out a reason for not attending the wedding. She didn't know how the latter was going to work out. Not with the other request.

In the email, Cara had also asked her to be a bridesmaid.
A bridesmaid! That was simply adding insult to injury.
Danielle didn't like to think about herself in these terms, but
wasn't she a bit *old* to be a bridesmaid? She felt like crying.
The only thing worse than going to this wedding was also
having to be a bridesmaid.

Plus, the whole situation was absurd. How could she be
a bridesmaid at this wedding? She barely had a relationship
with any of these people.

More to the point, how on earth could she get out of
this? What were her options?

Briefly she considered living in denial. She had done that
before after all. Just ignored reality, hoping it would go away.

And remember how that worked out? she reminded herself,
reluctant to revisit such a painful time.

No, she decided, thinking of her therapist's advice, she
had to tackle the issue head on, and come up with a plan.
If she had a plan, a solution, she could manage anything,
and she had to manage this.

Four months seemed like a significant amount of time,
but in reality Danielle knew that it would go by in the blink
of an eye. She wished that she felt something other than
dread at the thought of seeing her family.

There was no way that she could expose Zack to them
either. If he knew the extent of her issues, he would run a
mile.

And no matter how many years distanced her from them
or how she had changed, the mere fact was that like it or
not, Danielle was attached to her family through the invisible
rope that tied them to her, now and always. She couldn't
forget about that.

A little while later she heard the patio door open, and
temporarily her sun was blocked. She opened her eyes to

be met with Zack's tanned and handsome face. He stood above her, the sun at his back highlighting his blond hair and all-American good looks. He smiled at her, his teeth glowing white and perfect against his dark skin, his blue eyes sparkling.

Even in her current mood, Danielle couldn't help but smile back.

'What are you doing out here? I could have sworn I heard you talking to yourself,' he said in a flat South Florida accent, the kind that Danielle herself had taken so much care to develop.

She shielded her eyes against the sun and patted the chair next to her. 'Oh nothing, just enjoying the sunshine.' She wondered if she should tell him about the conversation with Cara, but decided against it. He didn't have to know about any of it. She rarely talked about her family to him anyway, and if this blasted wedding did happen, there was no way it would involve him. He was *not* going to meet her family, no way, no how.

'No way,' she muttered out loud, unbeknownst to herself.

Zack arched an eyebrow. 'Sorry?'

She swallowed hard. 'Just thinking out loud. That's all.'

Please don't press, she thought. She knew she was a terrible liar.

'Anything I can help you with?' he asked, but thankfully at that moment his BlackBerry chirped.

Saved by the bell, she thought, relieved.

'Oh, I have to take this, sorry – what do you think about going out to dinner later? Maybe head down towards Miami?'

She nodded and smiled. 'Sure. Go get that. I'll be right in.'

He touched her cheek, and then turned his attention to his phone. 'Cool.'

The moment Zack left she returned to her thoughts. She

felt slightly guilty for not telling him about Cara's call, but really, he was so cultured and worldly and completely removed from the kind of background she had that there was no way he would ever understand her family, or ever fully comprehend her history with them. It was just so complicated.

What's more, over the years Danielle had worked very hard to make herself the person she was today, and she simply wasn't prepared to let all that be stripped away. No way was she going to show Zack where she really came from.

If this wedding did take place close to home, she would bear the burden alone. She would fabricate a work trip; maybe create a client who was interested in property on St Lucia. That was it! Danielle sat forward as her mind raced. A quick weekend jaunt and then a deal that just happened to fall through at the last minute . . .

Easily done and Zack would be none the wiser about her nutty family or the skeletons from her past. Exactly how it needed to be.

Danielle hated to think of herself as unworthy of a good relationship, of something positive in her life . . . but she also knew who to blame for those feelings. Betty. All the therapy in the world couldn't beat out of her head the insecurities her mother had instilled, not to mention the still-painful highlighting of her shortcomings.

'What's up?' Zack asked, coming back out on to the balcony. 'You look stressed.'

'No, I'm fine, it's nothing. I'm just thinking about work and a client – a somewhat frustrating client. But how's your day been?' she smiled, hoping that Zack would take the bait.

'It's been good. Is there anything I can help you out with?'

Zack was so incisive when it came to business. He was a self-made man, with an empire that he had created from scratch encompassing some of the most lucrative business ventures in the US. He was involved in a variety of real estate and land dealings, hotels and entertainment, as well as finance. He was often compared to a young Donald Trump, although with better hair and without all the kids and ex-wives – an up-and-comer who was intent on taking the business world by storm.

Danielle cheered inwardly. She could start planting the seeds now about this client – the one with the interest in property in St Lucia. The one that she just might have to assist on the island on September 12 of this year.

'Oh, no I don't think so,' she said, straightening her shoulders, trying to project her usual confidence. 'Really I just think this client is a pain in the ass, or at least has the potential to be. Interested in Caribbean property, St Lucia specifically.'

'Well, that would probably be a nice commission,' Zack commented mildly. 'Who's the client? Anyone I know?'

'No, I wouldn't think so. Name is, um . . . Ben Richardson,' she said, thinking quickly, and combining the names of her brother and future brother-in-law.

Zack considered the name. 'No, I don't think I have heard of him. Who is he?'

Danielle fidgeted with her hands. She hated lying and now she was faced with a situation where she had to fabricate a person in order to spin a complicated story, all just to keep Zack from meeting her family. *Was it worth it?* she asked herself. She wondered for a moment what would happen if she just bit the bullet and let him meet them. She felt a shiver run down her spine. No, in this situation, the lie would definitely be better.

'Oh, I think new money, definitely. Seems like a young guy who has lots of ideas and lots of cash that he likes to throw around. Kind of tacky, you know the type.' She felt surprised by her answer and how easily the lie had tripped off her tongue; it had been effortless actually. Zack didn't hold tacky people in high esteem; therefore he wouldn't be interested.

Zack rolled his eyes. 'Shame to ruin St Lucia with more idiots. What is he interested in?'

'Oh, you know; ocean-front, marble floors, hot tub, stripper pole in the entertainment room, the works. Sounds like a cast member of *Jersey Shore,* doesn't it?' she added lightly, trying to drive home the idea.

'Does he have money to spend though?' Zack pressed.

She shrugged. 'Seems like he is willing to spend for this, but he's also alluded to the fact that price might be a sticking point,' she said vaguely, thinking of Cara's budget worries.

'Ugh. Send him to the Dominican or some other place. Keep him off our island,' Zack joked with a smile.

Danielle grimaced, thinking her boyfriend had no idea how true his words were or how she had echoed the same sentiment with Cara's initial phone call. Truthfully, there was only one island that she felt comfortable recommending to her family. Ireland. Where they were now and where they should stay.

'Well, I'll see what I can do. But there is a chance that I might have to go out there,' she said, trying to keep the nerves out of her voice. The last thing she wanted was for Zack to suggest that he should go with her.

There was a smile in his voice. 'Well, I would think so, if this guy wants to look at property . . .'

Danielle wondered if she should pre-empt by suggesting that he should come with her, only to stress how horrible it would be if she was working the entire time. Counter-intuitive, she knew, so she decided it might work, especially because she knew he hated trying to combine a business opportunity with a vacation.

'Yes, well, if I have to go, maybe you and I could make a weekend away out of it? Try to have some fun?' She smiled and crossed her fingers behind her back, hoping that her ploy would work.

Zack laughed as he sat down on the couch and stretched out his long legs. 'Right. Weekend away. Come on Danielle, you know better than that. Any time business is involved, it is impossible to separate it from any type of pleasure. While you are fantastic company, if you're running around showing some young, rich idiot property all over the island, how on earth could we possibly relax together? No, I'll hang back this time, thank you. Instead, if you have to go there, do it, close the deal, make some money and then you and I can have a real vacation. No work.'

Inwardly Danielle breathed a sigh of relief. Jackpot. It had worked exactly as she'd planned.

She sat down next to Zack on the couch and curled herself up next to him. Thank goodness he wasn't clingy. She had always hated having men around her who depended on her for their entertainment. Who felt like they had to be constantly on her heels. Zack was definitely his own man.

'However, if you have to go, you might as well show up in style, make sure this guy knows he's not working with some minor leaguer. You should take one of the planes. Maybe the Cessna,' he suggested.

Danielle's smile deepened. Wow, imagine arriving in a private plane to her sister's wedding on St Lucia. She tried to picture her mother's face as she stepped down the stairs of the Cessna onto the tarmac, outfitted in a beautiful and expensive designer suit, walking with purpose in twelve-hundred dollar shoes. Betty's expression alone would justify the trauma of attending and maybe make the weekend more bearable.

She felt bitterness surge through her veins. She would show her mother that she wasn't useless after all, she *had* made something of herself, and that someone worthy *did* want her in their life.

She looked at Zack, trying to dismiss the further notion of how satisfying it would be to introduce this handsome and wildly successful man to her parents.

No, she thought, squashing the idea, no matter what kind of payback it might give her, it just couldn't happen. Zack was too important to her, and there was too much at stake. He had to stay put in Fort Lauderdale while her family were anywhere in the vicinity of North America.

Zack plus the Clancy family equalled a recipe for disaster.

'Danielle?' Zack urged. 'So, what do you think, the Cessna?'

She realised he had been waiting on her reply and she had instead been staring at him blankly, as if in a trance.

'Oh, yes, that would be great!' she enthused quickly. 'I love that plane.'

Zack smiled and leaned down to kiss her. 'So spoiled . . .' he teased.

She grinned at him, suddenly feeling a lot better about everything. This might all just work out. She supposed she could survive her family on her own – just for a weekend – and if Zack thought she was meeting with a client, it could be a quick trip in and out of St Lucia. No big deal. Fly in on Friday night, leave on Sunday morning. She could deal with her family as long as it was for less than forty-eight hours, and there was nothing that they could do or say to her on her own that she couldn't take. Not even Betty.

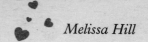

Danielle was stronger than that.

She felt a surge of confidence rush through her and experienced a release of some of the anxiety in her stomach. This was manageable. Anything was manageable as long as you had a plan.

And she had a plan.

Chapter 19

Cara couldn't sleep. Every time she tried to close her eyes and relax her brain, another errant thought would pop into her mind, causing her a fresh round of anxiety.

She couldn't get her parents' negative reaction to the wedding out of her mind, to say nothing of Heidi's complaints.

And it also hurt a little that Danielle hadn't yet replied to her bridesmaid request of two days ago. Shouldn't her big sister be excited – as Kim was – about standing beside her on her big day?

With the exception of Kim's reaction, this whole thing hadn't been going well at all, and this was before they'd even broached the subject with Shane's parents.

They had decided that calling them again and again would be of no use, so instead the following day – actually later today, Cara deduced after looking at the clock on her bedside table that read 3 a.m. – they would simply drop in on Lauren and Gene and tell them the news face to face.

In truth, this had been Shane's idea. Cara was dreading the visit and thought the previous suggestion of smoke signals seemed much more appealing.

She turned to her side, unable to get comfortable. Moments later she flipped on to her back, punching the pillow behind her head. She breathed heavily and considered getting up out of bed altogether. She hated insomnia; it was the worst.

Looking at the dark ceiling, Cara whispered, 'Shane . . . are you asleep? Shane?'

Shane let out a grunt and mumbled, 'Who could possibly sleep with all of that tossing and turning and noise?' He didn't sound happy. She heard a rustle from the other side of the bed and felt him move closer to her. 'What's wrong?'

She reached out, trying to scoot closer to him. She really needed some love and cuddling. All had definitely not been right in the world since this engagement, when it really should be a happy time. Shane pulled her close and kissed her on the head.

'What is it baby?'

'I'm really worried about going to see your parents. I'm scared of what's going to happen.'

'OK—' She felt his arms tense around her.

'And I am really stressed about how everyone is reacting to our idea for the wedding. I don't see how this can work out. It seems like no one is happy to just go along with our plans.'

'Seriously Cara, why are you worrying about this now? If people have their issues, they have their issues. Just ignore them.'

'That's easier said than done.' She pushed away and sat up in bed, turning on the bedside light. She was so frustrated by his nonchalance. This was important.

Shane sighed heavily, and squinted at the sudden onset of brightness in the room. He looked at his fiancée, who was looking thoroughly annoyed.

As if seeming to consign himself to the fact that sleep would not be an option until he listened to the grievances coming from the other side of the bed, he sat up.

'OK what?' He rubbed his eyes and yawned, while Cara shot daggers in his direction.

'How are you not upset about all of this?' she complained.

'This affects you too. Why am I the one that's stressed? Why am I the only one doing all the worrying?'

Shane raised an eyebrow. 'Upset about what? Worried . . . why exactly? Because some people are acting selfish and crazy?' He gave a short laugh. 'Sorry to say, that's not a new development.'

'I don't see how this doesn't bother you,' stated Cara. She was angry and what upset her more was that Shane seemed unaffected by the entire situation, and oddly resigned to the idea that what was going on was normal behaviour, just how families acted when a wedding was being planned.

'Cara, I'm not saying that, but don't you see, they want you to be riled up. They want you to be upset and drive you into a tizzy.' He ran a hand through his hair. 'The more concerned and upset you are, the more likely you are going to play into their hands and do what they want. I'm sorry, but I've always lived by the rule that you don't argue with children or idiots and quite frankly, at the moment your family is acting like both.'

She looked at him sharply. *Her family?* Did he just say it was *her family* that was to blame?

She turned her body to face him, pointing a finger. *'Excuse me? My* family? What about *your* family? They aren't exactly acting like the epitome of class these days either; they haven't even spoken to us in weeks. Not so well behaved, are they? Who do you think you are, saying that this is all my family?'

Shane sighed heavily.

'OK, I'm sorry but you took me wrong. I think that all of them are acting silly—'

'It's *your* family who stormed out on us at dinner, and it's *your* family who won't even talk to us. My family might be nuts, but at least they aren't controlling and domineering!'

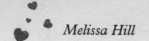

A cloud passed over Shane's face. When he spoke next, anger was evident in his voice.

'Right, right. My family is so controlling and domineering. Such a pain in the arse. I think it's fair to say that if we gave an inch to your mother, she would take a mile. I'm not sure of what your definition of controlling is, but in my book she pretty much lives up to it.'

'Right, and if it was up to your mum, we would have to invite every stuck-up snob in Ireland to our wedding. Just so your parents can get their share of ass-kissing and one-upmanship! What a bunch of crap, Shane. Honestly.'

'Oh, so now my parents are stuck up?' he repeated sarcastically. 'You know, they offered to pay only because they knew that your parents couldn't afford it. Don't hold that against me. Maybe if your parents were smarter, they wouldn't have had to remortgage the house for Heidi's wedding and wouldn't be up to their eyeballs in debt.'

'So my parents are idiots,' she shot back. 'That's pretty fair. You know Shane, I never realised you were such an asshole. Why don't you say what you really feel?'

'You want me to say what I really feel? Is that it?' Shane threw back the bedclothes and stood up. 'OK, then, you asked for it. Your mother worries more about what people will think than about the feelings of her own family. Your father should be focused on retiring, yet he is more concerned with spending money on stupid weddings that don't mean anything. Your sister Heidi is a spoiled, crazy child who seriously needs to be taken down a few pegs and her husband is so completely whipped that he is unable to form an opinion for himself. And from what I hear about Danielle,' he added nastily, 'she sounds like the only smart one of the lot of you for moving far, far away!'

Cara was shocked. Shane had really gone for it. She felt

as if he had just attacked her. Worst of all was that every one of those insults was peppered with the truth, and she knew it.

'You forgot Ben and Kim,' Cara said, hurt tears springing to her eyes. 'You wouldn't want to leave them out. Please, continue – you might as well ridicule us all while you're at it.'

Shane blanched, as if only then realising what he'd said. 'Oh babe—'

'I'm glad that you had the chance to get this all out now though,' Cara continued as if he hadn't spoken. 'I mean, why on earth would you want to marry into a family that you so clearly don't like?'

She turned away from him and swung her legs over the side of the bed. He reached out for her, but she pulled away. 'Don't,' she said simply, turning her shoulder to him.

'Cara, please. I didn't mean to say all of that – it was heat of the moment stuff, I really didn't mean it,' he pleaded.

She shook her head and willed herself to fight the tears. 'You know, your family isn't so perfect either.'

He nodded his head. 'I know, I know. I wasn't trying to say that they are.'

'They are very uppity, full of themselves. Your mother looks down her nose at everyone and everything. Your dad is so pompous and arrogant. Who the hell do they think they are? Acting like my family is some sort of lower-class peasants, completely beneath them.'

'Cara,' Shane said sharply, cutting her off. 'Please, let's not do this. Let's not attack each other. Or our families.'

'Well, you had the opportunity to do it to mine; I might as well tell you how I feel about yours.' But her voice lacked the conviction. Truthfully, she didn't have much of a problem with Shane's parents. While she might not necessarily have identified with them or their society-driven ways, she

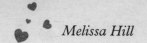

certainly didn't dislike them. She knew that her previous words about them lacked the vitriol that Shane's had carried about her family and truthfully, the ease with which he'd delivered his genealogical analysis stung her and deeply hurt her feelings.

'Babe. I am truly sorry. I was just mad. It was the heat of the moment. I don't mean that stuff. Please – I'm sorry.'

Cara regarded him silently before speaking. 'You know, they say that things spoken in the heat of the moment are usually true.' She lowered her eyes; she felt that she couldn't meet his. After all of the stress that they had been going through lately, the last thing they needed was this. She couldn't escape the feeling that everything had been fine before they got engaged. Now they were fighting over family issues, which they had never done before.

Shane tried again to reach out to her. 'Cara. Please. You know I love you and let's face it, your family isn't perfect, but neither is mine. Please honey.' His eyes pleaded with her to accept his apology.

She finally allowed herself to be pulled into his arms. 'What are we going to do?' she asked glumly. 'I don't want to stress about all of this. I don't want to fight with you.'

'I know, and this is stupid. I love you, honey. You know that don't you?'

Cara allowed the tears to come and buried her face into his chest. 'Shane, this is all such a mess.'

He stroked her hair and made comforting sounds. 'I know baby, I know. Come on, don't cry. I don't want to see you sad. I'm so sorry, I really am.'

'I know you are,' she sniffled. 'It's OK.' And she realised that she did forgive him. Shane wasn't mean-spirited and she knew that despite their faults, he liked her family.

It was just a fight. That's all it was and it didn't mean

anything. They were in this together, and nothing that their families could throw at them could affect their relationship. They were a unit, a couple, forging a life together. And every couple had their ups and downs, didn't they?

'Cara, we will get through this. No matter what. OK? Everything will work itself out, your family will come round and we will straighten everything out with my parents today. And think of the positive. It's not all bad news. You said Kim was excited.'

Cara snuffled again and nuzzled closer to Shane's bare chest. 'Yes, she was. She said she would be a bridesmaid, she said she couldn't wait for the wedding,' she mumbled.

'See, that's good. And pretty soon, once the surprise wears off, everyone else will realise just how much of a great time it is going to be, and want to get involved in all of it,' Shane said encouragingly.

Cara looked up to meet his eyes. She had tear-streaked cheeks. 'Do you think so?'

'I know so. You'll see. You'd have to be crazy not to get excited about a week in St Lucia.' He smiled. 'I know I am.'

Cara took a deep breath.

'So you're OK?' Shane asked.

She nodded. 'Yes. I just, you know, feel so tense about all of this. It's just not how I expected it would be, that's all.'

'Nothing ever is,' Shane said quietly. 'But everything will work out. And I know we will have an amazing wedding, not to mention the rest of our lives together.'

She put her arms around his neck. 'Thank you. I love you and I am lucky to have you.'

'I'm not going anywhere baby. I'm in it for the long haul.'

'Crazy family and all?'

He laughed. 'Yes. Crazy family and all. If you can put up with mine, I'll put up with yours.'

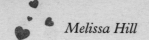

'Deal,' she giggled, already feeling better about things.

She had to think positive and not let the stress get to her. She had to keep her chin up, that's all there was to it. Shane was right. They would get through this, her family would come round. They would straighten things out with his parents later that day, and everything would get back on track.

Chapter 20

'You plan on doing *what?*'

Upon arrival at the Richardson residence Cara and Shane had at least been permitted entry into his parents' country estate, and somehow got through the short initial conversation that broke the ice and opened the floor for further discussion.

However, Lauren and Gene's expressions, as their son and future daughter-in-law told them about their plans in St Lucia, were a sight to behold. They looked as if they had just stepped in dog dirt.

'Mum, you heard me, Cara and I are having a beach wedding in St Lucia. On September twelfth,' Shane stated.

Since their argument the night before, they had promised to show a united front against any complaints that could be thrown at them by either side of their family. Or indeed against disdainful looks like the ones they were now getting.

'Yes Lauren,' Cara said confidently. 'All is confirmed and we have put down a sizeable deposit with the resort, so everything is ready to go.' Cara was suddenly concerned that she sounded defensive, when really all she wanted to do was state a fact.

Lauren narrowed her eyes at Cara. 'I care nothing about *deposits.*' The woman spat it out as if it was some form of low-class terminology, like *layaway*. 'This simply is not going to happen.'

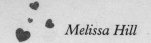

'Son,' Gene implored, finally speaking up. 'This really won't do. I won't have it.'

'Dad—'

'No Shane, your father is right. We do not approve of this and we certainly don't support it. You know our position, regardless of whatever notion you choose to operate under. You cannot expect us to participate in such idiocy,' stated Lauren primly, refusing to look at Cara as if this was all her idea, that it had been her decision alone to have their wedding in St Lucia, and Shane was merely going along with it.

'Mum, Dad, this was mine and Cara's decision and we are paying for your airline tickets and accommodation at the resort, so this is how it is going to be. Regardless of what you may think, I support this idea wholeheartedly.'

Lauren let out a burst of shrill laughter. 'Oh please. You grew up in this house, Shane. Do not try to make me believe that suddenly you think that some silly beach wedding is something that our kind would subscribe to.'

Cara's mouth dropped open. 'Excuse me? What do you mean by "our kind"?' What was his mother getting at?

Lauren turned on Cara in much the same way as a viper regards its prey before striking. Her nostrils flared in anger. 'Cara, what I mean is that I don't expect you to understand what goes into a *proper* wedding. Yes, yes, yes, you can spend plenty of money and put on a show, but a real society wedding is only identifiable by people who happen to move in certain circles. Members of society do not have beach weddings. They do not get married at *resorts*. All of it, the entire idea, is crass and common. But really Cara, you can't blame yourself. It's what you were born into.'

Cara paled. She was speechless. Had Lauren really just called her crass and common? Did her future mother-in-law actually just suggest that she couldn't help being tacky because of the family she was born into? Bloody hell, what was happening here?

'Now wait just a second Mother, you are completely off base and out of line. I demand you apologise immediately,' Shane shot back, the anger rising in his voice, and Cara noted how he was no longer addressing her by the more informal 'Mum.'

His mother turned on him coolly. 'Why? I have nothing to apologise for.'

'Talk about crass and common – how it is good manners to insult someone who has done nothing to you, or indeed, good manners to insult them at all?'

'Now that's enough, Shane.' Gene made quite a show of gruffly inhaling and pointing a finger at his son. 'I refuse to allow you to talk to your mother this way. You will apologise at once.'

'No, not until she apologises to Cara,' he replied, crossing his arms and refusing to budge on the issue.

Lauren sniffed in Cara's direction, refusing to meet her eyes. After a beat she spoke again. 'Cara, I'm sorry if you misunderstood what I was saying.'

Shane dropped his hands. 'That is not an apology, Mother. That is not how you say you are sorry. *You* are sorry that Cara *misunderstood*? What is wrong with you?'

Cara rushed forward, placing a hand on his chest, feeling that she needed to try and calm things down a little. 'Shane, really, it's fine.' But she was unbelievably hurt and felt close to tears. Lauren couldn't have insulted her any more if she'd tried.

'Cara, no, it's not fine at all. She is being disrespectful, not to mention rude. This is not acceptable behaviour and I won't have her treating you this way.'

Cara was insistent. 'Please Shane. Please. Let's just go.'

Clearly, her belief that she was an accepted member of the Richardson family couldn't have been more wrong. Had Lauren ever liked her? Had the woman ever approved of Cara's involvement with her son? She wanted nothing more than to get out of her sight and away from her accusatory gaze.

Lauren regarded the scene in front of her with obvious distaste. 'Shane, you have always been a good son. You always respected your parents and had good manners. I can't help but say that I am very disappointed in you, as is your father, over these outbursts and disrespectful displays of emotion.

And you, Cara. I have always liked you, really I have. And I was very pleased to hear about your engagement and looked forward to it being a big event in this family. But I must admit, I should have expected that something like this would happen. You could never know what is expected of us given our position. There is no way that you would have ever been exposed to any of this before, so I have to consider your ignorance about how things are done. But I have to say that I believe all of this to be your fault. You should have understood that it was your role to simply take our generous offer of support on day one, and that you were not in a position to turn it down. It was a subject that was non-negotiable.' She flicked at an invisible piece of lint on her skirt, while Cara suddenly wondered if they'd moved back in time somehow. What era did Lauren think she was living in, never mind what country? There were no formal class or societal divisions in Ireland, yet Lauren was behaving as if Shane was a member of the royal family, and they were attempting to go against protocol!

'Now you have dragged Shane down with you,' his mother continued. 'Brainwashed him into subscribing to some sort of trashy beach wedding. I don't have any idea what you have to hide, or why you have to run away to another country. I certainly don't know how you convinced Shane of such nonsense.' She turned her officious gaze on her son. 'And Shane, you used to be such a good man. So polite, so charming. I really don't think I know you very well any more. Not to mention I don't know how I will ever live this down. How can I tell my friends, our associates . . .' She turned to her husband, questions in her eyes. If Cara wasn't so shocked by the accusations being flung at her, she would have laughed at the theatrics going on here. Heidi could learn a thing or two about drama from Lauren.

Shane rolled his eyes. 'That's quite enough, Mother. Cara didn't brainwash me into doing anything, and we certainly have nothing to hide. Cara, come on. We are going.'

He held out his hand and Cara reached forward to take it. They started to turn and make their exit, but then Shane turned back and faced his parents. Cara fought the urge to drag him to the door; she didn't think ensuring he had the last word was the best option at this moment, and she was eager to leave.

'I'm going to say this once and I'm saying it for the record, so you both better take note. Cara and I are not changing our minds on this. This wedding is happening in St Lucia, whether you like it or not,' Shane said firmly. 'So, the way I see it, you have two choices. Either you can stay home and not be there, which at this point I honestly would be fine with. Or, you can come and join us in celebration of our special day. But I will tell you this,' he added, his tone ominous. 'If you do decide to come to our wedding, you better be happy about it and accept it. Otherwise, I don't want you there. Not at all. Cara and I are in love. We are going to be married. From now on, I will always choose her over you. Remember that.'

Shane turned and headed to the door, Cara in tow. While the entire scene was incredibly upsetting, she couldn't get the look that she had just seen on Lauren's face out of her head. While most mothers would have wept at the thought of being cut out of their son's life, Cara was almost sure that she had seen anticipation and excitement on Lauren's face.

Almost as if . . . as if she was eager for a challenge.

And the idea of that terrified her.

Chapter 21

'It's just not fair, Mum,' Heidi cried. 'Cara was completely unconcerned about how her wedding would affect me and the baby.' Betty's youngest then launched into a long and drawn-out tirade about why it was completely unacceptable, and how Cara's behaviour was stressing her out too, which was also incredibly unhealthy for her unborn child.

Betty was herself rather distressed that despite all their protestations, Cara still seemed unwilling to modify her wedding plans.

She just couldn't get her head around the idea of flying off to St Lucia to watch her daughter and Shane get married on some public beach, in a dress that possibly wouldn't even be a proper wedding dress.

'I am totally right. I know I am. Paul agrees with me. Don't you agree Mum? MUM!'

Betty tried to tune back in to the musings of her youngest.

'Sorry pet, what?'

'You didn't hear a single thing I said did you?' Heidi harrumphed. 'You weren't even listening.'

'No, of course I was listening,' Betty replied. Listening but only hearing white noise, as was often the case where Heidi was concerned. It was her own fault really. Heidi was her youngest and had been a complete surprise (as she and Mick had been sure that with Cara their family was complete), and as such she may have been indulged a little too much.

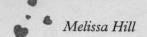

'So then? What do you think?'

'I'm not sure really; I'd have to think about it . . .' Betty honestly had no clue what Heidi had been prattling on about so she decided to try to wing it.

'You have to think about what would happen if I *went into labour early*? On St Lucia! What's there to think about? It would be a disaster!'

Oh Lord, Betty thought. She had created a monster by getting Heidi involved. The girl truly had been first in line when God was giving out the gene for theatrics.

'Heidi, no woman in this family goes into labour early,' she said easily. 'It just doesn't happen.' If anything, she thought, remembering her experiences, the Clancy babies were in no hurry to get out, oftentimes appearing well past due date. It had been the case with Danielle and Ben, and indeed with Cara too.

'But you don't know that for sure. These things aren't genetic and I could be completely different to you. Imagine going into labour on some foreign island? My baby's life would be ruined. Actually, it wouldn't even be Irish then, would it?' she added, biting her lip. 'It would have St Lucian citizenship, if there is even such a thing. I can't have a St Lucian baby, Mum. You have to talk some sense into Cara.'

Betty gave her a stern look. 'Heidi, that's quite enough. We really should be supporting Cara, not harassing her. We are a family. Therefore, we stand together to support each other in good times and bad. And this is a good time.'

Heidi's mouth dropped open.

Great, she thought, *now my mum isn't even in my corner*. Heidi felt morose. It was her against the world. No one cared about her pregnancy. Her poor baby; no one was the least bit bothered that he or she could be born St Lucian and not Irish. She patted her tummy.

'But Mum,' she pleaded. 'Just last week, you were annoyed about having to go to St Lucia too—'

'I was a bit taken aback, that's all. But we have to remember that this is Cara's day and if she wants us to eat live lobsters or whatever it is they eat on St Lucia – or dance naked on the beach – then maybe that is just what we are going to have to do.'

Heidi looked at her mother as if she had just lost her marbles.

'Shellfish? *Live* shellfish!' she squealed. 'Well there's no way *I* can eat live shellfish, there or anywhere else – it's lethal for a pregnant woman, and completely against all the rules . . .'

Kim pulled up in front of her in-laws' house in Greygates. Damn, she thought, spying Heidi's car. She briefly considered pulling away again, and just coming back later. Truthfully, she wasn't in the mood to put up with Heidi at the moment.

She sat back in her seat and closed her eyes as another wave of nausea overcame her, and she put her hand on the door, knowing that she wouldn't hesitate to throw it open and vomit in the street if she had to. She had already cleaned up the inside of her car after the day before when she couldn't disengage the automatic locks fast enough, and she wasn't planning on doing it again. It was bad enough that the horrible scent still lingered on the upholstery, one that she knew would only be removed by a bout with a professional valet.

She really shouldn't have eaten that cupcake – or the second one for that matter . . . The bad feeling passed, but Kim realised a thin line of sweat had broken out on her forehead.

This, she thought, *is the worst part of pregnancy*. She could take the rapidly expanding girth (which with this baby seemed to have happened even faster than the others), but the throwing up and all the nasty stuff that happened between conception and birth was the worst.

Especially this: the morning sickness. Kim willed it to be over soon, especially as she had a life to get on with, work to do, and busy days to contend with. She had no room for ceaseless vomiting. But she would be over the fourteen-week mark soon, after which it mercifully seemed to stop. It had with her others anyway, so she hoped she'd get lucky this time too, rather than be stuck with it for the duration of the pregnancy like some poor women. This time, though, it seemed to be so much worse than anything she had experienced while pregnant with Olivia or Lindsay. Although maybe it was just that Kim was getting older.

Yep, this pregnancy would definitely be her last. If Ben fancied any more children after Number Three, she thought, smiling, he would just have to find a surrogate.

She looked again towards the house as she wiped her brow with a tissue. The last thing she wanted in front of Heidi was to show any sign of weakness. Her sister-in-law would be only too delighted to feed off of something like that. She wondered how Heidi was getting on in the morning sickness department, but then, remembering their last conversation, in which her sister-in-law had chewed her out over the phone, Kim decided that actually, she didn't want to know.

She'd come over to Betty and Mick's to drop off a box of the aforementioned cupcakes, the ones that had caused all the trouble. The girls had dedicated the previous evening to baking the treats and had made their mother promise to put some aside for Nanna and Grandad. Kim had agreed to drop them off this morning as she was passing by Greygates on her way to an appointment with a client.

Indeed, she realised she could have just left them in the stockroom at work and watched them disappear, or even eaten them all herself (which she had come dangerously close to doing), instead of engaging on the errand over here, but Olivia had a mind like a steel trap, and was likely to remember to ask after them next time she saw her grandparents.

She got out of the car and walked up the steps. Already she could hear raised voices from inside, and she wondered what she was voluntarily walking into. Her stomach churned again and she paused, trying to regain her composure. She hoped to avoid confrontation today, with either her mother-in-law or Heidi. She just wasn't in the mood for it and unfortunately it was with these two women that Kim was always most likely to find it.

She tapped on the door lightly. 'Hello?' she said, trying to inject easy-going positivity into her voice. She let out a quiet burp and paused, hoping that air was all that was coming up.

'Betty, hello?' Kim called out again.

Standing at the doorway, she looked through to the kitchen. The first person she saw was Heidi, who (unsurprisingly) had her face set in a scowl. She turned in Kim's direction and the scowl deepened. Clearly, Heidi was as excited to see her as Kim was to see Heidi.

Betty quickly walked into view.

'Oh Kim, hello. I didn't know you were coming over. Oh, what do you have there?' her mother-in-law asked as she hustled forward to help Kim, who was struggling to balance the tray of cupcakes and open the front door at the same time. 'Here, let me take that box from you.'

'We were making cupcakes last night and the girls insisted that I bring some over for you and Grandad,' Kim replied with a smile. Her stomach let out another dangerous sounding groan, and she quickly – and thankfully – handed the tray of goodies off.

'Ah lovely,' Betty said, smiling. 'Are you feeling all right though? Your stomach sounds like you just ate a bear. I bet it's the morning sickness. Such a problem, such a problem, but all worth it of course. It's the natural way after all. Oh and Heidi's here. We were just discussing Cara's wedding.'

Uh-oh, Kim thought, so *that* was the ticking time bomb she was walking in on. She tried to plaster on a smile as she followed Betty into the kitchen. Maybe she could make this visit a quick one.

'Hey Heidi, how are things?' she said, waving a greeting.

'Hi,' Heidi replied shortly, and Kim immediately deduced by her tone that her sister-in-law was still in a mood with her. But then again, when *wasn't* she in a mood?

'So yes, I'm sure you have heard all about it of course? Cara's plans, I mean,' Betty asked. Kim tried to gauge the feeling in the room. She knew that what she had just been asked was a loaded question. How did she answer?

'Yes, Cara called me the other night,' she said simply, offering no additional information.

'Heidi and I were just discussing how we needed to be excited for Cara, support her and show a united front,' Betty continued.

Well, that's interesting, Kim thought, momentarily wrong-footed. Betty had just pulled a complete one-eighty turn in her opinion, judging by what Cara had told her about her mother's initial response to the news about the beach wedding.

For Cara's sake she was relieved that Betty had finally come to her senses; Cara adored her mother and Kim knew her parents' reaction had really hurt her.

'Well, I'm sure that Cara will be delighted that you want to be involved.' She also knew that Cara certainly needed the support, judging by the negative reaction she and Shane had also received from his parents. Poor thing had rung Kim in tears the other night after their visit to the Richardson house.

Heidi up to this point had been quiet, but her pointed gaze had not failed to be noticed by Kim. Her expression was hawkish to say the least.

'So I suppose that you are fine with all of this nonsense about going to St Lucia to get married? Even though we will both be in the last trimester? You do realise that don't you?' Heidi said pointedly. It was less a question and more an accusation.

'Only barely in your case, but yes, of course I know that Heidi,' Kim said, shrugging. 'It's not that big of a deal to me.'

Heidi rolled her eyes. 'So you don't care if your baby is born a St Lucian?'

Despite her dodgy stomach, Kim almost burst out laughing. 'Excuse me? What are you talking about?'

'Oh, I think Heidi might be a bit worried about either of you going into labour while over there,' offered Betty weakly.

'So how would my baby be a St Lucian if I went into labour on the island?' inquired Kim innocently. She had to hear this.

'Well, you are Irish if you are born in Ireland, you are American if you are born in America. So if my baby is born in St Lucia, it will obviously be St Lucian.' Heidi rolled her eyes as if she was explaining the nuances and intricacies of citizenship to a child.

Kim pressed her lips together. She had to say, her sister-in-law was really something. She could only conclude that

Betty must have dropped her on her head when she was a baby and had been feeling guilty about it ever since. Why else was her behaviour so readily indulged?

'Actually Heidi, I'm not sure if that is exactly how the laws of citizenship work. You might want to look that up.'

'Really,' Heidi replied sardonically, but Kim could tell she was annoyed. 'Still, you going into labour early would put quite the crimp in your plans, wouldn't it?' she added. 'Seeing as you would much rather have some doctor do all the work for you, rather than going to trouble of having the baby for yourself. Too posh to push and all that,' Heidi added nastily.

'Yes Kim, Ben mentioned something about that.' Betty chimed in. 'I've been meaning to talk to you about it, actually. What's all this nonsense about a planned C-section? It's a disgrace. You do know that such a thing completely goes against the laws of nature? Childbirth is meant to be painful, that is a woman's burden. After all, Eve had to go through it, so should the rest of us.'

OK here we go, Kim thought, infuriated. She was almost sorry now that she and Ben had been so open about their plans, given that so many people were determined to shove their oar in. But at the same time, it was no business of anyone else's and there was no way she was going to hide the decision, or act as though it was something to be ashamed of.

Still, she was becoming sick to the teeth of having to justify it, and now the last thing she wanted was a debate with her pious when it suited her mother-in-law about religion.

'Actually Betty, our plans in this regard are personal and entirely none of your business,' she said, working her hardest to bite her tongue. Her stomach moaned again and she felt bile rise in her throat. She really needed to get out of here – fast.

'I would think the approval of the family would be important to you on this matter. After all, it is my grandchild too,' said Betty.

Kim looked to from Betty to Heidi, who wore a maddeningly self-satisfied expression, knowing that she had essentially tossed Kim to the wolves.

'Betty, approval has nothing to do with it. I'm the baby's mother and given my experiences with the two girls, I know exactly what I'm getting into. Which is why this time, I get to call the shots.' She gave Heidi a withering glance. 'As for too posh to push, let's see how you get on yourself before you start casting judgement on anyone else.'

'I'll be just fine thank you. I have a detailed birth plan and I already know exactly what—'

Kim chuckled. 'A birth plan? Good luck with that. I don't want to scare you Heidi, but take it from me, once labour really gets going, any plans or notions you might have will have to go straight out the window. Which is exactly why I've decided not to leave anything to chance this time round.'

She thought she saw Heidi blanch and was beginning to feel guilty when her sister-in-law muttered, 'Drama queen.'

Kim's mouth dropped open. 'How dare—?'

'I don't see why you are still persisting with this silly business of yours either,' Betty put in, quickly changing the subject. 'It's not right being a working mother with three. You need to be there for your—'

'Persisting with my silly business?' Kim couldn't believe what she was hearing. Now she was getting the working-mother guilt trip! And as if Blissology was some tiny backroom set-up, instead of a thriving enterprise with an enviable turnover. 'Betty, if I remember correctly what Ben told me, you too worked after your children were born. And it's not as though what I do is some frivolous hobby that I can

209

abandon at a moment's notice. Not that I want to. And not only do I love what I do, but my having a career has no bearing whatsoever on my ability to be a good mother – if anything it complements it.'

Betty opened and closed her mouth and Kim knew that she had made her point. But as ever, Heidi decided to jump in with her tuppence worth.

'Really Kim, I can't see how what you do fits into the definition of a "good mother." I mean, it's your kids who are going to pay for your so-called career. I would much rather choose to have well balanced children than be going door to door like some kind of insurance salesman. Really, when the new baby arrives, I think you should re-examine your priorities'.

Kim had been trying desperately to bite her tongue, but she was tired and nauseated and had had just about enough of her husband's spoilt little sister. 'Heidi, I really don't think you can consider yourself an authority on anything motherhood or indeed career-related. It's not as though you successfully climbed the corporate ladder. And as for being a good mother – again, let's just see how you get on.'

Heidi's face flushed bright red, but she didn't dare reply.

'Anyway, I'd better get back to selling "door to door" as you put it,' Kim continued, abruptly turning to leave. 'Like such a bad mother, I simply wanted to drop off these cupcakes as a favour to my daughters; I didn't expect to get lectured.' Her stomach churned again and she knew she needed to get out of there ASAP.

'Nobody was lecturing you Kim, we were merely pointing out our concerns about the baby,' admonished Betty. 'I've already said it to Ben, and I'll say it to you now: what you're planning is not right and I do hope you will come your senses and—'

'Betty, I'm sorry but it's really none of your business,' Kim shot back, sick to the gills of interfering in-laws. 'The decision is made, I am having this baby whatever way I like and what's not right is you trying to interfere. You'll just have to get used to the idea. Just like you will with Cara's wedding.'

She pushed down on the door handle. 'And Heidi, for the record, if by any chance you did go into labour on St Lucia, I wouldn't be worrying so much about its nationality, I'd be worrying over the fact that it would be dangerously premature. In any case, I suggest you put on your big-girl pants and realise that this wedding isn't about you, it's about Cara. Therefore, your only role is to sit down, shut up and for once put a smile on your selfish face. All right?'

With that Kim walked out of the kitchen and through the house to the front door. Once she got outside, she broke into a controlled sprint to the car.

She was just about able to control her nausea until she pulled the vehicle around the corner, whereupon she threw open the door and promptly purged the two cupcakes that she had eaten before her visit to Betty and Heidi.

The problem was, she thought afterwards, that she wasn't sure if it was the baby, or the conversation with her bloody in-laws, that had made her sick.

Chapter 22

The following Saturday morning, Cara ran up the steps of the bridal dress shop just off Grafton Street. She had to admit, she was incredibly excited about this, especially in view of her recent stress concerning the wedding and, in particular, Shane's parents.

Regardless of anything else that was going on in the background, she knew today was going to be a great day. Kim was meeting her and they were going to look at wedding dresses, as well as bridesmaid dresses. A total girls' day out, just what she needed.

However, when she walked into the salon, she was completely unprepared to see her mother and Heidi. They were flanking Kim, who gave her a helpless look and mouthed 'sorry.'

'Mum, Heidi, what are you doing here?' Cara questioned, caught completely off guard by their presence.

'Heidi and I were out shopping for some baby things this morning. We stopped by Ben and Kim's to say hello, and we happened to catch Kim on her way out. I can't believe you didn't tell me, pet,' Betty said, looking hurt. 'As if I would miss out on shopping for your wedding dress with you.'

However, it was clear from Heidi's sullen expression that she was greatly put off from having a shopping day related to her and baby things redirected towards Cara and her wedding dress.

Cara smiled, pleased that Betty seemed so eager and positive; a huge change from the last time she'd seen her. She'd been so deflated about not having her mother along today to help choose her wedding dress – an important ritual she'd always anticipated sharing with her – but she just hadn't been able to face any more negativity. It had seemed easier all round to go with someone who was supportive of her wishes. But now Betty seemed genuinely happy about the prospect. Should she give her the benefit of the doubt?

'Fantastic. And great that you're here too, Heidi.' She hadn't spoken to her sister since Heidi's angry phone call shortly after she and Shane announced their plans.

Heidi, who had been staring at the ceiling, locked her gaze on Cara's face. 'Why's that?' she asked.

'Well, because if you do decide to join us in St Lucia, naturally I'm hoping that you will be one of my bridesmaids,' Cara said with a smile. 'I would have asked you before now, but the time didn't seem right, and the last time we spoke . . .'

A small smile jumped to Heidi's lips. 'Really? I thought that because you were so intent on having a small wedding, and wanting to run away overseas, maybe you wouldn't want me to be involved.'

Cara put an arm around her sister's waist and squeezed. 'Heidi, you are my sister. You, Kim and Danielle – I would love to have all three of you as bridesmaids, OK?'

She noticed Betty tense a little at the mention of Danielle, but decided not to dwell on it. Whatever was going on with those two would have to be put aside for the wedding. Much to Cara's relief, Danielle had since replied and confirmed that she'd be honoured to be her bridesmaid, so all was settled on that front at least.

'That sounds good. I'd love to.' Heidi allowed her smile to widen and Cara noticed that, unusually, it reached all the way to her eyes. She felt some of her earlier anxiety dissipate – maybe today *would* be fun.

A severe-looking woman in a navy blue suit and matching heels approached them.

'Cara Clancy?'

'That's me.' Cara smiled excitedly. She was going to choose her wedding dress today! 'Are you Bridget?'

The woman smiled tightly, as if it was her role to be the voice of reason when dealing with overzealous brides-to-be. 'Yes. We spoke on the phone last week.'

'Fantastic, thank you. This is my mother, Betty, my sister, Heidi and my sister-in-law, Kim. We're going to be looking at some bridesmaid dresses today, too.'

'Wonderful. Please follow me.'

The four women were ushered back to a large room with a raised pedestal in the middle, surrounded by mirrors.

Clearly designed with women in mind, the walls were a pale shade of pink, and gold leaf moulding graced the walls. The settees that they were led to were covered with mauve taffeta. The entire room looked as if it would fit well in an eighteenth-century castle.

The ladies took their seats and Bridget settled in front of Cara.

'Before we start, can I get you ladies some champagne?' she asked.

'Oh, yes please. That sounds wonderful!' Cara grinned.

Heidi shook her head regally. 'Just some sparkling water for me, please. I'm pregnant. So is Kim.'

'Ah go on Heidi, we can have a little glass,' Kim said, giving Bridget a nod.

Heidi turned on her with a shocked expression. 'Kim. You.

Cannot. Drink. Alcohol while pregnant,' she said enunciating each word carefully. 'You simply cannot.'

Kim waved a hand in Heidi's direction. 'Honestly, it's fine. I used to have the odd glass on both Olivia and Lindsay. Trust me, it's not a problem.'

Heidi turned angry eyes to Betty. 'Mum, tell her . . .'

Betty sighed heavily, but wisely stayed silent.

'Let it go Heidi,' Cara put in calmly. 'If you don't want one that's fine, but if Kim does, then that's her decision.'

Heidi rolled her eyes, and slumped in the seat. 'Typical. *I'm* the responsible pregnant woman here, but yet I'm the one who gets chastised!'

Bridget the bridal assistant shifted from one foot to the other, looking mightily uncomfortable.

So much for everything being fine, Cara thought with a sigh. This was going to end badly; there was no doubt about it. She cut in quickly. 'Bridget, champagne would be lovely, thank you. Three glasses please. And one sparkling water.'

'Of course. I'll be right back.'

Heidi kept her eyes firmly planted on the far wall. Cara rubbed her temples while Kim looked ready to wring Heidi's neck. Betty picked up a nearby bridal magazine and started leafing through it.

Still, the brief silence was encouraging. Maybe the subject would just be dropped, Cara thought hopefully. Maybe they could just all get along.

Betty looked up from the magazine, 'Oh, look at this, Cara,' she said, pointing at a photograph. 'Isn't it beautiful? You would look like a princess in this.'

Heidi and Kim momentarily forgotten, Cara looked briefly at the frou-frou Cinderella dress her mother was pointing at. Indeed it was a beautiful dress; a BIG, beautiful dress – but there was no way she could wear something like that in St Lucia.

'That's nice Mum, but I don't think it would do for a beach wedding. I'd roast in it. Like I said, I'm looking for something simple.'

'Well, there's no harm in trying something like that on, is there? Seeing as we're here . . . I'll check with Bridget – see if she has something similar.'

'Mum, no,' Cara insisted. 'There's no point; it's not what I am interested in.'

At that moment Bridget walked back into the room, holding a silver tray that carried three crystal flutes of champagne. There was also a bottle of San Pellegrino and a glass with ice for Heidi.

'Here you go ladies.' Bridget handed each woman a glass and Heidi looked icily at Kim as her sister-in-law accepted hers and took a sip, smacking her lips in appreciation.

Cara decided at that moment that the best course of action would be to ignore them both.

'So, Cara,' Bridget said, smiling. 'You said on the phone that your wedding will be taking place in St Lucia. That sounds wonderful!' she enthused, going into sales mode and focusing all her efforts on the bride-to-be. 'What do you envision for your Big Day? How do you see yourself?'

Cara took a deep breath. Finally, someone was just asking her what *she* wanted. Of course, she understood that Bridget wanted to sell her something, but the attention and focus was appreciated all the same. She thought back to her original vision, the dress she'd created in her mind when Shane had asked her the same question a few weeks before.

'Well, of course we'll be on the beach, and it will be quite warm. I was hoping for something very simple, flowing and sheath-like . . . like a white column of satin,' she said, smiling.

Bridget nodded. 'Sounds amazing. We'll need something that will catch the ocean breeze, light, feminine and elegant while at the same time comfortable and easy to walk in. I already have a few ideas in mind—'

'Yes, but we were also thinking something like this.' Betty spoke up suddenly. She pointed to the magazine she had been holding, and the same huge ballgown that she had shown Cara moments before. Bridget looked at Cara questioningly. It was apparent the woman was trying to figure out the dynamic in the room, or more importantly, who was paying for what. Which would be a big factor in deciding whom she would side with, from a sales perspective at least.

'That is indeed a beautiful dress . . .' she replied hesitantly. 'The train alone is cathedral length, about fifteen feet or so. So I'm not entirely sure if it is the best idea for a beach wedding . . .'

Cara was shaking her head. 'No Mum, I told you. All that tulle, and that heavy beading – it's just too much. And more to the point, it's not me. I don't want it.'

'You say that now, but you never know what you are going to like until you put it on. Don't you remember sweetheart?' she said, addressing Heidi. 'You came in thinking that you wanted one thing, and walked out with something completely different, didn't you?' Heidi nodded and for the first time Cara wondered if all of Heidi's apparent over-the-top decisions had actually been of her own making. Yes, she remembered her sister's wedding dress, the kind of big princess gown with a train, sequins, and very full skirt that *Betty* loved. Exactly the kind she was pointing out now.

'She's proof alone that you can change your mind, even if you think you're absolutely sure,' her mother encouraged. 'Do you have a dress like this in stock so we could take a look at it?' she asked the assistant. 'Along with the others of course. Let's just have a look and see, OK?' She spoke in a sweet tone, but there was steeliness behind it and Cara knew that her mother wouldn't back down until she had tried on the meringue. Well, couldn't she grant her mother that much at least?

Bridget looked to Cara for affirmation. 'OK, we'll take a look,' she conceded glumly.

The assistant nodded and disappeared once again from the room.

Cara, Heidi and Kim sat in silence, sipping their respective drinks while Betty hummed happily to herself.

When Bridget re-entered the room, she was followed by two more assistants who pushed a rolling clothes rail filled with white satin, lace and a variety of other fabrics.

Cara easily picked out the huge ballgown; it was clear that they had done their utmost to fit the dress in alongside the others, as it could have easily filled a rack on its own.

'So we've chosen several designs that we thought you might like, and that also fit with your vision,' Bridget said, looking only at Cara and working her hardest to avoid Betty's gaze.

The first dress she offered was a simple satin sheath, just as Cara had described. It had two delicate straps that criss-crossed at the back, tying into an elegant and understated bow. It also had the slightest of trains and as she looked at the dress, Cara could practically feel the sand under her toes.

'Oh, it's beautiful,' she cooed. 'I can't wait to try it on.'

Once she had disrobed and had assistance in putting the delicate satin over her head, she looked at herself in the mirror. While she wasn't sure if this dress was 'The One', they were certainly on the right track.

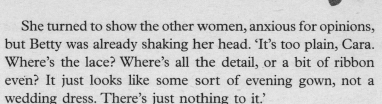

She turned to show the other women, anxious for opinions, but Betty was already shaking her head. 'It's too plain, Cara. Where's the lace? Where's all the detail, or a bit of ribbon even? It just looks like some sort of evening gown, not a wedding dress. There's just nothing to it.'

'Mum, I think it's gorgeous, very simple and light, exactly what I—'

'I do too,' Kim interjected, giving an encouraging wink. 'You look amazing.'

'Just try on this one – to compare,' her mother said, moving to the meringue. It was clear that Betty would not be dissuaded from her goal.

Bridget looked at Cara inquiringly, looking for approval to move on.

''OK go ahead,' she nodded. 'Might as well get it over and done with,' she added under her breath.

The two assistants approached her with the dress. It was made from yards and yards of taffeta and tulle, and Cara couldn't determine where the gown began or ended. Getting her out of the simple sheath, they began to help her negotiate her way into the monstrous gown.

Once they got her in, they started the process of lacing her up and using a little tool that helped them fasten the tiny buttons on the back of the dress. All the while Betty made cooing sounds behind her.

When the assistants were finally finished, Cara turned round to look at herself in the mirror.

Holy hell, she thought, trying to stifle a giggle, *I look like the Abominable Snowman!*

Off the shoulder, with intricate beading and design across the bodice, the dress ballooned into a massive skirt that was decorated with white sequins and lacework. Cara studied the reflection of the back of the dress in the mirror. The train alone was something to be reckoned with. She would need several attendants just to help her navigate it down the beach. She didn't even want to think of the weight that she would be carrying around in the humid Caribbean weather, especially once some damp sand inevitably found its way on to the train.

And while it probably would have suited her sister, or perhaps someone who was getting married at the likes of Westminster Abbey, it was definitely not Cara.

'Very nice but can you imagine dragging that around on the beach?' Kim chuckled, echoing Cara's thoughts.

'I'm sure it could be bustled or something?' Betty offered, campaigning blatantly for the dress.

'Ah Mum, you can't be serious. This thing is terribly heavy; I'd be killed wearing it in the humidity. Can we just agree that this dress is really not for me?'

Betty waved a hand. 'But it's beautiful. Just perfect – the kind of dress I've always imagined you wearing.'

'Mum, really, it's a little much, don't you think? It might be fine in a church, but not a beach,' Heidi chimed in and Cara smiled at her, grateful that she was taking her side on this one.

'You look like you're struggling already,' commented Kim. 'I'm about to break into a sweat just looking at you. Next please.'

Cara was only too happy to oblige, and as the attendants helped her out of the offending dress, she noted the disappointed expression on her mother's face.

'OK, which one next?' she asked, relieved to have got the big meringue out of the way.

Bridget walked forward with the next choice and Cara immediately felt her breath catch in her throat.

An elegant white strapless gown, it looked like something

a Greek goddess would wear with its sweetheart neckline and natural waist. The bodice was covered in ruched silk and the gathered skirt was made of a soft organza satin that created a romantic silhouette. Around the waist was a simple crystal appliqué that highlighted, rather than overdid, the style of the dress. The back scooped low and the skirt fell into a romantic and simple flowing train; nothing too heavy. This was a dress that would catch an ocean breeze for sure.

'This one just came in. It's from a new designer who is getting a lot of buzz. Kate Middleton is a fan apparently. What do you think of it?'

'Wow, it's gorgeous, Cara,' Heidi commented.

'Yes, try it, hurry,' Kim echoed excitedly.

Cara felt goose bumps up and down her arms as the dress's feather-light material was arranged around her. She closed her eyes in anticipation as they zipped her up. She had a feeling about this dress and was almost afraid to see how it looked, just in case it didn't suit. Please, please let it do her justice.

'Oh wow, Cara, do yourself a favour and open your eyes,' Kim urged.

She did. Her heart pounded with exhilaration as she took in her appearance. She barely recognised herself. The dress seemed to have been made just for her. In truth, it wasn't the simple sheath that she had originally envisioned, but this was *her* dress; there was no denying that.

'Say something,' Kim laughed.

'Oh my – I love it. I absolutely love it . . .' Her mouth still agape with fascination, Cara turned round and looked at the delicate flowing fabric behind her. Everything about this dress was simple and elegant. She imagined herself walking out on to the sand beneath a canopy of palm trees, the skirt swirling around her. She tried to imagine how much better the dress would look on her when she had sun-kissed skin. Yes, this was her dress – for her wedding to Shane on a beautiful beach on a paradise island.

She turned round to face the others, hoping that they loved it as much as she did.

'Mum, what do you think?' she asked, smiling.

Betty had removed a tissue from her purse and was dabbing her eyes lightly. 'Oh Cara—' she whispered.

Tears came to her own eyes, she was so taken aback at her mother's reaction. 'You like it?'

'Oh sweetheart, I love it. It was made for you.' Betty smiled happily. 'Forget all about the ballgown. This is the one.'

Cara turned back towards the mirror and looked at herself once again, doubly thrilled by her mother's approval. She wondered what Shane would think when he saw her in this. Her heart soared at the thought of becoming his wife in this gown, of committing herself to him for ever while she was wearing this.

'It really is stunning on you.' Bridget smiled.

'Thank you, Bridget.'

'Would you like to see any of the others or . . .?'

'No, no, I don't think so. I've been told you should always go with your gut when it comes to wedding dresses, and mine is screaming at me that this is the one.'

Bridget smiled. 'Yes, I have heard that theory works.'

'Is there a veil?'

She nodded and went back to the rack, a moment later producing a simple tulle veil with a crystal appliqué, similar to the one on the dress, decorating its bottom edges. She slid the comb of the veil into Cara's hair. It fell gracefully around her shoulders, falling right in the middle of her back.

She was sold.

'Bridget?'

'Yes?' smiled the saleswoman, already mentally calculating her commission.

'I'll take it.'

Chapter 23

Cara was feeling giddy. It had been a fantastic day. She had found her wedding dress, her family were (for the most part) getting along with each other, and she had indulged in champagne. Life was good.

She'd had three glasses at the bridal salon, and afterwards Kim had insisted on a celebratory late lunch, especially after they decided on the bridesmaid dresses, too.

Gold, Empire-line knee-length dresses that would look fantastic on all three women, even taking into account that two of them had ever-expanding tummies to contend with. As Danielle had always had an enviable figure and would look good wearing a sack, Cara figured her older sister would be fine with her choice, but she was going to email her the details, and a picture of the dress from the catalogue, just in case.

At the restaurant, she had allowed her wine glass to be filled a few more times and admitted that it was wise to let Kim drive her home while Heidi dropped Betty back at her own place.

'I can't believe I've found my wedding dress. Isn't it amazing I found my dress? Number three's a charm. Or is it third time's the charm?' she giggled at Kim as they drove home from the restaurant. 'I don't remember.'

'I believe it is third time's the charm. And yes, it's amazing and looked fantastic on you. Drop-dead gorgeous. What a

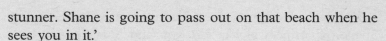

stunner. Shane is going to pass out on that beach when he sees you in it.'

Cara leaned her head back against the car seat. 'You know, I think I needed this,' she said dramatically. 'Something about this wedding to go right. Did you go through lots of drama before your wedding day?'

Kim smiled and patted Cara's knee. 'Let's just say that it wasn't smooth sailing, especially when Ben and I announced I was pregnant. My parents didn't take kindly to it really. My dad wanted to kill Ben, like he had compromised my honour or something. Poor thing had a hard time getting his head round the fact that I wasn't as pure as the driven snow, but yes, they all came round in the end.'

'Yes, but you and Ben were engaged already by then, and I don't remember anyone objecting to your wedding the way they are with ours,' Cara continued, looking to Kim for answers.

Kim smiled, keeping her eyes on the road. 'Like I said, it wasn't a walk in the park. Being the bride, technically it should have been my family who was in charge of things, but I have to admit, your mother had the tendency to over-step. That's between you and me of course. And my own mother drove me crazy.' She rolled her eyes. 'It's just part and parcel of it all, really. As for the beach wedding, I think your mother might be coming round, and barring that cheap shot about my drinking threatening to upend your dress shopping, Heidi might well end up onside too. It will work out,' she encouraged.

Thinking of Shane's parents, a sliver of worry shot through Cara's otherwise happy buzz. 'But what about Shane's parents though? They're still not speaking to us.'

Kim shrugged. 'They'll eventually come round too.'

'But what if they don't? What if they just continue to punish us? What should I do? What should Shane do?'

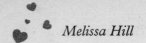

Kim looked at her as she pulled up in front of Cara and Shane's apartment block. 'Are you and Shane happy with each other?' she asked.

'Of course.'

'Exactly, you are a team, so there's little point in worrying about things you can't control. Just take it one day at a time. Now pull yourself together and powder your nose. I've got you home and I won't be blamed by Shane for getting you all drunk and messy.'

'OK, see you soon. And thanks for coming with me today.' Cara hiccupped loudly as she reached across to give Kim a hug.

'You're welcome. Now scoot!'

Cara got out of the car and laughed happily as she fished out her keys. This had been the best day yet and she couldn't wait to tell Shane all about it.

Lauren Richardson sat by a large floor to ceiling window in the library of her home. She studied the early evening sky and went over the conversation that she had had with Shane earlier. She hated that he was upset, but then again she had fully anticipated that he wouldn't take the information that she delivered too readily. In any case, when you truly considered it, she was really just trying to protect his interests – and the interests of the Richardson name.

She sighed and took a sip of the Bordeaux from the crystal wine glass on the side table next to her. Admittedly, she had always liked Cara and truth be told, she thought she and Shane were a good match. However, now that the wheels were apparently in motion on this so-called wedding ceremony, Cara simply had to come to her senses and move away from the ridiculous notion that some tacky beach wedding was appropriate.

Lauren felt her blood pressure rise at the thought of the ultimatum Shane had issued when they first told her and Gene about their wedding plans. She recalled his comment that they were to either take it or leave it and that he only wanted them there if they could act like they were happy about it.

Well, Lauren wasn't happy about it, and she certainly wouldn't pretend to be either.

Two can play at that game, she thought. She had to admit, she actually was surprised that Shane had so grossly under-estimated her. He seemed genuinely shocked at her request earlier. Whereas as far as Lauren was concerned, it was simply a trump card, and she was holding it.

She got up from where she was sitting and crossed the room to her desk, picking up the all-important documentation.

This was her security. This was how she would get the society wedding that she had dreamed about for her son.

Lauren thought back to the last few days. As soon as Shane and Cara had left after announcing their news, she hadn't wasted a moment in getting on the phone with her lawyer.

She picked up the papers that her lawyer had recently drafted.

It was a contract – a prenuptial agreement of sorts, really. It was a fantastic idea, practically foolproof if she was being honest. She thought again of the details in the specially customised legal document and smiled to herself. She didn't like to be devious, but really it was the only way.

What she was proposing was perfectly reasonable; what's more, she was putting all of the control in Cara's hands, and that – Lauren thought – was the genius bit.

She could pursue her wedding in St Lucia and suffer the consequences, thereby affecting Shane's future, or she could

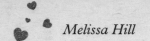

err on the side of caution and reason and have a proper, sophisticated wedding here in Ireland.

At that moment Gene walked into the library, holding a snifter of brandy in his hand. He swirled the amber liquid in the glass.

'You look like the cat that ate the canary,' he said, noticing the satisfied look on his wife's face. 'Do you really think this will work?' He sat down in the velvet-upholstered chair on the opposite side of the desk.

'Of course it will work. Only a fool would refuse and despite the current silliness, Cara is no fool. Besides, she wouldn't just be affecting herself, but Shane too.'

'What if Shane isn't concerned about that though?'

Lauren raised her eyebrows. 'Come on Gene. As cool as Shane plays it most of the time, and as unimpressed as he pretends to be by money and standing, he was completely concerned about it this morning. There's no denying that.'

Gene looked slightly uncomfortable, his conscience getting the better of him. 'Do you really think this is the best option, dear? What if it backfires and they want nothing to do with us? What if they are fine with cutting us out completely?' He set down his glass. 'Or worse, what if this causes them to argue and call everything off? In proceeding with this, aren't we denying our son his happiness?'

'Of course not. If anything, we are providing them with even greater happiness. Who in their right mind would pass up what we're offering?'

Gene shook his head. 'I don't think Cara is materialistic though. Neither is Shane.'

'Materialism and good sense are two completely separate things,' Lauren stated in a no-nonsense tone. 'Personally, I think the choice is simple.'

Gene ran a hand through his hair and considered the

situation, wondering if what they were proposing was perhaps too drastic. It was just a wedding at the end of the day. Still, he understood only too well what was at stake and how things worked in this country.

He looked at his wife and watched as she reread the document for at least the hundredth time since his good friend, Jarlath O'Connor, a contract lawyer, had sent it over. He had to appreciate the way her mind worked. It's too bad his wife had never gone into business in her own right; she would have made a killing – she was ruthless in her deter-mination to get what she wanted.

That same tenacity was what would undoubtedly get them out of their current bind. You couldn't navigate the Irish property circuit without a thick skin and an ulterior motive.

Lauren looked up to find Gene watching her. 'You aren't looking to reconsider, I hope?'

He jumped a little, startled by the warning in her tone. 'No, of course not.'

'Good.' Lauren smiled. She wondered if Shane had told Cara about the document yet. And if so, how did she take the news?

'Are you going to wait for Shane to tell Cara about our conversation?'

'No. I really don't care who tells her. In fact, I'm willing to bet that he's keeping this to himself at the moment, while he considers his options.'

Gene felt the guilt rise afresh in the pit of his stomach.

'Regardless,' Lauren continued. 'I am paying Cara Clancy a little visit soon. She and I are going to have a nice little mother- to daughter-in-law chat.' She smiled. 'And I have absolutely no doubt that we'll both be on the same page very soon.'

★   ★   ★

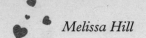 *Melissa Hill*

'Honey, I'm home!'

Shane looked up from the couch in the living room where he had been working on his laptop. Cara smiled at him and stumbled slightly as she closed the distance between the front door and where he sat.

Looks like she had a good day, Shane thought. She was glowing and smiling and looked genuinely happy. That was good, because he had had a somewhat less than stellar afternoon. But how to explain it all to Cara? He tried to push the thought away, at least for the time being.

'Good day?' he asked, trying to arrange his face into an easy-going expression.

Cara climbed on to the couch next to him and pushed his laptop aside. It was clear that she had had a couple of drinks while out wedding dress shopping.

She wrapped her arms around his neck and planted kisses along his jawline, making her way to his lips. 'I found it,' she whispered. 'A dress, *the* dress. It's really going to happen. I'm officially going to be a bride.'

She kissed him hard on the mouth, and ran her hands gently down his chest, Then her mouth moved to his neck. His lips found her mouth and she responded with more passion and need. Shane's hands worked the buttons on Cara's blouse, undoing them, removing the garment and throwing it to the floor while Cara took the more direct route of pulling Shane's T-shirt over his head, exposing his bare chest.

Cara shivered as his hands cupped her breasts and removed her bra. Then she pulled him on top of her on the couch.

'You know,' Shane teased, as he kissed her breasts and moved to her stomach, his hands skilfully undoing the buttons on her jeans, 'if you keep this up, I'm not sure you'll be able to wear white on our wedding day.'

'Way too late for that,' breathed Cara, moaning with anticipation as she arched her back.

Shane easily moved out of his jeans and pulled Cara up from the couch, her legs encircling his waist. He carried her from the living room to their bedroom where he collapsed on top of her on their bed.

She cried out as they began to make love with familiar and passionate movements, fully aware of what aroused and pleased the other, bringing each other to climax as a thin sheen of sweat covered their bodies.

Afterwards, lying in each other's arms, Shane traced a lazy circle across Cara's stomach. 'You know, I should send you shopping for wedding dresses more often. Gets you all hot and bothered. I like it.'

She smiled drowsily, some of the merry buzz from before wearing off a little. She felt warm and relaxed next to Shane. 'Yep, tulle and sequins really do it for me.'

Shane moved briefly to pull the duvet that had been cast aside up and over them. He cuddled down next to her once again. 'So did you find what you wanted? Are you happy?'

'Oh yes,' nodded Cara as she closed her eyes. 'It's perfect. I can't wait. It is just so perfect for what we've planned. I can already feel the sun on my skin and the sand between my toes.'

Shane stroked her hair, wondering if he should mention the conversation he'd had earlier that day. A conversation that he would rather not think about, truth be told. Still, he knew he had to talk about it with her. He just didn't know what their next course of action should be.

No, he thought as he watched his fiancée's contented face, *she's had a good day, she is happy, no need to add all this to it now.*

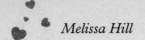

Cara looked to be drifting off to sleep. He studied her face and relished the peace that he found there; there were no lines, her forehead was smooth and unfettered by worry. He wondered how much longer that would last.

A pang entered his heart. His parents were important to him too, and if he was being honest, he wasn't altogether comfortable with the terms they were presenting. He couldn't deny that, but at the same time, how could he negotiate the problem he was faced with without either cutting his parents out of his life and drastically affecting his future or, worse, possibly losing Cara?

Unlike his fiancée, sleep wasn't going to come easily for Shane that night.

Chapter 24

'It's all so exciting. I've found an incredible dress, as well as the bridesmaid dresses, and they are just *awesome*. It looks like it all might just come together,' Cara told Conor happily on Monday morning.

After the wedding dress shopping, she had been in a great mood all weekend. She had slept fantastically every night and felt buoyed by her mother and Heidi's new-found positivity. The only snag was that now *Shane* seemed slightly on edge, and when Cara queried why, he'd shrugged and told her that he just had a lot on his mind with regard to work.

'And all your sisters have agreed to be bridesmaids?' asked Conor, who was sitting across from her sipping his coffee.

'Yep. Of course Kim said yes immediately, Heidi agreed to it the other day and Danielle's on board too, which is fantastic. Maybe all of my worries were over nothing.' She looked at her boss. 'Now all we need is for Shane's parents to come round and we'll be good to go.'

'Delighted it's all working out for you,' Conor said, before adding mischievously, 'Now is there any chance we could get some work done today?'

'I know, I'm sorry, I'll shut up.' Cara smiled guiltily. Conor was right; she'd been completely distracted lately, and she was hugely appreciative of him putting up with her. 'About that – look I know I've been a bit preoccupied lately, and I appreciate you not taking it out on me – or firing me even.'

Conor snorted. 'Fire my best employee?'

'Ah, don't you mean your only employee?' Cara laughed. 'Seriously though, I do appreciate it.'

'Hey, don't mention it. Besides, I understand that these things take up a lot of mental energy – for girls at least,' he added with a wink, and Cara made a face at him. 'Honestly it's no big deal. I'm just glad everything's working out for you guys, and that you're in a better mood these days. You don't deserve to have people on your back, harassing you like that. Although, if it kept up for much longer, I was thinking I was going to have to take matters into my own hands.'

'Er . . . how?' she asked playing along.

'Well, I'd have to give that spoilt sister of yours a good kick up the arse for one. And have a word in your dad's ear for turning his nose up at a trip to a fancy Caribbean island for another. Failing that, I was planning to challenge Shane to a duel for your honour, pistols at dawn, that kind of thing.'

Cara felt touched at the prospect of Conor standing up for her. He really was a great guy. It was a shame he wouldn't settle down; he would make some lucky girl very happy.

Then she was reminded of something. 'Conor, with all that was going on I can't believe I forgot to mention it before, but Shane and I would both love it if you would consider coming to along to the wedding. I mean, I know there would be a travel expense and everything, but if you'd like to come along, it would be great to have you there . . .'

In truth, Shane wasn't actually as keen about this as Cara was, but Conor had been so good to her all these years that she couldn't imagine *not* having him there.

'Actually, I had already assumed I was on the guest list,' he said, guffawing. 'And hey who cares about the expense – with all the nutters in your family, I couldn't pass up the chance of missing all the entertainment!'

Cara grimaced. 'Oh stop it. My new mantra from now on is "keep it drama-free". Whatever happens, it's all laid-back wedding planning from now on.'

'Well, I think that's a good theory,' Conor replied, but the conversation was interrupted by the bell at the front office door signalling that someone had entered.

They both turned to look, and Conor immediately moved from his perch on the end of Cara's desk to greet the woman who had just entered their office.

'Hello there; is there something I can help you with?' he asked pleasantly, and Cara could tell by his tone that he was immediately taken by the well-dressed, attractive older lady.

Unfortunately, this particular member of the female species was *way* out of his league.

'Lauren. What are you doing here?' she asked, slightly taken aback to see her future mother-in-law here. 'How are you?'

Conor took a step back as Cara came forward to greet Lauren. 'This is Shane's mum Lauren. Lauren, meet my boss, Conor Dempsey,' Cara said, making the introductions.

'Hello my dear,' Lauren replied, hesitantly accepting Cara's hug. Then she turned her cool gaze on Conor. 'Nice to make your acquaintance, Mr Dempsey.' She held her hand out formally without making any effort to close the space between herself and Conor, and he seemed to take this as his cue to move forward and participate in the formality, obviously unsure if she expected a handshake or for him to kiss her hand.

'Mrs Richardson, nice to meet you in person. I have heard all about you,' Conor said, all manners. Cara was impressed at his poker face. Yep, he'd heard plenty about Lauren recently, very little of it good.

'So Lauren, what brings you to this neck of the woods?'

asked Cara evenly, wondering about the purpose of the surprise visit.

Could it be that Shane's parents had also come to their senses about the wedding, and she was here to offer an olive branch? 'Did Shane tell you I found my dress at the weekend? And the bridesmaid dresses, too.' Cara was aware she was babbling, something she typically did when she was nervous. 'All very exciting. I'd love to show you if you'd like to see it before the wedding. Of course, you can't breathe a word about it to Shane,' she added, smiling, 'as it all still needs to be a surprise. Really, wait till you see it; it's going to be just perfect . . .'

Lauren smiled tightly and looked around the office, which was one big open space. Her glance rested on a door towards the back of the room.

'Yes, about that. Is there somewhere private we can talk?'

Cara's smile faded slightly and she looked at Conor, who cleared his throat.

'Why don't you take the back office, Cara? I'll hold the fort here. Just call if you need anything, OK?'

'Thanks.' Cara nodded and looked back at Shane's mother. 'Of course, Lauren, why don't you follow me?'

A tinge of worry entered her voice; she sensed that something else was up, and that this wasn't a conciliatory visit. Notwithstanding the fact that conciliatory was a dirty word when it came to Lauren Richardson. Leading her through to the small office in the back, she held open the door as Lauren regally entered the small space, making a full assessment.

Cara tried to see the office through the other woman's eyes. As she and Conor both usually worked side by side out front, this office was only used for client meetings. Truth be told, her boss wasn't the most organised person, and piles of paper and office files covered the majority of the desk space, the chairs and the floor. Lauren looked around, clearly wondering where she should sit amidst the mess.

Cara closed the door and realised that her future mother-in-law seemed to be expecting her to clear some space for her to sit. She duly grabbed a bunch of files and magazines off one of the two chairs, moving the pile from one place to another. She thought to herself that she would have to move it back after Lauren left. Somehow, Conor operated very well in his organised chaos and no doubt he knew exactly what that pile contained.

'There you go, sorry about that. Conor's sort of an artsy type,' she offered with a weak smile, but Lauren looked more repulsed than amused.

Cara's smile faded as she went about moving more paper and clearing a space so she could sit too. She could feel Lauren's eyes boring a hole in her back.

She had definitely gotten the vibe that this visit wasn't to be used as an exchange of pleasantries. Lauren's manner was all business.

As it was, her future mother-in-law wasted no time in getting down to the purpose of her visit.

'I came here today to discuss the wedding with you,' she said.

Cara's eyebrows rose and she smiled hopefully. OK. Maybe she had been right; maybe Lauren and Gene were indeed coming round and wanted to get involved in the details?

Lauren reached into her large Chanel bag and pulled out some papers. They looked formal, like something a solicitor's office would draw up.

'Cara,' she said, holding them out, 'I have with me today some papers that require your signature, and I believe that what I'm presenting will once and for all dismiss this ridiculous and crass notion of yours for a beach wedding.'

Cara furrowed her brow, taking the papers hesitantly. 'Excuse me?'

Lauren stared at her icily. 'It's quite simple really. Consider it a prenuptial agreement, one that has some extended terms to assist in your compliance.'

What the hell was this? And more to the point, did Shane know about it?

'Lauren . . . what? I don't understand. A prenup?'

Lauren motioned to the documents, which Cara was holding with trembling hands. 'It's all there. I believe the terms are quite simply laid out in language that is easy to understand. Why don't you go ahead and read it.'

Cara continued to stare at her as if she made no sense. *A prenup? Was this some kind of joke?*

'Go ahead, read it,' commanded Lauren.

Cara did as she was told and moved her gaze to the document at the top of the pile. She started to read, her brain trying to make sense of the many legal terms. As she continued to read, she felt her vision gradually begin to blur and her breathing become ragged and uneven.

The agreement was twofold, addressing both Cara and Shane.

If she and Shane went ahead with the wedding in St Lucia and refused to sign the agreement, Cara would be cut off from all Richardson money in the event that a divorce occurred in the future.

She would not be entitled to maintenance or any form of child support for any children that the marriage produced. This document would also trump any agreements previously set forth or considered in the future between Cara and Shane. Furthermore, if Cara decided that the beach wedding was the route she would take, she would not only be dictating her own future, but she would also be affecting Shane, as he would be cut off from the estate and written out of his parents' will entirely.

However, on the other hand, should Cara see 'reason' and go along with what Lauren and Gene wanted for their wedding, the couple would receive a substantial lump sum contribution towards their marriage, and an additional lump sum for every year married thereafter.

If a divorce should occur in the future, Cara would be taken care of, any children would be provided for, and Shane's inheritance would remain unaffected.

She came to the end of the document and saw that there was only room for one signature: hers. She rustled the stiff papers, going back to the beginning and reading through the document again, trying to digest just what was happening.

Surely this document didn't mean what she thought it meant?

Cara raised her eyes and met Lauren's. She willed herself to stay strong, but it was hard, especially when she considered the decidedly unfriendly face before her.

'Lauren, I don't understand. What is all this?'

Lauren's expression resembled that of a jackal that had just successfully cornered its prey. She smiled tightly, feeling triumph in Cara's obvious undoing.

'Oh I think it is quite simple really, even to someone like yourself. This is the way things are done in our family. Marriage, and all that it entails, is a contract, not only between two people, but between their families, in this case namely the Richardsons. Please be aware that our family name has much to lose if this marriage should go south, so to speak. However, we also believe that we have much to lose if it starts off on the wrong footing, namely with this absurd

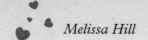

notion of a beach wedding. It is simply not going to happen, Cara. Surely you understand that now.'

Cara looked back at the document. Yes, she understood. She understood that her future in-laws were making an attempt to purchase her, and more deviously, any decision she made would also directly impact Shane's future, whether he was with her or not. She felt tears prick at the corners of her eyes.

She would not cry, not in front of Lauren, she thought to herself, steeling her posture as she returned her attention to the older woman.

'I'm sorry but this is complete and utter rubbish,' she said tersely. She wanted to be strong, she wanted to be brave and call Lauren out on her attempt to intimidate her, but the fact was she *was* intimidated. Still, she wasn't going to just sit there and say nothing. 'There is no way Shane is ever going to go along with this. Wait until I tell him what you are trying to do—'

'He already knows,' said Lauren, idly studying her manicure. 'We explained everything to him at the weekend. I'm surprised that he hasn't already discussed this with you actually; I would have thought it would have been foremost on his mind.'

At the weekend . . . Cara thought back. On Saturday evening, she had been so happy, so buzzed when she walked in the door after shopping for her wedding dress that she hadn't noticed anything off about Shane's mood or behaviour then. But she recalled his somewhat tense demeanour throughout the remainder of the weekend. Had he been telling the truth? she wondered as she thought about the excuses he'd made. *Had* he been stressed about work? Or was it about this? What did he think about it? And more to the point, Cara realised worriedly, why hadn't he told her?

She shifted her attention back to Lauren. 'I see . . .' She

was almost at a loss for words. Why wouldn't Shane have told her about this and why would he let her be blindsided by it? 'I'm sure he must be furious. I can't even imagine what he is going to do when I tell him that you came here and shoved this in my face.' Cara wanted to tear the papers up, wanted to set them on fire and then put the ashes through the shredder. She wanted to throw them on the ground and stomp on them until they disintegrated. She wanted to show Lauren just what she thought of her.

However, the other woman looked completely unfazed by Cara's obvious distress.

'Oh, if I know my son, he is probably going to advise you to sign the papers and then figure out a date for a wedding at the Club,' she replied smugly.

'No, you are wrong. I cannot be bought, and neither can Shane. We don't want your money, it doesn't mean anything to us,' Cara said with a conviction she didn't feel. About Shane at least, given that he hadn't taken it upon himself to give her the heads-up about this 'agreement'. Deal with the devil, more like, Cara thought darkly. 'I don't want it and I don't need it. I'm not for sale.'

'Well, that's all well and good, but what about Shane?'

She considered the question. Indeed, she didn't want a cent of the Richardsons' money, but if she was reading this contract right, whatever she decided not only affected her, but also affected Shane.

No, she reassured herself. Money wasn't important to Shane. He always said he didn't care a fig about his parents' money or their perceived status, that it was all just materialistic fluff. But, did he mean it? After all, this document said that she would be cut off, as well as any children that might come of the marriage, but Shane would be cut off entirely too even if the marriage ended.

Had Shane been telling her how he really felt? Cara wondered now. Or was he just posturing? Would he be upset if his parents followed through on their threat and cut him off from the family money for good?

Lauren seemed to be studying Cara's face, as if she knew exactly what was going through her head and could read every thought as it occurred. She smiled.

'What's wrong dear?' she asked tartly. 'Are you wondering if Shane might have been talking for talk's sake when it comes to how much he cares about his inheritance or family money? Thinking now that it might mean a little bit more than he lets on?' She rolled her eyes. 'The only people who say they don't care about money and that money doesn't buy happiness and all that dreary nonsense are the very ones who've have never had much of it. Shane knows better. Money is security, money is peace of mind. He is likely not only considering his future, but yours too.'

Cara wanted to close her ears. She knew what Lauren was trying to do. She was trying to plant the seeds of doubt in her brain, trying to turn Shane against her. But it wasn't going to work; Shane would never go for this.

Would he? Cara felt her confidence wilt from within.

But what if he did? What if he played into his mother's hands? What if he insisted that they keep the wedding here and have it at the K-Club or wherever his parents wanted them to have it? What would that mean for their relationship?

No, she wasn't going to be bullied, Cara decided. She wouldn't have it. Neither would Shane, there was no way.

'Lauren, you obviously don't know your son. He has refused your money before and I'd be willing to bet he is going to do it again—'

'A bet?' Lauren smiled, cutting Cara off again. 'What would

you like to wager? A wedding?' she said, her tone frighteningly enthusiastic.

Cara felt her stomach turn to jelly, but she pushed on. 'No Lauren. I'm going to prove to you that you are wrong. We are not signing this . . . document.'

'No, you are right, Cara. You and Shane are not going to be signing anything. You are. You and you alone,' Lauren clarified. 'Now really, I don't understand all the fuss. Gene and I are making you a very generous offer. Something that you should be happy about. What better wedding present could anyone possibly ask for than financial security? Really, all we are asking is that you hold the wedding on our terms. After all, you said it yourself, it's just one day. How bad could a beautiful wedding laid on by your very gracious in-laws be?' Lauren tried to smile sweetly, but Cara wasn't fooled. She had done exactly what she had come to do. There was an ulterior motive here, and Cara wasn't so sure that Lauren wanted there to be a wedding at all. If she was reading this right, it seemed like she would actually prefer it if she and Shane broke up.

Cara took a deep breath. 'Lauren, it's time for you to leave. And you can take this with you.' She flung the contract at her with such force that it accidentally ended up on the floor. Lauren's eyes followed it as she stood, but she didn't make a move to reach for it.

'Yes, you are probably right Cara. I am late for a luncheon with friends. As for that,' she said, waving her hand in the contract's direction, 'I'll leave that with you. I'd imagine you'll want to reread it. Preferably with Shane. In fact, I'm sure that you two have *much* to discuss together.'

Cara felt her cheeks burning and she turned her head, refusing to meet Lauren's sharp gaze.

'I enjoyed our chat, and I'll be so eager to hear what is

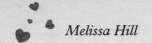

decided. I'm sure we can come to a mutually beneficial conclusion, aren't you? Goodbye, dear.'

When Cara looked up, all that was left of Lauren was the smell of her Chanel No. 5 perfume. That and the legal document on the floor, of course.

Reluctantly, she leaned forward and picked it up. She looked at the signature line. The lone signature line. Her decision. It was all on her. Her future, Shane's future. Now that she was alone, she allowed the tears to flow in earnest and she pushed the contract away as she buried her face in her hands, sobbing openly.

'Cara? What was that all about?' Conor rushed into the office and spotted her as she broke down. 'Hey, hey, are you OK? Cara? Talk to me.' He kneeled at her side and stroked her hair as she sobbed in frustration. 'Come on, whatever she did, it'll be OK, there's no need to cry.'

Cara shook her head and allowed herself to be held. Conor's embrace was soft and massively comforting. 'She hates me, she honestly must hate me. What did I ever do to her? Why is she doing this?'

Conor shook his head, thoroughly confused. 'What did she do, Cara? Please, let me help you.'

She cast the document in his direction. 'This, she brought me this. She wants me to sign it.'

Conor took the document as he got to his feet and sat back in the chair that had been vacated by Lauren only moments earlier. 'What is this?' he asked as his eyes began to scan the document. As the words began to sink in, Cara watched his face grow red with anger. 'What the hell is she playing at?'

Cara shook her head. 'It's horrible. She wants to buy me off. I feel so cheap and . . . dirty.'

'Well,' Conor said with resolution. 'You are neither, and

this is complete bullshit. You know it is. There is no way Shane is going to stand for this once you tell him. He's just going to have to put his parents in their place and tell them to take a running jump.'

Cara ran her hand through her hair. She grabbed a tissue from the box on the desk and blew her nose. 'That's just the thing. He already knows about it. They told him at the weekend apparently.'

'And he didn't mention it to you?' Conor questioned, obviously trying to put all the pieces together.

Cara shook her head. 'Not a word. Nothing. Why wouldn't he talk to me about this Conor?'

'He probably just didn't know how to tell you,' Conor assured her, but she could tell that he was wondering the very same thing. 'No doubt he was just as shocked as you are now. He probably didn't expect his mother to come here and tell you herself either.'

Cara shook her head. 'Perhaps. But Conor, what if he just didn't know how to tell me that he wanted me to sign it?' she offered, placing her worst fears on the table. 'If Shane wants me to sign it, it means he is scared about a future without the money, regardless of whether we stay together. In fact, I almost feel like the money is the primary thing here. I don't care anything about it. But if I go ahead with St Lucia, I am essentially cutting him off from his parents. How can I do that?'

She launched into another round of crying, this time out of frustration and confusion. Conor approached her and pulled her up from the chair, again putting his arms around her and letting her cry into his shirt.

'Hey, hey, now come on. It will all be all right. It's OK. You and Shane will talk about this and sort it all out. Come on,' he soothed. 'You guys are a team.'

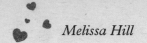

But Cara didn't feel so sure about that any more. Team members worked together after all. They didn't keep secrets from each other.

'Why don't you call it a day?' her boss suggested kindly. 'Go home and take it easy for a while so you're in a better frame of mind when Shane comes home from work, and then you can sort everything out with a clearer head.'

'But I have to work,' Cara said, pulling away and wiping her eyes, to no avail. There was no way the streams of runny mascara were going to come off with anything less than a good scrubbing. 'I'm already behind as it is and—'

'Right, and after this, I'm sure it will be a highly productive day,' Conor said wryly, trying to coax a smile from her. It worked. 'Honestly, Cara, go home. Calm down, wait for Shane to get there and have a good, long talk with him about it. I'm sure he is not going to be happy that his mother came here.'

Cara agreed that Shane would definitely not be happy, but she wondered if his annoyance would be about the way in which the document had been delivered, or the contract itself and the terms it demanded.

Chapter 25

Oh hell, Danielle thought, reading Cara's latest email, *my measurements? For a bridesmaid dress?*

She thought back to the last time she'd had to wear a bridesmaid dress and realised that it had to have been at least ten years – at an old colleague's wedding in Tampa. The dress had been a horrendous, baby-pink taffeta monstrosity. Hopefully Cara had better taste. She tentatively opened the attachment to the email – a picture of the dress in question – and nodded her approval.

'OK, not too bad, actually not bad at all,' she murmured softly as she examined the cute gold coloured Empire-line dress. While she wasn't overly fond of that particular look on its own, feeling that it was an all too convenient way for women to hide their tummies or round-the-middle bulge, she knew that Cara was considering the burgeoning waistlines of her other bridesmaids Kim and Heidi. 'It could be worse, and at least my boobs will look great,' said Danielle to herself matter-of-factly, gradually resigning herself to bridesmaid duty.

Despite being the oldest bridesmaid, she guessed that she'd look much hotter than the other two. Although Kim was a stunner, that was for sure. With her looks and famed devil-may-care attitude, Danielle got the feeling her sister-in-law would be pretty good at rocking the 'yummy mummy' look. As for Heidi, she couldn't be sure as she hadn't seen her in years.

And on that note, Danielle mused, it was time to schedule a chemical peel and a fresh round of Botox. She needed to make sure that everyone at that wedding would be impressed by her good looks and youthful appearance.

She read through the rest of Cara's email, which outlined what details the bridal store needed for the dress. She went into the kitchen and rummaged through a drawer for the tape measure she knew was in there somewhere. Finding it, she went to quick work measuring her bust, waist and hips. Pleased with the numbers, she worked out the conversion from an American size chart to the European equivalent.

Right at that moment Zack walked into the room. Danielle hurried to close the email and reduce the window on the computer screen, but too late – Zack had definitely seen something. Her fingers trembled as they moved across the keyboard.

'What are you up to?' Zack asked as he leaned down to kiss her neck. She felt his gaze turn towards the computer screen and wondered how much he had seen.

'Oh, nothing, just doing some online shopping.' She smiled, trying to turn round in her chair to divert his attention back to her face.

'What were you shopping for?' he inquired. Zack was sharp; very little got past him.

'Just a new outfit,' she said simply. It wasn't a lie, and Danielle hoped that he wouldn't ask to see it onscreen. 'More to the point, what are you up to?' she cooed coquettishly, in an effort to change the subject.

Zack chuckled as she stood up and encircled her in his arms. 'Hmm . . . what are you trying to hide?' he cooed. 'Someone sounds awfully guilty about what they were just doing. Spending some serious money were we?'

She giggled. 'Oh stop it.' Danielle never usually hid any

of her shopping habits; in fact, she was usually quite open about them, believing that her ability to indulge was a merely another testament to her success. She enjoyed showing off her Gucci watch, Balenciaga handbag, Manolo Blahnik shoes, or whichever other luxury items she'd recently procured. So it was understandable that Zack was going to be suspicious about her suddenly secretive behaviour.

'Is there a special occasion coming up I don't know about?' he asked, raising his eyebrows.

Sensing her opening, she smiled seductively. 'Well, I don't know . . . is there? And if there is, why would you want me to spoil the surprise?' She leaned forward and kissed him hard on the mouth.

'Interesting,' he said a smile in his voice. 'So is this an outfit to be worn inside or outside?'

'I guess that depends on how you look at it,' Danielle purred, pleased that she was able to divert his attention so easily.

'Maybe I could get a preview? Or at least help you with your measurements?' he offered, his words full of innuendo.

'Sounds like a plan. Why don't I meet you in the bedroom? Go and make yourself comfortable, while I tie up a few loose ends here.' She started to undo her blouse one button at a time, exposing a lacy and expensive purple La Perla bra underneath.

Zack's breath grew heavy. 'Don't keep me waiting long,' he said as he backed away in the direction of the bedroom. 'I have a meeting in an hour.'

While she would normally have been miffed if Zack had told her he was looking for a quickie before a business meeting, at the moment the only thing that Danielle could focus on was getting him to move in the opposite direction of her computer. And ensure that he was no longer interested in what she had been doing just moments before.

When he disappeared from view, she turned round quickly. Opening the laptop screen once more, she quickly typed in her measurements in a return email to Cara, offering to pay for the dress and saying that she would send her credit card information later, and pressed 'Send.' Then, she made sure to delete the email from her sent folder, as well as getting rid of the picture file of the dress.

Of course, now she would have to remember to order some sexy lingerie later in order to mesh with the story that Zack had just enabled her to create. She made a quick note, scribbling the words 'Agent Provocateur' on a sticky note and placing it on her monitor screen. If Zack wanted something saucy, she would give him something saucy.

She turned from the computer desk and composed herself. Momentarily switching her thoughts from the bridesmaid dress, Cara's wedding and all the anxiety that it was causing, she worked quickly to focus on Zack and get herself in the mood for a quick roll between the sheets.

Trying to push her worries from her mind, Danielle tried not to think about the extent that she was willing to go to, to keep her secrets secret.

Cara lay in darkness in the bedroom of her and Shane's apartment. She had a throbbing headache, which she guessed was from crying, and possibly dehydration due to the several glasses of wine she'd drunk when she got home just after lunchtime. She watched as the numbers on the digital clock blinked to 5.30 p.m. Shane would be getting home soon.

She had left work as Conor instructed; not that she was overly sure what to do with herself for the few more hours until Shane returned. She wasn't sure what to say to him on the phone so had switched her mobile off in case he called. This was definitely a conversation that needed to be had in person.

In the meantime, she had also phoned Kim to tell her what had happened. As expected, her sister-in-law had expressed outrage in all the right places, but still encouraged Cara not to jump to any conclusions until all was properly discussed with Shane.

Cara had been lying flat in one position for hours, thinking about what she was going to say and gauging her response to Shane's take on matters. Not that she had made much headway in that department, because her mind was swimming in an ocean of confusion.

Why hadn't he told her about this? Was it true that he was just unsure about how to broach the subject with her? Or was he having second thoughts about the plans they'd made, now that the die had been cast by his devious mother?

She hated thinking negatively, but it was unavoidable.

Now she just wanted to talk to Shane, find out what he was thinking and try to get some closure on this, one way or the other. She wondered though what she would do if he wanted her to sign that poisonous agreement.

She took a deep breath. She would worry about that later.

Time passed and she watched the light turn dusky outside her bedroom window. She knew she would hear the door open soon and her heart beat faster in anticipation and worry. Her mouth felt dry and she wiped her clammy palms on the duvet beneath her. She wished that she could just fast-forward through all this and see how everything would turn out without actually having to have what would undoubtedly be a difficult conversation.

A few minutes later Cara heard the front door open and she snapped to attention. Shane was sure to know she was home. Her car was parked out front and her briefcase and handbag were on the chair by the front door.

She listened as he went through the motions of putting down his laptop case and hanging up his coat. She heard him switch on a lamp in the dark front room and watched as the hallway was flooded with light. She stared at the door, hearing his footsteps move slowly and cautiously down the hallway towards their bedroom. Her stomach began to churn with anxiety and she swallowed hard, preparing herself for what she would say first.

Either he thought she was sleeping and didn't want to wake her, or he knew he was walking into a big pile of trouble, she thought to herself.

A moment later, her fiancé's silhouette appeared in the doorway. He knocked on the doorframe softly, as if he didn't want to disturb her if he could prevent it. 'Cara? Honey? Are you sleeping?'

She took a breath and paused, steeling herself and trying to prevent her voice from cracking. It was true she felt all cried out but there was always a chance that the floodgates could open again. Her eyes still burned from her previous crying bout and her body ached as if she was about to come down with a bad case of flu.

'No,' she said softly. 'I'm not sleeping. I need to talk to you.' She sat up against the headboard.

He stood still in the doorway as if trying to gauge what was happening. Cara guessed he had to know what this conversation was to be about. The tension in the room was palpable.

'Was there something you forgot to tell me after seeing your parents at the weekend?' Cara asked, her tone hollow. She flipped on the lamp next to the bed, making Shane fully aware of her tear-stained face and puffy eyes. 'Your mother called in to the office today to say hello. And she brought me this.' She tossed the legal document in his general direction. 'Apparently though, I don't have to tell you what it's all about, seeing as you already know. Don't you?'

'Dammit,' Shane muttered. 'Damn her.' Clearly he was talking about his mother.

'Yes Shane, damn her. Damn your mother for her interference and her insensitivity. Damn her for everything. However, that's neither here nor there. Just what do you think about this? I need to know,' she said, her tone clearly illustrating her hurt feelings and her anger at the actions of his family.

'I should have told you. Of course I should. But you were so excited about finding the dress . . .' Shane took a few tentative steps into the room and approached the edge of the bed. He picked up the document from the floor; it had taken on a crumpled look from all the handling it had had throughout the day. Cara didn't care; she would have blown her nose with it – or worse – if she could. 'Can I?' he asked, looking for permission to sit. She moved her legs slightly to allow him room.

'So? Your thoughts?' she urged again.

'It's complete bullshit—'

'Well I know that,' she said, her hackles rising slightly. 'But I'm not asking for an assessment of the situation. I am asking just what you think we should do about it?' She knew she was dangerously close to crying again, but Shane's delaying was driving her crazy. She felt her heart pounding wildly in her chest and she wished she could throw something, break something just to curb the feelings she was experiencing.

'Just hold on honey,' Shane offered, putting his hands out in supplication. 'Let me speak. I know you are mad. I was furious too, I am still furious.'

Cara crossed her arms over her chest. 'Well. If you were, you hid it well.'

He shook his head. 'The two of them blindsided me with this the other day, same way I guess my mother blindsided you earlier. I am sorry about that, she was completely out of line and she had no right to do that. But I hope that you can see through it too. She is trying to turn us against each other, trying to instigate a divide.'

'Well of course, I would have to be stupid not to see that, but it doesn't answer my question. Just what do you want me to do about this? Do you want me to sign it?'

Shane took a deep breath and lowered his eyes, his gaze resting on the floor. She waited for an answer, for an indication of what he thought, for anything, but it didn't come.

'Shane?' she urged, concern in her voice. 'Tell me what you are thinking?'

He sighed heavily again and finally met her gaze. The turmoil in his expression indicated the internal war that was waging in him. 'I don't know, Cara,' he said simply.

His answer made her heart drop to her stomach. 'What do you mean you don't know?'

Shane threw up his hands, running them through his hair. 'I mean, I don't know. I just don't goddamn know!'

Cara jumped. Her worst fears were coming true. Shane rarely raised his voice, or lost his temper. Oh God, this was all such a disaster . . .

Seeing the shock on Cara's face, Shane reached out for her.

'I'm sorry. I'm sorry,' he pleaded. 'I didn't mean to shout. I'm just so frustrated. I'm mad at my parents, not you. There is just a lot to consider here. There isn't an easy answer.'

She stared at him, gradually coming to an understanding of what this all meant. 'There is an easy answer, Shane. We just tell your parents to stuff their agreement. But you want me to sign it, don't you?'

'No, that's not what I'm saying, but . . . well, I just don't know what I am saying. I mean, I have been going over this in my head all weekend, looking for a way out of it, but my parents—'

'But you don't care about the money. You've always said it's not important. That's what you have always said,' she persisted, hoping against hope that he would agree with her.

He looked at her, and in that instant Cara knew. He was thinking about the money.

'So you lied to me,' she said sadly. 'Clearly money does matter.'

'No honey, it's not that. I mean, I don't care about the lump sum for the wedding present, or the yearly amount or anything like that. But—'

'You do care about your inheritance though,' she said simply.

'Cara, come on, you know me.'

'Do I though?' she countered. Things were starting to make sense now, but she decided to press on. She wanted clarification on another issue as well.

'Yes. Cara, come on. You know I don't care about all that society bullshit, but the inheritance – well it's twofold really. I get my trust when I am thirty-five and there's no denying that that would help you and me as we build a family, buy a bigger place—'

'But we can do all of that on our own. We're both hardworking intelligent career people, we don't need Mummy and Daddy's money . . .'

Shane looked guilty. 'There's other stuff,' he said solemnly in a tone that filled her with dread, because she knew it indicated that he'd been hiding something else. 'I made some investments with a view to the trust money, but this bloody recession and the turn the economy has taken, well, I've lost a fair bit. It's nothing serious, but if I can't rely on the trust money coming through . . .'

Cara stared at him, fully digesting what he was saying, understanding very well now that Shane had gambled on something on the back of his parents' money – something that he was now on the verge of losing.

Or worse, had already lost.

'I see.' She folded her hands in her lap.

'Cara. Honey, please.' He reached for her hands and she pulled them away.

'So what are you suggesting, Shane? What do you want me to do?'

He tried to avoid her gaze. 'I don't know. I mean, we've always said it ourselves, a wedding is just one day . . .'

She stared at him, hurt beyond belief. 'Yes, it is just one day, but it is *our* day. If I recall correctly, *that's* what we have always said. That's what we have been saying since the beginning. If we do this – go along with whatever your parents want – that won't be the case any more. We will have been bought and paid for. Your parents will own us, in more ways than one. They know that if they happen to disagree with anything else we do in the future, all they have to do is send another document our way that supersedes the last contract, and they have us. Under the thumb. We won't be our own people, not ever. We can't give in to them.' Shane looked miserable and she reached for his hand, hoping to convince him. 'And with regard to the investment, the market will turn around again, I'm sure of it. Whatever you've lost, we can make it back. We're young, it's a long way off until we retire; we don't have to worry about that.'

Shane was shaking his head and Cara stopped talking. 'Cara,

you don't understand. My parents are serious. We would be completely cut off. So would our kids, if we have them. That is a big deal—'

'Yes, but we would have each other. Like I said, we are both smart professionals and so far we haven't needed anyone or anything. My parents didn't have a trust fund or an inheritance and I'd like to think I turned out OK—'

'But say if something happened, in the future . . .'

Shane's comment surprised her. 'What do you mean?' But she already had an inkling of what he meant by that, and she was frightened of his response.

'Babe. Please. Neither of us is stupid, no one knows what the future holds.'

Divorce. Shane was thinking about their divorce. Before they even walked down the aisle. Who thought that way? Who had that on their mind before they even said 'I do'?

'So, we're not even married yet, but are already heading for divorce?'

'That's not what I meant.'

'It certainly sounded that way,' she replied, her eyes shining with tears. 'Who thinks like that? What's wrong with you Shane?'

'Look, plenty of people think like that in this day and age. And I'm not saying that is going to be us, I'm just trying to think about the what-if's, that's all.' His tone was gentle. 'Playing devil's advocate, I suppose.'

'Well, I'm trying to think about us planning our whole lives together, until death do us part. That's what's been on *my* mind. Not a back-up plan for when we get divorced. What do you care about more, Shane? You and me, creating a life for ourselves, or your intended financial security? Because I can tell you for certain that I'm thinking about us, not how *I* am going to survive on my own when we're finished. Unlike you, I have faith in us and I'm not so sure if you could say the same thing.'

'Of course I have faith in us—'

'Well, if you did, surely you would be just as confident as I am that we were going to get through life together, without your trust fund or your inheritance or anything else from your parents. But you are thinking in reverse. You're thinking about how you are going to get by either with me or by yourself.'

This was turning out horribly. Cara really wanted to throw up.

'Cara, no. That's not it, I'm just trying to look at things in a practical and sensible way—'

She shook her head. 'I don't want to hear it. It seems that the decision I was ready to make is not the one that you want me to make. I was going to rip this piece of paper up, throw it in the fireplace and torch it and then tell your parents that you and I don't come with a price tag. At least I thought we didn't.'

'Cara—'

'Don't "Cara" me, Shane. All throughout our relationship you've misled me, and not only that but you made me look like a fool in front of your mother today, me spouting nonsense about how money wasn't important to you, and that you'd soon tell her to where to stick her agreement. She clearly knows you better than I do,' she added, resignation in her voice. She couldn't believe that Shane was doing a hundred-and-eighty-degree turn about his attitude to money.

Now it seemed there was only one thing to say.

'You know Shane, there is one way that we can get round this entire situation. No more stress, no more worry.' Cara was surprised at the evenness in her tone; it was as if she was ordering a cup of tea.

'What's that?' Shane asked hopefully.

'Oh, I think you know.'

'I don't. Tell me, please. Honestly, if you can think of a way out of this—'

'We forget the wedding.'

'What?'

'You heard me. We call it off, you don't lose your inheritance and I don't become the one responsible for taking it all away.'

'You can't be serious,' Shane replied. The colour had drained from his face. Cara looked at him. Her heart was breaking and she felt as if she was in a dreamlike state, as if she was a third party in the room who was simply a casual observer, a fly on the wall to all that was happening.

She dropped her gaze to the floor. 'It's the only answer. Think about it. This engagement, all the wedding plans, have been a disaster from the very beginning. It's been nothing but refusals, and pushiness, and disapproval, and that was just from our families. And now this, from you. I really thought that you and I were on the same page. Of course, I was mad about this all day, and really very sad that your parents feel that they have to take this route with us, try to and buy us – buy me.' She sighed deeply. 'And while I can forgive you not telling me about the contract, I can't believe that you're even considering going along with it and giving in to their whims, their need to control things. This is becoming less and less about us, and what we want and value, and all about other people. Shane, I am not for sale. I am not going to budge on this. And it's not just about the wedding. It's about the principle.'

She raised her eyes to look at him. 'Maybe this is the universe's way of trying to tell us something,' she continued sadly. 'Maybe not getting married is the smartest decision.'

She loved Shane, so much, but she was also willing to face the fact that maybe this situation wasn't right, and they should just call it quits and move on.

'Cara, I love you—'

'I love you, too Shane. But I'm not sure if that's enough any more. Think about if we go through with this. What kind of future relationship will you have with your parents if you refuse them now? How will I ever feel comfortable around your mother? I doubt she's the forgiving type. She was so threatening today, you should have seen her. And then there's the money. I honestly don't think there is anything else I can say about that. You know how I feel about the subject. I don't want it. But it seems that you do.'

Shane opened his mouth to say something but Cara put up a hand and continued. 'Do I truly believe that you are as money-obsessed as your parents? No, I don't. But you are concerned enough about that investment you made that went south to put a value on the money you would be receiving in a few years' time. The rub is that you didn't tell me about it. That I am only finding out about this now. Why wouldn't you tell me something like that? I'm supposed to be your partner. Pretty soon, I'm supposed to be your wife – or *was* supposed to be,' she added, looking away. 'I just don't know why you would leave me out of stuff like this. It makes me wonder what else I don't know about.'

'Cara, I'm sorry, I should have said something, but I didn't think it was a big deal.'

'Only because you knew you had your parents' money behind you. But then this situation presented itself and you realised that of course I would have to be told.'

He shook his head. 'That makes me sound so devious – honestly, it wasn't like that.'

She bit her lip. 'In any case Shane, I can't be responsible

for making such a big decision. And I still want the St Lucian wedding – or I did.'

'Then we'll do it,' Shane said, sitting forward determinedly. 'We will tell my parents to just sod off.'

'And then we will be right back at square one,' she said, shaking her head. 'Worse, actually. Think of the long-term effects. If we had kids, would they ever know their grand-parents? And then of course, you are apparently worried about a divorce somewhere down the line. Shane, that is not how I work. When I said I'd marry you, as far as I was concerned I was making a lifelong commitment. To me, marriage means that we would be pledging ourselves to each other, and if problems presented themselves in the future, then we'd just work them out together, not head straight for the divorce courts.'

Her eyes started to water as she thought of the beautiful vision she'd had in her mind about how a life with Shane would be. It seemed so elusive now, something that wasn't hers and maybe had never been.

'Cara, this can't be it. I don't want this to be it. I don't want us to be over. I love you so much.' Shane's voice broke, a sob caught in his throat. 'I want you to be my wife. Please, honey. Please, let's just work this out.' He reached out to her and Cara allowed herself to be pulled in to his embrace.

She felt his warmth and breathed in his scent; everything about him was so familiar but now felt so foreign. She felt as if all truly was lost, and this was the end. She clung to him, as if she could stop time from moving forward, as if she needed to memorise everything about him because soon she would no longer have him in her life. She let the tears in her eyes spill forth and sobbed openly.

This is what heartbreak feels like, she thought. Every bone in her body wanted to forget about everything that had happened today, but the consequences weighed too heavily on her mind. She thought of the problems that would be caused if they just went ahead and did what they wanted. His parents had stripped them of that right, and she felt deep resentment flood through her body. If they got married, how on earth could she ever forgive his parents, his mother in particular? She would feel resentful of Lauren Richardson every day of her life. That wasn't healthy, she couldn't live that way.

Shane and Cara looked into each other's eyes. He kissed her, tenderly and slowly. He tried to appeal to her, show how much he needed her and wanted her, but Cara couldn't help but think that it felt like a goodbye kiss.

When the kiss ended, she pulled away slightly. She looked at her left hand and slowly removed her engagement ring.

'You should take this,' she said softly.

'Cara . . . no.'

'Shane, you know as well as I do that if we get married there are always going to be situations like this. One after another. I'm not trying to punish you, or make a statement, but I honestly don't know if I can live with your parents acting this way. Yes, I was marrying you, but I was marrying into your family, too.'

'Cara, I will tell my parents to mind their own business I swear—'

'We have tried that and look where it got us. I'm not prepared to live my entire life that way, Shane. There are no boundaries. I mean, I realise my family can be crazy, too, but they would never try to make us do what they want us to do through the means of a chequebook.'

She placed the ring in his hand but he shook his head.

'No, this is yours,' he insisted, although his tone seemed ever so slightly resigned that this was happening. That this was the new reality.

Cara sighed and bit her lip, fighting off a new round of tears.

'I'm going to go,' she said softly.

'No, no, I'll go,' Shane said, looking into her eyes, as if memorising every contour of her tear-stained face.

'Please really, I'm going to go to my mum's. You stay here. We'll – well I guess, we will work out everything later, what with cancelling St Lucia and everything,' she said, choking. She stood and looked around the room, the room in which, up to now, they had shared so many happy memories, and a stark realisation hit her. She and Shane weren't just cancelling the wedding; they were cancelling their life together.

There was so much to figure out. As a couple in love it seemed effortless to acquire things, to plan and weave your life together with the other person. So much harder to go about separating it all.

'I'll give you a cheque to cover my half of the lost deposit at the resort,' she offered sadly.

'Please, no,' Shane said. He held his head in his hands, his gaze firmly on the floor.

As Cara went round the room gathering clothes and fetching toiletries from the bathroom, Shane didn't make a sound. He couldn't watch her, feeling that that would make it all real. As it was, he pretended to himself that she was just packing to go on a trip, something temporary, something she would be returning from. But as each minute passed, it started to sink in that this was it, Cara was leaving, they were finished. Their relationship was over.

A thousand thoughts ran through his head. He considered getting on his knees, grabbing her legs and holding on to her, or blocking the door, refusing to let her leave. But he didn't.

When the moment came, she simply said, 'Shane?'

He looked up. She held a small suitcase and her handbag. She had washed her face, scrubbing the mascara off, leaving her skin red and raw.

'I'm going now,' she said. There was no malice, no anger. Just sadness. Regret.

'There's nothing that I can say that can make you stay. Is there?' he asked, hoping she would provide him with a solution to this problem.

Instead, she just shook her head.

'You know I love you,' he said, searching her face.

'I know, and I love you. But I don't think it's enough any more.' She turned towards the door.

'Cara?'

She turned around. 'Yes?'

'I'm sorry. I'm so sorry.'

'I know you are, Shane. So am I. I never would have thought that this would have happened to us,' she said. 'I would have never thought it in a million years.'

Chapter 26

The phone rang in his study, and somehow Gene Richardson knew that nothing good was to come from the call.

'Hello?' he answered warily.

There was a brief silence on the other end on the line. Finally, Shane spoke.

'I hope you are happy.'

'Shane? his father said, surprised by his son's tone. It comprised equal amounts of sadness, bitterness and vitriol. And all of those components were directed firmly at him.

'She left me.'

Gene felt something cold and hard sink down into his stomach. Without another word being said, he knew exactly what had happened and what his son was referring to.

'Cara?' he questioned dumbly. He liked Cara, always had.

'Yes, she left. Because of that despicable contract. Because of your interference. Thank you. Really, thank you, you have done such a good job. The wedding is off. Cara wouldn't sign it, but more to the point, she also wouldn't put me in a position where my relationship with you was ruined because of her. But really, she was wrong there, it didn't matter. Because our relationship is ruined anyway. I want you to know that. From now on, I want *nothing* to do with you or Mother.'

Gene had never been spoken to by his son in such a manner, and it disturbed him. He knew at that moment that he and Lauren had overplayed their hand. In their attempt to get their own way, they had set in chain a series of events that not only caused grief and hurt in Shane's life, but also very effectively turned their son against them. This was all their fault. They deserved this. Their interference had backfired on them spectacularly.

He should never have gone along with Lauren's idea. Of course he would have preferred to have his son get married here, in a big shindig at the K-Club and all that. But now there was no wedding, and he was lucky if he didn't lose – if he hadn't already lost – his only son for ever. Everything was falling to pieces.

'Son, I'm sorry,' he said weakly.

'I don't accept that. Why did you have to do this? Why couldn't you just leave it alone? I warned you not to interfere. I told you that this was about us, about what Cara and I wanted, but that wasn't good enough, was it? It seems Cara has proved herself to be much more genuine and nobler than you and Mother – better than any of us. But now she's gone. And it's your doing. Remember that.'

The line went dead. Shane had hung up on him.

Gene stared at the phone in his hand, feeling sick to his stomach. He placed the handset back on the desk and thought the entire situation through. This really was their fault. There was no denying that.

At that moment Lauren swept into the room, resplendently dressed for business in an Armani suit, even though it was eight in the evening.

'Who was that?' she inquired, taking note of her husband's drawn expression.

'It was Shane.'

She smiled. 'Ah, then I take it the decision has been made? When are they bringing the paperwork over?

'There is no paperwork,' Gene stated, still lost in his own thoughts.

Lauren frowned. 'What? What do you mean?' she demanded. 'Surely the girl couldn't be that stupid.'

Gene snapped to attention, coming out of his reverie and focusing on his wife.

'There is no paperwork because there is no wedding. It's all our fault, Lauren. What's more, she walked out on him and Shane wants nothing to do with us. He's not stupid you know. Neither is Cara. And apparently she isn't quite so money-hungry either. But she won't let Shane's future be affected because of her.' He put a hand to his head, as if the realisation was dawning on him. 'We lost, Lauren. You lost. Our selfish gamble has cost our son his happiness, and it has also cost us our son. I hope you are happy,' he spat.

Lauren felt as if she had just been slapped. The full weight of her actions began to pile up on top of her. She had never meant for this to happen. She'd merely thought that it would get Cara to come round to her way of thinking. As far as she was concerned there had been two options. She didn't think that Cara would eventually decide on a completely different one, namely calling off not just the wedding but also her relationship with Shane.

She felt her heart rate quicken as she thought of the repercussions of her actions. And now Shane had written them off too. He didn't want anything to do with his own parents! What had she done? In the effort to get her own way, she had essentially cut off her nose to spite her face.

'But—' Lauren started lamely. No matter how she thought about it, she couldn't figure out an angle, a trump card.

'No buts, Lauren. This is our fault. We should have just set aside our own stupid notions and let them be,' said Gene angrily. 'And do you know something? I don't blame Shane;

I would cut us off too if I had just lost the woman I loved. We cost him his happiness, and hers. You realise that don't you?'

Lauren swallowed hard. Yes, she knew that. She knew that this was all her fault. She hated to think about her son upset and unhappy. What mother could stomach the thought of her child suffering? And to know that she had caused it was even worse. Truthfully, she hated to think about Cara upset, too. She had never had a problem with Cara, and it was only recently that she had been vexed by the girl and her intentions. She cringed inwardly as she considered her actions that afternoon, about the way she had spoken to Cara. About the pain and suffering that she had caused.

Simply because she wanted to be the one who called the shots for the wedding. Because she and Gene had wanted to use it for their own ends.

She lowered her eyes and bit her lip, the guilt flooding her like a plague. And talk about diving straight into the role of the dreaded mother-in-law . . . Monster-in-law would be a more fitting title.

But maybe she could fix it, she thought, her mind going into problem-solving mode.

'What can we do, Gene? There has to be something we can do.'

'Any idea where we might be able to find a time machine?' he said sarcastically.

She bit a freshly manicured fingernail.

Gene looked at his wife. For all her ruthlessness and determination to get her own way, there was no denying that that she was now genuinely troubled by the developments. He wished they had considered this happening when first looking for a way to get what they wanted. If he'd thought that there was a chance of everything backfiring like this, he knew he would have never gone along with the idea. He might be very well focused on what the outside world thought of them and their standing in business circles, but at the same time, it wasn't worth sacrificing a relationship with Shane, or a future daughter-in-law.

'Well, I know the concept is foreign to you, and probably to me as well, but we could probably start with an apology,' he said gruffly. 'A real one, from the heart, to both of them. Although by now, we'll be lucky if either one of them could ever consider forgiving us.'

'So it seems the wedding is off . . .' mumbled Danielle as she read the latest email from Cara. She felt an automatic wave of relief rush over her but then immediately felt guilty. Imagine what Cara must be going through at that moment? After all of her planning and excitement over her big day, she was probably now dealing with over-whelming heartbreak.

Danielle's heart went out to her, and despite herself, she felt like picking up the phone to find out more and see if there was anything she could do to help ease Cara's distress. Cancelling a wedding was not an easy task. Never mind undoing all the arrangements already made, it must be so difficult to contend with emotionally too.

Scanning the email for more information as to the reasons for the cancellation, she saw that it was brief and to the point – in itself testament, she guessed, to Cara's upset. Apparently Cara and Shane had run into some kind of roadblock, there had been too many problems and complications, and Cara had decided that it was best if they just called off the entire affair. In closing, she apologised for putting Danielle out and hoped that she would end up seeing her soon.

See her soon? Danielle thought, wincing at the slight formality. In truth, and despite her anxieties, she'd been rather enjoying being up to date with the goings-on back home, albeit from a distance.

But while her heart ached for Cara's misfortune, she couldn't deny that the wedding cancellation eased the burden that lying to Zack had created.

Lying about a client who didn't exist in order to keep him in the dark about her travels had become a real challenge, especially since he loved talking business, even when it wasn't his own.

Now she would no longer have to lie and make up stories, and she felt as if she had a new lease of life of sorts. She no longer had a client who wanted to buy a house on St Lucia.

She thought about it and decided on the best way to present this new information to her boyfriend. At least the last lie that she would have to tell was more of a slight half-truth. Her client had cancelled, she would say, and backed out of the deal, so she no longer would have to travel to St Lucia.

Really it was barely a lie. All that she had to do was replace 'client' with 'sister' and it would have been the truth.

Danielle took a deep breath. Was it wrong that as well as feeling sorry for Cara she also felt relieved for herself?

She wondered what the 'complications' Cara had mentioned in her email were. Then she grimaced. She would be willing to bet that it had something to do with Betty.

Most of the problems began there after all. She just hoped that, if her mother was responsible for the wedding being called off, she felt appropriately horrible about it. Clearly Betty still hadn't learned to keep her nose out of other people's business or stop trying to control their lives.

Danielle bit her lip, again wondering if she should pick up the phone and talk to Cara, try and comfort her maybe. Not that she was much good at that kind of thing, but perhaps she should at least try . . .

At that moment, Zack entered the room, putting an end to Danielle's musings. He took note of her glum face as she stared at the screen of her laptop.

'What's wrong babe? You look like someone just cancelled Christmas.'

Caught by surprise, Danielle closed Cara's email and fought the urge to slam her laptop closed.

She thought quickly. 'Oh it's just . . . my client . . . the St Lucia one. Seems he no longer wishes to pursue his search for a beach home there,' she said, feeling her face flush.

God, she was a terrible liar.

Zack looked up, interested. 'Oh? And what reason did he give?'

'Well, it turns out he couldn't.' She tried to think quickly. 'He couldn't get financing. Major pushback from the bank apparently,' she said, spilling the words out.

'Pushback, eh?' Zack raised an eyebrow. 'Well, you know what that means; either bad credit or no money. I'm guessing probably both. People like that, in debt up to their eyeballs because they don't have any idea how to manage their finances. Really, these young guys, when they strike it rich, I am not sure why their handlers aren't instructing them to get with a financial planner ASAP. Otherwise they just blow all of their money on ridiculousness; booze, parties, expensive cars—'

'You are right, of course,' commented Danielle, barely listening to Zack's musing on the how-to's of financial planning and where people went wrong. 'How much do you stand to lose?' he asked.

She kept thinking to herself about her sister. *Poor Cara*, she thought. Guilt surged through her veins and she fought it back. She really didn't deserve this.

'Danielle?'

She snapped to attention. 'Sorry, what?'

'Where were you just now? Lost in another world?'

'Oh sorry, just thinking about stuff.'

'How much did you have wrapped up in this client? Surely it couldn't be that much forgone, other than time of course.'

'Oh, no, not much,' she said, thinking of the dress that would now, sadly, never be worn. She would really have to make sure that when it arrived in the mail she snagged it before Zack saw it. Especially as it screamed bridesmaid.

'Well, at least now I don't have to go to St Lucia,' she pointed out, some relief in her voice.

Zack picked up on it and smiled. 'Really, there's worse places you might have to go.'

'Yes, but you know I don't like travelling without you anyway,' she cooed, getting up from the desk and walking to Zack. She wrapped her arms around his waist and leaned in for a kiss.

He laughed. 'What has gotten into you? You travel by yourself all the time.'

She grimaced. Indeed, she did. She wasn't some type of co-dependent hanger-on but she was just so relieved that she could put all this family-related stuff behind her now. Most of the time, she felt as if she had her life under control, but when it came to her mother there was really no predicting the chaos could that could happen. At least now the Clancys would stay firmly planted in Ireland. Where they belonged. The way things should be.

'True, I guess I'm just feeling a little bit down about the whole thing. I thought I had everything under control, and

I was all ready to travel, and now nothing.' She smiled up at him. 'Maybe we should plan a weekend away sometime soon?'

He kissed the top of her head. 'We could drive over to Key Largo soon – it's always fun down there.'

'Sounds great.' That was fine with her. Zack could have suggested they drive to the moon and Danielle would have gone along with it.

After all, the world was her oyster again and she could go anywhere she wanted, without having to worry about the sky falling in.

Chapter 27

'What the hell is going on?' exclaimed Kim in lieu of a greeting as she rushed in the door at her in-laws' house, being greeted by the sight of a surprisingly composed Cara on the couch, surrounded by Heidi and Betty.

'Well, hello to you too Kim,' said Heidi pointedly.

Kim ignored her. 'What's this that I hear about the wedding being called off?'

Cara looked at her sister-in-law. Kim's pregnancy was starting to show and she had to admit, it was really complementing her appearance.

Heidi would probably begin to start showing herself soon, and Cara reflected on the fact that it seemed that life was blooming all around her now, and exciting things were happening. But not to her. She, on the other hand, was starting over. She couldn't picture what her life would be without Shane; she had been having a hard time coming to the realisation that this wasn't a dress rehearsal of a break-up. This was the real thing.

She was also feeling extremely tired of repeating what had happened. She'd confessed the whole sorry scenario to Betty and Mick, who'd insisted she move back in, and then retold the whole thing to Heidi when her sister had called over earlier and been surprised to see her there.

She looked imploringly at her mother and Betty duly chimed in, recounting the story behind the break-up to Kim in all its horrible detail. Kim, however, seemed determined to find a resolution.

'Cara, maybe he just made a mistake,' she suggested. 'Maybe he just spoke out of turn, put his foot in his mouth, that kind of thing.'

'Yes, I thought of that too,' said Cara sadly. 'But how am I ever supposed to get round this with his family? Say we did still get married, how am I ever supposed to forgive their interference?'

Kim smiled at her sister-in-law and took her hand. 'Honestly, you just learn how to let it roll off your back. You just forgive and move on – that's all you can do. You realise that some people are stuck in their ways and nothing you say or do is ever going to change them,' she said, with an almost imperceptible sideways glance at Betty. 'Remember, Shane is not the bad guy here. Sure he messed up, I understand that, but the ones who really need to realise that they need to take a step back and let their son live his life are his parents.'

Cara considered Kim's words. Evidently, she was speaking from experience and Cara wondered if the message Kim was trying to relay had been lost on her mother. Sure, there had been enough issues over the years where Betty had interfered in Ben and Kim's life, and it was true that Kim had done her best not to let it affect her.

Is that what I should do with Shane's parents? she thought to herself now.

'Have you spoken to Shane since you left?' Kim asked.

'No, she hasn't,' said Heidi, interrupting. 'And I don't think she should. What type of guy doesn't run after the woman he loves? Honestly, if I threatened to leave Paul, I would fully expect him to chase me down the street.'

Kim rolled her eyes. 'Cara, you know Shane is a good guy. You know he is. He just messed up a little.'

'That's what I said,' Betty offered. 'However, I would really love to give his mother a piece of my mind. The cheek of it . . . I have a good mind to pick up the phone to the stuck-up wagon and tell her exactly what I think of her.'

Cara put her hand up. 'That is exactly what you are *not* going to do, Mum. She already believes that we are crass and common. You are not going to say a word. You don't know Lauren and frankly, any argument between the two of you is just going to make it worse. Please let sleeping dogs lie.'

'But she offended you!' said Betty, bordering on hysterics. 'No one offends a daughter of mine.'

'Let it go Mum, please,' Cara insisted, exhausted.

'Have you cancelled the resort?' Kim inquired. She sincerely hoped that this hadn't been done yet. She honestly thought all of this could be fixed and she prayed that Cara hadn't done anything that couldn't be reversed just yet.

'No, not yet. I haven't had the energy.'

'I was just about to do it for her,' Heidi said eagerly. Kim looked at her and realised that once again Heidi was simply anxious about serving her own purposes. She was clearly not overly upset about having the wedding called off, because it meant she didn't have to travel to St Lucia.

Kim held up a hand. 'Don't do that.'

'But why?' Heidi retorted, rubbing her tummy protectively, as if Kim's raised voice might upset her unborn child.

'Because I have a feeling that this is a just temporary issue.'

'But they broke up—'

'Need I remind you, Heidi, that you threatened to break up with Paul several times during the planning of your wedding, and I think you even did once,' Kim said, and Heidi looked shamefaced. 'During that process,' she continued, 'nothing got cancelled. In fact, many of us were convinced that you would stand at the altar alone on the day if it meant getting your big day.' Kim was unimpressed with Heidi's lack of tact and compassion towards Cara and her plight.

'But—' Heidi started.

'No Heidi. We will not cancel anything. For once, stop thinking about your own interests and think about your sister, for goodness' sake.'

'Now girls . . .' Betty warned.

'Come on you two, don't fight. Please?' Cara pleaded tiredly.

Kim bit her lip. 'Sorry.'

'Really, I think I just need to have some time to think. OK?'

Kim nodded. 'Look sweetie, I know I sound like I'm in Shane's corner, but you know that I'm in yours, too. And that is because I think you two are perfect for each other.' She levelled her gaze with Cara, who sighed heavily.

'But Kim, think of all of the trouble surrounding the wedding so far. Right from the start there's been nothing but objections and resistance from almost everyone on the short guest list we have—' Cara glanced at both her sister and her mother and saw that both women looked suitably abashed. 'It seemed never-ending. And it was all so hard.'

Kim turned her attention back to Cara with a smile on her face and chuckled. 'Hard? Cara honey, I just want to inform you that marriage is hard. Yes, organising the wedding has had its up and downs but it's not all smooth sailing once you say "I do" either. I'm sure Betty and Heidi will agree with me on that?' she urged, and both women nodded.

'Sometimes I just want to *kill* Paul,' Heidi agreed with a sigh and the customary roll of her eyes.

'And honey, there have been many times over the years I've wanted to strangle your father too,' said Betty, encouragement in her voice. 'You know what he can be like, so stuck in his ways. And he can be so clueless about the simplest things, sometimes it's like looking after an extra child. But they can't help it,' she added wisely, 'they are men so of course they mess up. It's just an affliction of their gender.'

Kim laughed. 'Yes, and Cara, you are going to mess up sometimes too. No one is perfect and when you commit to living with somebody for ever, well, things happen. Sometimes I'm convinced that Ben's eyes will never be right again, what with all the rolling he does with them at some of my behaviour. But the point is, you get through it. You work on it. Yes, Shane's parents were wrong for doing what they did. And Shane is wrong not to have told you about whatever investments he made, but really, you guys are learning together. A lot of that comes from suddenly understanding that it's not just about you, that it's about the other person as well. Maybe you learned that lesson faster than Shane, but I can guarantee that he knows it now.'

Cara considered her sister-in-law's advice and felt her heart soften. She did make a good point, and Cara had never been one to hold a grudge.

'But what about him talking about the idea of divorce? What about that? What does that say about his faith in us?'

Kim shook her head, but Heidi beat her to an answer.

'I thought about it, before my wedding.'

Cara turned to look at her sister. 'What do you mean?'

'It just happened, like a thought that just pops into your head. Especially when you see things on TV or if you have a friend going through it and you think, what would I do if that happened to me? It's not as if you want to think about it, but it's just something that's there in the background. You can't honestly tell me that you have never thought about it, Cara.'

Cara shook her head. 'No, I mean, you can think about the concept of divorce of course, but I don't focus on it like it's sure to be part of my future.'

'I think what Heidi is trying to say that having a fatalistic notion isn't a bad thing, that it is normal,' offered Kim, trying to interpret her sister-in-law's rather jumbled thought process. 'You see something on TV when you are going through something similar, like if you are pregnant and watch a show about losing a baby or having one with a birth defect, and think, "God, what if that was me?" It's normal but it doesn't mean you are counting on it happening. It's just a scary thought, and maybe that's what happened. Maybe Shane knows someone who's going through a divorce and that's why it was in the forefront of his mind. Also when you're taking a huge step like marriage, it's only natural to let your mind drift to all the possibilities.' She patted Cara's shoulder. 'Really, there are risks involved with almost everything in life. But that's what makes it great. Without the risk of making a big decision, no one would ever be able to experience the reward.'

'It's human nature honey,' Betty chimed in. 'I've gone through many trials in my life, raising you, and Heidi and Ben and . . . Danielle,' she added, stumbling slightly. 'And even with your father. We have had fights that rattled the rafters, but we've never even thought about calling it a day. The dedication is working through the problems.'

'And I think you have that dedication and so does Shane,' Kim said, smiling.

Cara considered what they'd told her. Were they right?

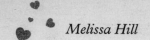

Should she give Shane another chance? Were his thoughts about divorce just simple fears, things he was afraid might happen? Would he keep her in the loop in the future and tell her everything? Could she trust him again? And what to do about his miserable parents?

Chapter 28

'Cara, you look like hell. Why are you here again?' Conor inquired as he observed Cara sitting at her desk, pale and exhausted-looking. She had dark circles under her eyes and he hadn't seen her eat in days, at least not while at the office.

He figured not much was different when she wasn't here, and while he knew it had been a very tough few days for her, he was starting to get concerned about her well-being.

'Because it's better than being at my mother's,' she replied. 'I forgot what it was like to live there.'

'You know the solution to that?' he said. She looked up at him, a silent question on her face. 'Make things up with Shane, of course.'

She shook her head. After her conversation with Kim and the others at her mum's house, she had been over it time and time again in her mind. How could she go back? Even if she could get over the issues there clearly were between them, how could she ever deal with his parents? She pictured his mother, probably happily sitting at some expensive restaurant in Dublin right now, drinking champagne and laughing over how she broke up her son and his fiancée.

Evil cow, Cara thought bitterly.

'Conor, you just don't understand,' she said. 'I'm the one who broke up with him. He probably hates me by now.' She started to tear up. That's all she felt like she did these days, cry. Cry over what would have been, could have been, *should* have been, if his horrible parents just knew well enough to stay away and mind their own bloody business.

She hated that she felt so angry over them, so bitter even. She had never considered herself an angry person, but now she felt like it all the time, when she thought about who was to blame.

If it hadn't been for Lauren and Gene, she would still be getting married to the man of her dreams in St Lucia.

'Oh please, spare me the dramatics; I thought that was Heidi's department. Shane doesn't hate you. You know that. And if you look like this I can only imagine what that poor sod is going through right now.'

'Thanks,' she said sarcastically.

'Cara, I mean it. Not that you look terrible, I mean you do, but I – oh shit, I didn't mean it like that. I meant that you are both miserable without each other, I know he must be. It's horrible to lose someone you love.'

She looked up at her boss, thinking she was so lucky to have someone so understanding in her life. Yes, it was one thing to have the support of her family, but it was quite another to have a friend like Conor. She placed a hand on his arm.

'Thank you, really, Conor, I appreciate it.'

He squeezed her hand. 'I just care about your happiness, that's all.'

She smiled. 'You know, for someone so jaded towards love, you sure seem pretty enlightened about the entire endeavour,' she teased, trying to lighten the mood.

He looked at her, and this time his expression was devoid of any teasing or sarcasm. 'Look, I just understand how miserable you can be when you miss the boat,' he said gently. 'It's something I don't wish on any man, that's for sure.'

Her smile vanished and she thought about what he'd said and how serious he'd sounded. Missed the boat? He wouldn't be talking about . . . suddenly Cara began to feel very uncomfortable. Conor reached out and patted her shoulder. 'Anyway, my point is—'

The rest of his sentence was cut off by the familiar sound of the bell, heralding the arrival of a customer.

Both he and Cara turned to see, only to be taken aback when they were greeted with the sight of Gene and Lauren Richardson. Conor jumped up from where he sat and turned towards the couple, standing in a protective stance between Shane's parents and Cara.

He strode towards them, his hands up, as if he was about to shoo them out the door. 'Now, I'll have none of this here, no more. I think both of you have done quite enough. Especially you,' he said, glaring directly at Lauren.

Gene took a position in front of his wife. 'Now young man, I don't know who you think you are, but—'

'I'm the boss,' Conor said, interrupting him. 'And I own this building. That means I get to say who stays and who goes. And you two are going.' He put his hands up once again, as if he could corral them out the door.

'Really . . .' Lauren blustered, unused to such harsh treatment. It was clear that she had never been kicked out of anywhere before. She tried to look around Conor's bulky frame. 'We just need to talk to Cara.'

'You have done enough talking. She is still wearing the scars.'

'Cara, please, call him off, we need to talk to you,' Gene pleaded with the woman who would have been his daughter-in-law.

Call him off? They were talking as if Conor was some kind of guard dog! Taking in the entire scene, Cara had to admit she was somewhat amused, even though she was worried by the couple's appearance at her office.

Didn't they understand it was inappropriate for them to interrupt her at work? Well maybe she would just tell them what she thought of them right now.

'Conor. Hold on, it's fine. I have something to say actually.'

Her boss looked over his shoulder as Cara got to her feet and made her way to the front of the office.

The Richardsons looked relieved. 'Cara, thank you, we have never been treated in such a manner . . .' Gene said, looking at Conor disdainfully.

'Stop, I don't want to hear it.' She looked to Lauren, a withering look on her face. 'Just who do you think you are? Where do you get off? Coming here, messing with my life, and messing with Shane's too. Do you have any idea how much misery you've caused?'

Lauren and Gene both took a tentative step backwards. They weren't used to such emotional displays amongst the circles they ran in. Yelling at another person in public, even if it was just an office, was quite unheard of and quite startling, too.

'Er well, Cara—' Gene began nervously, but she cut him off again.

'I don't know what I ever did to you. I don't know what I did that made you dislike me so much—'

'But dear,' Lauren interjected, 'We don't dislike you . . .'

'Really? Then you certainly have an interesting way of showing you care,' Conor put in. 'I'd hate to see what you do to your enemies.'

Cara looked at Conor gratefully and Lauren took a deep breath, as if steeling herself. 'You're right. I probably deserve that,' she conceded.

Cara's eyes widened in surprise. 'Excuse me?'

'It was wrong, Cara, what we did. What I did. I wasn't thinking about anyone, about you or Shane or what would make you happy. I was only thinking of myself and what I wanted,' she said, her voice barely above a whisper. 'Shane won't talk to us; he says he wants nothing to do with us. And I realise that I made such a mistake, a huge one.'

'Well, of all the great observations of our time,' Conor's voice was heavy with sarcasm. 'For all your protestations about class and society, you are nothing but a selfish woman with an unwarranted opinion of herself.'

Cara nodded, emboldened by Conor's rather heroic efforts to defend her, and she wondered if there was something in the fact that he, and not Shane, was the one doing so?

Lauren lowered her eyes and Gene patted her on the back. Cara looked at their pained and troubled faces, suddenly realising that all of their defences, their petty pretences, had been dropped. They were standing before her, beaten and bruised, sad parents who were being cut out of their beloved son's life.

Then, much to her horror, Lauren started to cry. Gene immediately moved to put his arms around her, all of his swagger and pomposity now absent. As she watched them, looking so shell-shocked and broken, Cara once again felt as though her heart was breaking. Her mother's words from her childhood echoed through her mind: *try to be the bigger person*. Shane's parents might have wronged her, they might have hurt her and trampled her feelings without a second thought, but that was the difference between her and them. They might have thought she was crass and common, but she knew that it was her behaviour and not her background that would identify her as a lady. 'Lauren . . .' She reached out and brought the woman who might have been her mother-in-law into her arms. 'Please don't cry.'

Lauren welcomed the embrace. 'Oh Cara. I know I was so horrible to you – and Shane. The point is; I came here to apologise.' She turned to look at her husband. 'We both came to ask for your forgiveness. Forget about our stupidity about the wedding; our motivation was coming from another place, a selfish place. We realise now that all we want is for our son to be happy, and there is no denying that he is happiest with you. Please, we hope that you will reconsider cancelling the wedding? If not for us, then for him.'

'Your motivation was coming from a selfish place?' Cara repeated, raising an eyebrow. 'What do you mean by that?'

Shane's parents looked at one another, before glancing uncomfortably at Conor.

'I'll leave you to it,' he said, taking his cue to give them some privacy. He looked at Cara. 'As long as you're OK?'

She nodded, intrigued as to what the Richardsons were going to say.

Once Conor had retreated to his desk and was out of earshot, Gene spoke again. 'Cara, Richardson Construction is as you know a family business, and has been for a long time. It was my father's business and I had hoped that one day Shane would take the reins from me, despite his protestations to the contrary.'

Cara nodded. She knew this was a sore point between Shane and the family; it had been as long as she could remember.

'But if it's not to be, it's not to be and he remains the sole heir in any case.' He cleared his throat uncomfortably. 'Anyway, the company like most has been going through a difficult time recently. Business is slow and the recession means that work has died down significantly.'

Lauren took up the reins. 'To cut a long story short, we wanted your and Shane's wedding to help rebuild our reputation within the industry. Society gatherings oil the wheels of the industry, but of course no one is throwing parties anymore, mostly because it seems in bad taste to do so without good reason. So our contacts are drying up and we had hoped that by having certain "influential" people on the guest list of your wedding that things might get moving again. You and Shane going abroad for a small intimate ceremony would have made this impossible.'

Cara shook her head. Of course. Moving and shaking. This was the Richardsons' world. The world of big business – wheeling and dealing and backslapping. Nothing like ordinary people who were merely trying to ride out the recession by working hard day to day.

'You wanted to turn your son's wedding into a business opportunity?' she said, flabbergasted. But yet, Cara had seen it before, had seen the pictures in the newspapers of an extravagant bash on behalf of the son or daughter of some big Irish businessman. It was sickening but it was indeed the way things worked in Ireland.

What was it that Shane had called them – 'The Golden Circle'?

Gene looked abashed and to her credit Lauren did too. 'We're sorry Cara – we've been so focused on trying to get things going again without losing face that we completely lost sight of how important the occasion was on a personal level, not just for us, but for you and Shane.'

'I realise how pathetic it must sound to you,' Gene said in a small voice. 'And yes, while the business is of course important to us, it's not as important as Shane and both your futures.'

'We have never seen Shane as happy as he is when he is

with you, Cara,' Lauren put in. 'He loves you and I know he is miserable now and it's all because of us. Everything you have been going through is our doing, and for that we are so sorry.'

Lauren sniffed again, and Cara tried to get her head around what the couple were saying to her. She was trying to figure out if there was some other angle to all of this, something she hadn't considered. After all that had happened it was difficult to trust them.

'Cara, we are begging you to reconsider. Shane was devastated after you left,' Lauren said.

Cara shook her head. 'But Shane lied to me too, about the money I mean. I don't want any of your money. Not now, not ever.' She raised her chin in defiance against their belief that she could be bought.

'We know and we were wrong to assume otherwise,' said Gene in supplication. 'And as far as lying goes, well, I wouldn't say Shane lied. He did make an investment in some stocks, but on my advice really. All of that is my fault. I told him it would be good for his future and I was wrong. I was wrong about a lot of things. I'm so sorry Cara. Really, my son is a good egg. Better than his old man, that's for sure,' he offered with a small smile.

'Cara, I always wanted a daughter, but it just never happened,' Lauren said. 'And Shane is a wonderful son, more than I could ever wish for. When you two told us you were engaged, we really were so happy.' She bowed her head. 'Unfortunately our desire to turn the wedding into a big shindig very quickly overshadowed everything else, and it was wrong. It was unforgivable of us to push ourselves into your day, and completely disregard what you both wanted, for our own selfish ends. I in particular know that now. I hope you will forgive us and most of all, I hope it's not too late.'

Cara considered the pleading looks on their faces, trying to forget that just moments ago she'd wanted to throttle them both. Were they telling her the truth? Did they really want the wedding back on, or were they just looking to get back in Shane's good books?

She considered another idea. 'And now? What about the wedding? I mean, there's nothing to say that Shane will even take me back, but if he did, what are your thoughts about St Lucia?'

Lauren and Gene looked at one another, weighing up their options. It was Lauren who spoke first. 'We have been to St Lucia before. It's a lovely island,' she said simply. 'Perfect for a wedding.'

'And the business . . .' Cara pressed.

Gene sighed. 'We'll find another way.'

Cara exhaled the breath she hadn't realised she'd been holding. She felt her heart soar. She turned to her boss, who was sitting at his desk, silently taking in the entire scene.

'Conor, I need a favour,' she said meekly.

He shook his head indulgently. 'Let me guess, errands to run and bridegrooms to woo?' he said with a wink.

'Something like that.' Cara winced apologetically.

Conor grinned. 'Go get 'em, sweetheart.'

Cara jumped from the Jaguar almost before Gene had been able to pull it to a stop in front of the apartment. She anxiously looked around for Shane's car and saw that it was there.

According to Lauren, they had driven past several times over the last few days, twice even attempting to stop to try to gain an audience, but he wouldn't talk to them. They knew he was home; they had heard the TV on as they stood on the other side of the door.

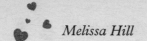

Lauren started to get out of the car too, but was held back by her husband. 'No Lauren, you stay here. Let Cara and Shane have their reunion. This isn't about us, remember?'

His wife looked abashed for a moment and opened her mouth to speak, but then remembered that his words were true.

Cara bounded up the stairs as if she was racing to beat time, working her hardest to close the seconds between when she and Shane would once again be together.

'Shane!' she yelled as she neared their front door. She barely had time to stop herself. She jiggled the doorknob. It was locked.

Damn! She'd left her keys at work.

Instead, she met it outright with her fist, knocking frantically.

'Shane? Open up, it's me!' she cried.

Seconds later the door opened. Shane stared at her in shocked silence. 'Cara?'

She looked at him and thought that he looked like hell. He had apparently been taking their separation just as hard as she had been. His skin was grey, his eyes bloodshot and his hair was all over the place. In all honesty he looked as if he hadn't slept in days. She threw herself in his arms.

'Shane, I'm sorry, I'm sorry for leaving, I love you so much. Please, will you take me back?' she sobbed, tears running down her cheeks.

Without saying a word, he pulled her closer and kissed her hard on the mouth, his hands finding her hair and moving along her body, as if he was trying to remember just how she felt, rekindling a memory.

'Oh Cara. I missed you,' he said eventually. 'And I don't care what my parents say or do. I don't care about any of it.'

'I know you do. I believe you.'

He pulled away and looked into her eyes. 'You believe me now. Why?'

'Because they brought me here. Your parents. They're outside.'

'What?' he said angrily. 'What are they doing outside? Talk about nerve—'

'Shhh . . .' she cooed, placing a finger over his lips. 'It's all OK. They apologised, they came to my office and said they were sorry—'

'Big deal,' he spat.

'No, Shane, no, I could tell they meant it. It was genuine. And what's more I accepted their apology and I think you should, too. I need you to, OK? They made a mistake and they accepted that. We are having our wedding in St Lucia. They understand that and they will be there. Look Shane, we are starting our lives together and this is how I want it. I want it to include your parents and my parents, our families. That's how it should be. That's the commitment we are making to each other, we are making a family and it includes everyone, OK?'

Shane stood, looking at her as if in awe. 'You really are the total package,' he said smiling. 'Do you know that?'

She shrugged and a smile played at her lips. 'What can I say? I try.'

'And I promise that I will never keep anything from you again. No secrets. You will know everything, no matter what, OK?'

She smiled, recalling her sister-in-law's wise words about lessons learned. 'Can I come in? We have a lot of catching up to do.'

He picked her up off her feet and kicked the door shut behind them, covering her neck with kisses.

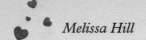

Cara laughed, and the sound felt comfortable on her lips. The familiarity of all of this was welcome after what had been a week of hell.

Suddenly she remembered something. 'What about your parents?' she asked, breathless, looking back to the door. 'They're waiting outside . . .'

'Let 'em sweat it out for a while,' he laughed, carrying his bride-to-be to the bedroom. 'Preferably a long while.'

Chapter 29

Danielle pulled her soft-top Mercedes into the driveway and took a quick look at her watch. It was late evening and the warm Florida sun was high in the sky at this time of day, before making its gradual descent into the horizon.

Maybe she could convince Zack to go for a swim with her in the ocean. They hadn't had a romp in the waves for some time, preferring instead to stay close to the climate-controlled pool on the back deck. She was gathering her briefcase and her suit jacket when her phone started to buzz. Her hands full, she tried to negotiate to see who it was before answering, but by the time she was able to read the display, it clicked through to voicemail. It was Cara.

Danielle raised an eyebrow, wondering what was up now. It had been over a week since she'd told her about the wedding being cancelled, and she wondered if now there was a change of plan. She'd call her back later.

But as Danielle neared her front door, she heard the landline ringing from inside the condo, and a burst of panic flooded through her veins.

Shit, what if that was Cara was calling the house – and double shit! What if Zack picked up?

Danielle dropped her briefcase on the front porch and launched a full-on assault on her purse for her keys. Why, oh why did she have a car that only required the keys to be somewhere in the vicinity of the driver and not actively in the ignition? Furthermore, her Louis Vuitton bag had a hook right inside its interior, perfect for keys, so why in the bloody hell didn't she *use* it!

The phone rang again. Maybe Zack was out back? Maybe he hadn't heard it?

She shook her purse violently and heard the keys jingle at the bottom. She opened the bag as wide as it would go, prepared to rip it to pieces if she had to. Finally, she found them and shoved the front door key in the lock, which finally granted her entry.

But the phone had stopped ringing.

The moment she walked in the door, a cold sweat already breaking out on her back and under her arms, she realised that she was too late. What's more, she also realised that she had been correct: Cara had indeed called, and right now she was talking to none other than Zack.

'Well, it's nice to talk to you, too,' her boyfriend was saying, smiling. 'Yes, I was beginning to believe you were a figment of Danielle's imagination too.'

She crossed the room with determination and held her hand out for the phone. He backed away, keeping his grip on the handset, his friendly expression turning to annoyance at Danielle's unexplained behaviour.

'Give it to me,' she hissed, gesturing.

He regarded her quizzically and held up a finger, instructing her to wait just a minute.

'Yes, I hope I get to meet you soon too,' he said. There was silence and Danielle focused in on the phone, willing Cara on the other end to finish up the pleasantries so that Zack would just give her the phone. At least before she said too much.

'Yes, I'm sure she'll be delighted to hear it. I'm sorry, what's happening in St Lucia?' he queried and Danielle felt her heart stop. She diverted her eyes from Zack's gaze, which was now steadily focused on her face. 'The wedding is back on? Really? That's wonderful news. Remind me, when was it supposed to be again?'

Danielle clenched her fists. She was caught. The cat was now well and truly out of the bag. How on earth would she explain this?

He raised an eyebrow. 'In September, I see. So soon. Well, fantastic that everything is going ahead, I'm so pleased. Yes, it will be lovely to have the entire Clancy family all together and I definitely look forward to meeting all of you,' he said, his voice full of sarcasm wholly directed at Danielle. She met his eyes and she knew that there were plenty of questions there, but there was also anger. He had put all the pieces together and she had been fully caught in a lie. She had a lot of explaining to do.

'Well Cara, it was very nice talking to you. Yes, it will be lovely to finally meet you too. I believe your bridesmaid has just walked in. Yes, here she is. Bye now, best of luck with the rest of the wedding plans.' His smile faded as he held the phone out to Danielle, covering the mouthpiece with his hand. 'It's your sister, Cara, calling from Dublin. Seems the wedding is back on. For September twelfth in St Lucia.' He raised an eyebrow. 'Such a happy coincidence that you no longer have a client to meet there, isn't it? Given that it would have clashed with this wedding?'

His voice dripped with mockery and she took the phone from him. 'Zack—' she started, but he held up his hand.

'You and I have plenty to talk about, but talk to your sister now. She is calling long-distance after all and I'm sure that you have *much* to discuss about the wedding.' He shook his head sadly at Danielle as she placed the phone at her ear, and she did her best to divert her gaze as she talked.

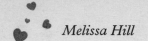

'Hello Cara? I'm sorry sweetie, but this really isn't a good time—' she began.

'Danielle? I just had to call you and tell you, the wedding is back on!' Cara squealed on the other end of the line, an ocean away. Of course Danielle couldn't help but feel happy for her, but at the same time, a cold dread rose up inside her as she thought about the nightmare in which she'd just landed herself.

Just like that, everything that she had planned, everything that she had tried to avoid was coming at her like an out-of-control train. Why couldn't Cara have just emailed the latest news in the same way she had been doing these last few months? Although she supposed she couldn't blame Cara; she was just excited to tell her and couldn't have known that Danielle would have been trying to keep the whole thing a big secret . . .

She had to think hard and fast to try to figure out a way out of this. 'Oh, that's such great news!' she enthused, trying not to betray her distress to an obviously delighted Cara. 'I'm so pleased and I'm sure you must be too. I can't wait to hear all about it but I really have to—'

'And Zack, I'm so thrilled that I got to talk to him – finally. He sounds lovely and I can't wait to meet him. But anyway, I am just so excited, everything got straightened out and your bridesmaid dress should be arriving any day now, so all we have to do now is make your travel arrangements. Oh, it's going to be so perfect and I can't believe we are all going to be together again. The whole family!' Cara chirruped happily.

'Yes, about that—'

'It's all finally coming together. After all that's happened Mum and Dad are completely on board now and so are Shane's parents – although that's a long story. Heidi's stopped her moaning for once too. Oh, we just can't wait to see you! It should be a good crowd; some of my friends are coming and Conor my boss . . .'

Danielle tuned out the words. As much as she wanted to share in Cara's joy, she was keenly aware of Zack still standing behind her, and she was anxious to end this call and get on with the difficult conversation she knew they were about to have.

'Cara, really I'm very happy for you that the wedding is back on,' she said gently, looking carefully over her shoulder to meet Zack's gaze.

Yup, he was pissed.

She swallowed hard.

'Will you let me know when the dress arrives, or if there are any problems with the sizing?'

'Of course I will.' Danielle didn't want to admit that the gown was already sitting in her wardrobe. And she had no idea if there was any problems with the sizing because – not expecting to ever have to wear it – she hadn't bothered trying it on.

'Yes, I'll give you a call when it arrives and we can talk about any other arrangements then, OK?' she said, angling to end the call.

'Brilliant. I can't believe it's so close now. I can't wait to see you. And Zack too. Tell him bye for me, OK?'

'Absolutely,' Danielle said tersely, hanging up the phone before Cara could say any more. She placed the handset down and took a deep breath, briefly closing her eyes as if that would help her balance her chakras.

'So,' Zack said from behind her. 'A wedding . . . in St Lucia . . . and in September too. What are the chances?' He put a hand in his pocket, a gesture that seemed casual but one which Danielle knew indicated that he was seriously ticked off. 'Frankly though, I'm struck by the similarities between your younger sister who it seems recently called off her wedding, and the client you lost when they backed out of the deal around the same time. But now, miraculously, your sister's wedding is back on. Does that mean your deal has a new lease of life too?' he drawled. 'That your client has, shall we say, reconsidered? And that you are once again going to have to run off to St Lucia in September?'

Danielle looked at her feet. 'Zack—'

'So am I to assume that you made that story up? The one about a client I mean.'

She didn't know how to get out of this, so she just nodded and continued to stare at the floor. She felt like a teenager again, caught out in yet another lie by Betty and Mick.

'I could ask why, but I am not an idiot,' Zack continued. 'It's obvious you didn't want me to meet your family. What is it, Danielle? Are you ashamed of me? Embarrassed? I didn't think I was the kind of guy that you should be afraid to take out in public. But maybe I was wrong. Maybe you aren't as serious about me as I am about you. Or how serious I *was* about you.'

She looked up, pleading in her eyes. 'No Zack, it's not that at all, it's not. It's just my family; there's a lot of baggage and most of the time I can barely tolerate being around them and—'

'Your sister seemed pleasant enough. And apparently they know enough about me.'

'That's only because I mentioned you a few times. It's not because I'm close to them. I haven't been close to them in years. In fact, I would rather they all disappeared and then I would never have to worry about any of it, or having to ever face . . .' Danielle felt close to tears and she realised she was on the verge of saying too much.

'Face what, Danielle?' Zack enquired, his tone now a mixture of hurt and curiosity. 'What are you afraid of? What are you hiding? Because I think it's pretty obvious that you are hiding something. And that worries me, because I always believed I knew exactly where I stood with you. That there was no bullshit.'

She felt a thin sheet of sweat erupt across her forehead. *Keep your cool, Danielle and for God's sakes shut your stupid mouth,* she thought.

'There is no bullshit,' she said tiredly. 'And I'm not hiding anything.' Zack didn't look convinced. 'You just don't understand what it's like,' she continued, trying to turn the tables on him. 'Why do you think I left Ireland all those years ago? And haven't you ever wondered why I hardly ever go back?' She looked away. 'It's because I am nothing like them. I don't get along with my mother, I haven't for years and I have nothing in common with any of them. I don't see why this has to be such a big deal.' She felt the bitterness rising in her chest, and she hoped that her feelings were visible on her face and would show Zack how she felt about her family clearly enough that he might not want to go to the wedding. Not that Danielle was counting on him going anywhere other than out the door. And she couldn't blame him. She'd be angry and suspicious too, if the tables were turned and she'd caught him out in a lie.

Still she felt determined to match his gaze, to keep her eyes steady on his, as if issuing a silent challenge. However, she failed, finally turning her eyes away under the pressure of his stare. She felt her inner resolve crumble and wondered how it had all turned so bad, so quickly.

Finally Zack spoke, breaking the silence. 'Well, if it's not such a big deal then I suppose you have nothing to worry about, do you? It will be just a nice family gathering on a paradise island.' He smiled. 'After all, a wedding is a happy affair and we have been together for some time now, right? So I'm thinking it's only appropriate that I meet your family. That's what happy couples do, right?' She turned her eyes towards him, not sure if he was mocking her or being serious. Yet there was no malice in his face. 'But let me tell you Danielle,' he finished ominously, 'I am very much looking forward to meeting your family. Every last one of them.'

Chapter 30

Cara could barely contain her excitement as on September 9, the plane taxied to the gate at St Lucia airport. She peered out of the tiny window, her face aglow at the fact that they were really here. For her and Shane's beach wedding. Finally, *finally*, things were going according to plan, and they hadn't looked back since Shane's parents had come onside.

'Oh wow, it looks amazing!' she gasped as she took in the stunning surroundings bathed in Caribbean sunshine. The glorious volcanic twin Pitons soared above the island, and she couldn't wait to reach the shore and set eyes on the white sandy beach. Palm trees swung lightly in the ocean breeze and Cara could almost taste the salt from the azure ocean they'd seen from the sky on the way in.

She smiled at Shane and rested her head on his shoulder. They had flown in a couple of days earlier than the rest of the wedding party. She did feel slightly guilty about not travelling with her parents, as Betty and Mick were both likely to feel nervous about their first ever flight, but Kim had assured her that she would keep an eye on them and (more importantly) make sure they got on to the plane in the first place.

'Just think, in three days' time, we will be man and wife. Can you believe we actually made it this far?' she laughed. It seemed as if the past few months were nothing more than a blurry memory now. She had replaced all the negativity of the earlier days with more recent positive experiences: making up with Lauren and Gene, her final wedding dress fitting, and the impromptu hen party Samantha and the girls (aided by Kim) had thrown for her last week. And she'd made a point of no longer thinking about the challenges that they had encountered up to now.

In the scheme of things, none of it mattered now; they had made it to St Lucia and were about to have the wedding of their dreams.

The plane came to a stop and the flight crew went about the motions of preparing the cabin and the passengers for arrival. Cara was so eager to get off the plane after the ten-hour journey, that she jumped anxiously in her seat.

'Hey, calm down,' Shane laughed. 'We'll be off soon enough.'

'I know; I'm just dying to get to the resort, throw on my bikini and get some sun.'

Shane chuckled. 'Don't forget about the cocktails.'

'Hmm, pina coladas . . . margaritas . . . I can't wait.'

This was definitely the way to do it, she reassured herself. A wedding in an amazing tropical-paradise location, poolside relaxation and guaranteed sunshine. Perfect.

'I think we're good to go now,' Shane said, rising as the line of passengers began moving towards the front of the plane.

She took his hand and gathered her carry-on luggage from the overhead bin. As they slowly inched their way towards the exit, Cara heard a man from behind her make a comment in a loud British accent.

'So is there any news on Gail?' he drawled. 'Does it still look like she's heading in this direction?'

Cara turned round to see his female travel companion staring at the screen of her iPhone.

'Looks like there is a chance, but it's still off in the Atlantic. They're saying it could turn north yet.' The woman looked up, and shook her head. 'Figures . . . of all the bloody weeks to plan a trip, we had to pick the one where a hurricane is brewing over the ocean.'

Cara blanched; she'd heard nothing about any hurricane, but then again, over the past few days her mind had been set on last-minute travel and wedding plans, and she hadn't been paying much attention to the news.

'I'm sorry, what did you say about a hurricane?' she asked.

The woman looked at her. 'Hurricane Gail started forming the other day off the coast of Africa, and is already heading this way.' She shook her head. 'She's fast too, worked up to a Category Five already. Could be big as Katrina,' she commented, somewhat nonchalant about all of it.

'That big . . .?' Cara gulped, alarmed. She was well aware of the catastrophic hurricane that had rocked the American Gulf Coast a few years previously.

'Yeah, but don't worry, they still think she might head north towards the Florida coast and skip St Lucia altogether.'

'Did you hear that, Shane?'

He nodded and pressed his lips together, his brow furrowing. 'Cara, there's nothing we can do about it. We'll just have to deal with whatever happens. We knew that it was a possibility when we booked, remember? Let's just stay positive and not worry about the things that are out of our control, OK?'

Cara shook her head, clearly worried. 'But what if it hits and we can't have the wedding on the beach?'

It didn't cross her mind that if a Category Five hurricane hit the small Caribbean island they would have bigger problems than whether or not they could have their wedding on the beach.

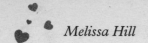

'Well, then we will just have to have it indoors,' he said simply, a determined smile on his face.

They reached the front of the plane and were immediately hit by a wave of warmth as they exited the doorway and walked down the stairs into the humid Caribbean climate.

Cara grinned in spite of herself and Shane smiled up to the sky as the sun hit his face. 'Come on bride-to-be, let's go get those cocktails and soak up some sun.'

Two days later, Cara and Shane lounged in their ocean-view room at the Paradise Oasis resort. The resort was simply incredible and their suite was the last word in comfort and luxury. They even had a jacuzzi in their top-floor suite that looked right out over the incredible Caribbean Sea, and for the last couple of nights they'd left the patio door open and had fallen asleep to the sound of the waves crashing gently on the shore. It was the most relaxing sound Cara had ever heard.

In fact relaxation was the last word in this resort, and she and Shane had been blown away when, the day before, they'd met with the wedding planner to go through the final details and check out the location for the ceremony.

As Cara had been insistent that they exchange vows right on the beach (she so wanted the wedding to be exactly as she'd first visualised it and feel the sand in her toes as she walked towards Shane), the wedding planner had shown them to a secluded spot right on the edge of the beach, on soft smooth sand looking towards the horizon with palm trees lining the shore. The wedding was to take place at sunset the next day. Absolutely everything was in place.

All that was left now was for the guests to arrive.

Cara idly flipped through the channels on the room's flat-screen television. They still had about an hour until they needed to head to the airport to pick up their families and were quietly relaxing, happily content from their activity the day before on the beach, where they had both frolicked in the sand and surf, and drunk plenty of rum and tequila.

Suddenly, Cara paused on the Weather Channel and Shane reached over to grab the remote control from her. 'Nope, none of that. You promised. It's beautiful outside. Nothing to worry about, OK?'

'I'm not worried. I just want to take a look.'

'I know what you are looking for though. Information on the hurricane.'

It was true. Although Cara was trying her utmost not to think about it, she kept hearing snippets about the weather from other guests at the resort, and had noticed some of the low-key preparations the hotel staff were taking, just in case. It gave her cause for concern.

'I'm just trying to stay informed, Shane.'

'Well, I'm sure the hotel will keep us informed.'

'Just let me watch. Two minutes, OK?'

Shane sighed and got up from the bed. 'Fine. I'm going to get ready.'

He left the bedroom, leaving Cara to her own devices. She listened and watched as the reporter on the Weather Channel started talking about Hurricane Gail. Its current position was south-east, and it was being projected that the storm was headed in a north-west direction, towards the Caribbean. However, there was still a chance that it would change course at the last minute, as hurricanes were apt to do, and go north instead.

Cara sat up in bed, wondering what would happen if the storm hit St Lucia. She didn't know anything about what to do in a hurricane and the thought terrified her.

So much for having everything ready to go. Would this

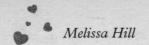

be yet another spanner in the works when it came this wedding? she thought and then immediately chastised herself for the notion. After all, a hurricane threw up somewhat bigger issues than just interrupting a wedding.

Shane entered the bedroom again after a few minutes. This time he took the remote control away from her and flicked off the TV. 'All right, that's enough. No more TV, not for today. Cara, everything will work out, I know it. We have got this far, no silly storm is going to get in our way,' he said, smiling.

She looked at her fiancé, wishing she shared his optimism. 'You're right. I know you are. I just need to put it out of my mind.'

Shane held out his hand. 'Come on then. Time for you to get ready.'

'I know. I'll try and forget about it, I promise. As you say, there's nothing we can do.' Still something was telling her that there was going be one last hiccup, and when it came to this wedding, fate hadn't quite finished with them yet.

She placed her hand in Shane's and got up from the bed. Despite her worries, she was excited and her skin glowed, thanks to a little help from the sun.

'The festivities start today once we collect the crew from the airport.' Shane smiled. 'It's time for some fun.'

The two of them watched from the terminal building, as the plane from Dublin via Heathrow taxied to a stop on the runway outside. Just as with the plane that they had arrived in two days before, the passengers would disembark from the aircraft directly on to the concrete runway.

Cara bounced excitedly on her heels. Although she'd enjoyed her and Shane's brief time alone, after all that had happened, she couldn't wait for everyone else to get here and see the resort, as well as what they had planned for their special day. Everyone was arriving on this flight, with the exception of Zack and Danielle (who were apparently coming in on a private jet later), and Lauren and Gene, who had decided to fly first class with British Airways instead of on the Virgin economy tickets Cara and Shane had booked for the others.

The couple watched as the first of the passengers began to disembark.

'Oh look, there's Mum – and Dad!' Cara exclaimed, pointing at her parents as they made their way down the steps. Despite her earlier protests, Betty looked as if she was actually well prepared for the warmer climate. She wore a flowing purple-patterned kaftan that danced happily in the tropical breeze. Cara gave a fond smile as Betty put a hand up to her head and caught her sunhat from blowing away as she looked around tentatively, as if half expecting to step off the plane and straight into the ocean.

Mick, on the other hand, looked as if he had just changed out of his usual corduroy trousers on the plane, instead opting for three-quarter length khaki shorts. To complement the look, and in typical Irish older male fashion, he had left on his socks and loafers, which dramatically clashed with his multicoloured Hawaiian shirt.

'Where on earth did your father get that shirt?' Shane snorted, holding back laughter.

'I have absolutely no idea.'

Next were Heidi and Paul. Cara's little sister wore a pink, Empire-line sundress, and held her tummy protectively, as if looking for the opportunity to shield her unborn baby from any tropical viruses or exotic animals that might suddenly attack as she exited the plane.

Paul, ever the obedient husband, carried both of their

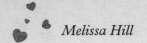

carry-on bags and tried to guide Heidi down the steps, as if she had never navigated such difficult territory before.

Cara's friends Samantha, Lilly and Maria emerged next, all laughing and in jolly spirits.

Probably drinking wine the whole way here, Cara guessed with an indulgent smile.

Another member of the Greygates crew then emerged. Conor was dressed casually in a pair of tan linen pants and a white cotton shirt. He had the sleeves rolled up to his elbows, was sporting a stylish pair of dark leather sandals and was smiling and chatting with Maria about something. Watching him putting on his sunglasses as he descended the steps, Cara had to admit that he looked unaccountably handsome, like a famous rock star.

'Look, leave it to Conor to entertain the girls,' she smiled. 'We're going to have to find him someone while we're here, otherwise it could be dangerous.'

'Yes I don't their husbands will thank you much for inviting them. Fun and frolics on a Caribbean island with Romeo Dempsey. I certainly wouldn't like it, I can tell you,' Shane said somewhat darkly.

'Ah stop it – Conor's not like that, you know that. And I'm glad they all made the effort to be here.' Although she knew that Shane had some reservations about Conor, there was no way she wouldn't have invited him to the wedding. Her boss had been so good to her – not just over the last few months but throughout all the time she'd worked for him. But she couldn't help but wonder, as she had recently, if there was something more behind that kindness? She hoped not, because while she adored Conor, she had never, ever seen him as anything other than a good friend.

Finally, bringing up the rear were Kim, Ben, Lindsay and

Olivia. Cara's nieces each carried little bags emblazoned with Disney princesses, and both girls were obviously ecstatic to finally be out of the aircraft. They leapt around on the ground excitedly as they grabbed their parents' hands, probably asking when they would be able to go swimming or play in the sand. Kim and Ben smiled happily at their children and at each other.

'Wow, I must admit when we were planning this, I honestly didn't expect Kim and Heidi to be so . . . well pregnant, I suppose. Kim especially; she looks almost ready to go into labour,' Shane commented.

'Don't even think about it. That's all we need,' Cara said, imagining premature deliveries and the drama they'd get from Heidi about St Lucian babies and whatnot. 'Anyway, they're both still a good while off.'

Once everyone had disembarked, Cara and Shane headed towards arrivals to meet them, and within moments the entourage came through.

'Mum, Dad, over here!' Cara called out, waving furiously.

The small party looked in her and Shane's direction, and the place immediately broke out into a cacophony of greetings.

'Cara, that was the longest flight in the entire world! And in such tiny seats! I didn't think we would ever get here,' Betty complained.

'Yes, and what's this I hear about a hurricane? Just what are we going to do if it hits here? We would have never had to worry about a hurricane in Ireland,' Mick complained, waving his hand across his face. 'Jeez, I'm kilt with the heat already.'

'Auntie Cara, Auntie Cara! Mummy said we could go swimming when we get to the hotel! Will you go swimming with us when we get there?' Lindsay squealed.

'Cara, you never told us your boss was so charming,' cooed Samantha. 'He had us in stitches all the way from London,'

'And I kept the lot of you in drinks too, don't forget that. I'm near broke,' Conor added, hugging Cara. 'I hope this resort is all inclusive.'

'Cara, honestly I didn't realise just how hot it would be. And so humid. I can feel water running down my back already. Does the resort have mosquito nets over the beds? I really cannot be exposed to malaria.'

'Heidi hush, you aren't going to catch malaria,' Kim admonished. 'And we'll get used to the heat in no time.'

'Well it's great to have you all here in one piece anyway,' Cara said happily, for once letting the protestations just roll off her. 'Now, all we have to do is wait for Lauren and Gene and meet up with Danielle and Zack, and then everyone will be all set.'

Kim grinned at Cara and held her arms out wide. 'Come here, bride-to-be, give me a hug.'

Cara smiled and obliged her sister-in-law. 'Crikey, all of you on one flight. Must've been fun – I can't imagine what went on,' she whispered surreptitiously in Kim's ear.

'Don't listen to a thing your mother says, she had a ball the whole way here. Ate all around her and drank Bloody Marys by the bucketload. She had the time of her life, and once Mick figured out how to operate the in-flight movies, he did too. How are you holding up, honey? Anything I can help you with?'

Cara rolled her eyes. 'Not unless you can control the weather. You've heard about the hurricane?' She bit her lip. 'I don't know what we'll do if it hits here before Friday.'

Kim patted her on the shoulder. 'Let's not worry about that. This wedding has seen much greater challenges than some silly storm. And if it happens, well we can all just stay indoors get drunk, and get you married off just the same. Besides, Gail, is it?' she queried. Cara nodded and Kim's smile widened conspiratorially. 'Heidi, Lauren . . . what's another bitch in the scheme of things?'

Chapter 31

Danielle's stomach clenched in a tight knot as the wheels of Zack's Cessna touched down on the runway of Hewanorra airport in St Lucia. She willed herself to keep control. She needed to appear calm, especially in front of her family and even more so now that Zack was present.

However, it was hard, because Zack was sitting across from her, observing her, much in the same way that a scientist would inspect a bug under a microscope. She felt as if he could read her every thought. It unnerved her.

'We're here,' he said simply, a hand cupping his chin.

She looked down and smoothed her Prada skirt, then picked a piece of lint from her colourful Pucci top and brushed it away. She'd had a fresh round of Botox a couple of days before, and her hair freshly coloured, and a pair of D&G sunglasses were now perched on her head. At the very least Danielle felt she looked the part of the rich, successful and glamorous older sister.

'So we are,' she replied, barely disguising the tension in her voice.

'Remind me again what your siblings' names are?' her boyfriend asked politely, as if he were about to enter a business meeting and wanted to know exactly who the key players would be.

'I'm the first child, Ben's next, then Cara and Heidi is the youngest.'

'And your sister-in-law is Kim, and the brother-in-law's name is . . .?'

'Paul is Heidi's husband. Shane is Cara's fiancé. Lindsay and Olivia are Ben and Kim's daughters,' she said, filling in the relevant information about her extended family.

'And your parents are Betty and Mick, of course,' he confirmed. 'Perfect. I'm looking forward to meeting them all.'

I'll bet, she thought. She almost wanted to smack the eager look right off Zack's face. Why did he have to put her through this, and why the hell couldn't she have been an only child?

'Well,' she said stiffly. 'I'm sure it will all be enlightening.'

'That's a good word, enlightening,' he commented. He shook his head as if puzzled. 'I have yet to understand why you are so reticent about your family.'

'Well, wait until you meet them,' Danielle said, avoiding his gaze. *You don't need to know,* she thought silently.

Moments later, the cabin attendant came to rouse them from their seats. She handed them each a hot towel to freshen up. 'I hope you enjoyed the flight,' she said, smiling, and Danielle couldn't help but smile back. This was so much better than flying commercial.

'It was lovely. Thank you,' she said, standing up. 'Well?' She turned to Zack. 'Let's get this over with.'

As she moved to pass him in the aisle, he pulled her close. 'Sweetheart, come here a moment. I know you are stressed, but please let me in. OK, I get it. You aren't close to your family, and while I am not really sure why that is, let's just make the best of the weekend. I am really not here to sabotage you. I'm here because I love you and I want to be part of what you are a part of. OK?'

Danielle allowed herself to be kissed, closing her eyes, wishing she could shut the world out at that moment. 'You just don't understand,' she whispered, more to herself than Zack.

'Understand what?' he pressed. 'That today you are a beautiful, successful, confident woman? Whatever's gone on in your past, whatever your relationship is or was with your mother, none of it affects you today. Come on Danielle, be the woman I know. Throw that chin out. Walk that walk. You don't need to regress to being a teenager, just because your family are in the same time zone. But whatever happens over the next few days, whatever I'm not getting . . . just try and let me in, OK?'

She studied Zack's face. He certainly appeared earnest and she thought for a moment that maybe she was worrying about nothing. Maybe this would be all right. Maybe he wouldn't judge. Maybe her family wouldn't drive him away.

Maybe, just maybe, her fears were unjustified.

She gave a small nod. 'OK, just promise me that you won't hold anything against me.'

'Hold what against you, Danielle? The family you were born into? No family is perfect. Believe me, I know that,' he chuckled.

'Well, it's just they can be a bit coarse, and loud and very Irish—' And that moment the cabin attendant opened the outer door and Danielle immediately heard voices calling to her.

She stepped out into the bright Caribbean sun and squinted to where her family – all of them – were waiting on the asphalt.

My God, how many of them were there? she wondered, lowering her sunglasses. Nerves instinctively flooded her stomach. She tried counting. There were too many people here. And to her they were all potential time bombs, ticking away, waiting to explode.

'Danielle! Wow, look at you, fancy-pants!'

She closed her eyes. Bloody Ben.

'Pulling up in a private jet, no less! Like a full-on celebrity!' Mick called out. 'Hey stranger!'

'Oh lord . . .' Danielle muttered, grimacing.

Zack let out a laugh. 'So they're excited to see you. Big deal, there's nothing wrong with that.'

'Maybe some of them,' Danielle said darkly. She didn't hear her mother shouting out her name . . .

Cara waved happily, and Danielle looked at the blur of faces, trying to identify who was there. She straightened her shoulders and walked with purpose down the stairs onto the asphalt, like Jackie O ascending from Onassis's boat.

Take that, Mum. Not looking so useless now, am I?

When she reached the bottom of the steps, she waited for Zack, who jogged down behind her, and took her hand. His staff would arrange to have their luggage forwarded to the resort, so all she carried was an oversize Chanel purse, the very latest, and the most in-demand of the season. She jutted her chin out, trying to convey the fact that someone would be taking care of the rest, fetching her luggage. This was how rich, successful people travelled.

She and Zack crossed the distance between her and her family.

Wow, those two are *really* pregnant, was Danielle's first thought as she caught sight of her youngest sister and Kim. She tried to remember the last time she'd seen them all and realised that she truly couldn't recall. Cara rushed forward, dragging Shane behind her.

'Danielle!' She threw her arms around her older sister's neck. 'I'm so glad you made it. This is Shane.' She introduced the handsome young man behind her. 'And you must be

Zack! I'm so excited to meet you. I'm Cara. We spoke on the phone.'

Zack smiled his winning, all-American, poster boy smile. He leaned forward to shake Cara's hand, but was instead met with a huge hug. 'Oh! Yes – nice to meet you too, Cara. Congratulations. I'm excited to be here, and to share in your special day. Shane, nice to meet you too and congratulations.'

Danielle smiled proudly. What a good guy, she thought, looking at Zack as he accepted Cara's hug and shook Shane's hand. He really did seem happy to be here. Maybe she should just lighten up?

'So come and see everyone. They all just got here, too,' Cara urged. 'Now we're just waiting on Shane's parents.'

'Er, right,' said Danielle nervously as she looked over Cara's shoulder at the rest of the group.

Zack came to her side. 'Relax,' he said under his breath. 'And smile. Cara seems great.' She cringed even as she placed a tight smile on her face and allowed herself to be guided forward.

'Danielle!' cheered Kim. 'So happy to see you again, it's been too long. Ooh love that bag. I just read a feature about that in a magazine on the way over. It's so roomy I thought it might be fun to use as a baby bag when the latest comes along.'

'Thank you.' Danielle reluctantly allowed herself to be greeted by Kim and Ben and her exuberant nieces, all the while introducing Zack to each member of her family.

'Auntie Danielle, you didn't say hello to Number Three!' Olivia admonished.

'Sorry, what?' asked Danielle, confused.

'She means this one,' Kim explained, pointing to her tummy.

'Right.' Danielle wasn't sure if Olivia actually expected her to bend down and speak to her mother's stomach. She simply smiled indulgently, always uncomfortable around children. 'And this is Heidi, and her husband Paul,' Cara continued.

Heidi extended a hand that had until then been glued to her tummy, and offered it to Zack, who greeted her warmly.

'Erm, congratulations on the impending arrival,' Danielle said to Heidi awkwardly. They'd never had much of a sisterly relationship, what with there being such an age gap, and truth be told they'd never really clicked, but manners dictated she said something, didn't they?

Heidi eyed her speculatively, sizing her up. 'Thanks, it's been a tough few months . . . but oh, listen to me blathering on – I know it's impossible for someone who's never had kids to understand.'

Much to Danielle's surprise this childless barb cut deep, and right then she remembered exactly why she and Heidi had never had much of a relationship.

Moving along quickly, Danielle turned to her father. 'Zack, this is my dad, Mick.'

'Honoured to meet you Mr Clancy,' Zack said politely and Mick beamed.

'Ah, call me Mick,' he said. 'Nice to meet you too and glad this girl of mine finally allowed you to mix with us.' Danielle felt herself relaxing a little – until she heard another voice.

'Well, Danielle, nice of you to honour us with your presence,' Betty said stiffly, not making any movement to move forward and greet her eldest daughter.

'Mother,' said Danielle crisply, working her hardest to match her tone. She took in the garish kaftan and wished that she could put a blindfold on Zack. 'Well, I am one of

Cara's bridesmaids after all, so of course I wouldn't miss it for the world.'

The two women engaged in a staring showdown until Zack moved forward, extending his hand to Danielle's mother.

'Mrs Clancy. I'm Zack Carter. It's a pleasure to meet you.'

Having locked her gaze on Danielle, Betty finally tore her eyes away to look to Zack. 'Yes, Mr Carter . . .'

'Please ma'am. Call me Zack.'

'Zack,' she said coldly. 'It is nice to meet you too. I was convinced for a while there that you didn't actually exist. It wouldn't be the first time my daughter's misled us about something.' She transferred her gaze pointedly back to Danielle, then quickly turned away, looking for someone else to talk to.

Danielle bit her lip and felt herself blushing. She swallowed hard, trying to bite back tears. Once again, her mother had won, thoroughly embarrassing her in the first five minutes. Jesus Christ, she had to be around that woman for the next three days. How on earth was she going to get through it?

'It's nothing, let it go,' whispered Zack encouragingly and Danielle felt relieved, realising that for once she had an ally. 'Don't worry about her.'

'Do you two have luggage to collect or anything?' Cara asked.

Danielle shook her head absently, still feeling the sting of her mother's comment. 'No, no, they'll have it sent it to the resort,' she said as she waved her hand in the direction of the plane.

Cara shrugged, but looked unsure as to who 'they' were. The elves, perhaps?

Chapter 32

'But of *course* the groom's family always throws the rehearsal dinner,' Lauren insisted, patting Cara gently on the arm. She smiled. 'We wanted to do something special for you. I realise that you already have reservations at the hotel restaurant and of course, whatever you want, but we insist on picking up the tab. We hope that is OK?'

Cara looked at Shane, who nodded in agreement.

'Well, thank you both,' she said to his parents. 'Really, that is very kind.'

Gene smiled and squeezed her shoulder. 'We are happy to help in any way we can, my dear'.

At least this time Shane's parents were asking permission to do something in relation to the wedding, and truth be told, Cara did welcome her in-laws' offer to pay for the rehearsal dinner, as the costs even for something as small as what they were doing were beginning to add up.

She smiled back at her very soon-to-be mother-in-law. Lauren was a changed woman since all that had happened in the preceding months. At least now all was on the straight and narrow.

And, most importantly, all members of the wedding party had safely arrived at the Paradise Oasis resort. Lauren and Gene were the last to arrive, not long after Cara had helped her family and friends check in to the hotel and settle in to their rooms.

'So now that we're all here, what's on the agenda first?' Lauren asked. 'Of course, I am eager to meet your family, and to assist your mother too. I'm sure that the job of mother of the bride is not an easy one,' she added pleasantly and Cara knew that this time she was being truly sincere in looking to help.

'And what is the contingency plan if this blasted hurricane hits?' asked Gene bluntly.

Cara winced. *The stupid hurricane again.* 'Well, we don't actually have one really. They're hoping it'll move off course before—'

'Well really, it's something you ought to be thinking about,' Gene harrumphed. 'The pilot on the way advised the first-class passengers that it was altogether likely to hit here.'

Lauren lightly tapped her husband on the shoulder. 'Not *now*, dear,' she said sharply.

Cara looked at Shane worriedly. 'Oh God . . . what do you think we should do?'

Shane shot daggers at his father, evidently annoyed at the fact that he had been the one to bring the dreaded subject up again. 'I think that we talk to resort management before doing anything else, don't you? Surely they know what to do if needs be – I'm sure they've been through many hurricanes before.'

Cara tapped her foot nervously. 'I just can't believe we have this to worry about now.'

'Now, now, it hasn't come to anything yet,' Lauren chided confidently. 'Don't worry Cara, I'm sure we'll be able to sort something out.'

As Cara and Shane escorted his parents to their suite, they were met by Cara's mother, who was pacing the lobby anxiously like a caged animal. Betty looked anything but calm, and the moment that she saw Cara approach she charged in her direction like a bull at a matador.

Catching sight of her mother, she secretly wished that Betty had changed out of her kaftan prior to meeting Lauren for the first time. She hated herself for thinking it, but really there couldn't be more of a contrast between the two women; Betty in her multicoloured, oversized tent and Lauren in her chic linen trousers and Givenchy top.

Putting this to the back of her mind, she decided she had bigger things to worry about at the moment.

'Cara! They said that the hurricane is on its way!' Betty cried. 'That its course is now set, and it's definitely going to hit St Lucia! Do you think that we need to evacuate? Do you think we should get out of here? I've never been through a hurricane before – what if we all drown? This is a national emergency, maybe we should call the embassy and they can helicopter us out – oh hello,' she said stopping short as she suddenly noticed Lauren and Gene's presence. 'I'm Betty Clancy, Cara's mother.'

She extended her hand to Lauren, and the two women sized each other up fully. Cara swallowed hard, hoping that there wouldn't be any problems. Up to now, Lauren and Gene hadn't been at all shy about expressing any preconceived notions about her family in the build-up to the wedding. And Betty had also had plenty to say for herself about Lauren's part in the troubles she and Shane had had with them recently.

But at that moment, neither woman seemed to be expressing any outward animosity.

Lauren stepped forward and grasped Betty's hand with one of her own, patting her on the wrist with the other. Cara had to admit, she was impressed; that was practically a knock-down embrace in Lauren's world. 'It is so nice to meet you, Mrs Clancy. I have heard so much about you and I must apologise for our not meeting sooner,' she cooed.

While her voice was stately and she very much spoke with her usual upper-crust accent, she was nonetheless welcoming and polite.

In turn, Betty beamed. Whatever she might have thought previously about Shane's snooty mother seemed to have vanished like smoke.

'Oh of course, well, I am sure that you are very busy, and I completely understand that you have so much going on. I am so excited to finally meet you too. Please call me Betty. Of course, we are all going to be family shortly. That is, if this hurricane doesn't spoil everything.' Betty's smile all too quickly returned to a grimace of pure worry.

'Try not to concern yourself about it, my dear lady,' said Lauren, her voice dripping with authority. 'We'll figure this all out. Come with me.' She put her arm through Betty's and led her off towards the front desk, barking orders the entire way. 'You there, young man! I need to speak with the manager immediately.'

Cara had to smile, amused by the force of nature that was Lauren Richardson. *Did she really think that she could control the course of this hurricane?*

'Anyway, as things stand, and until we hear otherwise, we're just going ahead with what has been planned,' Shane said pointedly to his father. 'We will deal with the weather as it happens, that's all that we can do.'

Cara looked at her fiancé with some scepticism. Personally, she rather hoped that his mother might be a force of nature after all.

If there was anyone who could fight off Hurricane Gail, it just might be her future mother-in-law.

Danielle lounged on a sunbed by the pool, watching her nieces play in the water with Kim and Ben. Zack was still getting settled in the hotel room, and trying to find a good Wi-Fi connection.

She looked at her sister-in-law, who was very, very pregnant but still shamelessly and proudly wearing a Gucci Black bikini. She had to admit too, she was pulling it off. But then again, when you looked like Heidi Klum, you could pull off anything from a bikini to a paper bag.

Danielle smiled briefly; she had to admit, from what she'd seen of her so far, Kim did seem kind of cool.

'Hey Danielle! Would you do me a favour?' Kim called out from the water.

'Yeah, what do you – erm, I mean sure!' she replied, struggling to retain her American twang. She had noticed that even in the few hours she had been back around her family, the accent of her native land kept coming back unintentionally. 'What do you need?'

'Can you order a couple of margaritas, one for me and Ben and one for yourself if you fancy it. And some blueberry slushies for the girls.'

'No problem.' Danielle duly waved down a waiter at the other side of the pool, but couldn't help feeling Heidi's dark gaze on her from the next bed over.

'Problem, Heidi?' she asked. It hadn't taken her long to get reacquainted with her sister, who was clearly quite the prima donna.

'You really shouldn't be encouraging her,' the younger woman said shortly.

'What are you talking about?'

'The margarita. She's pregnant, remember. As if she wasn't making it obvious enough,' she added, patting down her own decidedly more demure pool kaftan.

Danielle shrugged. 'I'm sure it's fine. It's not like she's doing shots or anything. Besides, it's her business,' she continued, her tone brisk. She had no patience for women like Heidi who had it in their minds that they were the authority on everything. Clearly it was a good thing that they'd never been close.

The waiter approached and Danielle ordered the drinks and looked at Heidi out of the corner of her eye. 'Plus, a couple of shots of Patron, extra chilled,' she added defiantly. The shots were for her alone, but she couldn't resist winding up her younger sister by making her think she was ordering extra for Kim.

Just then, a squeal from across the pool diverted Danielle's attention. It was coming from one of Cara's girlfriends; she'd been introduced to them earlier but she couldn't remember their names.

Some guy standing at the edge of the pool had just tossed the girl in. A rather cute guy too, she realised, taking in his nicely defined biceps from the back. He was wearing a tight pair of black swim trunks and it looked like he was a devout follower of a very good workout, she observed.

Then the same guy turned around to face the pool, a huge grin on his handsome face, and Danielle's heart almost stopped.

Suddenly, everything around her became a blur. She felt the blood drain from her face.

Now her heart was beating so quickly she didn't think it would be possible to slow it down, and her knees felt weak as she tried to get around the fact that the one man in the world she had never expected to see again was standing only a few metres away. A man whom she hadn't seen in more than two decades.

What the hell? Why was he here? At Cara's wedding, of all places . . .

Conor Dempsey, possibly one of the biggest skeletons in Danielle's closet, was here in St Lucia.

And for some reason seemed to be a guest at Cara's wedding.

Just at that moment Cara emerged into the pool area. Danielle hadn't had a chance to catch up with her properly since she and Zack arrived, and she knew that Cara and Shane had been busy helping everyone get settled in and making last-minute arrangements for the wedding.

Cara strode confidently towards the end of the pool where her friends were laughing and joking. She was wearing a pale pink bikini that accentuated her light tan, and Danielle felt briefly envious of the fact that Cara looked even younger than she actually was – more like her early rather than late twenties – whereas she herself was unfortunately starting to show her age. She glanced down at her swimming costume, suddenly self-conscious now that Conor was here.

Danielle tried to push the thought from her mind as she watched Conor playfully catch Cara round the waist and heave her into his arms, threatening to throw her in the pool.

Laughing, Cara screamed and pounded on his chest, demanding to be let down. Instead, though, he started to swing her above the water, acting as if he was going to let her go any minute. Cara howled with laughter and, finally, Conor placed her back on her feet. She hugged Conor around his middle and he delivered a little peck to the top of her head.

What the hell? Clearly, Cara and Conor were very close friends, and watching all that made Danielle very uncomfortable.

'That is not cool,' she said under her breath, trying to calm her thoughts. She closed her eyes and tried to just relax and not think about it, not for the moment. She needed to try and balance her chakras, relax and enjoy the sunshine.

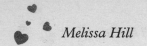

Once that was done she could try to get her head straight and think about what to do next.

A moment later the waiter arrived and delivered the drinks, along with the extra shots of tequila she'd ordered. Danielle waved to Kim to come to the side of the pool, where she handed out the margaritas and slushies. Returning her attention to the rest of the group, she noticed Zack had just made his way down to the pool deck. He took in the scene, apparently deciding where to go.

For some reason he headed directly towards Conor.

'Holy hell,' said Danielle under her breath. Those were two people who should *not* have an opportunity to get to know each other.

She jumped up from her position on the lounge chair and wrapped a sarong around her waist. *At least I look hot in a one-piece,* she thought, considering her expertly toned stomach. Grabbing a shot of tequila, she threw it back and sucked on a lime as a chaser. She glanced briefly at the second shot, shrugged and thought, *what the hell?* Downing it for good measure, she stood up and walked with confidence towards her boyfriend, and her, well . . . ex-*something*.

'Nothing like liquid courage,' she said under her breath as the tequila burned its way down her throat and she considered how much would she have to drink to make it through the next few minutes – let alone the weekend – in one piece?

Cara looked up and smiled as she saw her approach.

'Hi, Danielle, wow, you look amazing – like a fifties Hollywood icon or something,' she said, and Danielle kept putting one foot in front of the other, while she tried to work out if this was actually a compliment. Then Cara grabbed her arm and pulled her forward. 'There's someone you haven't met yet I think. She tapped Conor, who was still fooling around with the three other women and had his back to her, on the shoulder. Danielle steeled herself for the inevitable, knowing that she was powerless to stop what was about to happen next.

'Conor,' Cara smiled. 'I want you to meet my big sister Danielle. Danielle, this is my boss, Conor.'

He turned around quickly, immediately meeting Danielle's gaze head on. Suddenly, everything around her came to a stop. Despite the temporary buzz from the tequila, she felt the blood drain from her face and her knees go weak as his gaze locked on to hers. She thought she noticed a slight wrinkle of confusion in his face but just as quickly it was gone. Conor's expression remained cool and collected, and Danielle struggled to keep her feet planted firmly on the ground, although she had the overwhelming desire to run.

Conor spoke, an ironic smile playing on his lips. 'Of all the bars in all the world . . . Danni, how the hell are you?'

Chapter 33

'And so, it makes us so proud and happy to be welcoming Cara as a daughter and a new member of our family,' Gene said later that night, addressing the small group in the private dining room where the rehearsal dinner was being held. 'And also to welcome all of you. We are so happy to be a part of this wonderful celebration in this stunning location. Cheers to Shane and Cara!'

Everybody raised their glasses, saluting the happy couple in a toast. Shane and Cara exchanged a smile and a brief kiss and returned the fond gazes of the people around them.

So far, so good, Cara thought. The rehearsal on the beach earlier had gone according to plan, even as she did her best to try to ignore the wind that seemed to be picking up around them, and the growing waves that grew more restless as they crashed on the shore. She wondered if maybe, just maybe, the weather would hold off until after tomorrow night? Come hell or, erm, high water (although no, scratch the high water bit), she wanted to get married on that beach.

'Thank you Gene,' she said, getting up from her chair and hugging the man who would hopefully become her father-in-law in less than twenty-four hours.

'Pleasure dear,' he said, returning the embrace.

Cara sat back down, delighted with the way things were going so far. She had to admit that everyone was getting along swimmingly. However, she couldn't help but notice that Danielle did seem somewhat on edge, especially when Conor was in the room.

It had transpired at the pool earlier that the two already knew each other, which was a surprise, as Conor had never mentioned it to Cara before. When she'd asked earlier how they knew each other, both had been vague, saying something about being in school together and sharing mutual old friends, which Cara supposed made sense. Danielle had been away from home so long she'd almost forgotten her sister had had a life in Greygates too.

But it seemed that Conor hadn't actually realised that she and Danielle (or Danni as he seemed to know her) were related, as Cara and her boss had only become acquainted after his return from London, long after Danielle had moved away from home. Cara was sure she'd mentioned her older sister on occasion, but evidently he hadn't made the connection.

Lauren stood up and took command of the room. 'I also have something to say, Cara,' she said, turning to her. 'Now, I am not sure if you have your "Something Blue" just yet and of course, if you do I understand. But I wanted to give you a gift of my own. Something that was given to me for my own wedding day. It seemed only appropriate that I now pass it to you since I never was blessed with a daughter, at least by birth. Come here Cara – you too Shane.'

Cara turned her attention to Lauren and got up as requested. Her mother-in-law to be turned back to the table where she had been sitting and retrieved a dark rectangular velvet box.

'Now of course, if you don't want to wear this, I understand, but I just thought . . .' She handed the box to Cara.

Cara took it and looked at Shane, somewhat puzzled but delighted at the same time. Opening the box slowly, she saw that inside was a delicate sapphire-studded necklace, sparkling beautifully beneath the overhead lights. It wasn't big or gaudy, but simple and classic, a fine stream of sapphires sitting in an invisible, white gold setting. But regardless of its simplicity, Cara knew this necklace would have cost a fortune. Indeed, she did already have her 'something blue,' some sexy underwear to wear beneath her dress, but she decided that a little more couldn't hurt.

'Oh my goodness, Lauren. It's beautiful . . .'

'I know you're dedicated to having a simple, no-fuss beach wedding,' Lauren said somewhat self-consciously. 'So if it's too much and doesn't fit with that, I understand.'

'Lauren, it's amazing, thank you. I'll wear it proudly.' Cara was blown away by the wonderful effort Shane's mother was making to be a part of the day and the festivities without being pushy. It made up for all the hassle of before. 'Mum, come and see.' She passed around the jewellery box to show everyone and received a chorus of oohs and ahhs.

'It's really gorgeous, Cara,' smiled Danielle as she showed her. 'It will look amazing with your dress.' Cara smiled brightly at the vote of confidence from her glamorous older sister. She'd shown Danielle her wedding dress earlier, delighted by their new-found closeness since they'd started communicating again for the wedding.

From across the room, another voice sounded.

'Excuse me,' Conor called out. 'I wonder if I could say something?'

At this Danielle looked up sharply. Was it Cara's imagination or had her sister's tanned complexion turned white? She glanced from her to Conor, wondering what she was missing.

'What's the matter?' Cara inquired, sitting down in an empty seat next to her in the hope of teasing some information out of her on this history between her and Conor.

'Nothing, why?' Danielle replied, wide-eyed.

'But—'

'Shh!' hissed Heidi from the other side of Cara, turning her attention to Conor.

Conor cleared his throat and looked around the room. 'I just wanted to have a quick word if you all don't mind. I know I am not a member of the family and am here just as a guest but . . .' Danielle threw back the remainder of what was in her wine glass, and looked to Zack to refill it from the bottle to his left. He obliged her willingly.

Cara watched her sister with growing interest as Conor went on. 'Anyway, I just wanted to thank everyone, Mr and Mrs Clancy, and Mr and Mrs Richardson and especially Cara and Shane, for inviting me here and making me feel so welcome. I've known Cara a long time now and she is very special to me.' He smiled at Cara, who blushed, not sure what to make of all this, given what she'd suspected recently. Nonetheless it was true; of course she and Conor were so much more than boss and employee; they were truly good friends. And how lovely of him to get up in front of all these people and say something so nice. She just hoped Shane didn't mind.

As if reading Cara's thoughts, Conor turned to Shane. 'Mate, you are a very lucky man. I can only hope to meet someone like her some day. So keep a watch out,' he added with a wink. 'And make sure you marry her tomorrow, because otherwise I might try to steal her away.'

Cara gulped and everyone else laughed except Danielle, who at that moment choked and began coughing violently into her napkin.

Cara looked at her sister, as Zack began gently pounding on her back. 'Are you OK?' she asked, concerned.

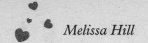

'Sure,' Danielle finally said, when the coughing fit had ended. 'Something just went down the wrong way.'

'Here's some water,' offered Zack.

'It's fine. I just . . . I just need to go to the restroom. I'll be back soon.' Danielle stood up abruptly and hastened from the room.

'What's the matter with her?' Cara asked.

Zack shrugged. 'I think she's just a little tense.'

'Yes, I sort of gathered that,' she replied.

The question was, Cara wondered, tense about what?

Later that night, Cara and Shane said their goodbyes and separated for the night, having decided to take the traditional stance of not seeing each other until the wedding ceremony.

Full of excitement and nervousness, Cara lay in bed, trying to sleep but unable to switch off. Her mind was crammed with thoughts about the wedding day itself, the rest of her life with Shane, the growing inevitability of stormy weather and also about her family, specifically Danielle.

Her mother and sister had been careful to avoid one another at the resort so far, but Cara worried that their close proximity would eventually come to a head.

If there was going to be some kind of blow-up between them, she sincerely hoped they at least managed to wait until after the wedding. She couldn't allow anything else to go wrong just now.

And she wondered why exactly Betty was always so disparaging of Danielle when her sister seemed so nice and had no airs and graces about her whatsoever. Cara had always suspected Danielle must possess a somewhat self-absorbed Heidi-style personality, but in fact, other than looking very alike the two of them couldn't have been more different.

Since her arrival Danielle had gone out of her way to ask if there was anything at all she could do to help in the run-up to the ceremony, proper sisterly and indeed bridesmaidly behaviour, unlike Heidi who'd been skulking around with a face on her that would cut diamonds.

Cara hoped the short stay would give them the opportunity to get to know one another better and maybe become closer. She liked her older sister a lot and whatever had gone on between her and Betty in the past didn't mean that Danielle shouldn't be close to the rest of the family.

But she couldn't help but notice that Danielle seemed very much on edge all the time, and she hoped this wedding wasn't forcing her to confront any demons where their mother was concerned.

Or indeed with anyone else, she mused, thinking about Conor. There was some kind of history there too; that much was obvious.

And what should she make of Conor's speech earlier and the recent inkling that he might have more than friendly feelings for her?

Exhausted with all her thinking, Cara finally drifted off to sleep in the wee hours of the morning, her brain demanding rest.

At seven a.m. she was abruptly awakened by urgent knocking on her hotel room door. She sat up quickly in bed and was immediately met by the sound of a large crack of thunder from outside the window.

What the hell . . .? she thought blearily, temporarily confused as to where she was and what she was doing here. She looked at the other side of the bed. Where was Shane? Then it all dawned on her. She was on the paradise island of St Lucia, and what's more, today was her wedding day!

Cara grinned brightly, but another loud clap of thunder suddenly brought her straight back to reality. Oh no!

Panic rose in her throat as she jumped from the bed and raced to the window.

'Cara, are you up? Open the door,' Kim called from outside before she'd had time to open the curtains.

She rushed to the door and flung it open, allowing Kim to rush in. 'What's going on?' she asked, hustling back to the window and throwing open the curtains.

It was a nightmarish scene. Driving rain pounded on the window, and a violent wind bent the palm trees on the other side of the glass to dangerous angles. Thunder roared across the sky and lightning flashed wildly. The sky itself was an inky looking colour that bore down on the tropical landscape like an unfeeling and uncaring menace.

Hurricane Gail had arrived.

'It's . . . it's a hurricane,' Cara gasped, unable to believe what she was seeing. A hurricane today, on her wedding day, of all days.

Kim stood next to her. 'Well, not quite yet, but she'll be here shortly. This is just one of the outer bands. Or at least, that's what I was just told by the front desk.'

'But it's my wedding day. I'm supposed to get married, out *there*, today!' Cara pointed to the beach, barely visible in the murky distance. Her eyes started to well up. She couldn't believe this. Her day was ruined. It couldn't be possible, not after all she and Shane been through to get to this point. It was if this wedding just wasn't supposed to happen.

Kim sighed. 'I'm sorry sweetie, but I don't think your beach wedding is going to happen now, at least not today. The hotel is advising everyone to take cover in the storm shelter. For our own safety, while we wait this thing out.'

'But what about the wedding?' Cara whispered lamely, searching wildly for a possible solution to this gigantic problem.

'I'm sorry Cara, but our main priority now is to get ourselves to safety.' Kim looked out of the window and sighed ominously. 'Before things really get bad.'

Chapter 34

A few minutes later, Cara found herself being led down grey concrete stairs through the dingy inner catacombs of the hotel. This was a part of the resort that tourists were clearly not supposed to see, other than in the case of an emergency, which this obviously was.

'Where are we going?' she asked dejectedly, the full weight of everything that was happening resting heavily on her shoulders.

Ever the organiser, Kim had taken charge of making sure that Cara's wedding dress, bridesmaid dresses, shoes and other wedding-related paraphernalia were taken down to the storm shelter with them, just in case.

Now she followed her sister-in-law ever downwards, her parents and the rest of the family bringing up the rear and helping transfer some of Cara's belongings along with their own. 'Everyone in the hotel is headed down to the storm shelter. It's the safest place to be,' Kim told her.

'Everyone?' Cara repeated, her eyes filling with unshed tears.

'Yes, honey. Everyone. Shane will be there. Don't worry.'

Cara stopped in her tracks, and Heidi ploughed straight into her backside. 'Come on Cara, keep moving,' she said gruffly, as she tried to manage the three dress bags that contained the bridesmaid dresses. 'You know, I really shouldn't be carrying so much weight, and these dress bags are heavy. This whole situation, the weather, the weight, the stress, it's bad for me and the baby.'

'It's not as if I engineered the storm just to put you out, Heidi,' she shot back through gritted teeth. 'And it's kind of stressful for everyone right now.'

She turned again to Kim. 'Shane's going to be in the storm shelter? But I can't see him before the ceremony. It's bad luck for the groom to see the bride before the wedding.'

Kim smiled and reached out to grab Cara's hand, pulling her forward once again. 'Frankly speaking Cara, I think you're much more likely to have bad luck if you don't get your butt to this storm shelter pronto. We'll meet the rest of them down there. Now come on.'

When they reached the shelter, an employee of the resort was standing in the doorway.

'This way everyone, please, come in,' he directed them. 'You have nothing to worry about. This is standard procedure with weather like this. It is simply the safest place to wait out a hurricane. Please understand we are monitoring the situation on the ground as well. Know that your well-being and safety is of the utmost importance to the staff at the Paradise Oasis Resort,' he intoned loudly as hotel guests (many in pyjamas who looked like they had literally run from their beds down to the storm shelter) shuffled wearily about, trying to make sense of what was happening. Many carried a selection of bags and personal possessions, as if they were worried that they would find their belongings washed away when (or if) they were able to return to their hotel rooms.

The Clancy family staked out one corner of the large storm shelter, joining the Richardsons, who were already there – Shane looking glum, but brightening a little when he saw their approach. Cara had since given up worrying about whether or not he saw her today. For the wedding to happen, they were going to need a miracle.

Although the room was dark and unwelcoming it wasn't uncomfortable as the resort had provided plenty of chairs, blankets, pillows and other necessities for their use.

Nonetheless, Cara just couldn't stop thinking that this was so not how she'd pictured the morning of her and Shane's wedding day.

'I can't believe this is happening,' she moaned into Shane's chest.

'It will be OK, honey. Try not to worry about it just now. It's just a temporary setback. We will leave St Lucia married, I promise.' He pulled her close and she gradually relaxed into his embrace, glad that at least they were together.

Just then Danielle and Zack arrived and shuffled over to the group. Cara noticed that her older sister looked a bit the worse for wear; it appeared that all the wine she had drunk the night before had taken its toll.

The only available space was an area close to Betty, and Danielle sat down next to her, unaware of her mother's look of faint disapproval – her attention seemed once again to be on Conor, who had just sat down directly across from her, close to Cara and Shane.

'Do you want some water, sweetheart?' Zack asked and Danielle nodded tiredly.

'What's the latest from the hotel management?' Lauren asked in a booming voice.

Shane looked at his mother. 'They say this storm is fast moving. By tomorrow it could all be over and so we could possibly have the wedding then,' he suggested and Cara brightened a little.

'Admittedly the timing is unfortunate, but really, it's better we all stay safe now,' Gene agreed.

'Hey, if you really want a wedding today Cara,' Conor offered, trying to lift the mood, 'We could always find a priest and get you married down here.'

Cara blew her nose. 'I'm not getting married in a storm shelter, Conor.'

'It would be sort of romantic, in a way. What do you think?'

'Don't be an idiot, Conor,' Danielle berated him, shaking her head in annoyance. Zack returned and handed her a bottle of water and she drank it down greedily.

'What? It was just a suggestion . . .'

Betty leaned forward and patted Cara on the knee. 'Pet, try not to worry. Really it will be OK. We'll just have to wait it out. The hotel says this is the safest place to be at the moment. Although I can't help thinking that this kind of thing would never have happened in St Joseph's . . .'

Suddenly Heidi's eyes widened, as if something had just occurred to her. 'What if there's flooding?' she gasped, her tone panicked. 'What if we are locked in here and we all drown?'

Danielle shook her head. 'That's not how a storm shelter works, Heidi, and Mum's right,' she said, glancing briefly at her mother. 'You just wait out a hurricane. If it's a fast moving storm, it'll just keep going, right over us. It will be over in no time.'

Conor raised his eyebrows. 'Quite the expert, I see.'

'I live in Florida, Conor. By the beach. I have been through hurricanes many times before,' she said disdainfully, and turned her head, signalling that she didn't want to talk to him any more.

'Well, I suppose we can think of it this way Cara,' Conor continued jokingly. 'At least now you have another day to reconsider.'

Cara punched him in the arm. 'I am not reconsidering.'

Shane laughed. 'Hey, back off my woman, Dempsey. I warned you . . .'

'May the best man win then. Cara, my offer from last night still stands,' Conor said with a wink, and Cara knew he was trying to lighten the mood, as she and Conor had barely spoken last night. 'Leave this guy and run off with me.'

Across from her, Cara noticed Danielle suddenly stiffen and, looking at her sister's beautifully manicured fingers, she realised that they were clenched tightly. Danielle looked as though she was about to explode. What the hell was wrong with her? She looked at Conor. Was that it? Was she jealous or . . .

'Seriously Cara,' Conor was still teasing, 'maybe the storm is a sign—'

Then all of a sudden, Danielle jumped up from her chair. 'Shut up! Stop it! Not another word, please! I can't stand it—'

The group lapsed into silence as all eyes turned to Danielle.

'Danielle?' Cara began gently, using the same tone you would use if you were trying to convince someone not to jump off the top of a skyscraper. 'What is it – what's wrong?'

Her sister's tone was clipped. 'It's Conor, he shouldn't talk to you like that. It's not right.'

Crikey, she was jealous, Cara realised. Now she was seriously worried, wondering if Danielle might have picked up on an aspect of Conor's behaviour that she'd been hoping didn't exist. 'Conor and I are good friends, he's my boss – what do you mean, it's not right?' she said.

'Babe?' Zack inquired, his voice full of concern. 'Come sit down.' He reached for Danielle's hand, but she pushed it away.

Conor looked confused. 'Hey, it's just a joke, Danielle. Cara and Shane both know I'm joking, don't you?'

'Of course. Although with your reputation Dempsey, you never know,' Shane jibed. 'I'd still be reluctant to leave any woman alone in a room with you. When I think of that time in the office when I walked in on you two—'

'Jesus Christ, stop it,' Danielle commanded and Cara heard a sharp intake of breath coming from nearby. She looked to her left and saw that Betty was staring at Danielle, a look of horror on her face.

As if she'd just realised something.

What the—? Now Cara was seriously flummoxed.

'Sweetheart, please why don't you sit down,' Zack urged again.

Danielle pinched her nose and closed her eyes. 'No . . .' she whispered, but it was as if she was talking to herself, steeling herself for something. She looked at her mother, then at Cara and finally back at Conor.

'I don't know what kind of relationship you two have . . .'

'We don't have a relationship Danielle, other than friends and colleagues of course.' Cara felt that she needed to re-assure her.

'Are you kidding me?' Heidi put in smartly. 'They are always flirting with one another. Seriously if I didn't know better—'

'That's not true.' Cara whirled on her sister, suddenly terrified that she had somehow, unknown to herself, invited Conor's affections, if that were indeed the case.

Danielle slowly turned her gaze on Conor. 'Please don't flirt with Cara any more, Conor. Really, it would be better if you didn't.'

Conor looked equally baffled. 'Why? What business is it of—?'

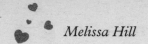

'It is my business,' Danielle said flatly. 'Yours too.'

'Mick . . .' Betty grabbed at her husband as if understanding that something terrible was about to happen. 'Do something.'

For some reason, a deep feeling of unease crept into Cara's stomach. There was something going on here, something that she wasn't privy to. Why was everyone behaving so strangely? She looked at Betty. 'Mum?'

Conor frowned. 'I'm sorry. I don't think I quite caught that.' His eyes searched Danielle's face, as if he would find some sort of answer there.

'Danielle,' Betty pleaded. 'No . . .'

Cara looked at her mother, who was shaking her head at Danielle, a beseeching look on her face. Mick, in turn, wore a look of concern.

'No Mum. This is wrong.' Danielle turned to Cara, who saw that her big sister's eyes were shining with tears. 'Cara, I don't know how to tell you this . . .'

'Tell me what?' Suddenly Cara felt very scared.

'Danielle? What's going on?' Zack asked, trying to make sense of the sudden change in family dynamic.

Danielle ignored him. She couldn't take her eyes off Cara. 'I—'

'It's OK, Danielle.' Betty stood up and put a solid hand on her oldest daughter's shoulder. Danielle looked close to breaking down. 'This isn't how I would have chosen it, and certainly not in a place like this, but—' She looked at Danielle, who nodded softly.

'Sweetheart, I'm sure you remember hearing that Danielle here was a bit of a tearaway when she was younger,' she began and Cara looked at her, momentarily puzzled at the shift in topic.

Betty patted Danielle on the shoulder. 'She was young

and foolish, and when she was sixteen things got out of control.'

'Out of control . . .' Cara repeated, puzzled.

Conor was staring confusedly at Danielle while Cara struggled to figure out the subtext of everything. Yes, everyone knew that Danielle had been a bit of a wild child. But what had that got to do with Conor . . .?

Then suddenly, Cara understood. 'Oh wow,' she said, staring from Conor to Danielle. 'You two—' So there *was* history between Conor and her sister. Ancient history but it must have been serious enough at the time. When she was sixteen he would have been a good five years older than her. A relationship would have been pretty scandalous all right, particularly to her parents and in a small community like Greygates.

'She was very young, way too young for the kind of responsibility that—'

'Jesus Christ . . .' Conor said, his face suddenly paling. 'You mean . . .'

Danielle just continued to stare from him to Cara, all the while shaking her head.

'You can't be serious,' Conor was saying.

'Responsibility, what kind of responsibility?' Cara asked, but suddenly, other details swam into focus.

Danielle and Betty's strained relationship. Her sister's departure from the family home when Cara was just a baby.

Suddenly it hit Cara with the force of a speeding train. Oh no – it couldn't be – it couldn't *possibly* be . . .

'You got pregnant . . .?' she said to Danielle hoarsely.

Her sister could only nod, her eyes shimmering with tears.

'Yes.' Betty confirmed. 'She was only a girl herself, and completely immature, in no way equipped to be a mother.'

Danielle shook her head. 'I . . .'

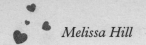

'Hold on, what happened to the baby then?' Heidi spoke up. 'Did you give it up for adoption or—'

'I suppose that's one way of looking at it,' Cara said slowly, and by the way her mother and Danielle were looking at her there was no doubt in her mind as to what had happened. The walls seemed to close in on top of her, and suddenly she couldn't breathe.

'I'm sorry,' Danielle whispered tearfully. 'I had no choice.'

'Cara, you were loved right from the start by me and your father,' Betty was saying. Nobody had yet said the words out loud, but then again nobody needed to. The truth was plain as day. *She* was Danielle's baby.

She heard Conor emit a low curse. The tension in the room was palpable, and Shane moved closer and gently put an arm around Cara's shoulder.

'You became mine and your father's,' Betty continued. 'You have always been mine. You are my sweet daughter. I have never thought of you any differently.'

Cara just sat there, speechless, unable to take it all in.

'What are you all bloody talking about?' Heidi demanded. 'What happened to the baby?'

'The best thing possible happened to her,' Danielle said, finally finding her voice. She looked at Conor. 'It was a mistake, but I never told anyone. No one, except me, knew that you were her father. Cara, I'm sorry, I am just so sorry.'

Conor had a look of sheer unadulterated anger on his face. 'So that's why you disappeared back then? You just upped and left without a bloody word. Not even a goodbye . . . I didn't even deserve that! And what's more, you don't think I had a right to know?'

'You and Conor . . .' Zack was scratching his head. 'And you're saying that Cara is . . . your daughter?'

'Cara, please say something,' Danielle pleaded when Cara just sat there dumbfounded. 'I am so sorry. I have always felt so awful, always guilty, and that's why I left. I just messed up so much; it was always something with me. I was no good at taking care of you – most of it ended up falling to Mum. It wasn't that I didn't care, it was just – I didn't know what to do, I . . .' She looked at her mother. 'What you said back then, that I would never have been any good at it – you were right.'

'You were just a child yourself,' Betty repeated gently and Cara was struck by this sudden softening in her behaviour towards her eldest daughter.

'So one day she told me that it wasn't fair to any of us and that we needed to make a decision,' Danielle continued. 'I wanted to take care of you Cara, honestly I did, but I was no good. So I moved out of home and got a place in the city. But I couldn't take being so close to you and facing my failures every time I was around the family, not to mention feeling so guilty that Mum and Dad had to step in. So eventually, I moved abroad. And I suppose that's why I stay away. Over the years I thought I'd succeeded in blocking it all out and just considering you my sister, but now coming here, and then seeing Conor . . . It's just too much. I'm so sorry.' Danielle slumped in her chair, everyone's eyes upon her.

Betty sat next to her and patted her back in a motherly fashion that Cara had never before seen her use with her eldest daughter. 'Didn't I try to tell you that confession would be good for the soul? It's OK now. No more secrets.'

And in that moment, Cara understood that the root of Betty and Danielle's problem was that her sister (her mother?) had never revealed the father of her baby. It was the kind of thing that would have driven her mother mad;

the notion that Danielle wouldn't tell or, even worse, that she hadn't known. And in a way, Betty was obviously comforted by the fact that while Danielle might have been a tearaway back then, at least she hadn't been sleeping around.

But Conor . . .

Now Cara felt sick, given her recent worries about his possible feelings towards her. How much more wrong could she have been?

'No,' Conor said, pointing a finger at Danielle. 'I can't believe this! This is not OK, not OK for anyone. Danielle, you selfish— this wasn't just all about you, you know!'

'Conor, please—' Danielle looked up as tears streamed down her cheeks.

'Stop it. You can't just do this; drop a bomb on me, on Cara, on everyone! What you just said changes everything! You think you can just confess and dump your secrets and then go on your own merry way? It doesn't work that way, Danielle! Cara and I . . . Jesus Christ, we're probably going to need years of therapy because of you. God, you haven't changed, not one bloody bit. Still you go around ripping people's hearts out, torturing people who care about you.'

Danielle cried openly and looked at Cara, who still sat in stunned silence.

'Cara, please say something,' Danielle pleaded.

Where Conor was a raging storm of anger, Danielle looked devastated, worn out.

Cara shook her head. 'I'm not sure what I am supposed to say . . .' She turned to Conor. Her father. Her *father* for goodness' sake! 'The woman who broke your heart; the one you missed your chance with. It was Danielle, wasn't it?'

He looked at her hesitantly, as if he was afraid he would see his own eyes staring back at him.

Then she turned to Danielle.

'I just don't understand. Was it that you didn't want me?' she asked hoarsely. 'I'm not sure how to think of you right now and what I am supposed to feel. You all have lied. Am I supposed to call you Mum now or something?' Her eyes swam with tears as she considered the women sitting across from her. She shoved her face into Shane's shirt and began to sob. Conor looked at her, but didn't move to comfort her. He appeared to be afraid to be too close to her.

Danielle shook her head violently. 'No, no, Mum is your mother, of course she is. Please understand, I was so young. Mum knew I wasn't capable, and she was right. The truth is I still wouldn't be capable. I wasn't cut out for kids. I'm not like Kim or Heidi or Mum. So I made sure you got the best possible mother.' She looked affectionately at Betty, who had tears in her eyes. It was as if years of tension and resentment were crumbling away in the face of the truth. 'And what's more is after that, I never felt as if I belonged any more, with this family I mean. And Conor, I just didn't want anyone to know. I didn't want to change your life. I didn't want to make you feel like you were beholden to me or something.'

'You still could have told me,' he said bitterly.

She nodded, acquiescing to his statement. 'I could have and what good would that have done? Cara became their baby – it was better that way. She's always been their baby.' Cara looked at Betty and Mick, who were holding hands and looking deeply sorrowful.

'That's true pet,' Mick told her. 'We've never seen you any differently.'

'I don't fucking believe this,' Conor put his head in his hands, clearly awestruck by all that had been revealed.

'And Zack. I'm sorry, for not telling you,' Danielle went on sadly. 'I know it was wrong, and I don't blame you if you want nothing to do with me.'

Zack looked at her, his eyes full of gentle compassion. 'Stop it honey. What did I tell you before we got here?' She looked up, meeting his gaze. The tension had been erased from her face, as if all of the stress and worry that had consumed her for years had suddenly been released. 'I told you that it didn't matter what had happened in your past, that I am only interested in who you are today. I love you Danielle, and I think you have punished yourself for too long. In fact, I know you have.'

He pulled her close and kissed her on the top of the head.

'Well fan-fucking-tastic,' said Conor sarcastically. 'At least you get a happy ending.'

Suddenly Cara felt as though the four walls were closing in on her. 'I have to get out of here,' she said, panicking. Shane exchanged a look with his parents, who were staying resolutely silent.

'Sweetheart, no you can't,' Betty knelt down next to her. 'I know you're upset but—'

'Upset? I've just found out that I've been lied to all my life!'

'No, please – your father and I, we love you, all of you. Cara, nothing's changed, you are my daughter, always have been.'

Cara bit her lip, willing herself not to break down. How could she ever move on from this? How could things ever be normal again?

'I need to think. I have to get out of here. This isn't how it's supposed to be.' But where could she go? She was trapped in a room with people who, at that moment, she desperately wanted to escape from. How on earth could she have a wedding that involved all of them? Especially given the fact that she didn't even know who *they* were any more.

'Shane, get me out of here. Please.'

Chapter 35

Heidi watched as Cara, led by Shane, got up and left the group and headed towards the other side of the room. Where she expected to go, Heidi wasn't sure. She wondered if she should go over to her and say something.

But what? She looked at her mother and Danielle sitting across from her. They had *lied*, and so had her father. They had lied to Cara, to Ben, to all of them. Their entire existence as a family was a lie.

Was this why Cara had always got special treatment, why she'd always been the golden girl as far her parents were concerned?

Heidi didn't know what to think.

As if it wasn't bad enough being stuck in this stinking dungeon; the dead, humid air was making her feel nauseated and sweaty, and she hated being confined to small spaces, especially with so many other people.

Still, she had to admit that the resort and indeed St Lucia had been miles better than expected, and she was beginning to think that Cara had the right idea after all in having her wedding in such a gorgeous location.

Until this bombshell.

Heidi was finding it difficult enough to get her head around it all, so how on earth must Cara be feeling? she wondered, in a rare moment of empathy with her older sister. Who it turns out wasn't actually her sister but her *niece*.

Suddenly, Heidi's nausea intensified, and she felt herself break out in a cold sweat.

A wave of panic engulfed her and she reached out for Paul's hand as she felt a tightness around her middle; the baby was clearly responding to her discomfort. What felt like indigestion ploughed through her and, more frighteningly, a cramp caught her hard, as if she had just been punched in the stomach.

'Oh God!' she cried, doubling over, holding on tightly to her tummy.

'Honey, are you OK?' Paul said, moving closer to her. He put his hand on her back, leaning down, trying to meet her eyes.

'It's a cramp,' she said weakly. 'It . . . oh but God, it hurts.'

'What can I do?' her husband asked, caressing her back. 'Is it passing?'

'I think so,' said Heidi through gritted teeth as she exhaled slowly. She counted the seconds in her head. However, at that moment another cramp tore across her midsection, catching her off guard. 'Oh shit!' she cried out, terrified.

She was still ten weeks from term, but according to the instructor in her antenatal class anyone could go into labour prematurely. What's worse was that she was thousands of miles away from home, her doctor and her birth plan.

Oh God, her birth plan!

Paul looked at his wife, unsure of what to do next as she started to sweat profusely, fighting through increasing pain. 'Could you be in labour?'

'I don't know Paul!' she said, starting to cry. 'I've never done this before.'

Suddenly everyone seemed to turn their attention on Heidi, temporarily diverted from the drama of Danielle's revelation.

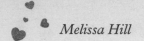

Kim, evidently sensing that something was up with Heidi's baby, quickly found her way to the other woman's side.

'Heidi?' she said softly, leaning down to her. 'What's happening? What are you feeling right now?'

'I don't know. Cramps, it's bad. It hurts.' Heidi breathed out heavily. 'Am I in labour, Kim?' she asked, afraid to hear the answer. This was her worst nightmare. 'It's too early!'

'How many weeks are you again?' Kim inquired, keeping her voice steady.

'Thirty,' Heidi said, without having to pause for thought. Kim's face was unreadable. 'OK. Hold on. Betty, can you get me some blankets and a pillow? I want Heidi to lie down flat and see if that helps.'

Betty obliged and Kim helped Heidi down, allowing her to rest on her back with a pillow under her knees and one at her lower back. Then she crouched down to Heidi's level.

'It will be OK Heidi,' her mother encouraged, but Heidi turned away, focused only on Kim. She didn't want to be around her mum right now; she couldn't look at her without thinking about all that had just happened.

'Should I see if the hotel has a doctor down here?' Lauren asked.

Heidi looked weakly to Kim. 'Am I going to have the baby here, Kim? On the floor? This isn't my birth plan. I was supposed to have soothing classical music and candles – Oh Paul!' Heidi started to sob.

'Shh, Heidi, you are just scared, and there's nothing to be scared about. And don't worry about the birth plan, sometimes babies have their own plans. But first, I want you to answer some questions for me, OK? And relax. That's really important. If you are stressed, the baby is going to be stressed.'

'I know!' she cried. 'That's what I have been trying to tell everyone this whole time, and this family of ours, they are completely bonkers—'

'Shh, don't worry about the family right now, don't think about any of it. Just think about you and your baby, OK? Now close your eyes and breathe in and out, in and out.'

Kim's tone was decidedly soothing and Heidi duly closed her eyes, and tried to stay calm as per her instructions. 'OK. I'm thinking about the baby.'

'When did the cramps start?'

'Just now, just as everything was happening.'

'OK and where did they start exactly?'

'In my tummy Kim,' Heidi said, resisting the urge to add a 'duh' at the end of the statement.

'I know that, but where. Like lower? Or at the top of your abdomen?' Kim's hand ran across Heidi's stomach, looking for information on where the pain had originated.

Heidi thought for a minute. 'I think it was lower.'

'OK. You didn't feel your waters break or anything, did you?'

Heidi shook her head. 'No, nothing yet. But I haven't checked.'

Kim chuckled. 'You would know if your waters broke. I needed four towels with Olivia, I thought it would never stop.'

Heidi giggled nervously. 'No, definitely nothing like that.'

'Have you had any cramps since moving down here, to the ground?' Kim wiped a hand across Heidi's brow gently. Heidi had to admit, it felt nice, especially because she felt so hot and sweaty.

'No, it feels better now.'

'OK Heidi. That's good.' Kim sat back. 'I think you'll be fine. It's still very early days and I think you just had a case of Braxton Hicks, known as false labour. I've had it myself. It can usually be stopped by changing position, like we just did.'

'So he's not coming early?' Heidi opened her eyes.

'He?' Kim repeated, raising an eyebrow.

She nodded. 'Yes, we are having a boy.'

She smiled. 'You never said anything . . .'

'You never asked.'

Kim shook her head. 'Point taken. I'm sorry.'

'I didn't think you were that interested, because you've been telling me to stop being silly and to stop going on about it all the time.'

'I know, and that was wrong of me too,' said Kim softly. 'I hope you will forgive me. I have to remind myself that everyone is different, especially when it comes to this. I know I can be a bit dismissive about certain things, especially when it's something I've been through before.'

Heidi smiled a little. 'I know, and I suppose that I can be a bit – dramatic sometimes.'

Kim arched an eyebrow. 'Sometimes?'

Heidi laughed. 'Actually, I can probably be a real pain. But it can be a bit scary you know.' She met Kim's gaze. 'Thank you Kim, I was . . . I was really worried,' she admitted reluctantly.

'Understandable, but it's fine honestly. You'll both be fine.'

Heidi closed her eyes again. 'I guess it must have been very scary that last time for you – with Lindsay I mean.'

Kim looked at her. 'It was. Very scary. I wasn't sure if either of us would make it.'

'I didn't understand . . . why you wanted to do it a different way this time. Before now I mean,' she said, referring to Kim's plans for a C-section. 'Being honest, it's the first time I've really thought about the baby, and how frightened you can be for it, especially when you don't know what's going to happen.'

Kim nodded. 'That's why in some cases, control is good. Still, I think you'll be fine. You come from a family of strong women, your mother especially.'

Heidi followed Kim's gaze to where Betty was sitting.

'So what do you think about this thing with Cara? What happens next?' There was no denying that Heidi still felt as if her world had been rocked.

'I don't think it changes anything, not really,' Kim replied.

'I guess . . . I guess I always wondered why Mum and Dad preferred her so much over me,' she said, before she could think too much about it. 'Now I know.'

Kim looked at Heidi as if seeing her for the first time. 'I don't think parents favour any one child over the other,' she began, but then paused as if realising something. 'Although, I guess we instinctively react to the one who might need us that bit more.'

'You think that's all it is?' Heidi asked, slightly amazed at herself for confiding her feelings about this to anyone, least of all Kim.

'Absolutely. You'll see, when you have your own.'

Heidi sighed afresh. 'This family is totally messed up now.'

'Not really,' Kim said. 'We are all family, Heidi. And this stuff with Cara and Danielle and your parents – it doesn't change that. There's a lot more to sisterhood than biology.'

'But we can't go on as if nothing happened,' Heidi replied, trying to get her head around what Kim was saying.

'No, I suppose not. But maybe it means that all of us talk more, and become closer. Family is family, you can't change that, no matter how hard you try. If anything, maybe this brings Danielle back closer to the rest of us. Maybe it'll mean a new beginning.'

Heidi thought about it all, but still wasn't so sure. 'Kim,' she said, shaking her head, 'you always did have an interesting way of looking at things.'

Chapter 36

On the other side of the room, Shane wrapped his arms around Cara as she cried out all of her shock and frustration. He was completely unsure of what to say. After all, what was the proper protocol for handling a situation where your fiancée finds out that her older sister is actually her mother?

'I just don't know how to go on from this, Shane. I feel so betrayed.'

'I know honey. I . . . I just don't know what to say. I don't have an answer.'

'They all lied to me. My entire life.'

'Cara, let's think of it this way. They lied to give you a good life.'

She moved back and stared up at him, her cheeks tear-stained. 'How do you mean?'

'Well,' he said hesitantly. What *did* he mean? 'Your sister, I mean your – I mean Danielle – was just a teenager when you were born. Think of how different your life would have been if you had been raised by anyone other than your mum. Your real mum, not Danielle. Danielle might be biological but that doesn't mean she's your mother.'

'But it's so weird. And Conor too – it's just so . . . sick . . .'

'I'll give you that. And I have no idea how you must be feeling about it all.'

'I feel like everything has changed; how can I just go on with everyday life? Maybe we should call this wedding off . . .'

'No, you are still you. You are the same person, irrespective of what's just happened. You are Cara, the woman I am going to make my wife the moment that this bloody hurricane passes over us.'

'You mean the one in here, or the one outside?' she said, smiling a little.

'I mean it Cara, we will get through this. You and me. Because we are a team.'

She shook her head sadly. 'Why would you want someone with so many issues?'

Shane laughed. 'Last time I checked, it wasn't you with the issues, it was everyone else.'

'I don't even know what to call them any more. I mean my mum is my grandmother and my dad—'

Shane shook his head. 'No she's not. Betty is your mum and you would be doing her a disservice by considering her to be anything else. She raised you, she made you who you are, helped you become the woman you are, the woman I fell in love with. She did the right thing. And Danielle, she is still your sister. She wasn't ready to be a mother, and it takes a brave woman to admit that. Conor might have called her selfish, but really what she did was anything but. She gave you a future, allowed you to be raised by a woman who had your best interests at heart.'

Cara took a deep breath and considered his words. Of course, he had a point, but then again, there was another loose end in all this.

'And what about Conor?' she asked. She hated thinking about what he must be going through now.

'I think that you and Conor will work it out. You have always been good friends, and maybe it's just fate that you started working for him when you did and developed that great relationship you have. Maybe this was all meant to be.

Fate might have a cruel sense of humour, downright sadistic if you think about it really, but maybe she thought that having this all out in the open was better for everyone involved. No more secrets, remember?' he smiled, and she recalled their own vow to not keep anything from each other.

'And you still want to marry me, after all this?' She looked at him doubtfully. She wouldn't blame him if he wanted to run for the hills.

'Not a doubt in my mind.'

'Not even when considering the thousands we are going to have to spend on therapy for me after we get back home?' she said archly.

Shane smiled and pulled her into his arms and Cara rested her head against his chest. She could hear his heart beating; steady, constant, unwavering. A constant. That was what she needed in her life.

She sighed. 'You know Shane, you really are the whole package.'

'Only when I'm with you, honey. Only when I'm with you.'

They both stood still, content in their embrace, feeling as if at that moment they were the only two that mattered, that existed. The rest of the craziness could just bugger off.

Then a tentative voice interrupted them.

'Excuse me? Cara, is it possible for you and me to have a little chat?'

It was Conor. He wanted to talk. To his daughter.

'I'll be over there if you need me,' Shane said encouragingly. He gave Conor a brief pat on the shoulder as he moved away.

Cara shifted from one foot to the other. To say that she was uncomfortable with this situation would have been a gross understatement. She could barely meet the eyes of the person, the man, who had, only moments previously, been her good friend and boss.

'So, um,' Conor said, fumbling for words. 'I suppose we need to talk, eh?'

'I suppose.'

'So it's been quite a day.'

'You think?'

He took a deep breath and ran his hands through his hair. 'Look Cara, I knew nothing about this, not at all. If you think I did—'

'No Conor, really, I know you didn't, you're not that good an actor.' She couldn't help it; she smiled. 'What I don't understand is, I don't know how you didn't know – or make the connection – that Danielle and I were related.'

He shrugged. 'Well of course I knew you had an older sister who lived in America. But back then I didn't know anything about Danielle's family background, and she went by Danni at the time. Anyway it was all so long ago, a lifetime ago, and I guess I tried to forget about her by the time I came back from London, so maybe that's why the penny never dropped.'

'And you loved her.' It was less of a question and more of a statement.

Conor nodded. 'I did. We were both very, very young, Cara. Danni was very spirited, your mother was right there. I mean, Betty – the one who raised you, um . . .'

'Go on,' encouraged Cara. She didn't want to think about logistics at that moment.

'Well, she and her mother fought a lot, I remember that much. She was always sneaking out, heading my way. I was quite mad for her really. She was such a free spirit, she just did whatever she wanted. She was so full of excitement and adventure. All the guys I hung around with were in love with her. She was like oxygen. And then suddenly, she was gone from my life. Now I know why. I remember hearing from around that she'd moved to the city, and then not long after that I myself went to London so . . .'

'And what about now? Do you still have feelings for her?'

'Being honest Cara, it was a lifetime ago and we were just kids. Yes, I was crazy about her back then, but we're two completely different people now.'

Cara nodded, understanding. 'I'm not sure how to think of you right now,' she offered, wondering about his thoughts on the subject.

He sighed. 'Truth be told, I'm in the same boat.'

She bit her lip, construing his words to mean that he probably wanted out of here as fast as possible, and away from her.

'Conor, if it's any help, I'm happy to offer my resignation. Right here, right now on the spot. I'm sure you don't want me around the office. I think that would be a bit too much. And for the record, I also completely understand if you want to catch the first flight out of here.'

He frowned. 'Would you shut up Cara?'

'What?' she said gently. 'I'm giving you an easy out. That's all.'

'I don't want you to leave the job, and I'm not going to leave either. Look, I realise this is not a normal situation, but maybe we just, you know, roll with it.'

'Roll with it?'

'Why not? I consider you a friend, and I hope you think of me as the same, but this honestly explains a lot.'

'Like what?' she asked, curious.

'Like, well, the protective feeling I seem to have whenever you are around and how I want the best for you and for no one to ever hurt you. I feel close to you. I think you are an incredible woman.'

Cara smiled. 'Fatherly concern?' she said, trying to keep the laughter from her voice.

'Would you shut it?' Conor laughed. 'I mean, look, maybe we aren't father and daughter from a relationship standpoint, but maybe there is something there that my sixth sense identified when I met you. Some type of instinct. Maybe there is a part of you that reminds me of Danni, but at the same time, you're your own person, the whole way through. Does that make sense?'

She nodded, appreciative of his comments. Appreciative that he was willing to still be a part of her life. She had to admit, she was certainly surrounded by some wise people. Maybe they could help balance out the crazy.

'Yes, Conor. It makes sense.'

'And look, it's not like I am altogether just fine and dandy with all of this. This has been a serious shock to the system. And I am probably going to have to check straight into a mental hospital when we get back . . .'

'Join the queue,' she said.

'But I suppose what I'm saying is, if you are willing to accept all this, so am I. And maybe, I don't know, we can figure out how to make it fit into the rest, work and all. Maybe we can figure out our relationship. I can't guarantee it will happen overnight, but I suppose we will figure it out as we go along.'

Cara looked at the floor and thought about the whole situation. Indeed, it was all too bizarre for words. But then again, what exactly was normal anyway?

Again, she tried to find the humour. 'So, I have a question about how this all works . . .'

Conor looked nervous. 'OK, fire ahead.'

'So say I needed some money . . .' Cara met his eyes, a smile breaking out on her face.

He snorted. 'You go to your other dad. Smart-ass.'

Chapter 37

The storm that had both literally and figuratively borne down upon the wedding couple and their guests eventually passed.

The group, amidst all of the new information that had been presented to them and the revelations that had been made, were able to return to their rooms late on the evening of September 12.

'So what's a day in the scheme of things? Especially when you have the rest of your lives together,' Kim laughed as, the following morning, she straightened the veil on Cara's head. 'And lucky number thirteen too!' she winked.

Cara stood by the window, bedecked in all of her wedding finery. She smiled at Kim, realising that while the entire family dynamic had shifted, at least nothing had changed between the two of them. 'You know, I think I am going to need more than an unlucky number to stop me from getting married today.'

'Well, you have made it through plenty of obstacles at this stage. Family issues – to say the least – a prenup and potential deal-breaker, an almost break-up with your wonderful fiancé, a hurricane and then finding out your boss is your dad . . . I'd say you had a trial by fire.' Kim's eyes sparkled with mischief. 'You know, if I was a bookmaker, I would place more than a few hundred quid on your marriage. I think you and Shane can get through anything.'

Cara pulled Kim close to her, tears sparkling in her eyes. 'Thank you.'

'For what?' Kim said, as she returned the hug.

'Just for being you.'

Kim waved an arm. 'Oh stop it.'

From across the room, a knock sounded on the door. Cara and Kim turned as Heidi peeked her head into the room. 'Knock knock . . .' she called out.

'Is it time?' Kim asked, as Heidi, looking pretty in her bridesmaid dress, walked to Cara's side.

'It is,' she replied. Since her little scare the day before, Cara had noticed that her younger sister had been much more at ease and relaxed, and she guessed she had Kim to thank for that too.

'All right then. Let's go get you married,' Kim said, tucking her arms into Cara and Heidi's.

As they were about to leave the room, Betty and Danielle entered, a new peace between them that was plain for all to see. It seemed confession truly was good for the soul and, with the identity of Cara's father finally revealed, Betty's worst fears about her daughter had been assuaged and her long-held disapproval evaporated.

Danielle and Cara had since had the opportunity to discuss at length the events of all that time ago, and while Cara still felt unbelievably hurt and betrayed at being misled about her parentage all this time, she was doing her best to try to understand and come to terms with Danielle's decision. It was strange, but despite all she'd learned, she still couldn't view her as anything other than her sister.

Trying to put herself in Danielle's shoes back then, she wondered if she herself would have been able to take on the huge responsibility of caring for a young baby, especially when Betty seemed so determined that she wasn't able for it. And they both knew how forceful their mother could be with her opinions. Danielle hadn't a chance really. Still, she couldn't argue that she'd had a wonderful upbringing and Betty and Mick had done an amazing job. She was thankful to Danielle for that much at least.

And she was looking forward to getting to know her sister better. Now that the secret was out, the ice had very clearly thawed between Danielle and Betty, and Cara hoped that this would all go some way to healing rifts and the Clancys being a proper family once again.

'Oh pet, you look beautiful,' Betty cried tearfully. 'Oh no, I think I'm going to cry!'

Cara walked over to the woman she realised would always be her mother. 'Thank you, Mum. For everything. I love you.' The two women embraced and as Cara pulled away, she looked at Danielle. 'Thank you too'.

Danielle looked at the ground, still unable to meet Cara's gaze. 'I'm not sure what for,' she said nervously.

'You made a tough decision. I can't imagine being put in that place. But you did make the right one when all is said and done. I am lucky to have such a family.' She embraced Danielle, who also began to sniffle. Cara pulled away and laughed. 'Now don't you cry too, OK? Come on, let's get out of here quick! I want to get married before anything else can go wrong.'

The sun was heavy on the St Lucia horizon as Cara walked barefoot down the aisle of white sand, a balmy breeze on her skin, her beloved father by her side.

Mick patted her arm. 'You are a vision, Cara. Do you know that? I want nothing but happiness for you and Shane. I've wanted happiness for you your entire life.'

'Thanks Dad and I know that,' she smiled as she looked

into her father's face. No, nothing had changed really, only for the better.

The truth might be out in the open, but her family as she knew it was much the same.

Besides, there would always be new surprises, new additions; weddings, babies, everything life encompassed.

She looked up ahead to where Shane stood in a pair of khaki linen trousers and a white cotton shirt. He was barefoot and his fair hair ruffled in the breeze. His eyes shone with love as his gaze took in Cara, dressed in white and walking towards him, their day exactly as they had pictured it so many months ago.

Shane's parents sat with the others on chairs placed in the sand, holding hands, all pretences dropped, all worries about society a million miles away. There would be other opportunities to make the business work, and Shane had already confided that he was planning on taking a more active role in his parents' company when they returned to Dublin, so as to help them on their way. With luck this would also help towards restoring his lost investments, which were indirectly tied up with Richardson business interests.

None of that mattered today though, not in lieu of their son's happiness. Lauren smiled happily as she noticed the delicate sapphire necklace on Cara's neck as she passed.

Yes, this was exactly as it should be.

As they neared the front, Mick shook Shane's hand, wishing him luck.

He turned to his daughter and kissed her cheek, telling her that he loved her before returning to his seat inbetween his wife and Conor Dempsey.

Cara held tightly to Shane's hand as the waves crashed on the sand before them. Regardless of the previous day, the beach sparkled anew, as if the rains from the storm had given new life and new hope to the island.

'Cara, you are the most beautiful thing I have ever seen,' whispered Shane and she smiled, in that moment completely content and at peace. She knew that this was where she was supposed to be, and she didn't have a doubt in her heart about how right this all was.

She thought about all that had happened, everything that had taken place.

All of it had led directly to this moment and Cara took heart in the idea that this day was part of fate's plan too. She thought about all of the people around her. Some she had loved since she was a child; some had entered her life in recent years, and with others she had only just realised how important they would be to her future.

Regardless, they were all her family and she knew they loved her.

The minister in front of them began the ceremony. 'Cara, do you take Shane to be your lawfully wedded husband? In sickness and health, for richer for poorer, in good times and bad for all the days of your life, until death do you part?'

Cara held Shane's hands in her own as her veil caught a breeze from the Caribbean sea. The setting sun illuminated her face as she said with confidence, 'I do.'

'And do you Shane, take Cara to be your lawfully wedded wife? In sickness and health, for richer for poorer, in good times and bad for all the days of your life, until death do you part?'

'You better believe it,' he quipped, which elicited laughter from the little group behind them. 'I mean, I do.'

'Then it is my honour to pronounce you husband and wife. Shane, you may kiss your bride.'

Shane pulled Cara close to him and covered her mouth

with his. The kiss was deep and full of promise, for the past, present and their future together.

When they broke away and turned to their family and friends they were met with cheers and applause. Cara took in the scene, her eyes shining as she considered the faces of each and every guest smiling back at her: her sisters, her parents, her in-laws, her friends and Conor. Each of them was a part of her, and now a part of Shane too. No matter what happened, no matter what the future presented, she knew her life was better because of each and every special person in it.

Actually, her in-laws had been right, she realised then; this wedding wasn't just about the two of them; it was about all of them. And she was fine with that.

'Happy, Mrs Richardson?' Shane smiled, looking down at his bride's happy face. 'We finally made it.'

'Couldn't be happier,' she smiled back. 'Now what are we waiting for? Let's get this party started.'

Epilogue

Cara smiled at her mother sitting in a nearby pew as, bouquet in hand, she slowly walked up the aisle of St Joseph's church. By the beaming smile on Betty's face she could tell that her mother was overjoyed her wish had finally come true.

A big church wedding at home in Greygates, although admittedly the guest list today was also small.

As she continued her parade, she saw Kim waving from the other side of the church, a smiling, pudgy baby in her arms. Olivia and Lindsay were fussing over him, while Ben sat proudly alongside his family. Number three had made his appearance six months ago – some three weeks before due date – which meant that her sister-in-law's hopes for a stress-free delivery hadn't quite come to pass.

But as Kim herself would say, babies often had their own plans.

And speaking of plans . . . Cara's gaze shifted to where Heidi and Paul sat contentedly with their gorgeous baby girl, Amelia. Another unexpected occurrence given that her sister's ultrasound scans had indicated a boy, but again leave it to a Clancy to throw a spanner in the works.

Cara was amazed at the change in her sister recently; it was as if motherhood and its inherent responsibilities was exactly what Heidi had needed to calm her down and cast aside her self-absorption. In the end Amelia was indeed born at a private hospital, though the scented candles and Debussy soundtrack had been abandoned within ten minutes of the first contractions, and Heidi freely admitted to all and sundry – even Kim – that she'd screamed for every last painkiller known to man.

Cara winced a little, realising that she would have to face a similar scenario in just under seven months' time. She and Shane hadn't yet shared their good news with the rest of the family, although she was sure that Conor – who witnessed her frantic races to the bathroom every morning at work – already suspected. But if he did have any suspicions he hadn't yet shared them, evidently waiting for Cara to confide in him whenever she was ready to.

It was strange how little their relationship had changed given what they'd learned. She still considered him her boss and great friend, and felt that the extra biological connection had enhanced their relationship rather than strained it. Although she did feel somewhat more proprietorial towards him in turn, especially since he'd started dating someone a couple of months back. Cara had been anxious to meet the woman, and having given her the once-over, eventually proclaimed her suitable enough to tame 'Clooney'.

When she reached the top of the altar, and went to join her beloved Shane, she turned and smiled at the bride's final approach.

Radiant was not the word to describe Danielle today. She looked utterly stunning, the beaded figure-hugging fishtail dress defining her gorgeous curves, and the white colour setting off her deep Floridian tan, but in demure contrast a white veil covered her smiling face as she saw Zack waiting for her at the altar.

And as Cara took the bridal bouquet from her sister, she

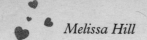

again looked back towards the guests and sought out the tearful faces of her parents Mick and Betty, realising just how symbolic this moment was for the entire family.

At last, Danielle Clancy had come home.

Melissa Hill
The Charm Bracelet

Holly O'Neill knows that every charm bracelet tells a story.

Many years ago she was sent one with just a single charm
attached. The charms have been appearing ever since,
often at challenging times, as if her mysterious benefactor
knows exactly when she needs a little magic in her life.

As a result, Holly's bracelet is her most prized possession.
So when she finds someone else's charm bracelet, she
feels she has to try to reunite it with its owner. Even if the
only clues she has to follow are the charms themselves.

On a search that will take her all over New York City at
Christmas, Holly becomes ever more determined to piece
together the details of this other charmed life. But what
she doesn't know is that her quest may also lead her
somewhere she never, ever expected . . .

HODDER

Have you read Melissa Hill's magical novel

Something from Tiffany's

Treat yourself . . .

Every girl deserves a little . . .

It's Christmas Eve. And on Fifth Avenue in New York
City, two very different men are shopping for gifts for
the women they love.

Gary is buying his girlfriend, Rachel, a charm bracelet.
Partly to thank her for paying for their holiday of a
lifetime to New York. But mainly because he's left his
shopping far too late. Whereas Ethan's looking for
something a little more special – an engagement ring for
the first woman to have made him happy since he lost
the love of his life.

But when the two men's shopping bags get confused, and
Rachel somehow ends up with Ethan's ring, the couples'
lives become intertwined. And as Ethan tries to reunite
the ring with the woman it was actually intended for, he
finds it trickier than he expected.

Does fate have other ideas for the couples? Or is there
simply a bit of Tiffany's magic in the air . . . ?

HODDER

We love a happy ending. But, almost more
than that, we love the promise of a new beginning.

Join us at www.hodder.co.uk, or follow us on Twitter
@hodderbooks, and be part of a community of escapists
who enjoy nothing more than curling up with a good book.

Whether you want to find out more about this book,
or a particular author, watch trailers and interviews, have
the chance to win early limited editions, or simply browse
our expert readers' selection of the very best books,
we think you'll find what you're looking for.

And if you don't, that's the place to tell us what's missing.

We love what we do, and we'd love you to be part of it.

www.hodder.co.uk

 @hodderbooks

HodderBooks

HodderBooks